Bolan fisted the Desert Eagle, rode out the grenade's blast

With the killzone secure, the Executioner sprinted toward the alley, ready to back up an old friend with whom he'd spilled more blood during his War Everlasting than he cared to remember.

A moment of eerie silence had fallen, followed by a chorus of anguished cries. Damn!

Before Bolan could take another step, a roar reverberated throughout the canyon of buildings, followed by the tortured sound of grinding metal and a loud crash. A massive front of singeing heat whooshed out, forcing him to involuntarily cover his face.

What the hell had happened to Jack?

D0837014

Don Pendleton's Mack Bolan®

Point of Betrayal

A GOLD EAGLE BOOK FROM

W❖RLDWIDE®

TORONTO • NEW YORK • LONDON
AMSTERDAM • PARIS • SYDNEY • HAMBURG
STOCKHOLM • ATHENS • TOKYO • MILAN
MADRID • WARSAW • BUDAPEST • AUCKLAND

First edition September 2005

ISBN 0-373-61507-8

Special thanks and acknowledgment to
Tim Tresslar for his contribution to this work.

POINT OF BETRAYAL

Rapidity is the essence of war; take advantage of the enemy's unreadiness, make your way by unexpected routes, and attack unguarded spots.

—Sun Tzu,
The Art of War

The rules of engagement are simple. Hit hard.
Hit fast. Don't give killers time to think or to counter.
Strike them with the only things they understand and deserve—lethal force.

—Mack Bolan

To the men and women of America's security
and intelligence services, who put it on the
line every day to keep us safe.

PROLOGUE

Baghdad, Iraq, April 2000

Tariq Riyadh stared into the face of a madman and felt rage building. Everywhere he turned in the city, his birthplace, his home, it was the same. Saddam Hussein's damnable face, his arrogant smile following Riyadh and his fellow countrymen as they went about their lives, trying to coexist with a murderous dictator who cared more about power than people. For years, Riyadh had watched as Saddam ground Iraq, a resource-rich, well-educated society, under his boot heel, killed its people with impunity, made Riyadh's homeland a polarizing force on the geopolitical landscape.

All that changed this night.

The still-warm desert breeze blew over Riyadh's face, tousled his salt-and-pepper hair. He stared at the painting of Saddam erected on a neighboring building and smiled at his enemy. The paintings, monolithic testaments to Saddam's arrogance and narcissism, dotted the country, as innumerable as grains of sand in the desert. Like his fellow countrymen, Riyadh suffered daily under Saddam's mocking glare, through the ever-present paintings, through the eyes of the Republican Guard, through Saddam's network of spies, all ready to kill for the slightest treachery, real or perceived.

Riyadh knew his first order come morning would be to tear down the paintings, bring them together in a pile and burn them in a huge funeral pyre marking the passing of an oppressive regime.

He squeezed his left arm against his rib cage, grateful for the reassuring bulk of the Beretta 92-F he carried in a shoulder holster. If all went according to plan, he'd use the weapon only once, a single shot into the dictator's face, watch fear replace Hussein's smugness. Change history with a single squeeze of the trigger.

Riyadh smiled and excitement tickled his insides. He stood on the balcony of his apartment, watched as troop carriers, soldiers and citizens milled about him ten stories below. If he shut his eyes and listened, Baghdad sounded like any other teeming metropolis at night. Honking horns, sirens, relentless footsteps, voices—all were audible even at this height. Perched several stories above it all, he couldn't feel the fear, the repressed anger that gripped the country, gnawed at it like a cancer. It was the righteous anger of an oppressed people, a people with no voice because it had been stolen by a despot.

Riyadh wanted to rule Iraq, to transform it into a progressive state that other countries would marvel at, perhaps even mimic. And he would get his chance to do just that. The Americans' promise had been explicit—with Saddam gone, Riyadh would step in as Iraq's president, run the government until Iraq stabilized and then the people would choose their own leader in democratic elections. Pride surged through Riyadh as he realized he'd bring freedom to his people and they would love him for it. He had no doubt they would do the right thing, elect him as president. Over and over.

The impending revolution also would make him a rich man. Unbeknownst to the Americans, Riyadh had been in contact with the Russians and the French, via their intelligence agents, and they had agreed to secretly buy oil from him. He'd undercut the OPEC countries, reduce their clout in world affairs, give rise to a new power in the Middle East. And if he lined his pockets in the meantime, then who was to complain?

Riyadh heard footsteps from behind and turned. A tall man with close-cropped, blond hair and a ruddy complexion stepped from Riyadh's well-appointed penthouse onto the terrace. Obviously a Westerner, the man had been traveling as a journalist, had even filed stories under the byline Daniel Gibbons for Liberty News Service. Riyadh knew better. Liberty News Service was a ruse, a part of the Central Intelligence Agency's massive overseas propaganda machine. And Daniel Gibbons was really Jon Stone, a CIA agent.

"It's almost time," Stone said. "Come inside. We need to talk."

Riyadh nodded. Lighting a cigarette as he moved, he stepped inside the apartment, closed the sliding-glass door behind him. A rush of air-conditioned air hit him, cooling the sweat that had formed on his brow and down his spine. He loved his country's dry, hot climate. But as a member of Iraq's parliament and the son of a wealthy oil family, he also enjoyed the comforts of air-conditioning. Another man stood in the room with Stone, a mirror image of Riyadh, minus his graying hair, the crow's feet etched into the corners of his eyes, the soft middle from too many dinners with Iraq's political elite.

"My brother," Riyadh said, "it is so good to see you."

"And you," Abdullah Riyadh stated.

Stone fell heavily into a chair, causing it to slide back a

few inches. Riyadh stared at him and, with great effort, kept his expression neutral. He found Stone boorish, overbearing. Stone, though well educated, lumped all Arabs into a single pile and regarded it as he would dung. In Riyadh's mind, Stone had seemed an unlikely man to coordinate a coup in the Middle East. Despite the man's shortcomings, though, he had pulled together the operation with an attention to detail, an efficiency that elicited a grudging respect from Riyadh. Indeed, he was a social clod, but a strategic genius.

Stone's upper lip curled into a sneer as he spoke. "You two done having old home week, or do I have to waste more time before we can get down to business?"

Angry heat radiated from Riyadh's face, but he gave Stone a curt nod and sat in a chair opposite the bulky American. Moving with a grace that Riyadh no longer possessed, his brother stepped between them, settled into a nearby couch.

"Our boy is staying at the royal palace tonight," Stone said. "He'll arrive in a caravan, probably the third car from the front. My sources place him there between 0100 and 0200. He has a late meeting with the foreign minister. Then he'll go to one of his other houses, stay for two hours, then head to the palace."

"You're sure it will be him, not one of his doubles?" Riyadh asked.

Stone's face turned a deeper shade of scarlet. He leaned forward as he spoke, underscoring his words by pounding an index finger against the table.

"As a matter of fact, Riyadh, I'm not sure. I can't guarantee anything. But I am giving you the best information I have. We've been dropping wads of cash all over Baghdad trying to find this bastard. I've got the best intelligence possible. But if you want a sure thing, walk away now because I can't give it to you and neither can anyone else."

"I understand," Riyadh said.

"It's real easy," Stone said. "The target will be most vulnerable while he's on the street. They're going to try to sneak him inside, so he'll forgo the full motorcade. Instead it will be one Hummer in front, the presidential Mercedes in the middle and another Hummer in the middle. My source told me there are going to be helicopters nearby. If something happens to your boss, they're going to swoop in and blast everything in sight. That's why I gave you the rocket launchers. Incinerate the Hummers, trap the Mercedes in the middle. Take out Saddam's car. My people will deal with the air support. Got it?"

"Yes," Riyadh said, "of course."

"Do not deviate from the plan."

"I understand. But what about us?"

"Hide. I'm going to have my hands full getting my own people out of Baghdad. You just have to last a few hours and it's cool. By morning, the United States and Britain will step in and offer troops to help stabilize the country—all by your country's invitation, of course. We've got others inside your government and military to keep things solid after he goes down."

"And I will be appointed interim president?"

"None other," Stone said. He slipped an envelope to Riyadh, who picked it up and started to open it. "Later," Stone said. "It's coded instructions to make clear any details we didn't cover here. You just have your people in position when it all goes down. We're counting on you. Understood?"

"Clearly."

Stone came to his feet and Riyadh did likewise. "I thank you for your help," Riyadh said. "More importantly, my country thanks you."

He held out his hand and Stone ignored it.

"Look," Stone said, "let's get one thing straight—as long as I walk away alive and Saddam goes out horizontal, I don't give two shits what happens to you or your country. Washington cares. I don't. The way I see it, I'll probably be back here in five years, helping someone else overthrow you because you can't handle the power, either. So take your olive branch and shove it."

Stone turned and let himself out. As the door slammed shut, a smile tugged at the corners of Riyadh's mouth. Stone was insufferable, but a necessary evil. Just like Riyadh's alliance with the United States. Let Stone shoot off his mouth so long as he helped Riyadh attain his goals.

"We should kill him."

Riyadh turned, regarded his brother. The elder man dismissed the notion with a shake of his head.

"No," Riyadh said. "We need him and his people. To kill them would kill our cause."

"We've made a pact with the devil, Tariq," Abdullah said. "These people are not our friends, they are puppet masters. And once we have done the hard work, they will cut the strings, leave us to die. Please do not tell me otherwise."

"Have vision, my young brother," Riyadh replied. "We do not need friends, we need allies. Our goals and America's are the same. That makes us allies. In politics, you learn that sometimes you must work with those you do not like if you are to achieve what you want.

"Stone's a killer. You and I, we are freedom fighters. Stone's friends are soldiers, good men. But he's a murderer. He knows tonight blood will spill and it fills him with joy. Hopefully, he will not be disappointed."

CHRIS DOYLE GUNNED the Jeep Cherokee's engine, wheeled the vehicle through the military checkpoint and breathed a sigh of relief. The soldiers had given him and his vehicle a cursory look, checking under seats and sifting through his camera bag. They hadn't looked hard enough to find the compartment hidden in the rear of his vehicle, the one containing weapons, radio equipment, black clothes and camou paint. Doyle had made small talk with the men, a pair of foot soldiers, and slipped each of them an impressive amount of Iraqi dinars, enough to expedite the search without arousing suspicion. After all, he had a deadline to meet.

Doyle had told the soldiers he was a French photojournalist for a nature magazine, in the country shooting photos of Iraq's deserts and the swamplands feeding off the Tigris and Euphrates rivers. He had the forged papers, a dozen digital memory Archers filled with pictures, and a murderous sunburn to back up his claim. Because he'd spent most of his time in undeveloped areas, he'd been allowed to travel without a government monitor.

Goosing the Jeep's accelerator a little harder, he settled into the leather bucket seats, checked the rearview mirror. A pair of stationary headlights glared back at him, and he caught glimpses of the guards' silhouettes as they busied themselves with a new search. They seemed disinterested in him, which was exactly how Doyle wanted it.

Hopefully, in a few hours when all hell broke loose, they'd forget they ever met him, not an unlikely scenario. Doyle was nondescript and grateful for it. Average height and weight. Mouse-brown hair cut to an average length. Soft chin. Dull hazel eyes that masked an oceans-deep intelligence that had earned him full-ride scholarship offers to three Ivy League universities. His dull appearance had made him effective first as a Force Recon soldier and later as a CIA assassin and paramilitary operative.

Motoring deeper into Baghdad, Doyle drummed the balls of his thumbs against the steering wheel, began humming an old blues tune. In his mind, he traced the song's rhythm pattern, thought longingly of his electric guitar stored in his apartment in Langley, Virginia. When was the last time he'd been home? Six months. Eight? He usually lost count after three. By then he'd sunk deep enough undercover that Chris Doyle had ceased to exist, resurrected only for occasional phone calls to his handlers back at Langley. Otherwise he lived someone else's life. Today a photojournalist. Last year, posing as a United Nations translator so he could kill two Russian diplomats stealing American secrets to sell to rogue nations.

Each time, a perfect kill. Each time, three more stepped up to replace his slain targets. It was as though he was helping thugs and terrorists become upwardly mobile.

Doyle ground his teeth together, felt acid bubble up in his stomach. Face it, he thought, you're pissing in the ocean and drowning at the same time. He checked the rearview mirror again. Rather than look for pursuers, though, he studied his drawn, haggard face. Bottom line, he was losing his edge. He'd seen his work undone one too many times, either by enemies or friends, to believe he was making a difference. After tonight, he may say to hell with all of it.

Assuming, of course, that he survived tonight.

Twenty-five minutes later he reached a small bank of three-story buildings, the ground floor occupied by retail and the upper floors by apartments. Doyle parked the Jeep curbside, doused the lights and waited. Five minutes passed and Doyle became increasingly nervous. His contact was three minutes late, the man's apartment sat dark and Doyle was sitting in the open, alone and unarmed. Doyle had decided against carrying weapons on his person, in case soldiers decided to search him.

Five minutes turned to ten and the sinking feeling in his gut continued to deepen as he sat in his vehicle, exposed and waiting. He started to feel as inconspicuous as a man jogging naked through Times Square in New York.

The digital phone resting on the seat next to him trilled once. Keeping his eyes trained on his surroundings, Doyle grabbed the phone and activated it.

"Bonjour."

"Hey, Frog boy, what's the word?" Great, it was Stone. Doyle switched to English but maintained his French accent.

"Monsieur Gibbons, how good to hear from you."

"You get the picture?"

"I have many pictures, but not the one you want."

"Where the hell is it?"

"I could not find the right subject. Perhaps I was mistaken in my approach?"

A pause. "Maybe. You think you should try again?"

Doyle shrugged as though Stone could see him. "I can take a few more minutes, scan through my images. Perhaps I have something else that might meet with your approval. This picture, it is critical?"

"Damn straight it's critical. I've got a deadline to meet. We need this exclusive picture to make a memorable package. You know what I mean?"

"Of course. But I must tell you, there also are issues with this particular subject. You realize that, don't you?"

Stone paused, his breath coming in audible, angry rasps at the phone. Doyle imagined Stone's tiny, ratlike eyes skittering back and forth as he processed the news.

"Okay. That is a problem."

"Perhaps we should meet for coffee to discuss the issue."

"Usual place?"

"I look forward to it."

Stone killed the connection and Doyle deactivated his own phone. He scanned the streets once again, saw no one. A cold fist of fear buried itself in his gut, stole his breath. "The picture" had referred to Brahim Azar, a soldier assigned to Saddam's security detail. Azar was supposed to give final confirmation about Saddam's intention to sleep at the royal palace. The plan had been simple—Azar would watch for Doyle's vehicle and come down to the street when he saw it. If the mission was a go, he'd light a cigarette and then buy a newspaper from a nearby vending box. If not, he'd buy a newspaper and disappear back inside.

As it was, their source was a no-show and Doyle couldn't help but fear the worst.

Maybe the guy had been conscripted to work late.

Or maybe the mission had been compromised. Regardless, it looked bad. Resting his left hand on the steering wheel, he reached for the ignition key with his right hand.

An engine hummed from behind, growing louder as it closed in on the SUV. He looked up, saw a large vehicle pulling in behind his own, brakes groaning as the heavy vehicle ground to a halt. Doyle muttered a curse as halogen floodlights exploded to life, bathing his SUV with a white glow. Moments later a helicopter hovered overhead, pinning the SUV under a pair of searchlights.

A voice amplified by a loudspeaker boomed from behind. "This is the Republican Guard. Do not attempt to start your vehicle or you will be killed."

Doyle reached for the best option at hand.

Langley, Virginia, CIA headquarters

"DO YOU THINK the mission's been compromised?"

"My best source misses an appointment, even though he just has to walk down one flight of stairs," Jon Stone said. "You do the math, Simmons. He's been made. We're compromised."

"Calm down, Stone," said David Simmons, a retired Marine officer and mission controller for the Iraq insurgency group. "What does Doyle say about all this?"

"Not sure," Stone replied. "We just got off the phone a few minutes ago. He's en route to my position. He was on an unsecured portable phone so we couldn't talk freely. Besides, who gives a shit what Doyle says? I'm the field commander on this little op, not him."

Because you're a damn psycho, Simmons thought. But he said, "At ease. I just wanted to hear his field report since he was at the rendezvous site. Are you getting any other signs that the mission has gone south?"

"One of Riyadh's crew also failed to show up. Doesn't answer his phone, either. He may have lost his nerve or he may have turned on us. Hard to know for sure."

"But you're checking?"

"Stephen Archer and one of Riyadh's people are en route now. I expect a report soon."

"What about the others?"

"Ready to go. They're just waiting for the word. So what is it?"

"Hang tight. I need to go up a level for this one."

"I won't wait long."

"Ten minutes."

Killing the connection, Simmons hauled himself to nis feet, wincing as he stood erect. Pain seared his midsection, reminding him of the cancer eating away his insides. The oncologist had diagnosed it earlier that month, declared it inoperable. In the best-case scenario, Simmons had two months to live, perhaps three. Within a month, he guessed, he'd be admitted to a hospice where he could quietly wait to die. Setting his jaw, he walked past the banks of computers, the hurried workers that populated the control center. He kept his face stoic as he went. He'd decided to keep his illness a secret as long as he possibly could. If his superiors knew of its extent, he'd probably be put out to pasture within a matter of days. He could sit on the sidelines and watch as someone else within the Agency oversaw Saddam's downfall; he could watch as they took the credit.

Like hell.

Glass doors hissed as they parted in front of Simmons. He moved quickly down the corridor, stepped into a secure elevator at the end of the hall and within seconds was silently ascending to another level of the CIA's sprawling complex.

Slipping off his glasses and squeezing his eyes shut, Simmons rubbed the bridge of his nose with his thumb and forefinger. As he did, his mind wandered to the Gulf War. He'd led a team of Marines into southern Iraq to pinpoint artillery batteries for coalition bombers. Getting past the ersatz soldiers had been easy enough. Most had looked too scared to wipe their nose let alone take on a group of heavily armed Marines, especially a group backed by the thunder and hellfire of coalition fighter jets. Within an hour the group had reached the batteries and prepared to pinpoint them with handheld laser-targeting instruments.

After that, it all had gone to hell. A Republican Guard unit had caught them on their rear flank, taking out two Marines before the American fighters could respond in kind, cutting down the Iraqi soldiers in an unrelenting storm of gunfire. Sixteen Iraqi soldiers had died in the encounter, two Marines. It had been two too many, as far as Simmons was concerned.

He clenched his jaw. Simmons had never lost a man in the field, ever. After that night, war had become intensely personal.

Stepping from the elevator, he walked down a corridor, following it as it jogged left then right. He passed through another pair of bulletproof glass doors, into a control room similar to the one he'd left behind downstairs. After the requisite security checks, he crossed the room and slipped into another, smaller room where several men and women in business suits sat at a large mahogany table with polished brass inlaid trim.

Simmons ignored the other six and focused on a big bear of a man seated at the head of the table. CIA director James Lee returned the stare.

"Good news, David?"

"No, sir."

"Tell me what's wrong. And for God's sake, pull the rod out of your ass and stand like a normal person."

It was only then that Simmons realized he stood at attention, legs and back bolt upright, arms and hands stabbing toward the floor. Old training died hard, he thought. And he'd caught himself in more than one stressful moment falling back on the order and discipline of the military.

"It's the operation, sir. We need to talk."

He paused while Lee dismissed the others in the room.

"Sit down, David."

"I prefer to stand, sir."

"Fine. Just tell me what's wrong."

"You told me to inform you of any irregularities, right?"

A worried look passed over Lee's features. Leaning forward in his chair, he rested his elbows on the table and stared intently at Simmons. "Yes. Yes, I did."

"One of the informants failed to make a rendezvous."

"His whereabouts?"

"Unknown."

"So we may have been compromised?" Lee asked.

Simmons shrugged. "It's possible. But I can't say that with certainty."

Looking up from the table, Lee met Simmons's gaze. "Well, what can you say with certainty?"

"That the informant missed the rendezvous."

"You already told me that. But what the hell does it mean?"

"Hard to say. The guy might have gotten cold feet. He might be waiting at his girlfriend's house, hoping the whole thing just blows over. It's hard to find people in Iraq willing to cross Saddam."

"Can we track him down?"

Simmons shook his head. "Not a good idea. If we make too big a stink, we raise everyone's suspicions. Whole thing goes to hell after that."

"Well, give me something I can work with here. Can we accomplish this mission without him?"

"Possibly. He had the itinerary information. He could place Saddam within a five-minute window. Without that, we may have to expose ourselves for longer periods, probably forty-five minutes to an hour."

"What's your comfort level with this?"

Simmons pondered this for a moment. In an operation such as this, with a paranoid target like Hussein, any deviation from the plan was cause for alarm. "Stone, Archer and Doyle are three of our best operatives. They adapt quickly to adversity. We've been training the Iraqis for six months. They're good to go."

Lee's eyes narrowed. "You didn't answer my question."

"I'm comfortable. As long as my men get the air support they need, they can pull off this mission."

Lee leaned back in his chair. Lacing his fingers together into a double fist, he stared at his thumbnails, as though lost in thought.

"You bearing a grudge?"

"Sir?"

"I know about the op in '91. You lost men, good ones. Is that clouding your judgment?"

Anger colored Simmons face and heated the skin of his shoulders and arms. His hands clenched into fists. Lee's bluntness took him by surprise. "Of course not. I won't put my men in harm's way just to settle a score."

Lee came to his full six-foot, four-inch height and stared down at Simmons. "You're right," he said. "You won't."

A lurch that had nothing to do with the cancer passed through Simmons's belly. "Excuse me?"

"No mission. Not tonight, anyway. My orders from the President were explicit—a surgical strike. Quick and deadly. No hint of American involvement in this, period. The Middle East is a goddamn tinderbox as it is. We don't need to put a blow torch to it by creating another Bay of Pigs. My gut says to abort the mission. If you were using your damn head, you'd see the same thing."

"Sir—"

"I want those people out of there. Tonight. End of conversation. Don't get greedy. You'll have plenty of other opportunities to plug this bastard before retirement rolls around."

"Jim—"

Lee held up a hand to silence Simmons. "Make the call. I want our people out of Iraq within twelve hours. If you hand me a problem, I'll hand you back more trouble than you can handle."

Squelching an impulse to punch Lee in the solar plexus, Simmons snapped ramrod-straight to attention and fixed his gaze on an invisible spot on the wall. "Yes, sir," he said.

"I knew I could count on you, David."

From his peripheral vision, Simmons saw Lee smile and more rage bubbled up from within.

Lee ignored his subordinate. Hooking his jacket with two fingers, he hefted the garment and slung it over a narrow shoulder. A moment later he was gone and Simmons was alone, numb.

His stomach burning as he exited the meeting room, Simmons reached into his shirt pocket and extracted two painkillers. He'd been warned not to exceed the dose, that it might impair his coordination, his judgment. So what? According to Lee, his judgment was already flawed and Simmons's body hurt like hell.

Returning to his own command center, Simmons considered Lee's words. Lee was a flaming jerk, but he made a good point. A botched coup attempt in Iraq only would solidify support for Saddam Hussein, make him a sympathetic figure on the Arab street. And the coup's backer, America, would walk away with egg on its face, a superpower unable to topple a two-bit dictator.

You'll have plenty of other opportunities to plug this bastard before retirement rolls around.

Smug bastard. Lee had no idea what it was like to face death, to feel your heart slam so fast, so hard, that it felt as though it might explode at any moment. He pushed paper all day, moved agents and paramilitary operatives around like chess pieces on the board, one eye on his strategic plan, the other on the next promotion. Not all CIA directors had been that way, but this guy was and Simmons hated him for it.

He picked up the satellite phone and set it in his lap. With the diagnosis of cancer, he thought constantly about death, realized he'd leave nothing behind. His career had been heroic, but shrouded in secrecy and bereft of recognition. His ex-wives hated him and had trained his daughters accordingly. He'd lost contact with most of his military buddies, and only occasionally socialized with the other CIA employees outside of work.

During the last decade or so, the closest thing he had to family had been his Force Recon team. Those men had admired and trusted him, following him into hell time and again.

He'd repaid them with death, leading them into a deadly mission and returning home with a handful of survivors.

"Sir, are you okay?"

Simmons looked up and saw a young woman, her amber hair pulled into a ponytail, a wireless headset wrapped around her head. She was one of six technicians and intelligence analysts in the room.

He waved her away. "I'm fine, Dana. Head just feels a little light, is all."

"If I may say so, you look tired, a bit pale."

"I said, I'm fine. Dammit, leave me alone."

The volume of his voice surprised him. The woman stiffened, jerked back a bit as though burned, her pretty features hardening into a cold stare.

"Yes, sir. Jon Stone called two minutes ago, just before you returned."

"I'll deal with Stone."

In his mind, his voice dripped with disdain, like venom trickling the length of a cobra's fang. Stone was an undisciplined killer, a wild cannon. Maybe he dazzled the brass with his dual master's degrees and his record of successful missions. Simmons knew better. He knew that every time Stone walked into a mission, he drew innocent blood. Women. Children. Stone cared little as long as he got results. Same went for his buddy, Stephen Archer.

If Simmons's voice betrayed his hatred, the woman in front of him showed no signs of it. And what if she did? To hell with her and everyone else. Simmons was dying. And the way he saw it, a dying man ought to be able to say whatever the hell he wants.

"Sir, did you hear what it I said?"

The room came back into focus for a moment. "Huh?"

"They lost contact with Doyle, sir. He was supposed to check in with Stone and they lost contact with him."

Simmons sat upright in his chair. Doyle not checking in? Something about that bothered him, though he couldn't place what. Why was it so damn hard to think?

"Get out."

"Sir?"

"Get out. All of you. I need to speak with Stone."

The analysts and technicians filed from the room, leaving Simmons alone.

Raising the satellite phone, he began to punch in Stone's code. Knowing he might need to dial it at a critical moment, he'd burned the code into his memory, doing so until he could recite it in his sleep. Still, he had trouble bringing the numbers on the keypad into focus. They blinked and blurred as he tried to pin them down under his index finger.

Finishing the number sequence, he leaned back in his chair, waited for Stone to pick up.

The agent's voice sounded far away, angry in Simmons's ear.

"Where the hell you been, man?"

"Do it," Simmons said.

"What?"

"You heard me. Lee says it's a go. So, go"

IHMAD JUMA STEPPED from the room and wrinkled his nose, a vain attempt to expel the stenches of vomit, blood and human excrement that clung inside his nostrils. He shut the door behind him, hoping to seal behind it the memory of an old friend who still lay inside, mangled and dying.

Correction: an old friend who had turned traitor. That made the man an enemy, and his impending death a cause for celebration. Perhaps if Juma told himself that long enough, eventually he'd believe it.

Juma moved with clipped, precise strides that belied his twenty years as an Iraqi military officer. As he continued down the hall, he realized the air felt irritatingly cool against his forehead and armpits. He extracted a handkerchief from his fatigue pants. Wiping the cloth over his forehead, he traced the edge of his severe widow's peak and scrubbed away the sheen of perspiration that lay below it.

The screams and pleadings of Brahim Azar echoed in his mind, as unrelenting as the desert sun. He shook his head violently to shoo them away, then caught himself and looked around self-consciously. None of the passing soldiers seemed to notice his momentary distress, eliciting a silent prayer of gratitude. He'd witnessed more tortures, beatings, rapes than he could recall. The memories of these events flashed past his mind's eye like a high-speed kaleidoscope, one blurring into the next with almost blinding speed. Years ago the images had disturbed him, yanking him from sleep, prompting violent outbursts against his family. But now he prided himself on his aloofness in the face of others' agony.

Still something about watching an old friend suffer had disturbed him deeply, wrenching his guts and searing his soul with the unwelcome fires of guilt, self-hatred.

Several minutes later he stood in front of the great leader, in one of the man's numerous private offices. Silence and cigar smoke hung heavily in the air, the latter stinging Juma's eyes. His stomach continued churning, this time because of nerves. He'd been close to the leader many, many times, but never the focus of the meeting. The news was grim, and Juma couldn't help but wonder whether delivering it might cost him his life.

The great leader sat in a high-backed chair, facing a wall. Waiting for an invitation to speak, Juma eyed his surroundings. Bookcases lined the walls, ornate brass lamps shone brightly and a television carrying Iraqi state news reports blinked in the background.

"You bring me information?"

"Yes, sir. Of utmost importance."

"Speak."

"A small group of men, including some within the government, have conspired to kill you. They planned to do it tonight."

"Who are these men?"

"I have their names here, sir." Juma pulled a manila folder from under his left arm and handed it to one of the guards, who, in turn, set in on the great leader's desk. "They planned to kill you tonight at the royal palace. Tariq Riyadh is among them."

"The Americans?"

"The infidels also are part of the plan, yes. They have operatives within the country, all of them posing as foreign journalists, even as we speak. As for our own countrymen, I have dispatched teams to hunt them down, arrest them."

"No."

"Sir?"

"Let them come en masse. We'll kill them together, like a pack of wild dogs. Make an example of them."

"Yes, sir. Their families?"

"Kill them, too, of course."

CHRIS DOYLE STEPPED from the SUV, walked into the lights of the Iraqi jeep. He squinted to block out the white glare. Clutching his identification papers in his left hand, he held both hands overhead and wore a grin he didn't feel.

An Iraqi soldier, one hand clutching the pistol grip of his submachine gun, approached Doyle and snatched the papers from his hands. Releasing the submachine gun, the soldier grabbed Doyle's arm, spun him and shoved him hard against the vehicle. Over the rumble of the jeep's engine, Doyle heard the rustle of paper as the soldier pored over the American's identification documents. Doyle's heart speeded up and he forced himself to take deep, even pulls of the exhaust-tinged air to keep his thinking clear.

"You are French?" the soldier asked.

"*Oui*. I mean, yes," Doyle said, switching to Arabic.

"It says here you are a journalist. Where is your monitor?"

Doyle shrugged, smiled. "I am a nature photographer. The information ministry decided I didn't need an escort in the swamplands. I am unimportant."

The soldier grunted, continued poring over the forged papers. "The information ministry obviously erred," he said without looking. "Wouldn't you agree?"

"I was supposed to meet with my monitor tonight before I return to my hotel. He was going to check my pictures. I cannot take my film from the country without his approval. Please, I do not want problems."

"When are you leaving?"

"One week," Doyle lied.

The soldier's machine gun hung loose on its strap from his right shoulder. Spare clips were sheathed on his belt. Doyle watched as the soldier, a stout man in camouflage fatigues and a beret, traced a stubby finger across the paper until he reached the line bearing Doyle's departure date. A moment later the soldier refolded the papers, stuck them in his shirt pocket.

The stout man locked eyes with Doyle. "Why are you here?" he asked.

"I told you—"

"I mean, in this neighborhood. After dark. According to your papers, you're staying at the Continental Hotel, which is nowhere near this place. Why are you here?"

Doyle felt his palms moisten, his mind begin to race.

Crossing his arms over his chest, the American agent leaned down toward the soldier. He gave the man a conspiratorial wink, hushed his voice as though sharing with an old friend. "I've been away from civilization for a while," he said. "I'm here looking for a little companionship. I was supposed to meet someone."

Prostitutes frequented the area. Doyle expected the man to understand, perhaps cut him some slack. Instead the man shot him a look that screamed disapproval.

Great, Doyle thought, three hundred, fifty thousand soldiers in Iraq. I get the one puritan.

"I thought you were going to meet your monitor."

Doyle grinned. "There's always time for this, my friend. You know?"

"Whom are you freelancing for?"

"Liberty News Service."

The man opened his mouth to reply, stopped when the door of the white Toyota Land Cruiser opened. A tall, lanky soldier armed with an AK-47 stepped from the vehicle and approached them. With the headlight glare at his back, the man's face was black as night until he came to within a few feet of Doyle. At the same time, the Soviet-made chopper, which had been cruising overhead in wide, lazy circles, gunned its engine and disappeared into the night, the beating rotors diminishing to a distant hum.

"Who is he?" the tall soldier asked. Doyle recognized the Republican Guard insignia on the man's tunic and felt a cold splash of fear roll down his spine.

"A journalist," the first Iraqi replied. "He should not have stopped here unaccompanied. He was told to report directly to his monitor."

Giving Doyle an appraising look, the soldier spoke over his shoulder to his comrade. "A journalist? For whom?"

"I'm freelance."

"He's with Liberty News Service. He told me that."

A glint of understanding sparked in the Republican Guard soldier's otherwise impassive stare before snuffing itself out. His lips curled into a smile that didn't reach his eyes.

"Let him go," he said.

The first soldier started to protest, but the other man held up a hand to stop him. "His papers. Give them to him and let him go. We must not delay him any longer."

In less than a minute Doyle was back in his car, stuffing his forged papers back inside his pants' pocket and watching the Toyota Land Cruiser roar down the road. Doyle's heart hammered against his rib cage and adrenaline caused his hands to shake. He puffed on a cigarette to help calm his nerves.

Something was wrong. *Let him go,* the man had said. No looking at the papers, no shaking Doyle down for a bribe, nothing. Doyle knew he should have felt relieved. He didn't. He felt like a condemned man taking the first step on his last mile.

Keying the SUV to life, he piloted the vehicle to his rendezvous with Stone.

FORTY-FIVE MINUTES later Chris Doyle met Jon Stone and Stephen Archer at an abandoned factory, poorly lit with boarded-up windows. The place stank of machine oil, dust and Archer's wintergreen chewing tobacco. Doyle had armed himself back at the hotel. A .40-caliber Glock pistol rode in the small of his back, obscured by his shirttails.

"You sure no one followed you here?" Stone asked as he shut the door behind Doyle and locked it.

Doyle shrugged. "Reasonably so. I changed clothes, walked several blocks and took one of our standby cars.

Switched papers so I look like a Russian national. That's why it took me so long to get here."

Stone nodded, apparently satisfied.

Doyle turned and uttered a curt greeting to Archer, a small, bald man whose skin bunched in heavy folds at the base of his skull. Archer grunted, tamped down his tobacco with the tip of his tongue. The little man stood off to one side, splattering the floor with thin, brown streams of tobacco juice and swirling them with the toe of his boot so they made odd patterns in the dirt. At first, Doyle had considered Archer disengaged, perhaps even stupid. Just like everything else Doyle seemed to encounter, it all was an act. Archer could read and explain complex research reports issued by the Massachusetts Institute of Technology or defuse a nuclear warhead without taxing his mind.

Doyle carried his equipment bag on his shoulder. Slipping it off, he set it on the floor carefully. An uneasy feeling in his gut told him something was wrong.

"What's the extraction plan?" he asked.

"Washington says it's a go," Stone said.

"What the hell?"

Doyle whirled toward Stone, found him standing less than eighteen inches away, arms crossed over his chest. Stone coiled and uncoiled his steroid-enhanced pectorals, biceps and triceps, causing them to writhe under his shirt like a bag of snakes. Consciously or unconsciously, it was his way of telegraphing his physical power, an intimidation tactic he employed regularly.

"Simmons says it's a go," Stone said. His expression seemed to dare an argument and Doyle was only too happy to comply.

"Is he crazy? We've been compromised. We're as good as dead if we go through with this."

Stone shrugged. "We don't know we've been compromised. There could be a logical explanation as to why he pulled a no-show."

"Like what?"

Stone grinned. "He likes the ladies. Maybe he was getting laid."

"I planned to hand him thirty thousand in Iraqi dinars. I think he could keep it in his pants until he got the money."

"Calm down, Doyle. You sound like a damn old woman."

Anger burned hot in Doyle's cheeks and forehead, but he kept his voice even. "You tell Riyadh that our contact disappeared?"

Popping his gum, Stone stared at Doyle for a minute. "I don't talk to Riyadh about anything unless I think it's a good idea. These people are spooked enough without me scaring them some more. They're about ready to overthrow their leader, upend their country. A handful of guys against a man with an army at his disposal. You know what Saddam does to traitors?"

"I know."

"He kills their whole family. Wife, kids, parents, even distant relatives. He tortures them, rapes the women. Scorches their skin with branding irons. Like cattle. Cuts off their—"

"Goddammit, I said I know."

Doyle suppressed a shudder. Maybe it had been a trick of the light, but he swore a glazed look settled over Stone's eyes as he'd discussed Saddam's atrocities. Doyle never had trusted Stone, had balked at the notion of working with him. Stone was as unstable as hell. He always made missions happen, nearly always got results. That seemed good enough for Simmons and James Lee, the CIA director.

Stone continued. "We spent a year building up these guys. They hate Saddam and that's good. But they used to fear him too much to do anything about it. Half these guys figured he was invincible. That any move against the man would cost them their families. We finally got them over that. Now you want me to scare them again just because one guy disappears?"

"Yes."

"Forget it," Stone said with a gesture. "I want these people to have their heads where it should be. Same goes for you."

Doyle scowled, clenched his jaw until it hurt. He stepped a couple of inches closer to Stone and spoke through clenched teeth. "Don't worry about me," he said. "I'm here because I believe in this mission. If Washington says 'go,' I'll go. But if you want blind obedience, forget it. I'm loyal, but I'm not stupid."

Deep creases formed in Stone's forehead and anger glinted in his eyes, but he nodded. "Suits me. I don't give a shit why you do it, as long as you do."

"We go to our second alternative," Doyle said.

Stone's face flushed red. "We can't change now," he said, his voice a growl.

"They may know what we have planned. The alternative is audacious enough that it might work."

Archer spoke up. "He's right, Stone. If we're going to do it, we might as well stick it up their ass. Hit 'em where they least expect it."

Stone whipped his head toward Archer. "You just stick to your motherboards and let me handle the strategy," Stone said.

Archer held up his hands in appeasement, flashed a gap-toothed grin. "Just sticking my two cents' worth in, okay? You're the strategy genius. I mean, hell, look at where we are so far."

Doyle sensed the tension crackling between Stone and Archer, watched it with morbid interest. The two men, equally deadly, always seemed a step away from killing each other. Doyle often prayed for that day, but didn't want to be there when it happened.

Stone turned back to Doyle. "Make these girls get their damn gear on. Let's make this shit happen."

"THERE'S BEEN a change of plans," Jon Stone said.

The words caused a film of perspiration to break out on Tariq Riyadh's forehead and a cold splash of fear to roll down his spine. A change? At this point? It was unthinkable. What the hell were the Americans trying to pull so close to the moment of success? Perhaps it had been a trick to expose Riyadh and his people. Perhaps Stone and his crew were double agents and the whole plan, the promises of American cooperation, an elaborate ruse to flush out traitors. Saddam was just paranoid enough to try such a thing.

"Did you hear me?" Jon Stone asked. "There's been a change."

"Yes, of course I heard you. Tell me more."

"Forget it. Just send your little brother and his people over here. We need to go to Plan B."

"Why?"

"Dammit. Just do as I say. It's not safe to talk."

"You said these phones were secure."

"They are."

"Then what's the problem?"

"You think I owe you an explanation? I don't owe you shit."

Though he did his best to control it, Riyadh's fear had turned to anger. He'd tried being diplomatic with this bastard, but to no avail. He wanted his country to be free, wanted to enjoy the power that came along with it. But every man had his limits. He leaned against the bar, lit up a cigarette and waited.

Stone broke the silence. "Riyadh, when this is all over, you and I are going to go round and round."

"When this is all over, I will eject you from the country."

To Riyadh's surprise, Stone laughed. "Well, you little bastard," Stone said, "you really do have a spine underneath those expensive suits. Look, it's like this. We lost a source tonight."

"Lost how?"

"Didn't show up."

"We've been discovered."

"Settle down. We don't know that. Stop jumping at shadows, for God's sake."

Sandwiching the phone between his shoulder and his ear, Riyadh reached under his jacket, withdrew his pistol from its holster and checked the load. A glance at the door told him the dead bolt and the chain were in place. Not that either would do much good against Saddam's Feyadeen soldiers or his secret police.

Stone continued. "Our source didn't know all the specifics of the plan, but he gave us Saddam's itinerary and the motorcade information. That might be enough to put them on to us."

"Might," Riyadh said sarcastically.

"Yeah, smart-ass, 'might.' You want to push the panic button? Go ahead. I'll have my people out of here and in Jordan in a few hours. And you bastards can find your own way out."

"I'm listening."

"We figure the target will hang in his bunker tonight. We can't get him once he's inside the main underground complex, but there are a couple of weak spots in the tunnel system. We ambush him and his people there. Kill the whole lot of them and we're golden. Don't worry. We drilled for this contingency."

"Why not just bomb the bunker if you know he's going to be there?"

"And attribute it to who? God? Officially we're out of the assassination business."

"I see your point."

"I don't care what you see. Just send your people to the rendezvous. And you get underground. Once this goes down, we'll need you to step in."

"Fine."

"And one other thing, Riyadh."

"What's that?"

"I'm on to you. I did some checking, found out you're looking to make a little cash on the side selling Saddam's chemical and biological agents to the Russian mafia and the Libyan government."

Riyadh smiled. The spy had been spying on him. The man was boorish, but smart, resourceful. Riyadh couldn't help but feel a grudging respect for the man.

"And what will it cost to buy your silence?"

"We'll discuss that later. After we finish this op. Who knows? Maybe you'll get lucky and someone will kill me before it's all said and done."

"I should hope not," Riyadh said, not meaning it.

The phone clicked as Stone terminated the call. Riyadh holstered his pistol and went to get his brother.

DRESSED HEAD TO TOE in a black khaki bodysuit and combat boots, Abdullah Riyadh smeared black combat cosmetics to his cheeks and forehead in tight, circular strokes. Then he picked up the Heckler & Koch MP-5, slammed in a magazine and charged the weapon, realizing how it had become an extension of himself. He could field strip it, reassemble it, blindfolded, just as he could countless other weapons. He had learned to enjoy the feel of the weapon, the sense of power it gave him. The American, Chris Doyle, had trained him to handle it, to fight empty-handed. It had taken more than a year, but Doyle and the other Americans had turned Abdullah and his forty-nine comrades, a mixture of defectors and angry patriots, into a tightly knit band of warriors. Unlike Stone, Doyle had taught the men not just to fight, but to survive, to live long enough to enjoy their freedom. Though outwardly tired and cynical, Doyle seemed to care about the men he was teaching.

Hearing footsteps from behind, he whirled and saw the three Americans approaching. Other men, all outfitted in attire similar to Abdullah's, stopped their preparations and also stared at the trio.

"Okay," Stone said, "you girls ready to save the world, or what?"

Abdullah ignored him. Instead he looked at Doyle, who flashed a tight smile.

"We are ready to move?" Abdullah asked.

Doyle nodded. "It's a go."

ABDULLAH RIYADH CROUCHED beside the tire of a large troop carrier as he lay in wait for the Republican Guard soldier. Fear constricted his lungs, causing them to ache for oxygen as though he'd just run a marathon. He pressed his knees together to keep them from shaking and gripped the knife clutched in his right hand so hard that it caused his knuckles to throb.

Twenty yards away lay a critical target for the mission. Abdullah knew all too well that Saddam's network of tunnels and bunkers was almost legendary, both inside and outside Iraq. Fewer people knew of the dozen or so well-guarded emergency exits connecting the tunnels to the surface, all of which led into innocuous structures such as small groceries or apartment buildings. If it ever struck Iraqi civilians as odd that Republican Guard soldiers might fortify such seemingly useless structures, Abdullah knew they swallowed their curiosity. Their very survival depended on such compliance.

At his back lay a one-story structure, a former restaurant apparently sagging under its own neglect. The windows and doors were boarded-over and parts of the red-brick exterior had been scorched black by fire. In stark contrast, the structure bristled with security cameras and halogen spotlights, rated the attention and protection of a handful of elite guards.

During the past thirty seconds, another portion of the crew had successfully killed power for the surrounding four blocks, including the target building. According to intelligence and best guesses by the Americans, Abdullah and his group had ninety seconds once the lights went out to cover the open ground surrounding the building and breach its defenses before backup generators restored power, resurrecting alarm systems, security cameras and lights.

Abdullah knew he and his crew were living on borrowed time. During the past five minutes, his teammates, using a lethal mix of knives, garrotes and poisonous darts, had slain ten Iraqi soldiers, each identified as Republican Guard by the red triangle on his shoulder patch. With the area pitched into darkness, Abdullah had donned a pair of night-vision goggles, plunging his world into green. Four more soldiers closing in on the building, all of them Egyptian mercenaries recruited for the job by Jon Stone, were similarly equipped and considerably more dangerous than Abdullah could hope to be.

The soldier cleared his throat. The sound snapped Abdullah from his thoughts, caused his shoulders to tense. Using a handheld television with a tubular camera lens protruding from it, he snaked the lens around the carrier's front end, caught a glimpse of the soldier. The man stood, staring straight ahead, apparently fixated on a grove of date palms situated fifty yards ahead. The soldier held a wicked-looking SMG in his left hand, its barrel canted at a forty-five-degree angle as he scanned the area.

Abdullah watched as the soldier pulled a walkie-talkie from his belt, raised it to his mouth. Setting down the television, the young Arab rose up in a crouch, trying hard not to jostle his MP-5 or other equipment as he did. Blood thundered in his ears, making it harder to hear the soldier's transmission.

"Position ten," the soldier said.

A pause, followed by a muffled response reached Abdullah's ears.

"All clear," the soldier said.

Relief washing over him, Abdullah snatched up the television, secured it on his belt, listened. The soldier had turned and was moving back toward the main building. Rounding the carrier's front end, Abdullah fell in behind the soldier, closed the distance between them with just a few steps. Reaching around, digging fingers into the man's fleshy jowls, he gave his adversary's head a twist and dragged the knife blade across the man's throat, severing muscles, tendons and arteries.

Blood spurted from the gash and he went limp, dead before he hit the ground.

Sheathing his knife, Abdullah let the soldier fall into a heap. Folding the man's arms and legs in on his torso, the young Arab stuffed the soldier underneath the armored troop carrier, bunching his remains behind the tires so he'd be less visible.

Returning to his feet, Abdullah stared at his hands. The warm blood glistened bright green on his palms. His stomach rolled with nausea and his head momentarily grew light as the enormity of his actions struck him. He'd killed a man, willingly, mechanically. For a moment the realization and the physical sensations overshadowed everything else around him.

A voice exploded in his earpiece. "Abdullah! Left!"

The young man whipped around, bringing up the sound-suppressed weapon as he did. He spotted a pair of shadows approaching. Each brandished an assault rifle, the barrel tracking in on Abdullah. Without thinking, he triggered the MP-5, drilled the man closer to him with quick burst to the abdomen. Even as he did, his second attacker fired his own weapon, the muzzle-flash tearing a hole in the darkness, the report shattering the silence. Even as Abdullah tried to process the sounds, recognize them as gunshots, he whirled toward the second attacker. He cut loose with another burst from his weapon, simultaneously felt something grab hold of him, stop him cold. Pain seared through his right arm even as the gunshot registered in his mind. His knees buckled, slammed hard against the concrete.

The soldier, face obscured by night-vision goggles, readjusted his aim. Abdullah willed his arm to rise, realized it no longer responded to his commands. Streams of gunfire ripped through the air overhead, causing him to flinch. A storm of bullets ripped into the Iraqi soldier, pounding him back several steps, burrowing into the man's body armor, but stopping short of his flesh. Although not mortally injured, Abdullah saw the man whipsawed about by the bullets' force. Another burst smacked into the man's face, knocking him backward as though tackled from behind.

A pair of Abdullah's comrades, both Egyptian mercenaries, raced from the shadows and helped him to his feet while a third stayed behind the troop carrier and laid down cover fire. Weapons chatter and muzzle-flashes erupted around Abdullah. Bullets sizzled just past his head, chewing through concrete and ricocheting off the armored hide of the vehicle at his back.

He felt fingers slip into his shirt collar. Someone dragged him to his feet, roughly.

"Go," said one of the mercenaries.

Abdullah nodded, backpedaled toward cover. Even as he did, he used his good hand to snatch the Beretta 92-F from his hip, snapped off three shots at another soldier. The first two rounds flew wild, screaming past the man's head. The third, fueled by sheer luck, drilled into the man's mouth, tunneled through his spinal cord before exploding from the back of his head.

His arm throbbing, his head lightening with blood loss, Abdullah continued moving. God had smiled on him with that last shot, that much he knew. He triggered the pistol again, watched muzzle-flashes pop lighter green in his field of vision. With the Egyptians' guidance, he made it behind the large troop carrier.

"You're okay?" the mercenary asked.

Abdullah nodded. "I can treat this myself."

"You're lucky," the man said. "The bullet came out the other side. But you're losing a great deal of blood."

Abdullah waved him away. "Fight. We came here to fight."

The mercenary grinned. "Yes, we did. And I came here for a paycheck. Unfortunately we find ourselves at odds."

The man jabbed the barrel of his pistol into Abdullah's forehead. Abdullah raised a hand to swat it away but never connected. Then his world went black.

Amman, Jordan

TARIQ RIYADH SAT at a table in the corner of the hotel bar, nursed his third whiskey. The hotel catered mostly to Westerners and a pianist tapped out an old jazz standard, the melody competing with the dull din of collective conversation, broken only by an occasional burst of laughter. Riyadh watched as the cigarette pinched between the first two fingers of his right hand, burned down to the filter. Discarding it, he lit another. What the hell? he thought. I have plenty of time.

A big man dressed in a summer-weight navy-blue suit, eyes obscured by a pair of mirrored aviator shades, drifting through the crowd. Clutching a glass mug of amber beer, he approached Riyadh's table, dropped into a chair without invitation. Anger burned in Riyadh's face, knotted his stomach, as he stared at the man, who was looking past him at a wall. With his eyes hidden and his mouth set in a neutral line, Jon Stone was as inscrutable as ever.

"They've killed more than three hundred," Riyadh said. "The entire team, except for the mercenaries, are dead. They've also been hunting down members of their families, killing the men. I've lost four cousins and two nephews within the last week. One of them was twelve"

"Sorry," Stone said, not meaning it.

"Sorry? Sorry gets me nothing."

Stone shrugged and swallowed more beer. "It happens, man. You knew the risks going in. You don't like how it worked out? Tough shit."

"You knew the mission had been compromised."

"We suspected. There's a difference."

"Without distinction."

"Did you know the Egyptian mercenaries had gone rogue?"

"Maybe."

"But you went anyway. Why?"

"Orders."

"Whose?"

"None of your damn business."

Riyadh thought for a moment of the 9 mm Smith & Wesson hidden under his light jacket, discarded the notion. He couldn't shoot Stone, not here, not now. Even if he could best the man in combat, he knew he'd never make it out of the lobby without being arrested or shot by the armed guards protecting the hotel. Neither was an acceptable option. He had too much to accomplish.

"I'm making it my business," Riyadh said.

Stone had shifted in his seat, sitting sideways so Riyadh faced his profile. He cupped the rim of the mug with his fingertips, swirled it around the table in long, lazy circles.

"Take it somewhere else, asshole. You made your bed, now lie in it. You don't like how things worked out, tough. Truth be told, I don't care what you think."

"Perhaps you should start caring," Riyadh said. Apparently, Stone caught the change of tone in Riyadh's voice and fixed him with a hollow-eyed gaze.

"Really?" Stone said. "And why is that?"

"We both know about my little transgression with Saddam's weapons. We also know you shook me down for a percentage of the money. I believe your country would consider that treason."

"No one would believe you."

"I have proof."

"What kind."

"None of your damn business," Riyadh said, a smile ghosting his lips.

His hand still clasped around his drink, Stone unfurled his index finger and pointed it at Riyadh as he spoke. "If you report me," Stone said, "you go down, too."

Riyadh shrugged and ground out his cigarette. Setting both elbows on the table, he stacked his forearms atop each other and leaned in close to Stone.

"There's a difference, Stone. I have nothing to live for, nothing to lose. Thanks to your bungling, I have no family, no home, no country. And if you think you can solve this problem by killing me, you'd better reconsider."

"And why is that?"

"I have an audio copy of our previous conversation in Iraq attached to more than four dozen e-mails addressed to everyone from the CIA director to the White House to the managing editor of the *New York Times*," Riyadh explained. "If I don't check in every twenty-four hours, my people send out those e-mails. There are more than a dozen people spread out all over the globe, each with the same information, each with the same orders to distribute the information should something happen to me. You'd never stop them all."

Stone drained his glass, shoved it away. His lips curled into a snarl as he spoke. "You little bastard. You could bury me with that stuff."

Riyadh knew the admission cost Stone, and he made no attempt to hide his pleasure. "There are few things I'd enjoy more. Who approved the mission?"

"James Lee, the director."

"As I thought."

"Okay. So are we even? Are we done?"

Riyadh shook his head, grinned. "Done? Hardly, my friend. I'm just getting started."

CHAPTER ONE

Islamabad, Pakistan, the present

His hooded head bowed, his body shrouded in heavy robes, the big man shuffled down the street, arms crossed over his midsection, apparently trying to preserve what little heat he could. He stuck close to shadows cast by nearby buildings, stumbled and limped along as though physical pain accompanied every movement. A frigid January wind whipped down the street, carrying with it discarded scraps of paper and the smells of meat, vegetables and spices simmering in neighborhood kitchens.

In furtive glances, the man's eyes, like chipped blue ice, scanned the cityscape as he closed in on his destination.

A pair of hard-eyed men, each brandishing an AK-47, blocked his path, but the man continued on. As he approached, they stepped aside, each staring at their feet as he passed. From his peripheral vision, the hooded figure saw one of them shiver as though touched by Death itself.

Mack Bolan's face remained impassive as he moved. Though his life was steeped in violence, he took no pleasure in intimidating others, experienced no intoxicating rushes of power or pride. That was the province of the men he sought, men who abused others simply because they could.

Besides, Bolan knew that in war—particularly his War Everlasting—things never were as they seemed. Only fools declared victory prematurely.

Case in point.

A pair of shadows fell in behind Bolan, grew larger as their owners closed in. With his peripheral vision, the Executioner glanced into a nearby storefront window, saw the two men he'd just passed move in on him. Neither had unlimbered his assault rifle, but one of the men had produced a long knife from under his heavy coat.

Unbidden, Bolan's heart sped up and his senses came alive. His pursuers' gaits remained steady as they came up from behind, but maintained some distance. In this case, Bolan neither wanted nor needed any combat stretch. He planned to take out both men in short order, disable them before they could unleash their firepower on him, or, more particularly, on an innocent bystander.

At the request of an acquaintance, Bolan had come to Pakistan for revenge, but not a bloodbath. If even one innocent fell during his campaign, it would be deemed a failure.

Bolan's pursuers accelerated their approach. The soldier counted down the microseconds, waited for them to pass the point of no return. The hairs stood on the back of his neck as one of them came within grabbing distance. Simultaneously whirling and folding at the knees, Bolan's hands came into view, clutching the Beretta 93-R and the .44-caliber Desert Eagle. One of his attackers lurched forward, grabbing handfuls of empty air and stumbling under his own momentum. Bolan moved from his path and the man crashed to the ground.

A glint of steel caught the Executioner's eye as the other

attacker brought down his blade, the razor-sharp edge slashing a collision course with Bolan's flesh. He fell backward, rolled and came up off to his adversary's side. The silenced Beretta coughed once, spitting a thin line of flame. The 9 mm Parabellum round slammed into the man's face, hitting the soft area at the bridge of his nose and driving him backward. Bolan's opponent dropped his knife.

A scream sounded from somewhere, but a burst of autofire from Bolan's other attacker quickly drowned it out. The man still lay on the ground and was aiming the Kalashnikov rifle in haste. The bullets passed overhead as shell casings flew from the weapon, littering the ground around the man.

Bolan cursed inside. The wide-eyed man's rifle was spitting rounds everywhere, instantly raising the odds of innocent casualties. Bolan had hoped to take one of the men alive, to turn him into an intel source. With his erratic counterattack, the man had taken that option off the table.

The big American raised the Desert Eagle and fired two rounds. Even as the thunder from the big-bore handgun shattered the afternoon, reverberating off cars and buildings, the hollowpoint rounds tunneled into the other man's midsection, pinning his lifeless body against the wall.

The soldier rose to his full height and slipped his weapons back into the special holsters built into the sleeves of his robe.

Sirens wailed in the distance, heralding the arrival of police and emergency crews. He heard more screams from down the street, coupled with angry voices. He recognized both men from his briefing with Hal Brognola, head of the Justice Department's Sensitive Operations Group, a day ago. They were foot soldiers, toadies for Bolan's real quarry, international terrorist Ramsi al-Shoud.

But this was their neighborhood and they likely had friends and family here, people who loved them and would be only too happy to put a bullet in Bolan's brain in retribution for his actions. He could understand their grief and anger all too well. And he wasn't simple-minded enough to believe that just because the dead men in front of him were terrorists that their whole lineage had been tainted. Bolan no more wanted to shoot a grieving family member on the offensive than he would a police officer.

That didn't mean he planned to stand here with a bull's-eye painted on his back.

He had important work to do in Pakistan, and he needed to get on with it.

Holstering his weapons, he slipped his hood back over his head and left the killzone, navigating his way through a series of side streets and alleys. Passing a small tearoom, he heard a group of men speaking loudly, trying to drown out one another as they sipped hot beverages and smoked tobacco from water pipes. The Executioner continued at a dead run, feet barely making a sound, body hardly sagging under the weight of the robes and the weapons he carried underneath.

He had one other place to try. Al-Shoud's money man, Pervez Shallallab, lived in an upscale neighborhood only a few blocks distant. The man employed a heavy guard and Bolan likely would have to eliminate the foot soldiers protecting him, slowing his progress and forcing him to raise more of a ruckus than he'd hoped before hitting the head man.

When circumstances dictated it, Bolan didn't mind unleashing a boisterous campaign of hellfire and confusion. But al-Shoud was slippery, a survivor who would sacrifice his own mother before allowing an assailant to get within striking distance. In other words, a nauseating coward. The Executioner knew he was racing the clock to get to al-Shoud before he disappeared, living to terrorize another day. Making a lot of noise would only confound those efforts.

Minutes later, as dusk began to settle over Pakistan's capital, causing the temperature to plummet, Bolan reached his quarry's home. Ensconced in nearby shadows, the soldier scanned the ornate home and the reinforced iron gates that secured it. A trio of black Mercedes, engines running, headlight beams knifing through the wintry gray, waited in the driveway. Was the man coming or going? There was no way for Bolan to know for sure.

A well-lit street separated Bolan from Shallallab's estate, making a stealthy approach that much more difficult. He knew he'd have to ditch the hooded robe, switch to the combat blacksuit hidden underneath and sneak into the grounds. It could add several minutes onto his approach, but Bolan knew it couldn't be helped. If these men knew about their dead comrades, they'd be on the lookout for an intruder.

A pair of fighter jets flew over low enough that Bolan almost could read their markings. The jet engines' whine momentarily drowned out all noise and set Bolan's teeth on edge. As the sounds echoed for another moment in his ears, he smelled cologne, heard the faint scrape of a shoe sole disturbing gravel.

Unleathering the Desert Eagle, Bolan whirled. A bulky man stood behind him, a pistol clutched in a two-handed grip.

"Your mistake," the man said, grinning.

Fire and sound exploded from the pistol. Bullets pounded against Bolan's chest like a sledgehammer, the blunt force stealing his breath, causing white flashes of pain to erupt in his vision. His mind raced as an overloaded nervous system tried to assimilate the fiery sensation spreading through his chest. The soldier reeled back, his legs rubbery, and fell to the ground. His skull hit the pocked asphalt, but the pain seemed little more than a distant echo of the pain created by the impact of the bullets.

The man closed in, sighted down the pistol. Bolan knew the kill shot was a heartbeat away.

Stony Man Farm, Virginia

FORTY-EIGHT HOURS EARLIER, Mack Bolan, sitting in Stony Man Farm's War Room, studied a photo of former CIA director James Lee. From the chin up, Lee looked as if he were sleeping, eyes shut, but not squeezed tight, mouth parted an inch or so, as though snoring. From the chin down, he looked as though a bear had clawed out his throat, leaving behind a shiny mess or ragged flesh and spilled blood. Bolan stared at the close-up digital image of Lee's face and felt his stomach knot at the sight.

The Executioner already had seen accounts of Lee's death in both the *Washington Post* and the *New York Times*. He had a cursory knowledge of the situation. Lee, the former CIA director, had been gunned down in an alley in Islamabad less than twenty-four hours earlier. A four-man squad of Diplomatic Security Service officers, all highly skilled with weapons, had also been killed. An unidentified woman had been rescued by local police.

Surrounded by Stony Man chief Hal Brognola, mission controller Barbara Price, pilot Jack Grimaldi and armorer John "Cowboy" Kissinger, Bolan clenched and unclenched his jaws as he memorized the image down to the smallest detail. The fallen man's left hand rested next to his head, a smooth, gold band encircling the third finger.

"He had a family," Bolan said.

Brognola cleared his throat, nodded. "Wife, two kids. The kids came later in life, and the youngest is still in high school. I knew Jim. He was a good guy. Bit of a politician, but he believed in what he did, cared about his country. He didn't deserve this."

"No," Bolan agreed, "he didn't. What do we know?"

"You're staring at the exit wound from a 9 mm hollowpoint round," Brognola said. "Judging from the powder burns on the back of his neck and the path of the bullet, someone stood over him, put the barrel against his neck and fired. Jim knew it was coming."

"He was dead instantly." It wasn't a question; Bolan was trying to piece together the facts, picture things just as they went down. What he saw in his mind's eye thus far made his blood boil. "Who found him?"

"Pakistani state police. Since he was an American citizen, they called in the local FBI team to help investigate. They recovered the round that took out Lee, along with a few dozen stray slugs and shell casings. It was a damn bloodbath, Striker."

Bolan nodded, but kept his icy blue gaze locked on the picture. "How many nut job extremist groups are claiming responsibility?"

Brognola leaned forward, pushed a folder Bolan's direction. The soldier trapped it under his big hand and dragged it toward him, found it to be about the thickness of a rural community's telephone book. Setting the dossier on his lap, he fanned it open and gave its contents—stacks of paper, several with photos held to them with a paper clip—a cursory glance. He knew he'd have plenty of time later to pore through it. He shut it and returned his attention to Brognola, the head of the Sensitive Operations Group.

"To answer your question," Brognola said, "five extremist groups have taken credit."

"How many are credible?"

"That's the real question," Brognola said. "Four of them are little home-grown groups. Got some AK-47s, some whacked-out ideals and plenty of bad intentions, but not the expertise to pull off something like this. Forget about them." To punctuate his point, the big Fed waved his right hand dismissively. With practiced ease, he snatched up his cigar from his ashtray, clenched it between his teeth and started chewing.

"You said four don't have what it takes. What about the fifth?"

"That's where things get more plausible," Brognola said. "Barb?"

Using a nearby laptop, Price changed the image on the screen. "This is Ramsi al-Shoud." A brown-skinned man with raven-black hair and an unruly beard and mustache of the same color stared at the assembled group. The man's hair had receded well off his forehead, but he'd let it grow down to his shoulders.

Price continued. "Al-Shoud is a former Pakistani army officer. More recently, he was an officer with Pakistan's intelligence service where he spent a lot of time arming, funding and training extremists so they could terrorize India. It's estimated that he's directly or indirectly responsible for the deaths of more than two hundred Indian citizens. He also helped give aid and comfort to the Taliban before we went to war with them."

"You spoke of his affiliation with the Pakistani government in the past tense," Bolan said.

"Right," Price said. "The CIA knew about his behavior and had for years. Once Pakistan allied itself with us after September 11, we strongly encouraged them to fire him. They grudgingly complied and retired him four years ago."

"I take it he hasn't been puttering around the house, playing with the grandkids," Bolan said.

Price smiled. "Hardly, Striker. He's just taken his hate show on the road, but without official sanction, of course. He hates Americans, wants them expelled from the country. We believe he's behind a recent car-bomb attack on our embassy in Islamabad."

"Kill anyone?"

"Twelve Pakistanis, no Americans."

"I assume that's our fault, too," Bolan said. He caught the bitterness in his tone and scowled. He'd seen so much innocent slaughter in the name of religion and nationalism that his anger toward extremists groups sometimes spilled over.

"The Pakistani government fired him," Price stated. "But won't take it any further. Al-Shoud still has lots of powerful friends and the president's office worries that arresting or killing the guy might incite the extremists and lead to a coup."

"Is he even still in the country?" Bolan asked.

Price nodded. "He splits his time between Islamabad and Waziristan, a territory located near the border of Afghanistan. The U.S. has sent CIA paramilitary teams after him, but he always gets away, probably because his contacts keep dropping a dime on us. The Company also has tried bribing various Pashtun leaders in Waziristan into turning him over. Apparently he has enough money or power to counter us.

"Or both," Barbara said. "With his intelligence contacts, he's been able to get everything short of nuclear missiles. That and the embassy bombing already had made him a priority target, putting him in the Agency's top twenty-five covert targets."

"That all changed," Brognola said.

Leaning back in his chair, the Executioner clasped his hands behind his head and studied al-Shoud's features, memorizing even the most minor details.

"What about the woman?" he asked. "The newspapers said she'd been rescued, but that she'd been whisked off to a U.S. Army base for a debriefing. Has she told us anything of any value?"

Price tapped another key on the laptop. An image of a pretty woman with pale blue eyes, an athlete's tan and shoulder-length blond hair popped up on the screen.

"This is Jennifer Kinsey," Price said. "She was Lee's assistant and traveling companion. She's a former CIA agent, but more recently has been assisting Lee with his diplomatic work. During the last year, they've traveled through Syria, Iraq, Afghanistan and Pakistan. She speaks four languages and has a law degree from Stanford. She's supposed to be a rising star in foreign-service circles. Most people don't know of her CIA ties."

Bolan nodded. "But her background as an agent should be a good thing. With her training, she must have remembered something. Has she given us any good details?"

Brognola plucked the cold cigar from his mouth, tapped an end against the table. His cheeks flushed red and a scowl spread over his features. He jabbed the stogie back into the corner of his mouth, spoke around it.

"Her rescue was a little creative storytelling on the CIA's part," Brognola said. "Actually, Kinsey's MIA. The evidence techs found some stray hairs, a woman's shoe, a ripped gold chain and a torn piece of fabric from an expensive suit. They also found some of her blood, but only in small patches."

"So you don't know whether she was kidnapped—"

"Or she escaped," Brognola finished. "That's right, Striker. If I was a betting man, though, I'd say she escaped. These guys weren't taking any prisoners."

"So you're asking me to find her?"

"We're asking, is all. Alive or dead, we want to know what happened to her."

"Okay."

"But that's just a small part of the mission."

"Lay it on me, Hal."

"The President is very concerned about this. When a terrorist can kill the former CIA director, in broad daylight, on a busy street, and take four federal agents out with him, it sends a bad message to the perpetrators and any copycats."

"I assume the Man wants me to deliver a message of my own."

"Yes," Brognola said. "A very nasty one."

Islamabad, Pakistan

HIS CHEST RIDDLED with pain, Mack Bolan summoned his strength, rolled to one side and took himself off the firing line. The robe, heavy with ballistic plating, slowed his movements just enough to dull combat-hardened reflexes.

A bullet chewed into the concrete near him. Bolan fisted the Desert Eagle and was bringing it around to fire as the other man readjusted his own aim. The warrior knew in his heart he'd never make the shot, but he had to try anyway.

Even as his gun hand whipped around, Bolan heard a staccato whisper from behind the shooter. The man stiffened and, an instant later, a swarm of bullets burst through his chest, leaving a trail of blood and bone fragments in their wake as they buzzed into the darkness.

A male silhouette, distinguished by a ball cap and submachine gun, emerged from the darkness. Bolan trained the weapon on the man, but held his fire.

"Easy, Sarge," Jack Grimaldi said. "Just me."

Relief washed over Bolan and a smile ghosted his lips. Using his free hand, Bolan hugged his ribs as he rolled onto his side, climbed to his feet. Pain seared his muscles, bones and joints as he rose to his full height, melting away the grin.

"You okay?"

Bolan shrugged. "As well as can be expected. I thought you were going to stay with the airplane."

"The hell with that," the pilot said. "You stopped answering your radio, and that made the airplane seem kind of insignificant."

"Thanks. The radio took a bullet earlier."

"Forget about it," Grimaldi said. "Did Cowboy's ballistic robe work okay?"

Bolan nodded. "The thing's heavy as hell, but it stops bullets."

"So, who's this clown?" Grimaldi asked, nodding toward the shooter's crumpled remains.

Bolan walked to the man and, using the toe of his boot, rolled him onto his back. The man was Caucasian, with hair blacker than the Executioner's, his bloodless lips locked open in shock. Bolan didn't recognize the man, and said as much.

"He sounded American, though," the soldier said. "His accent sounded east coast, from what little I heard."

Kneeling next to the man, Bolan pulled a small digital camera from the pocket of his combat suit and snapped a couple of pictures of the man's face.

"I'll send these back to the Farm later," he said. "When we get back to my laptop."

"Couple of pinups for Barb," Grimaldi said. "I'm sure she'll enjoy that."

Before Bolan could reply, he heard a flurry of activity coming from the financier's compound. The sounds of a facility heading into lockdown reached his ears. Slamming car doors, voices, engines coming to life. Not surprisingly, the gunshots had announced his approach. He'd hated to waste the time shooting the man's picture, but finding an American running interference for an Islamic extremist group sent up a massive red flag to Bolan, one that he couldn't ignore.

Cursing to himself, Bolan turned to Grimaldi, flashed a series of hand signals. The ace pilot nodded and was already separating himself from Bolan so they didn't present a concentrated target. The soldier dragged the heavy robe over his head, revealing his black combat suit and web gear. He grabbed the Beretta 93-R from its sleeve holster, slipped it into his shoulder leather. He discarded the robe and moved into the shadows cast by a nearby building. Holstering the Desert Eagle, he filled his hand with an Ingram Model 10, minus the sound suppressor.

Gliding along a brick wall, he peered around the corner and saw a trio of men, each toting an AK-47, coming his way. Bolan couldn't help but be impressed. From what he saw, each man wore a headset and two of the men hung back, using nearby cars for cover as the third closed in on the alley. Hardly Special Forces tactics, but definitely better than anything he'd encountered thus far.

Bolan momentarily wished his own radio hadn't been damaged, but purged the recriminations. Make the best with what you have, he thought. Adapt. He had to think like the enemy. He knew Grimaldi, a battle-hardened veteran, would do likewise. He turned to the pilot, signaled him to watch their backs. The pilot nodded and turned his attention toward their rear flank.

Just as he did, a car screeched to a stop at the other end of the alley, effectively blocking them in. Electric windows hissed down and the black muzzles of assault rifles popped out, the weapons spitting flame and lead.

A thrill of adrenaline passed through Bolan. He focused on the gunners in front of him, left the other threat for Grimaldi to handle.

Caressing the Ingram's trigger, he cut loose with a salvo that blistered the air just next to the approaching terrorist. Acting with surprising presence of mind under fire, the man shifted positions and shot back at Bolan. The rounds pounded into the bricks just behind the soldier, peppering his face with reddish grit and slivers of mortar.

The bits of debris tore at Bolan's cheeks, opening the skin

and drawing trickles of blood, but thankfully sparing his eyes. He fired again, this time dragging the weapon in a wider arc, as though dousing a raging fire. Rounds smacked into nearby cars, perforating metal, puncturing windshields. A string of bullets pounded into the shoulders and chest of the shooter, who was approaching in a crouch. The man stopped cold, then jerked for a moment under the Executioner's merciless onslaught.

Bolan's combat sense screamed for him to look up. Even as he did, he was on the move, crossing the trash-strewed alley with long strides. Another shooter, a heavyset man with a long, unkempt beard and a lion's mane of black hair, was drawing down on the warrior from a fire-escape landing. Even as he came into the crosshairs of the man's AK-47, Bolan raised his own weapon, tapped out a pair of bursts that tore into the man's girth, knocking him back against the wall, killing him.

Reloading on the run, Bolan drew down on another of his attackers, drove the man undercover with a quick burst. At the same time Bolan heard an engine roar, saw a small caravan of cars exit the building. Bolan's heart sank for a moment.

Target lost. Game over.

Like hell.

He'd just adapt again.

Scanning the streets for bystanders, Bolan saw none. He could at least be thankful for that much, he decided. With the streets apparently clear, he decided to unleash a little controlled chaos.

Laying down his own cover fire, Bolan pinned his attackers under a withering hail. Shell casings fell around his feet and the popping of autofire in such a small space rang in his ears. At the same time, the warrior yanked a flash-bang grenade from his web gear, pulled the pin, but held the lever.

Breaking cover, he sprinted from the confines of the alley to grab a little combat stretch. At his back, he heard the rattle of subgun fire and thought fleetingly of Grimaldi, vowed to get back to him as soon as he defused the immediate threat.

Bolan's sudden shift in position apparently threw off his attackers, gained him precious seconds. As his own gun locked dry, he tossed the grenade into a space roughly between the two men. In the meantime, the hardened fighters had already begun to recover from the change and were shooting in their adversary's direction. The Executioner hurled himself to the ground in between a pair of parked cars. Knee and elbow pads absorbed much of the shattering impact of flesh and bone against concrete, but Bolan still felt flesh rip away from his open palm as he used it to help break his fall.

Letting the Ingram fall loose on its strap, Bolan fisted the Desert Eagle, rode out the stun grenade's sting and then hauled himself to his feet. Cocking back the big Israeli pistol's hammer to ease the trigger pull, the soldier stepped from between the cars, weapon leveled in front of him in a two-handed grip. One of the men, face buried in a V created by bending his left arm, fired wildly with a stubby black handgun. The Desert Eagle cracked once, the muzzle-flash illuminating Bolan's hardened features. The Magnum slug chewed through the air, caught the man in the forehead and knocked him back.

One down.

Bolan saw the other shooter, dazed by the white flash, trying to find a lost weapon. He triggered the Desert Eagle, its shattering report again splitting the night, and the round sliced a crimson line along the man's shoulder, eliciting a cry and causing him to settle back on his rump.

The Executioner stepped up close to the man, kicked away his AK-47. "You speak English?"

The man looked terrified. "Yes. I studied in America."

"You and I are going to talk," Bolan said.

"Yes, yes," the man said. "Talk."

Bolan pushed the man to the ground and rolled him onto his stomach, bound his hands behind his back with plastic handcuffs. The warrior came up in a crouch, started for the alley, ready to back up an old friend with whom he spilled more blood than he cared to consider during his War Everlasting.

Moving along a building, he stopped just a few feet from Grimaldi's combat zone. A moment of eerie silence had fallen, followed by a sudden chorus of anguished cries. Damn!

Before he could take another step, a roar reverberated throughout the canyon of buildings, followed by the tortured sound of grinding metal and a loud crash. A massive front of singeing heat whooshed out, smacked Bolan front-on forcing him to involuntarily cover his face.

What the hell had happened to Jack?

JACK GRIMALDI RAISED his silenced Ingram, unloaded a quick burst at the car blocking his path. Bullets skittered and sparked off its black metal skin, smacking into nearby walls.

Shit, he thought, armored to the teeth.

Orange-yellow muzzle-flashes flared from a pair of assault rifles protruding from the car. Grimaldi dropped into a crouch, caressed the Ingram's trigger. The hellstorm of bullets thudded against the car and gave the shooters pause, buying him precious seconds in which to maneuver.

Judging by the open windows, the car had no gunports and for that, at least, Grimaldi counted himself lucky. Considering the odds, he'd take any advantage he could get. His first hastily placed burst drilled into a fortified car door, just below the window rim. The bullets bounced away, but threw the shooter off balance, prompting him to withdraw inside the vehicle. Firing on the run, Grimaldi tapped out two more bursts that sailed inside the car. An anguish scream sounded from within the vehicle, indicating he'd injured or killed one opponent. That left three more shooters, one in the driver's seat, two more positioned outside and behind the car, using it for cover.

With quick, sure steps, the pilot crossed the killzone, acquiring a new target on the run. One man, crouched behind the car's front bumper, was drawing a bead on Grimaldi. A quick burst caught the enemy in the shoulder, chewing through fabric and flesh before knocking him backward. Grimaldi knew the man was down, but probably not out, particularly if he had a backup piece that he could fire with his one good hand.

Reaching a small alcove created by a doorway, the Stony Man pilot inserted his slender frame inside the cramped space, riding out a concentrated barrage of autofire as he did. Unzipping his leather bomber jacket, Grimaldi reached inside, snagged a fresh clip, reloaded his weapon. He inventoried his personal armory—one remaining clip for the Ingram, a .40-caliber Glock in a shoulder holster and a .44-caliber Charter Arms Bulldog snugged in an ankle holster, a last-minute gift from John Kissinger before leaving for the mission.

He was loaded for bear, sure, but so were the two men, and perhaps a third, trying to kill him. Death, Grimaldi could handle, but he was the barrier standing between these men and his old friend. If they wanted to get to Striker, they'd have to do it over the ace pilot's dead body.

It sure as hell wasn't the first time someone had tried.

Peals of gunfire echoed throughout the alley, intensified, telling Grimaldi that the men had seized on his pause to reload. Whipping the Ingram around the corner, he fired blind, emptying one-third of a clip in his attackers' direction. Chew on that, you bastards, he thought. He followed up with a second, more intense burst. Judging by the pause in return fire, he'd driven them under cover, at least for a moment.

A slight shift in the building's shadow caught his attention. Even before it clicked in his mind, instinct warned him of immediate danger. Still crouching, Grimaldi folded his body around the corner, saw a gunman slipping along the length of the building toward him. He triggered the Ingram. The stubby weapon roared to life, spitting jagged columns of flame, a cloud of acrid smoke. Rounds drilled into the approaching man's chest and throat, stopping him cold and pushing him backward. The man's assault rifle clattered to the ground as he crumpled in a dead heap.

Even as the dead shooter fell, Grimaldi was turning his attention to the hardman situated behind the car. A hand popped up over the trunk and Grimaldi saw that it clutched something.

Grenade!

Firing low, Grimaldi swept the Ingram in a tight arc, dispatching a swarm of .45-caliber rounds underneath the car. The way he saw it, this was his best bet. If he gunned for the hand, he had a better than average chance of hitting it. If he tried for the man's crouching body, and more specifically, his legs, the pilot improved his own odds of survival.

He hoped.

As the Ingram clicked dry, he heard the man scream. Shifting back into the doorway, Grimaldi folded in on himself. If he was lucky, the guy had dropped the grenade, releasing the spoon and activating the explosive. The man and the armored vehicle would absorb most of the explosion and shrapnel.

If he was lucky. If not...

The weapon exploded, sending waves of heat and shrapnel buzzing through the alley. A grinding noise, metal on concrete, followed and Grimaldi had to assume the explosion had knocked the car up on its side.

Grimaldi reloaded his weapon and got to his feet. He peered furtively around the wall, trying to present as small a target as possible. He saw the vehicle on its side, corpses spread around it.

He felt something behind him, turned, his muscles tensing for another confrontation.

"Easy, Jack," Bolan said.

Grimaldi relaxed, grinned. "Easy? Easy my ass. This is some of my best work."

MINUTES LATER Mack Bolan shoved his POW hard into a chair, causing it to creak and slide back several inches. The man, a Pakistani dressed in jeans and a gray athletic sweatshirt, glowered at his captors. A few extra minutes of drawing breath apparently had emboldened him into thinking he was in the clear.

Bolan was about to show him the error of his ways.

"Shallallab. Where was he going?" Bolan asked.

The man sat mute.

"Was he going to see Ramsi al-Shoud?"

A flicker of recognition lighted the man's eyes before fear doused it back out. He remained silent.

"Where is al-Shoud?"

Nothing.

Grimaldi spoke. "The problem with you, Striker, is, you give people too damn much leeway."

"Shut up, Ace," Bolan growled.

"I'm just saying—"

"I'm just saying shut up. So shut up."

"Maybe he doesn't speak English."

"He speaks English."

Grimaldi turned back to the man. Raising his voice, he asked, "You speekie English?"

The man looked insulted, but said nothing. "I think you're wrong," Grimaldi said. "He doesn't speak English. Hell, he doesn't seem smart enough to speak his own language."

"Bullshit," Bolan said. "He spoke English like a pro ten minutes ago. He's just playing stupid."

"Doing a good job of it, too," Grimaldi said. "So I suppose we're going to sit here all night, coddling this dumb-ass until he decides to talk. Him. A guy that doesn't speak English. I'm telling you, you're wasting your damn time with this."

Bolan made a grim face, turned away from the prisoner. "So what the hell do you suggest?"

"Remember Kabul?"

"Don't even go there with me, Jack."

"See that's what I'm talking about. You're too soft on these people."

"And you're mental."

"I'm just saying it worked in Kabul. It'll work here. That guy suddenly remembered his English really good after we did that to him."

"I'm not letting you cut this guy's balls off, Ace. It's not going to happen."

Bolan glanced over his shoulder, saw the man sitting stiff, eyes about to pop out of their sockets.

"What about his ears?" Grimaldi asked. "Can I cut them off?"

Bolan thought about it for a moment. Finally he nodded. "Okay," he said. "That's not so bad. You know, you can't just go around cutting off a guy's privates. Not right out of the gate, anyway. You gotta at least give him a chance to cooperate. It's only fair."

Grimaldi pulled a switchblade from his jacket pocket. He clicked it open with a metallic snick, held it up to the light so it glinted.

"But the ear's okay?"

Bolan shrugged. "Knock yourself out."

An evil grin twisted at Grimaldi's lips. "Righteous," he said.

The words practically exploded from the man's lips. "Please," he said. "I will talk about Shallallab and al-Shoud. I want to tell everything."

And he did.

BOLAN AND GRIMALDI climbed aboard a Black Hawk helicopter and slipped into the front seats. Each man carried a heavy gear bag packed with weapons and equipment, Bolan had laid his next to his seat, allowing him to perform a last-minute weapons check during the flight.

His right foot positioned on the gear bag to keep it from shifting in flight, Bolan loaded his Heckler & Koch with a sound suppressor and attached extra clips to his web gear. Grimaldi ran a preflight check on the craft.

"I'm glad that guy talked," Grimaldi said.

"Me, too," Bolan said. "I was afraid he'd call our bluff."

"Who said I was bluffing?" Grimaldi joked.

Bolan shook his head. "Forget it. An old tomcat like you could never do that."

"Your buddy didn't tell us a lot," Grimaldi said.

Bolan nodded. "Foot soldier," he said. "Probably doesn't know a whole lot."

Fifteen minutes later, the Black Hawk was aloft with Grimaldi guiding it expertly toward Waziristan, a Pakistani territory.

Straining against the harness holding him in place, Bolan

reached into his equipment bag and withdrew a laptop. The pressure of the straps against his recently bruised skin, even through the Kevlar vest, kicked up jolts of pain. He winced, ground his teeth and ignored it. During his War Everlasting, the soldier had suffered much worse, and had the scarred flesh to prove it.

Setting the laptop on his thighs, Bolan popped it open and powered it up. Within minutes he'd lock into a Stony Man computer dump system via an encrypted wireless connection. A digital camera would eventually carry his and Grimaldi's images electronically to the Computer Room. After a few more keystrokes, Aaron "The Bear" Kurtzman appeared on the screen.

"Striker," Kurtzman said.

"You get the coordinates I sent earlier?" Bolan asked.

"Right," Kurtzman replied. "I ran them through the National Security Agency's database and liberated a few things for our use. I'll send you the satellite pics while we talk. But your guy told the truth. There's something there, an encampment of some sort, right on the Pakistan-Afghanistan border. It was an al Qaeda camp at one time before a CIA paramilitary team shut it down a few years ago. After the team arrested the inhabitants, seized all their computers and documents, a couple of F-18s bombed the buildings to rubble."

"Our boy told us they've been setting up the place for months," Bolan said. "On the surface it looks like an agriculture operation, with animals and the whole thing. They do all their training inside a series of nearby caves to help avoid satellite scrutiny. No outdoor firing ranges, or anything like that. They do a lot of hand-to-hand combat training, classroom work, that sort of thing. There's also a large concrete building that houses their command functions."

Kurtzman nodded. "That tracks with what I found out.

The intelligence community had tagged the site as suspicious because of its history. But without any hard intel, they had to knock it pretty far down on the priority list. Plus, it's a crappy target."

"What do you mean?"

"Guess al-Shoud and his people brought their families along with them. Women, kids, elderly."

Bolan's brow furrowed, his lips formed a tight line as he considered the implications. "Lots of innocents on the firing line," he said finally.

"Right," Kurtzman said.

"We don't have much of a choice in this one," Bolan said.

"Just laying out the facts," Kurtzman replied. "Hey, Hal wants to speak with you."

"Go."

Kurtzman disappeared from view. An instant later Brognola's weary features appeared on the screen. Since Bolan had last seen him, the big Fed had lost his necktie, but judging by the coffee stain on his right breast, he still wore the same shirt, now unbuttoned at the collar.

"Striker," Brognola said, "what's the word on Jennifer Kinsey?"

"Nothing yet," Bolan stated. "The man we spoke with knew nothing about her."

"Could he have been lying?"

Grimaldi cut in. "He was pretty motivated to be honest."

Brognola drank some coffee from a foam cup. "I don't even want to know what that means."

"That's why we wanted to find Shallallab," Bolan said, "the finance guy. He's high enough up that he'd know whether she was there. Al-Shoud considers him a confidant."

"But you've got a good fix on al-Shoud?"

"Yeah," Bolan said. "Bear says we've got apparent innocents in the way. I plan to make this a soft probe until I learn more."

"Keep Barb and Aaron posted," Brognola said. "I won't be around."

"Why?"

"We have an antiterrorism summit at an undisclosed location," Brognola replied. "Heads of state from Egypt, Jordan, Morocco, Kuwait and Saudi Arabia are expected to be there. So are their intelligence chiefs. We're going to share information, try to expand cooperation, all that sort of thing."

"Hal the politician," Grimaldi said.

Brognola smiled around his stogie. "Yeah, I'm loving it, too," he said. "I'd stand naked in Times Square, but it's a command performance. The Man wants me there, so I'm going."

"Barb'll take good care of us," Bolan said.

"I have no doubt," Brognola said. "Look, the minute you get a line on Jennifer Kinsey, let us know. If she's still among the living, we'd very much like to bring her home."

Bolan nodded. "Feeling's mutual. We'll do what we can."

"No doubt, Striker," Brognola said. "Just watch your ass. Al-Shoud's operation may be small, but he's not small-time. Most of his men are former intelligence agents who've pulled some serious black ops in India. Badasses all. If this turns nasty, do your best—hell, do your worst—and come home."

"We're on it," Bolan said. Killing the connection, he and Grimaldi began scanning the satellite images and other intel provided by Stony Man's cyberteam, preparing themselves for what needed to be a short, precise confrontation.

CHAPTER TWO

Jennifer Kinsey saw the U.S. Embassy compound from about two blocks away. Another block ahead of her, state police armed with automatic weapons had blocked all roads leading to the embassy with wooden sawhorses and officers. She guessed the Marines and Diplomatic Security Service agents also had doubled up their efforts since James Lee's murder.

A shudder that had nothing to do with the biting cold seized her. Unconsciously she pulled the burqa's heavy fabric tighter around her, as if doing so would protect her from homicidal bastard that had pursued her now for how long? Three days? Four days?

Underneath the thick black robes, she still wore her navy-blue business suit and white silk blouse, both stained dark crimson by James Lee's blood. She chewed at her lower lip for a moment as unbidden memories of Lee's death flooded her consciousness.

Almost immediately, she shook her head to purge the memories. Stay strong, she told herself. If you want to fall apart, that's fine. God knows you deserve it. But do it after you've gotten inside the embassy. Not before. You've been through worse and you'll survive this, too. Just stay strong.

Kinsey bowed her head and started walking. She had bought the burqa from a young woman. It had cost her all the two hundred dollars in emergency cash that she carried in a small belt under the waist of her skirt, but had been a worthwhile purchase. In her right hand, she clutched a .25-caliber pistol that she normally kept strapped to her thigh. She could handle much more substantial ordnance. But the State Department frowned on their people carrying weapons, regardless of what hellhole they sent you to. So, from her way of thinking, carrying a smaller weapon was a compromise of sorts. The stubby weapon was no good at distances, but she knew she could jam it into an attacker's throat or eye and inflict plenty of damage.

She hoped it didn't have to go that far.

She began threading through the sea of people gathered outside the embassy. It took a conscious effort to not push past people, particularly men who'd stand in a woman's way on principle. It rankled her to be so passive, to walk seemingly without a purpose, to yield to anyone. Jennifer Kinsey hadn't climbed the ranks of the CIA or the State Department by being submissive. She'd fought tooth and nail for every promotion, every letter of commendation.

Now she was fighting for her life.

A man bumped into her, knocking her off her feet. She fell to the ground, banging her knees and skinning her hands. Her cheeks grew hot with anger as she stayed on all fours a moment. The man continued on, not bothering to offer a hand or to apologize. She chewed her lip and took a deep breath to clear her head. Let it go, she told herself. Get to the embassy and tell them what you saw.

Of course, she didn't expect them to believe it. She hardly believed it herself. That a group of Islamic extremists would attack her and Lee—or any American, for that matter—came as little surprise to Kinsey. Any U.S. diplomat who stepped into the country and expected a warm welcome, needed her head examined. Or at least needed to read a damn newspaper.

But Lee had been slain by a comrade. Not a friend, but one of his own.

Several of his own, in fact.

Hugging her arms tightly around her midsection, Kinsey found herself within forty yards of the nearest police checkpoint. She hurried toward it.

Again she could smell the smoke, hear the voices.

See the face.

It had been sheer pandemonium. The limousine's front end pinned against the wall, shoved there by another car. When Kinsey first felt the impact, heard the grind of metal on metal, the explosion of radio traffic from the security team, she wondered if they'd been the target of a car bomb.

In some ways it might have been better that way, she thought.

The DSS agents had put up a valiant fight, of course. Stay in the car, they'd said. We'll call for help, fight these guys off.

A swarm of militants, all dressed in civilian clothes, most armed with AK-47s, faces obscured by hoods, had set upon Lee's vehicle almost immediately. The DSS agents had given little ground, burning down half a dozen of the bastards in the first few seconds of the fight. They were well trained, well armed, quite simply, the best.

But Kinsey was convinced that a person couldn't be trained to survive a live frag grenade dropped just out of reach, particularly when an opponent was willing to sacrifice a few of his own men to kill you.

Grabbing an abandoned 9 mm SIG-Sauer, Kinsey had stepped from the vehicle, staking herself as the last line of defense between Lee and his attackers. Old habits died hard, she supposed. And she'd fought like the damn devil to nail a few of the guys, hoping against hope that help would arrive. Her life for Lee's. It had seemed like a fair trade at the time.

She'd exhausted the SIG-Sauer's fifteen rounds in no time. With those gone, the remaining militants had set upon her, beating her with rifle butts, fists and feet.

"She goes alive," a voice had called out. "She's mine."

The words had caused Kinsey to freeze, a sensation she was unaccustomed to. Turning her head, she saw a big man standing near the shattered limo. He looked at her as he aimed a Browning Hi-Power at the back of a kneeling Lee's neck.

"I said, she's mine."

Jon Stone. Here, in Islamabad. Killing his former boss. Why?

She had shuddered at the words then and did so now. He turned his attention to Lee. She kicked one man in the balls, crushed a second's windpipe and fled. The gunshot that murdered Lee rang in her ears as she'd run away.

She still wondered—no, obsessed was more like it—about whether she'd done enough to save Lee. What she knew for sure was that Stone, a former teammate, had assassinated a government official and probably wanted to do likewise to her.

So she could second-guess the hell out of herself all she wanted—later. After she took care of the job at hand.

The closer she came to the police checkpoint, the less regard she had for maintaining her disguise. Maybe it was fatigue or hunger. She hadn't slept at all and had only eaten a few scraps of food along the way. Maybe she just wanted the sweet relief of her home territory.

Regardless, she almost missed the warning signs.

A Pakistani man came in close, a blade clutched in his right hand. He grabbed her arm and stepped just a few inches away. He kept the blade pointed into her stomach.

"Come with me," he snarled.

In response she shoved the stubby pistol into his groin and fired it. Blood spurted over her hand, hot against her cold, chapped skin. With the muzzle shoved hard against him, his body and his clothing absorbed most of the sound. A shocked look overtook his features and he stumbled back.

A glint of steel flashed to Kinsey's right. Taking a step back, Kinsey caught the faint impression of a man stepping in on her, knife cutting its way to her. She brought her arm down hard, letting her wrist collide with her opponent's and knocking the jab off course.

The man pressed his attack, swinging the knife blade at her in wide slashes. By now, people had begun to see the altercation and were clearing away, most looking elsewhere. Kinsey sidestepped the knife thrust, bringing her almost face-to-face with the man. Bringing up the pistol, she jabbed it into the soft flesh under the man's chin and fired it.

As the man folded, she heard a screech of tires as a car came around the corner in a skidding turn. Hooded men stepped from the vehicle and began to rake the air with autofire. People screamed and scattered or dived for cover.

Kinsey tried to use the pandemonium to her advantage, melting into a wave of fleeing people. Looking up, she saw a big Caucasian threading his way through the oncoming throngs of people toward her.

She raised the small handgun to fire. As she did, something struck her skull, causing a white flash of light to explode behind her eyes. She stumbled forward and a swimmy feeling overtook her. She whirled to retaliate and found herself looking into Stone's dead-eyed stare.

"Hi, Jen," he said. A massive fist struck her once more in the temple and she sank to her knees. A moment later everything went black.

CHAPTER THREE

Waziristan territory, Pakistan

Crouched behind a line of boulders, Bolan panned his binoculars over the village of mud huts and sized up his adversaries. His breath escaped in white wisps and needles of cold plunged through the fabric of his combat blacksuit and into the skin underneath. Three men, two carrying AK-47s, the third an Uzi, acted as sentries for the gateway leading into the walled village.

Craters and shattered stone from past wars dotted the landscape that lay between Bolan and al-Shoud's stronghold. Bolan watched as one of the men fired up a cigarette, the lighter washing his face in a flickering orange glow. Another sentry, apparently the ranking member, cursed his comrade and swatted him on the arm. The stricken man groused but dropped the cigarette, stomped it under a booted heel and stalked off into the darkness.

A handful of tattered tents stood next to the mud huts and behind it all stood a large, featureless building of concrete brick. No fires for cooking or warmth burned. All the structures, except for the brick building, stood dark. Like Bolan, the three men clung to shadows, occasionally glancing at a dirt road that wound its way into the camp, as if they expected someone.

Bolan had kept the camp under surveillance for hours, but hadn't yet found anything of substance. If Kinsey was alive—and Bolan wanted to believe she was—it was going to take an intense search to find her.

The Executioner felt the hairs on the back of his neck prickle. Deepening his crouch, he turned and cast a wary glance. A fourth sentry, this man a good three inches taller than Bolan, walked the road heading to the camp. As he marched, the man scanned the area around him, his gun muzzle following the line of his gaze. Bolan's breath caught in his throat as the sentry's eyes settled on his darkened form.

The gaze lingered for a moment. The warrior felt his grip on the Beretta harden and his finger curl around the trigger. The man's next move would determine his fate. To Bolan's relief, the guard turned his gaze back on the camp and kept moving toward it.

During his hike up the mountain, Bolan had counted three guards and had left all three standing. That had been by design. He knew the events earlier in Islamabad would have al-Shoud's fighters on edge as it was, ready to strike at the slightest provocation. And leaving a trail of dead bodies in his wake would only prematurely alarm the Executioner's opponents and give them time to fortify their positions. However, the strategy also forced him to watch his back more carefully than usual.

The guard hurried up the trail and stopped when he reached the others. Bolan heard the muffled tones of the man's voice but couldn't distinguish his words. The terrorist warriors nodded their heads as the man spoke, and at least two broke into smiles and clapped one another on the shoulder.

"Striker?" It was Jack Grimaldi.

Bolan keyed his headset. "Go."

"Spotters caught a chopper coming your way. ETA is seven minutes."

"You sure it's coming here?"

"Anything's possible, but it's a safe bet. The craft has no visible markings and only minimal exterior lighting. I checked and it's definitely not one of ours. It could be weapons smugglers or terrorists not associated with al-Shoud. But my gut says you're about to get visitors."

"Clear," Bolan said. "May be the break we've been looking for."

"Understood. What have you got there?"

"Four guards, all armed," Bolan said. "Three more roaming the grounds. Unknown on how many inside. You ready to swoop if I need you?"

"Right. You said you wanted a fast taxi ride, so here I sit. Just me, a combat chopper, and a strike team of two dozen special ops soldiers who, by the way, are getting a little impatient."

"Tell them to stand fast," Bolan said. "They're here for mop-up, nothing else. This is a situation where the fewer guns we have, the better off we'll be."

Grimaldi whistled. "I'm sure that message will play well. If you hear gunshots, you'll know what happened. Any sign of our lady fair yet?"

"Negative."

"Al-Shoud?"

"Same."

"Think she's still alive?"

"Hard to say. If she is, al-Shoud knows where to find her. Regardless, he and I are going to have a heart-to-heart."

"My guess is he's going to do most of the talking."

"Most likely."

"Stay hard, Striker."

"Always."

Bolan heard the thrumming of helicopter blades in the distance. The guards returned to view and began turning on halogen spotlights, illuminating a flat area that Bolan guessed served as a landing pad.

Within less than a minute the helicopter, a Russian-made Mi-17, swooped in overhead. The whine of its engines pierced the silence. As it settled to earth, rotor wash seized snow, dirt and small stones, and flung them into the guards' eyes, forcing them to wrap their forearms over their faces. White cones of light emanated from the craft's bottom as it lit up the makeshift helipad. Bolan slipped deeper under cover to avoid detection and waited for the chopper to land.

A side door slid open and a big Caucasian with thick blond hair stepped from the craft. His booted feet sank several inches into the snow, but he still covered the ground in confident, graceful strides. Camouflage battle fatigues and a rumpled field jacket covered his bulky frame. A Colt Commando hung from a strap looped over his right shoulder.

He turned and his big hands reached inside the aircraft and almost immediately connected with something. Grinning, the man pulled Jennifer Kinsey, an olive-drab field jacket draped over her designer suit, hands bound in front of her by steel handcuffs, out of the craft. As she kicked out to get her footing, the man dropped her into the snow. As she glared at him, he shook his head and laughed.

Bolan studied her through the binoculars. A bruise swelled under her left eye, and she wore a couple of small cuts on her cheeks. But she was alive. For now, Bolan considered that enough.

For now. Soon she'd be free. Or Bolan would be dead. He wasn't going home empty-handed.

The large man reached down, gathered the fabric of her coat collar in his hand and yanked her to her feet. Bolan saw a satisfied grin play on the man's lips as he brought her erect and shoved her forward, causing her to stumble. The guards neither laughed nor made a move to stop the rough treatment. Four men all dressed similarly to the big man and brandishing assault rifles stepped from the chopper. They followed Kinsey and her tormenter inside.

Bolan keyed the headset. "Ace?"

"Go, Striker."

"She's here."

"Roger that. You going in?"

"Right. Standby. I'll call for a pickup."

Grimaldi acknowledged the radio traffic. Bolan killed the connection. The warrior sheathed the Beretta and unlimbered the sound-suppressed Heckler & Koch MP-5. Bolan came to his feet and, using rocks strewed about the terrain for cover, closed in on the village.

The crunch of hard-packed snow crushed underfoot reached Bolan's ears. He whirled, spotted a fifth gunner crouched next to a boulder. The man already had locked Bolan in his sights. The Executioner lunged left and crashed into the ground, the icy snow yielding under his weight. Flame blossomed from the sentry's weapon and bullets pounded the area around Bolan. Small geysers of snow erupted from the ground as rounds chewed a path toward Bolan.

Taking aim, Bolan stroked the H&K's trigger. The initial burst sailed inches past his target's head. The guard held his ground and laid down another withering hail of gunfire. Correcting his own aim, Bolan fired two more bursts from the

SMG. The rounds drilled into the man's belly, causing him to stiffen and stagger back before he collapsed to the ground.

Shadows loomed behind Bolan and in the absence of gunfire, he heard more assailants crossing the snow toward him. The Executioner rolled into a prone position, propping himself up on his elbows and clutching the MP-5 in both hands. He tapped out a short burst that chewed into the man's chest and stomach. Caught by the 9 mm stingers, the man staggered back and his body went limp. Dropping his weapon, he fell to his knees, pitched face-first into the snow.

More autofire flashed around Bolan. Bullets tore at the smooth, snowy surfaces and sparked off exposed rocks. He was on his feet and running for another position. He switched his weapon to full-auto and laid down a sustained salvo for cover as he ran.

He caught motion to his right, whirled and spied a pair of shooters trying to acquire him as a target. Orange muzzle-flashes burst from their weapons and lead sizzled the air around Bolan, lancing between his legs and passing close to his ears and shoulders.

As grim as hell, the warrior brought around his MP-5 and unloaded a burst at the nearest man. The leaden storm ripped ragged holes in the man's chest, shaking him like a leaf in the wind. As the first shooter fell, Bolan whirled toward the second. Having seen his comrade fall, the man redoubled his own efforts, emptying his rifle in a sustained assault on Bolan.

The Executioner snap-aimed the subgun and loosed a murderous gale of autofire. The onslaught pounded the man's center mass and drove his battered corpse to the ground. Smoke curled from the MP-5's barrel, mixing with the clouds formed by Bolan's frozen breath.

The big American snapped a new magazine into the weapon. Legs pumping, he surged toward the encampment, dropping two more gunners as he continued his death march. More gunfire blazed a trail toward him, forcing the warrior to thrust himself beneath a wooden donkey cart. A shower of hellfire pounded into the ancient vehicle, creating a spray of splinters. Bullets tunneled into the ground around him.

The warrior plucked a frag grenade from his web gear and rolled from under the cart. Popping up from behind it, he spotted two of the shooters—a pair of Caucasians in camouflage fatigues—laying down a relentless hail of lead. Yanking the grenade's pin, Bolan heaved the weapon toward the shooters and dropped back under cover.

An orange blast erupted, punctuated with a hellish chorus of agonized screams. Bolan was up and running again, this time beating a path for the helicopter.

A pilot stepped into view, pistol raised in front of him. Bolan's subgun came to life, stitching the guy from left hip to right shoulder. The bullets' impact thrust the man back into the chopper, knocking him from view. Grabbing a thermite grenade from his gear, Bolan activated the bomb and tossed it inside the craft. As a second followed in right after the first, Bolan wheeled and put some distance between him and the chopper. Reaching a line of rocks, he vaulted, hit the ground hard and launched into a side roll.

The dual grenades ignited one right after the other. Roiling clouds of flame erupted and ripped through the craft. Within a heartbeat, the fire ignited the craft's fuel tanks and blew it into a supernova of flame, glass shards and twisted metal.

Bolan took the blitz up a notch and beat a path for the brick building. The MP-5 held in front of him at shoulder level, he weaved a path through the cluster of huts. He detected no signs of life from within, no cooking odors or fires, no noise.

The source had claimed the place was filled with innocents, but Bolan had seen no evidence to support this. He considered that a stroke of luck.

He flattened himself against one of the huts and peered inside. He saw blankets, dishes, utensils, radios and a laptop scattered around, but no people. He checked two more structures and found the same.

Bolan edged along another of the small houses, bringing himself within a few yards of the concrete-block building where he'd seen Stone take the woman.

A shadow from above overtook the Executioner. Raising his weapon, he spun just in time to see a large, robed man— apparently one of al-Shoud's fighters—leap from a roof and fall toward him.

The man dropped into Bolan, wrapped his arms around the warrior's midsection and took him to the ground. The attacker straddled him and sent a fist rocketing for Bolan's face. The soldier rolled with the blow, letting it graze his cheek but mitigating the damage. Bolan tried to swing the MP-5 around so he could drill his adversary, but found his arm held fast in the other man's grip.

Bolan's left arm struck out hard, burying a fist into the guy's soft belly, once, then twice, each blow driven hard into the man's diaphragm. Breath exploded from the man's lungs and his grip on Bolan's wrist loosened. The soldier pressed his wrist against his opponent's thumb until the Executioner's gun hand slipped free. With lightning-fast movements, he cracked the man in the jaw with the MP-5 and sent him sprawling.

His appetite for hand-to-hand combat spoiled, the man grabbed for a pistol. Bolan's MP-5 coughed out a trio of bullets that struck the man in the throat and robbed him of any remaining fight.

Bolan reached the brick structure and flattened himself

against the wall, taking a moment to familiarize himself with the single-story structure layout. Kurtzman had told him that it had popped up within the last year, supposedly as part of an aid project for the village. The cover story was that it was to serve as a school and a community shelter.

Bolan dropped the MP-5 and fisted the Beretta and the Desert Eagle. He glided along the building's edge until he came within yards of a door. He heard the click of a door latch and, a moment later, the steel door opened. A woman half walked, half stumbled out, a baby clutched to her. A bearded man, his red hair trimmed into a crew cut, stood behind her, his forearm wrapped around her throat as he used her for a human shield. She clutched a bundle to her bosom—a baby.

From behind his human shield, the man aimed an autoloading pistol at Bolan. The soldier's eyes darted around as he sought a decent shot with Beretta.

He saw nothing.

JENNIFER KINSEY WINCED as Jon Stone hit her square between the shoulder blades. The blow launched her into a room that resembled a makeshift command center, with a bank of television monitors, computers and other high-tech equipment.

Kinsey felt Stone behind her before he touched her. When he did make contact, it was painful. He drove a fist into her kidneys, driving her to her knees. Grabbing a fistful of her hair, he forced her back to her feet.

Stone took a few steps forward, wheeled and pinned her under his cold stare. He nodded over his shoulder at the security monitors as they conveyed the carnage unfolding outside. A big man had waded into the middle of Stone and al-Shoud's gunners and, from what Kinsey saw, had unleashed hell on them.

"Friend of yours?" Stone asked.

Kinsey shrugged. "Maybe. Does he scare you?"

Stone's lip curled into a sneer. "Nobody scares me, honey. You should know that."

"James Lee must have scared you. Or you wouldn't have killed him."

"Lee was a paper pusher. Killing him was just business."

"Business for who?"

"Get it straight—I ask the questions, you answer."

Kinsey's eyes narrowed. "Simple rules for a simple man."

"You know, for a lady, you got some real clangers. Who knows you saw me?"

"Everyone."

"Care to elaborate?"

"No."

Stone stepped forward, crowding Kinsey. She felt her heart slam in her chest and her lips go dry as he did. He pressed his Glock to her forehead, used it to sweep aside a lock of her hair. The muzzle left a cold trail on the skin it touched. Despite her bravado, Kinsey was scared. Stone was a sociopath and he'd kill her without remorse. Her only lever, the only thing keeping her alive, was information.

That and Stone's propensity toward underestimating women.

Kinsey was a trained agent. She could hold her own against any man. Stone knew this about her but chose to bind her hands in front of her, leaving her in a position to strike out at him.

More motion flashed on the television monitors. A glance told Kinsey that the lone warrior had blazed through the exterior guards and was making his way through al-Shoud's compound.

"You tried to contact someone. Who was it?"

Kinsey shook her head. "No one."

His moves a blur, he cracked her once in the jaw. Her head snapped back hard and a coppery taste filled her mouth.

Blood.

Son of a bitch.

Kinsey spit crimson onto Stone's left thigh, stared up into his eyes, even as one of her own swelled shut from an earlier blow.

"Honey," he said, "I can do this all day."

"Go for it," Kinsey replied.

Stone's face reddened. His right hand snaked out and steely fingers closed around her throat. Kinsey felt her airway constrict and an ugly croaking noise escaped from her lips. Even as her heart began to race and panic set in, threatening to overtake reason. Stay strong, she thought. He can't kill you. He needs information.

As black spots filled her vision, Kinsey's thoughts slowed, became more disjointed. Stone heaved her across the room with a powerful thrust of his arm. Her throat open, she automatically gagged for breath. She collided with the wall, the impact forcing out what little air she'd regained. Sliding down the wall, she came to rest on her rear. She shook her head to clear her blurred vision.

Gagging, she raised her cuffed hands to her throat in a protective move as Stone came at her again. This time, she caught the motion of his foot snapping out, a kick headed straight for her temple. She rolled with the blow so only the edge of his boot caught her skull. It still hurt like hell.

Stone took another step forward, paused. To hell with it, Kinsey thought. I'm not going to let this bastard manhandle me. I'd rather die fighting.

Stone halted, looked toward a pair of his men. With a nod, he ordered them to gather Kinsey up from the floor, hold her arms. He closed his hands into mallet-sized fists.

One of Stone's thugs grabbed Kinsey's collar and brought her to her feet. A second man, a thin smile creasing his pocked face, closed in on her from the other side. Outstretched hands came within inches of her upper arm.

Teeth clenched, Kinsey fired her right leg out in a front snap-kick that caught the approaching soldier in the groin. She drove the leg with enough force that her shin collided against his pelvic bone, causing the man to exhale the contents of his lungs and double over. Her calf went numb. Cocking back her leg, she kicked a second time, this time going for broke, driving her feet higher than before. The outer edge of her foot smashed into the man's nose, pulping it in a spray of crimson.

The man holding Kinsey's arm pulled her back, taking her off balance. Instead of resisting, she threw her weight into him, pushing him back farther than he'd anticipated. He went off his feet and she came crashing down on top of him. As they hit the floor, he slammed his forehead into Kinsey's own. A white flash exploded in her eyes and she grunted with the pain.

He released his grip on Kinsey and she rolled onto her back, dazed. She felt the meager contents of her stomach push up at the back of her throat.

Her vision blurred by tears, her muscles shaking with adrenaline and fatigue, Kinsey saw Stone's big form coming back into view. He centered the Glock's barrel on her forehead. His finger whitened as he took the slack out of the trigger.

CHAPTER FOUR

The scratch of fabric rustling against itself, the creak of leather, sounded from somewhere to Bolan's left. He tore his gaze away from the frightened woman and her captor and looked over his shoulder. He saw a gunner approaching, walking diagonally toward him. Bolan raised the Desert Eagle and locked it on the approaching hardman.

The guy halted several yards away from Bolan and centered a machine gun on the warrior's torso.

Bolan willed his mind to stay calm as he considered the situation. He couldn't risk a shoot-out, not with two innocents on the firing line. As good as he was, he knew he couldn't fire the MP-5 fast enough to take out both men, not without catching the woman in a cross fire.

Bolan's combat sense called to him, but he considered it too little, too late. The danger was obvious. His choices limited.

"The gun, asshole," the man with the hostage said. "Drop the gun. Now. My boss wants to talk to you."

"Listen to him," the other guy urged Bolan.

The Executioner held his gun hand steady. He locked eyes

with the woman, tried to give her a reassuring look. He saw something flicker in the eyes, saw her look down at the bundle in her arms. The baby. Of course she'd look at the baby. What mother wouldn't, right? So why did his combat sense tell him he was missing something?

"Drop it!" the bearded gunner repeated.

Blood pounded hard in his ears. Everything—sounds, images—slowed to half speed. Still, his gut said he was missing something. What? The gunmen? He saw them. The woman? The baby?

The baby.

Hadn't moved. Hadn't cried.

Bolan's stomach knotted and his compassionate gaze hardened. In almost the same instant the woman's expression changed. Her eyes narrowed as they shared his realization. Her hands, still wound up in the blankets, came up, arms extending. A portion of the blanket fell away, revealing a dark shape.

Gun!

Bolan lunged sideways. Both the woman and the bearded man who'd acted as her captor tracked Bolan with their gun muzzles. An explosion of yellow flame shredded the blanket as autofire burst through it. Bullets lancing the air around him, Bolan triggered both weapons in midair. The Beretta hurled out three rounds in what sounded like a single cough. The bullets blazed through the woman's ribs, rending vital organs and snuffing her life immediately. The Desert Eagle thundered simultaneously. The bullets tore into the man who'd approached Bolan from behind. The hollowpoint slugs bent the man at the waist like a jackknife and shoved him backward. He was dead when he hit the ground.

The bearded gunner staggered a bit, but held the woman's corpse tightly to him as a shield. The barrel of his SMG tracked in on Bolan, prompting the warrior to unload a second triburst into the man's face that exploded out the other side of his skull in a shower of blood and bone fragments.

Bolan slipped inside the building and started down a corridor. As he approached a corner, a moving shadow caught his attention. The warrior halted and a moment later one of al-Shoud's men stepped into view, an assault rifle at the ready. Bolan's left hand snaked out and he grabbed a fistful of the man's shirt. With powerful movements, Bolan yanked the terrorist off his feet, heaved him into a wall and filled his stomach with a blast from the Beretta. The soldier took the corner and nailed another terrorist with the Beretta's sting.

Another of al-Shoud's fighters had dropped to one knee and was trying to acquire Bolan as a target with his AK-47. The assault rifle cracked once, the bullet sizzling just past Bolan's ear. He triggered the Beretta, which delivered a stinging rebuke. The 9 mm Parabellum rounds ripped through the man's shoulder and sent his assault rifle skittering across the floor.

Bolan crossed the distance between himself and the guard. Clutching the man's shirt, the soldier lifted his injured opponent from the floor, slammed him hard against the wall and jammed the Beretta's hot muzzle into his chin.

"Open that door," Bolan whispered in Pashto.

The man spit in the Executioner's face. "Go to hell."

With a rough shove, he thrust the guy, headfirst, toward the steel door. He grabbed the man by the collar and shoved his face into the retinal scanner. The automated lock beeped and the door hissed open.

The Executioner cast the man aside and pushed his way into the next room.

Gunfire erupted, lashing out at Bolan. He surged through the doorway, snapping off shots from the Beretta as he went.

His eyes fixed on the surveillance monitors, Jon Stone watched the black-clad warrior plow through the guards. A dull ache radiated from Stone's mouth as he clamped his jaws shut to contain his rage. His pistol still was trained on Kinsey's face.

Stone looked down at her. "He one of yours?"

"If he was," she said, "I wouldn't tell you."

Stone tightened his finger on the trigger, but Kinsey's gaze never wavered. The bitch was tough, he'd give her that. She'd eluded capture like a pro, put up a hell of a fight until the very end. Even now, despite the slightly widened eyes and the almost undetectable quiver in her lips, she planned to go out with her pride intact. He couldn't help but feel a little disappointed. He loved it when they begged for their lives, loved having the ultimate power over life and death.

To hell with it, he decided. There'll be others.

The orders had been explicit—kill Lee and any witnesses. Kinsey, with her list of contacts, was particularly dangerous to Tariq Riyadh, which by extension made her dangerous to Stone.

A voice called from behind. "Stone, we've been breached. What's going on here?"

Stone turned to see a small man dressed in mud-brown tunic and pants, his face twisted in anger. It was al-Shoud.

"It's all under control," Stone said. "Just shut your damn mouth and let me handle it."

The smaller man came to Stone's side, stopped. He glowered at the woman, then returned his attention to Stone. "Why is she still alive?"

"I had questions."

"Questions? Of what sort?"

Stone heard more shooting outside. He looked up, saw the intruder had mowed down more of al-Shoud's men. He was getting too damn close.

Stone turned back to the smaller man. "Dammit, this isn't the time. Get the hell out of here. Or grab a gun and make yourself useful, you little fanatic. I don't care what you do. Just get away from me before I blow your head off."

Al-Shoud, whose eyes stared level with Stone's collarbone, poked a finger into the bigger man's chest. "You do not give the orders, I do. Now why is this woman still alive?"

Stone felt rage supercharging his body. The little man was screaming at him. The tip of al-Shoud's index finger nearly bent as he jabbed it into the sinew and bone of Stone's massive frame. A red haze filled Stone's eyes as he watched the smaller man whip himself into a frenzy, his words melting together into a single high-pitched whine.

To hell with this, Stone decided. The guy had served his purpose and Stone had fulfilled his promise—killing James Lee. Stone raised his pistol, jabbed it into the man's face, triggered it. The weapon barked once and the man's head disintegrated in a red haze.

A cry sounded from behind Stone. He whipped around, saw two of al-Shoud's men stepping away from their posts, each bringing his weapon to bear on Stone.

The Glock cracked four more times in Stone's grip, leaving them dead.

Stone detected motion to his right. He looked down, spotted Kinsey scrambling across the floor, distancing herself from him. Raising the pistol, he caught her dead to rights, prepared to squeeze the trigger.

Before he could fire, the steel security door banged open, grabbing everyone's attention.

"The door," he yelled to his own men. "Get the damn door."

To hell with it, Stone decided. As gunfire rang in his ears, he rolled across the floor, which was littered with shell casings, shattered glass and wood splinters. Coming up in a crouch, he chanced a look over his shoulder and glimpsed the blacksuited commando laying waste to a squad of highly trained mercenaries and terrorists. Stone hated to turn and run, but experience won out. Chances were, the guy had backup— extra soldiers, air support, the whole nine yards. If so, Stone didn't stand a chance. And, like any good soldier, he knew when to retreat.

But things weren't over between him and this icy-eyed SOB. Not by a long shot. He slipped from the building, the din of gunfire still ringing in his ears.

CHAPTER FIVE

Alexandria, Virginia

Doyle chased the last piece of Kansas City strip around his plate with a fork. Spearing it, he popped it into his mouth, began chewing. He looked up in time to see his wife, Nancy, smiling at him, green eyes regarding him warmly.

"Skip lunch again?" she asked.

He nodded. Covering his mouth with a cloth napkin, he said, "Had a magazine piece to get out the door. Hoping this will turn in to something really good. The editor likes me, I like him. If I can get a couple of regular assignments, it might take some of the stress off."

"What stress? We make plenty of money."

Doyle washed down the beef with a swig of ice water. "Uh-uh. You make plenty of money. I made so little last year, the panhandlers were giving me cash. I don't carry my share of the load and it sucks."

Scowling, she reached across the table, took both his hands in hers. "What I make is yours. You know that. You hated working for the State Department, and I hated your being gone twenty weeks out of the year. Your quitting the government has been a godsend for our marriage."

"But not for our bank account."

"I don't care about the money," she said, her scowl deepening slightly. "You know that. I want you to be happy. I want us to be happy."

Doyle returned her smile and placed his hand on top of hers. "Hey, I am happy," he said. "I've never been this happy. I swear. Just ask my last three wives."

Pulling a hand free, she gave him a gentle swat on his forearm, smiled. "You rat."

He shrugged. "I told you before, I'm a curmudgeon."

"It's probably because you don't sleep," she said.

"I was tossing around again last night?"

She nodded. "You yelled once, too. Scared the devil out of me."

"I say anything you could understand?"

"Something about a woman named Heidi. And you mentioned massage oil. Should I be worried?"

Nancy let the words hang between them for a moment before she surrendered to the grin fighting to come out. She laughed and Doyle found himself laughing, too. He had to admit, it felt good to lighten up a little, to enjoy a night out and a little conversation. It felt good, but it did little to untie the small knot forming in his stomach.

That he'd had another outburst while sleeping worried him. The shrinks in rehab had warned him of this, calling it posttraumatic stress disorder or some such thing. He called it a whopping pain in the ass, one that refused to go away.

From the start, he had resolved to keep his CIA career secret from Nancy. The way he saw it, it was his only chance of having a normal life. She was gorgeous, successful, loving, a person who wouldn't swat a mosquito if it was sucking her last pint of blood from her body. Would she want to be with a man who'd spent the last decade running around the world assassinating people?

Doubtful, damn doubtful. So he talked only about his career as a reporter for Liberty News Service and later his job as public information with the State Department. He kept the cloak-and-dagger stuff precisely where it needed to be: tucked away in a small corner of his mind, where he could forget the bloodshed, the betrayals, the battles. Still, things tended to bubble to the surface, as they had last night. And that worried him.

"Do you remember what it was?" Nancy asked. "Were you having a bad dream or something?"

Doyle gave a mock shiver. "Probably the dream where you just keep asking me for sex, over and over again. Scared the hell out of me."

Even in the flickering candlelight, he saw the smile drain away from her eyes. "I'm serious, Chris. Ever since you got out of rehab, you've been like this, thrashing around, crying out."

He shrugged, forced himself to maintain eye contact as he lied. "Probably just work stress," he said. "That's all. Things are moving a little slow. It's got me a little worried."

"Are you sure that's all there is?"

"Of course, I'm sure. What am I now, a liar? Let it go, for Christ's sake."

It was only after the words came out that he realized he'd raised his voice. He looked to Nancy, who was chewing her bottom lip, probably weighing whether to retaliate. He wrapped her small hand in his. "Hey," he said. "I'm being a jackass. Sorry. I guess I'm more stressed than I let on."

"It's okay," she said, nodding. "I shouldn't have pushed the issue."

"Hey, you're my wife," he said, lightening his tone. "You're allowed to check up on me. Anytime. I mean that." Even as he said the words, he felt pangs of guilt overtake him. Yeah, he thought. Ask me anything you want. I may even give you an honest answer.

"So this stress," Nancy said, her voice halting, "I mean, how are you doing with the, you know."

"The drinking?"

"Yes."

"Fine. I hardly even crave the stuff anymore," he said.

"I was worried that with all the stress, that you might—"

"Start drinking again? Nah, those days are behind me. Besides, I'm obnoxious enough without the juice. Right?"

"Not really," she said, unable to contain her smile. "But at least you don't spend the night hugging the toilet anymore."

"I like the toilet."

"I like having you in bed, with me."

"So does this mean we can have make-up sex tonight?"

Shaking her head, she pulled her napkin from her lap, set it on her plate. "Is that all you ever think about, sex?"

"I thought about a sandwich a couple of weeks ago."

"Well, that is progress," she said.

As Nancy hugged his arm, snuggled in close to his side, Doyle looked at her, smiled and exhaled, letting the tension drain from his body. The click of her heels and his dress shoes striking concrete echoed throughout the parking garage as they wound their way throughout, searching for their car.

A cold tingle passed down Doyle's spine. He wasn't immediately sure what triggered the response, but he also chose not to ignore it. Pulling his wife a little closer, he swept his gaze over the surrounding parked cars, lined up on either side of them like rows of imperfect teeth.

He saw nothing, but the sensation buzzing through his spine remained. He knew better than to ignore it. After years in the field, Doyle had developed a sixth sense about things, the ability to sense danger before it befell him. It had saved his life more than once, but now he wondered whether it was a relic, a holdover from his old life. He was out of the game. He'd left that life behind, opting for something quieter but ultimately more satisfying.

A dull scrape reached his ears, caused him to turn. A big man in an ankle-length coat, ragged jeans and black cowboy boots was approaching from behind. The white shimmer of an overhead light bulb reflected off the forehead of the man's watermelon-shaped head. The scraping repeated itself as the man's coat dragged along the rear bumper of a Buick sedan.

Probably sensing something, Nancy stiffened a bit.

"Honey, what's wrong?" she asked.

"Shh," Doyle said. "Just my imagination. I'm having bad dreams now while I'm awake."

Or so he hoped. The man looked threatening, but hadn't made a move against Doyle. So why panic Nancy unless it became absolutely necessary? It probably was the damned stress disorder shit again. The longer he stayed away from the sauce, the more pronounced it became.

But...

Before the couple proceeded farther, another man stepped from behind a van and blocked their path. Built like a football linebacker, the guy, a steel pipe gripped in one hand, tapped the pipe steadily against his open palm.

Her eyes wide with fear, Nancy turned to him. Doyle saw a question forming on her lips. Before she could speak, he held a finger to his lips, silencing her. Stopping dead in his tracks, he swept his wife behind him, guiding her into the space between two parked cars. The guy with the pipe stopped three parking spaces away from Doyle, while the other man positioned himself equidistant in the opposite direction.

Doyle's heart slammed against his rib cage. Unconsciously he licked his lips, which had gone dry with fear. His hands balled into fists, but hung at his sides. Energy coursed through his arms and legs. He made a conscious effort to stand still. He knew which way it could go, but he didn't want it to go that way. Not here, not in front of Nancy.

"Yo, man, help a guy out with some money?"

Doyle flashed the guy a smile, gave a slight shrug. "Sorry, guy," he said, "I'm all tapped out tonight."

Steel Pipe took another step, shortening the gap between them. From the corner of his eye, Doyle spotted the other man do likewise.

Cocking his head, Steel Pipe gave Doyle an appraising stare. The guy's stony face shifted to Nancy. His gaze lingered what seemed like an excruciating amount of time on her.

Doyle felt an angry heat rise from his skin as muscles tensed underneath his jacket. Don't even go there, you bastard, Doyle thought. But he kept the grin plastered on his face.

"What about her?" Steel Pipe asked, nodding at Doyle's wife.

Doyle shook his head. "Forget it," he said. "She doesn't have any money, either. We spent it on dinner."

The guy shot Doyle a gap-toothed grin. "I'm not talking money, boy. I'm talking some ass. I want to spend some time with your woman. What do you say, Nick?"

The other guy snorted out something vaguely like a laugh, but said nothing. Doyle heard Nancy make a small, scared sound. He wasn't surprised. She was a good person, kind, loving, accepting. She was completely out of her element here.

Not Doyle.

God help him, the situation fit Doyle like a glove.

"You heard me, man. I want to spend some time with your lady."

Doyle's voice came out quiet, cold. "I don't think you want to go there."

"Man, who are you to—"

Before the thug finished, Doyle surged forward, bridging the gap between them. Muscles coiling, releasing, his foot fired out in a front snap-kick that he buried in the guy's groin. His cheeks swelled, turned purple. The man staggered forward, trying to hit Doyle with a wild swing. It didn't connect. The guy's mouth had popped open as he gasped for breath. Jamming his thumb into his opponent's mouth, Doyle hooked the first joint on the space between the man's cheek and his upper jaw. His opposite hand grabbing the man's forehead, fingertips digging into the guy's temple, Doyle yanked his hands in opposite directions.

Bloodied fingers encircling the pipe, Doyle shot his leg out in a side snap-kick that hurled the other man into a concrete support column. He fell to the ground, blood glistening as it poured from his shattered mouth.

Whipping around, Doyle saw Boots raising a revolver, drawing down on him. Doyle heaved the pipe at the guy, catching him in the forehead and throwing off his aim. The gun barked once, but the bullet flew astray, hitting a car window.

One.

Even as the guy readjusted his aim, Doyle slipped between a pair of cars. He considered going to Nancy, to shield her with his body, but decided against. He didn't want to draw the fire toward her. If anyone took a bullet, it'd be him. But if something happened to him, what about his wife?

Don't go there, he told himself.

The gun barked several more times as the man panic fired,

the bullets breaking out windows, punching through steel and rubber as the guy tried to overwhelm his opponent with quantity rather than quality.

Grudgingly, Doyle had to admit it was about to work. Even as the sixth shot's report echoed through the concrete surroundings, Doyle was on his feet. Rounding the corner of the car, he caught the guy emptying spent brass from the revolver's cylinder. Doyle dug into his pocket, palmed a stainless-steel pen, as he plunged ahead. As he surged forward, he swung the pen in a swooping arc, jammed it into the guy's already injured eye. Dropping his gun, the man screamed and stepped back, hands automatically covering his face to protect it. Enraged, Doyle worked the man's midsection, bare fists sinking into the man's soft middle. As the thug raised his fists to retaliate, Doyle's fist shot out a last time. The first two knuckles of his hand spearing into the man's injured eye socket. A primal scream escaped Doyle's lips as the final blow connected.

He heard a gasp behind him. Wheeling, he saw Nancy's hand resting on her chest, palm down, fingers splayed open. Eyes wide with shock told Doyle all he needed to know.

Things never would be the same.

CHAPTER SIX

Somewhere over the United States

Working the warm, soapy water over his hands, Tariq Riyadh starcd again at his new face and wondered whether he'd ever get used to it. It had been months since the cosmetic surgery, since he'd sacrificed his face, his identity, his history, in exchange for a new life and a chance at revenge. With still-wet fingers, he touched the corners of his eyes, made smooth under the surgeon's knife, traced his fingertips along the contours of his cheekbones, also surgically enhanced. Colored contact lenses had turned his dark brown eyes hazel and he'd shaved his head bald.

Riyadh dried his hands, wadded the towel and threw it away. The whine of the 707's engines grew louder as the craft gained altitude, the corresponding pressure change pinching his inner ears. The Arab stepped from the small washroom and headed for his seat, hands smoothing wrinkles from his suit jacket as he moved. The cabin was nearly empty, except for a half dozen burly, armed men seated around.

Riyadh returned to his seat, started to reach for his newspaper, when a hand on the shoulder caused him to stop. He looked up and saw a man, a tightly curled microphone wire dangling from his ear and a handgun holstered on his hip, standing next to him.

"Mr. Aziz will see you now," the bodyguard said.

Nodding, Riyadh got to his feet and followed the man into the plane's front section. A heavy security door hung open, lashed to one wall with a small chain. A haze of smoke hung in the hot, dry air, causing Riyadh's nose to wrinkle as he stepped inside. He felt a tickle of fear pass through his stomach as he swept his gaze over the room, sought out Jamal Aziz, the man who had sought him out several months earlier and promised to help change his life forever.

Aziz was a small, meticulous man with a head of thick gray hair and brown eyes so dark that, from a distance, they looked black. Upon seeing Riyadh, Aziz came to his feet, flashed a smile that Riyadh found neither pleasant nor warm. But he liked the man's money and that was enough reason for him to return the smile.

"My friend, welcome," Aziz said. The baritone rasp of his voice served as an amusing foil to his small form. But Riyadh knew better than to underestimate the man in front of him.

After his initial contact with Aziz, Riyadh had done some checking. He'd found very little information of substance. But what little he'd learned taught him that the man was wealthy and powerful. An invaluable ally if he liked you, a deadly adversary otherwise. Riyadh considered himself fortunate to be in the former group.

With a sweep of his hand, Aziz gestured toward a chair. "Please, sit."

Riyadh complied. Settling into the chair, he crossed his legs, folded his hands on his lap and smiled, allowing the other man to speak first. Aziz, he knew, was a man used to being in charge. So Riyadh would mind his manners, until it no longer made sense to do so.

Aziz exhaled a cloud of smoke, parted it with a wave of his hand.

"The mission in Pakistan was successful? James Lee is dead?"

"Yes."

"Excellent. This makes you feel better?"

"Better, of course, my friend," he said. "But it pales to the joy I will feel when we move into the next phase. That will be truly gratifying."

"Agreed. All is ready, then?"

Riyadh nodded. "The money has changed hands. The weapons have been trucked into Utah."

"The warriors?"

"Stone finished training them two weeks ago. They are entering the United States even as we speak. We have others who already have been training in Utah."

Aziz smiled, clapped his hands. "Perfect. I knew you would handle this with precision."

Pulling a crumpled pack of cigarettes from his pocket, Riyadh shook one into his hand. Slipping it between his lips, he opened the stainless-steel lighter's hood with a thumbnail. "You've been generous with your money and your connections," Riyadh said. "I could not have killed James Lee without your help."

Aziz nodded, encouraging Riyadh to continue.

"Would it be rude to ask why? You're obviously a man of means. Why would you want to involve yourself in all this?"

Aziz seemed to weigh the question for a moment. His face hardened as he spoke. "As an Arab, I can do no less," he said. "The Americans continue to spill our blood for their own benefit. Whether it's for oil or security, they bully our countries, take our resources, kill our people. I have watched this happen over and over. I cannot sit by as it continues to happen."

"I see."

"Then you also understand how important this is to me. And you must understand the importance of honesty between partners, particularly as they work to liberate their home."

The small hairs on the back of Riyadh's neck brushed against his starched shirt collar. "I would have it no other way."

"And that's why you didn't tell me that al-Shoud had died? At the hands of your own man?"

Riyadh's throat constricted and sweat beaded on his forehead. "I did not think it important," he said, his voice taut. "Al-Shoud was a small part of a larger picture.

Aziz gave him a cold smile. "Perhaps you should let me determine what's important. That might be in all our best interests."

"You are right, of course. My apologies."

"I must be able to trust you, Mr. Riyadh," Aziz said. "I will give all I have to your cause. My fortune is yours to use against the Great Satan. Allah has blessed me with great wealth, great power, and I give it freely to those who are worthy. But in return I must demand rigorous honesty. It's the only condition I request, but it is nonnegotiable."

"It's only fair," Riyadh stated.

"The woman. The one who's missing. Tell me about her."

"Jennifer Kinsey? She's a low-level diplomat. She once worked for the CIA alongside Stone and Lee."

"She poses no threat?"

Riyadh shook his head. "None. She's a bureaucrat. Nothing more."

"And the man who attacked al-Shoud's camp. What do we know of him?"

"Very little, I'm afraid. He took out more than a dozen guards before it all was said and done. A cleanup team followed behind, moved all the relatives to a camp for debriefing."

"Any surveillance photos?"

Again, Riyadh shook his head no. "All our security images are captured digitally and backed up on offsite servers. Someone hacked into the system, drained all its information. We know nothing of him—yet."

"Did the hackers get any information that could compromise us?"

"No."

"This man, the one from Pakistan, he could cause us more problems."

Riyadh considered this for a moment. "Minor problems, perhaps," he offered. "But Stone is working his sources in U.S. intelligence. We hope to identify the man within the next twenty-four hours. Once we do that, we can hunt him down and kill him."

"And if that fails?"

Riyadh remained silent as he contemplated this.

Aziz continued. "I don't like loose ends. I need assurance that this man no longer will bother us, that he and others in U.S. intelligence suspect nothing of our plan. We are at a very critical, very dangerous phase of the operation. There's no room for error. You must find this agent, this soldier, and take him out."

"Don't worry," Riyadh said. "He's as good as dead."

JAMAL AZIZ WATCHED the other man exit the cabin, felt an indescribable joy well up within. He was transmuting others' hate into gold and knowing the pending results made him damn near giddy with anticipation.

Leaning back into his seat, he rested his head against the headrest, settled his arms on the chair's armrests. A pair of slender, feminine hands reached from behind the seat and began kneading the tiny muscles of his shoulders. Closing his eyes, he sighed contentedly.

The world stood on the precipice of hell, and it made Aziz feel good.

Within days, he'd inflame his homeland of Egypt, along with most of the Middle East. Within days, the common people of the Middle East would hate the United States more than ever. And those who'd been willing to give the world's superpower the benefit of the doubt also would turn.

As would Arab leaders—those who survived through the end of the week, anyway.

With Riyadh's help, Aziz planned to sow discord, nurture it until it grew into something much worse. Eventually, the anger would explode into violence. If not immediately, then soon enough. Of course, he realized that not all Arab countries, particularly those weak enough, misguided enough, to have forged a relationship with America would turn on that country immediately. But eventually they'd have to. Even the most autocratic of nations had to listen to its people, if the people were ready to stage a violent overthrow.

He'd already laid the groundwork for such uprisings. Aziz had used his considerable resources to arm, train and fund militant groups operating in Egypt, Jordan, Saudi Arabia and other U.S.-friendly Middle Eastern countries. These men were ready to deal death upon their home governments until they fell to their knees.

At the same time, he and Riyadh had set in motion a sequence of events sure to devastate the Middle Eastern psyche while causing America to hang its head in shame.

Aziz felt the woman's hands slide gracefully down his

arms. She rubbed the tension away from his upper arms, but remained silent as she did, probably awaiting an invitation to speak. As a woman should, he decided.

Listening to the hum of the 707's engines, Aziz recalled when he first heard of Riyadh's plans, brought to Aziz through an intermediary. Riyadh's ideas had been rough, but contained a germ of genius that only Aziz, with his superior analytical skills, his penchant for organization and detail, could bring together.

Of course, their motives differed. Riyadh wanted to stick a knife in the United States' heart, twist hard, punish that country for betraying him. Aziz considered himself a simpler, more pragmatic man, not one given to mixing emotion with business. He had given Riyadh what he knew the man wanted to hear—a speech of freeing the Arab lands from the Great Satan, and all that rubbish.

In reality, he cared little about geopolitics. He wanted money and he wanted to win. When everything came unhinged, when the U.S. and the Middle East found themselves awash in blood and fire, then Aziz would know he'd won.

Taking a sip of ice water, he sank back into his chair, enjoyed the rub down and thought of his impending victory and the accompanying windfall.

It had always been so for him. The son of a wealthy Egyptian family, he grew up with everything a young man could want or need. His family made a fortune in construction, shipping and oil, at least publicly. But it also earned millions by smuggling diamonds, Egyptian artifacts, people and guns in and out of Africa and Asia. Aziz considered himself lucky. Indeed, he never wanted for anything, ever. He'd studied business in the United States. Upon his return to Egypt, he joined his family's business, eventually overseeing its shipping and logistics operation. He grew the family business from a force in Egypt to a major international corporation. That he used his fleet of planes, trucks and freighters to move drugs, guns and stolen technology around the world helped him achieve these results.

It was during this time that he encountered the Paladin Corp., a Virginia-based defense contractor, and its chief executive officer, Daniel Perkins. Paladin had launched a hostile takeover of Aziz's business, taking what had rightfully been his and his family's for generations. Within the span of months, he'd walked away with tons of money, but had lost all he'd worked for.

It was only later that, using his network of contacts, he'd discovered the truth about Paladin. It was a front for the Central Intelligence Agency, not an independent business. Paladin developed weapons and surveillance aircraft for the U.S. government while also generating cash to underwrite covert operations for the CIA. From what his sources had told him, the CIA had decided that his business was much too successful, especially for a man who had befriended international terrorists, gunrunners and organized crime figures. The best solution, the CIA had decided, was to take it away, leave him some shut-up money and use the business for its personal purposes.

Aziz sighed as the woman applied pressure to his forearms and wrists, her touch gentle but firm. A sweep of black hair, silky and fragrant, spilled into the space next to Aziz's head, brushed his cheek as the woman peered over the chair, scanning his face for some sign of approval. He gave her a tight smile of encouragement, went back to his thoughts.

He knew the takeover should have angered him. It hadn't. As the American saying went, Aziz never got mad, just even. When all was said and done, he'd actually felt a grudging respect for Daniel Perkins, the man who'd engineered the takeover, and Paladin Corp. It almost amused him, both that U.S.

intelligence considered him a threat and that Perkins had gotten the best of him.

He assured himself again that this wasn't about revenge. He couldn't operate on such a visceral level. No, to him it was just a game. He considered it a challenge to best Perkins, the CIA and Paladin Corp. He wanted to win, and he wanted to bag a trophy in the process.

He planned to do just that. During the past several months, he'd set up dozens of dummy corporations in the United States, Asia and Europe, all of which were charged with buying up shares of Paladin. With the accompanying unrest in the Middle East, aided by a flood of false rumors pumped into Wall Street, Paladin's shares would plummet in value. After all, with its huge operation—correction, Aziz's huge operation—in the Middle East, the company stood to lose a fortune if that area fell apart. Particularly once people learned all the details of the next day's bloodletting.

The stock would plummet, allowing him to buy it for at least half its value. Within days, he'd not only regain his family's business, but also the entity that had taken it over. And with dark clouds forming over the Middle East, an American defense company only could rebound, especially one such as Paladin that boasted cutting-edge surveillance planes and satellites, items the U.S. government would need if it were to face greater conflict in the Arab world.

A self-satisfied smile spread across Aziz's features as he contemplated the progress thus far. Already Perkins and Lee were dead, both by seemingly different circumstances, but ultimately assassinated. Giving the order to kill the men had been a function of pragmatism rather than revenge, as far as Aziz was concerned. Those two men, above all others, were capable of unearthing his takeover bid, of derailing the carefully orchestrated events of the next few days.

They had needed to die so that his idea might live. It was simple.

That Stone had let the CIA woman escape twice worried the Egyptian. After all, he knew she was well-trained, good enough to have been Stone's comrade. But still, she was only a woman and shouldn't have gotten the best of Stone. That a woman had the possibility, no matter how remote, of bringing Aziz's plans crashing down around him bothered Aziz. There were some things a man couldn't tolerate, and losing to a woman was one of them.

And what of this American who'd come to her aid? Clearly he was a federal agent, and obviously a capable one at that. But he could be dealt with, just as the woman would be dealt with.

He needed a specialist and knew just who to call.

"Phone," he said.

A second woman, an Asian, came to him carrying a mobile phone. Taking it from her, he punched in a number, waited a few beats for the other party to answer.

On the third ring, someone answered, "Yes?"

"I have a situation."

"What sort of situation?"

Aziz told him of the man who'd attacked Stone and al-Shoud in Pakistan.

"I can handle that," the man said.

"Fine. The usual terms, I assume?"

"I've raised my rates. It's ten percent more." Aziz almost could hear the smile in the man's voice.

"As you wish."

"You're feeling generous today. That's quite a bit of money."

"Obviously I consider it a good investment," Aziz said, "or we wouldn't be having this conversation."

"Of course."

"You will send me the target's picture?"

Aziz shook his head, as though speaking to the man in person. "I don't have that, I'm afraid. We were unable to get his picture. We do, however, have a physical description of him which I will forward immediately."

"And I should begin the hunt where?"

"Salt Lake City. If he goes there."

"If?"

"Yes, if. I want you to shadow a man, Mohammed Nasrallah. If he gets to this man, then you must take the target out."

"How will I know?"

"Nasrallah will tell you when to act. Until then, don't worry about it."

"I never worry. I trust you'll send the money in the usual fashion."

"Of course. Unmarked account in the Cayman Islands. You will get half up front, half upon completion of the assignment, as per our standard agreement."

"Wonderful."

"I look forward to hearing your results."

"It's already a foregone conclusion."

"I hope that's the case."

Aziz ended the call. A tickle of excitement, persistent and pleasant, buzzed around his stomach as he imagined the possibilities that lay ahead of him. Riyadh and he had placed powder kegs underneath the U.S. and the Middle East, affixed short fuses to them. The resulting explosion would forever alter the geopolitical landscape, sentence scores of innocents in both the East and West to death.

Now he just needed to strike the match.

CHAPTER SEVEN

Mack Bolan watched as a Special Forces medic applied an alcohol swab to Jennifer Kinsey's cut cheek.

The sting caused her to wince, but she said nothing. In an instant her expression turned from pained to inscrutable as she rested her gaze on Bolan.

"I need to get back to Washington," she said.

Bolan nodded. "Soon enough. First, I have some questions I need to ask."

Kinsey chewed on her lower lip for a moment. "Okay," she said. "Shoot."

"The big guy who brought you here. Who is he?"

Kinsey hesitated and gave Bolan an apprehensive look. "Who do you work for?" she asked. "Are you with the CIA?"

Bolan shook his head. "Right government, wrong agency," he said. "I'm with the Justice Department. In a manner of speaking."

"What manner might that be?"

"The clandestine kind."

"You have a name? Or should I just call you the Black Knight. You did, after all, ride in here and save the damsel in distress. The helpless little woman."

Bolan detected a trace of bitterness in her voice and shook his head. "Looked to me like you did just fine. After all, you were outgunned and unarmed."

Kinsey held up her wrists, marked with red rings from the handcuffs, and frowned. "And bound. Don't forget bound. At least they didn't tie me to the train tracks for God's sake."

Bolan allowed himself a grin. "At least."

"So what's your name?"

"Matt Cooper."

She gave Bolan an appraising look. "Okay, Matt Cooper from Justice, what the hell brings you here?"

A no-nonsense tone slipped into Bolan's voice. "Later. Right now, I want to know about your host. Who is he and why did he bring you here?"

Before she could reply, the medic gathered his things and got to his feet. "The cuts and bruises are mild," he said. "But you took some hard shots to the chest and head. Get yourself to a hospital ASAP and get some X-rays. Until then, lay low."

The woman's eyes narrowed, her lips tightening into a bloodless line as the medic spoke to her. Bolan sensed that, when it came to orders, the lady was more comfortable giving than receiving. She nodded and thanked him, anyway.

The medic spun on his heel and waded into a nearby cluster of soldiers who were searching the monitor room. To his right, Bolan saw two Special Forces soldiers, bearded, with Kalashnikov rifles strapped on their backs, searching al-Shoud's corpse, presumably for weapons and documents.

"Why'd they kill James Lee?" Bolan asked.

She stiffened at the mention of Lee's name. She took a deep breath, exhaled audibly and turned to Bolan.

"Jim was an American and a former CIA man. That creep was a terrorist. The two were working at cross-purposes. Doesn't seem too damn mysterious to me."

"The guy who dragged you off the helicopter didn't look much like a terrorist. Not in the homegrown sense, anyway. He looked more like a soldier."

Kinsey met Bolan's gaze. "So we're back on that again, are we?"

"Yes, we are."

Bolan let the silence hang between them, while Kinsey stared off into space. With the fingertips of one hand, she lightly stroked the red marks on the opposite wrist.

"His name is Stone," she said. "He used to work for Jim."

"When he was with the CIA?"

"Did that guy look like a fucking diplomat to you? Yes, when he worked at the CIA."

"Sorry," Bolan said without meaning it.

"Stone—his full name's Jonathan Stone—worked for Lee until a couple of years ago. We all did."

"Who's 'we'?"

Kinsey stared at Bolan for a moment. "I'm not sure I'm cleared to say anything," she stated.

"I'm cleared to hear it. If you want, I can do my little dog-and-pony show. Hand you my credentials, have your boss call my boss, who will call his boss, who will say it's okay. I'd like to say I have nothing but time here. I don't, but we can play it that way, if you want. It's your call, Jennifer."

Kinsey folded her arms over her chest and gave Bolan a hard stare. "Jon Stone worked for Lee for about five years. He did a lot of special ops work. Stone's about as subtle as an atom bomb, so we primarily used him for wet work and training insurgents in rogue nations so we could effect regime changes."

"He's a good soldier?"

Kinsey nodded. "In the technical sense, yes. He can handle any weapon he touches. Fights like a mother lion guarding her cubs. He can take a group of dirt farmers and in six months transform them into deadly guerrillas."

"Sounds like there's an implied 'but' in there."

"Here's the but—he's crazy," she said. "He's a sociopath. All he cares about is Jon Stone. If it had occurred to him, he would have strapped these mothers and children to him like Kevlar. Force you to make a hard choice."

"It wouldn't have been a difficult choice," Bolan said.

"Oh, right. I forgot. You're the good guy. Just how many people did you drop when you came in here? A dozen?"

Bolan felt his jaw clench. A burning sensation welled up inside his gut, threatened to spill forth as an angry reply. Remaining stone-faced, he let the comment ride. The way he saw it, the fact that she was vertical and breathing was testament enough that his methods worked.

Kinsey looked down at her lap and shook her head. "Sorry," she said. "You saved my life. I ought to cut you some slack. If I was a good damsel in distress, I'd throw myself at you."

"I'd settle for more information," Bolan said.

Kinsey looked up at him and flashed him a tight smile. "You're really not going to put up with my bullshit, are you?" She didn't wait for a reply. "Lee had a covert team called Thunder Hawk. It was Jim's personal plaything. Whenever the President asked for a covert op, he dispatched the group and let them work their magic. Hostage rescues. Assassinations. They took on everything he could throw at them and made it happen. It started out great."

"Started?"

She shrugged. "After a while, personality conflicts got in the way. Stone had a habit of using missions to line his own pockets. Jim didn't know that, of course. At least not at first. Stone always produced results. And if Stone and his people ripped off a terrorists account in the Cayman Islands or sold a dead African president's diamonds on the black market, who was going to tell?"

"I presume that Stone didn't leave much in the way of witnesses."

"That's an understatement. You want to talk to his targets or their family's? Better have a séance. Not that it was always like that. At first, he'd take out a specific target. But the longer he went, the more he started killing anyone he could. Wives, sons, daughters. He left no witnesses."

"And Lee looked the other way?"

"Look, Stone got results, okay? Kill a terrorist or a financier in Saudi Arabia, save one hundred lives somewhere else. If the kids or the wife caught a bullet in the process, too bad. Guilt by association, right?"

"You don't believe that."

She remained silent for a minute. When she continued speaking she didn't look up. "Anyway, Stone's methods started splitting the unit. Some of the guys figured their authorization to kill also gave them a green light to torture and steal. You know, absolute power corrupts absolutely, and all that stuff."

She raked back some of her hair, tucked it behind her ear. "But the other guys didn't see it that way. Sure, they were cynics. But cut through the crap and you found people who believed in what they were doing. They hated to see Stone abusing his power. But most of them were reluctant to say anything. Stone enforced a strong code of silence. If you broke it, he didn't take it out on you, he took it out on your loved ones. No one wanted that kind of responsibility hanging over them."

"So Lee never knew."

She shook her head vigorously. "Absolutely not. Jim had

his faults. He was ambitious, a bit of a politician. But his morals were sound, and he never would have tolerated that crap had he known about it."

"When did Stone leave the CIA? Or did he?"

She nodded. "He left years ago," she said. "We had a mission go bad, really bad. The President ordered the group disbanded. Stone quit and disappeared for a couple of years. Most of the guys were reassigned or they quit. But Stone had had too much leeway to go back to being someone's stooge. He couldn't handle it. Correction, he didn't want to handle it. Plus, he was damaged goods. No supervisor would touch him. So he took his skills elsewhere."

"In other words, he went rogue. Whom does he work for?"

"Anyone who can pay his bill. He's taught Islamic terrorists, Colombian insurgents, Russian mafia. You name them, Jon has put a gun in their hand, taught them to kill and made a fortune in the process."

Motion in his peripheral vision caught Bolan's attention. He looked, saw Grimaldi approaching, a stainless-steel Thermos and foam cups clasped in his hands.

"Hey," he said to Bolan, "is this a private party or I can I join in?"

"Who the hell's he?" Kinsey demanded.

Bolan ignored the question. "You were going to tell me about Thunder Hawk's last mission."

Her cheeks turned crimson. "The hell I was. That's top secret. It's bad enough I told you what I have without dumping my guts about specific missions. You don't have that kind of clearance."

Pulling the foam cups apart, Grimaldi lined three up on a nearby table, filled each with coffee. A smirk played across his lips as he listened to the exchange. "Lady," he said, "he's got all the clearance he needs."

Kinsey gave the pilot a pointed look. "Like I said, who the hell are you?"

Bolan held up his hands, palms forward, in a peacemaking gesture. "We're here to help. If you need to call your people, make sure I'm okay to hear what you've got to tell me, fine."

Bolan unhooked a secure mobile phone from his belt, handed it to her. She paused, looked at him for a moment before palming the phone and stepping away from them.

Bolan stared after the woman as she grabbed some distance, his mind focusing for an instant on her pleasant curves. She dialed in a series of numbers, paused as she waited for a connection and began to speak. She occasionally stole a glance in Bolan's direction, covering her mouth each time she did.

"She thinks we can read her lips," Bolan said.

"I'd like to try," Grimaldi said.

Bolan flashed his friend a tight smile. "Forget it. She's been through enough without suffering under the onslaught of the patented Grimaldi charm."

"Better women than her have faltered," the pilot replied. "Are you sure this is such a good idea, telling her to call her handlers? She already seems skittish as hell. Probably wouldn't take more than a word or two to shut her up."

"Or to get her to talk," Bolan countered. "She's a pro. She may not like me. But if she gets the word from the right people, she'll talk to me."

"And if she doesn't?"

Bolan shrugged. "I'll sic you on her. Like you said, she'll never hold up under your charms."

"I couldn't agree more. I gotta go check on something."

Grimaldi lit a cigarette and walked away. Bolan leaned against a table, sipped his coffee until Kinsey returned. He noticed her features had softened somewhat.

"The right people say you're okay," Kinsey said. "I didn't realize you came with such high credentials."

"Thunder Hawk. What happened to it?"

Grabbing one of the foam cups of coffee, she settled into her chair. "The group made a mistake, a big mistake. It cost a lot of people their lives."

Bolan nodded, encouraging her to speak.

"In 1999 and 2000, Jim sent most of the group to the Middle East to do some cloak-and-dagger diplomacy. We—Stone, actually—took a group of Iraqi dissidents and Egyptian mercenaries, trained them to work together, so they could carry out a mission."

"Which was?"

"Assassinate Saddam Hussein and his inner cadre of officers. Saddam was holding a high-level meeting in Baghdad and we had good intel placing him right down to the hour and minute. The team was supposed to raid the meeting, kill as many of these folks as possible and decapitate the Iraqi government."

"And then what?"

"We had a high-level politician on our side. At least as high level as one can be under a dictator. If Saddam went down, this guy promised to help us. In exchange, we'd put him in charge of the interim government, probably make him the country's prime minister or something. At least that was what we told him."

"I don't have to ask whether the coup worked."

Kinsey shook her head. "It was a fiasco from the word go. One of our assets sold us out to Saddam. We lost all the insurgents. Their families went out right behind them. The government killed everyone and buried them in unmarked graves. It was a complete failure and embarrassment."

"But quiet."

"Saddam clamped down on it. From what we learned later, after the second Persian Gulf war, Saddam considered going public with the coup attempt. You know, speeches, public hangings, the whole bit. Ultimately he decided against it."

"Why?"

"Put yourself in his position. He had few real allies and those only wanted him for money or oil. His strength lay in scaring the hell out of people and putting up a strong front to the world. If word got out, at least in his mind, he'd be disgraced and weakened."

Bolan nodded. "That much makes sense. If people had nothing to lose, they might decide to play the odds, see if they could knock him out of power."

"The murders were awful," she said, her voice tightening. "We had satellite photos. Old men, women and children digging their own graves. NSA gave us the photos, but wasn't sure what to make of it. We never volunteered the information."

"Of course not," Bolan said.

Her head whipped up and she gave him a hard look. "What the hell does that mean?"

A cold edge crept into Bolan's voice. "Just keep talking," he said. "What happened to Thunder Hawk after all that? Did you folks catch the blame?"

Kinsey paused, choosing her words carefully.

"Not exactly," she said. "The mission was a fiasco, but it really wasn't the team's fault. Jim ordered the whole thing scrapped, but the team went ahead anyway. Seems the mission controller had a hard-on for Saddam, some bad blood from the first Gulf War, and wanted to take the old man down. Jim told him to cancel, but he went ahead anyway."

"Sounds like treason."

"Doesn't matter. He died three months later from cancer

and was an invalid for a month before that. Guy never saw the inside of a jail cell."

Thoughts whirled through Bolan's mind as he tried to piece together the disparate pieces of data. So a black-bag operation went bad and a few people got reassigned. Hardly grounds for killing a high-profile figure like James Lee. Even with what he knew, it still made no sense. He said as much.

"What I'm laying out for you is the truth," Kinsey said. "Stone hated the CIA for disbanding the group. It cost Stone leverage and money. He had ample motivation to hunt Lee down and kill him. That's how I see it, anyway."

Bolan scowled. "So a highly trained CIA man goes underground, stews for a while and resurfaces just to kill his former boss. It just doesn't play."

Forming a V with the first two fingers of her right hand, Kinsey pointed them toward her eyes. "I was there and saw the whole thing. I got dragged halfway across the country by that slug. Don't tell me he wasn't involved."

Setting down his coffee, Bolan crossed his arms over his chest. "Of that I have no doubt," the warrior said. "I just can't believe he went to all this trouble because Lee fired him. If what you say about Stone is true, he doesn't strike me as the type to waste time and money hunting down an old boss."

"So what do you suggest?"

"That he has other motives. Perhaps even some help. What else do you know about him?"

"He spends a lot of time in the Tri-Border region. He has a school there."

"A school?"

"A merc school. And he sells weapons. A couple other former members of Thunder Hawk stuck with him, guys by the name of Archer and Card. They did a lot of his dirty work when the good guys got out of line. Rumor has it that Archer once shot a cowering child to draw an assassination target out of hiding. Card's record isn't much better."

"World's going to be a better place without them," Bolan said.

"If you can get them."

"When," Bolan corrected. "They're dead. They just don't know it yet. What about this politician—the one who helped Stone and the others—what happened to him?"

"He's dead."

"Care to elaborate?"

She held out her empty foam cup and Bolan refilled it. "He went into exile shortly after the failed coup. Lived in Jordan for a time and then dropped out of sight. We figured Saddam's overthrow in 2003 would bring him out of hiding. It didn't. I don't think he wanted to associate himself with anything remotely American."

"He was bitter."

"He lost his entire family. Wouldn't you be bitter?"

Bolan's throat thickened for just a moment. Grim experience told him precisely how he'd react to such a tragedy. "Yes."

"Back in 2003, before the war, we tried hard to find this guy, Tariq Riyadh, grill him for whatever intelligence we could. He avoided us like the plague. We even offered Stone big money to track him down. Stone declined."

"Doesn't that strike you as odd?" Bolan asked. "Stone turning away an easy payday, I mean?"

"Hell, yes, it does."

"But it didn't at the time?"

"We were trying to gather intel to launch a major air-and-ground offensive against Iraq. Second-guessing a psycho former field agent was not high on my priority list."

"Fair enough."

"So Riyadh went AWOL from life. And after the war, we really didn't think about him at all. When you've got troops able to search through Saddam's sock drawer, it's not like some disaffected former asset adds any value. We didn't exactly have a shortage of government officials to interrogate."

"So he's dead?"

She nodded. "For a while now."

"How?"

"Suicide. He shot himself in the mouth."

"You saw the body?"

She shook her head. "Killed himself in Damascus, Syria. We found out about it three months later. Since no one knew about the attempted coup, his death was little more than a side note. He was a former Iraqi politician who killed himself. End of story. Forget about him. He died angry and penniless. My guess is they buried him in a pauper's grave in the desert. Just like the rest of his family. He's not a factor in this."

Bolan drained his coffee cup, tossed it aside. Pressing his palms against his eyes, he rubbed them in small, circular motions. The caffeine did little to ease the dull ache of fatigue pounding in his eyes. Nor did it help him to think more clearly.

Chances were, Jennifer Kinsey was right. Riyadh was dead, his body moldering in an unmarked grave. Bolan needed to play the odds on that one because he had neither the time nor the inclination to chase ghosts.

He'd vowed to hunt down and kill those responsible for James Lee's death and he was damn close to succeeding.

Grimaldi's voice sounded in his earpiece. "Striker."

"Go ahead."

"Troops say there's no sign anywhere of Stone. Looks like he had another way out of here. Maybe a vehicle stashed."

"Understood."

"You want to advise on our next move?"

"Tell them to keep looking. If we lose him here, I've got another place we can look."

"Hope it's a little warmer."

"Closest you can get to hell and still be breathing."

CHAPTER EIGHT

Alexandria, Virginia

His eyes still gritty with sleep, Doyle stared at his feet as he descended the stairs of his town house. The sweet smell of gourmet hazelnut mixed with the white haze of cigarette smoke encircling his head as he puffed his second smoke of the day.

Stepping into the kitchen, he poured himself a cup of coffee, gathered his robe together and tied it off. Hefting the hand-made ceramic coffee mug, he sipped at the coffee. After the near-mugging in the parking garage, he'd grabbed Nancy and brought her home. She had started to dial the cell phone to call the police. He'd snatched it from her and told her no. She'd been too shocked to argue.

They'd ridden home in silence, but as she'd thawed, the torrent of questions came. Where did he learn to fight like that? Why not call the police? Was he hiding something from her? It'd been 4:00 a.m. before he'd fallen into a fitful sleep, leaving him feeling depleted. Even worse, an emotional chasm had opened between him and Nancy. She'd shrunk from his touch and seemed scared of him. Was it the shock of the attack or seeing her husband nearly kill two men?

Having drained his coffee mug halfway, he returned to the kitchen and refilled it. Just as he put the carafe back on the heater plate, the doorbell rang.

Doyle scowled, checked his watch. 7:00 a.m. Who the hell stopped by this early? Certainly none of his friends. They knew approaching him before 10:00 a.m. was like grabbing a steak from a starving Doberman's mouth. Nancy's friends? Hell, they were either at the gym or ushering the kids out the door.

His brow furrowed and his breathing kicked up a notch. What if it was the police? Or friends of the two guys he'd beaten last night? He didn't care about himself. But if they tried to hurt his wife—

He left the thought unfinished. He was overreacting, he told himself.

Maybe.

The doorbell rang again.

Crossing the room, Doyle glanced through the peephole and felt his stomach sour.

Son of a bitch! It was him. Of all the people.

Leaving the chain on the door, Doyle opened it a few inches and stared out. A small man, dressed in an impeccable black suit, a hand cocked on each hip, stared back at Doyle. The man flashed Doyle his best attempt to smile—lips split apart, white-capped teeth exposed. He looked to Doyle as though he was passing a kidney stone.

"You going to make me stand out here all morning, Doyle, or what?"

"Given my druthers, Cam, I'd just as soon leave you out there. Maybe give you a damn jockey outfit and a lantern."

"You son of a—"

Doyle cut the statement short by slamming the door. Unhooking the chain, he reopened the door but blocked the entrance, trapping assistant CIA director Cameron Roberts in the hallway. A pair of security agents, each dressed as impeccably as Roberts, flanked the CIA officer.

"C'mon in, Cam," Doyle said. "But leave the monkeys out there."

"You heard the man," Roberts said over his shoulder. "Stay outside."

After Roberts entered, Doyle slammed the door and slid the chain into place. If it bothered Roberts to be sealed inside with a man who hated him, he gave no outward hints of it.

"What do you want?" Doyle asked.

"We need to talk. I've got some critical intelligence information to share with you."

Yanking the cigarette from his mouth, Doyle clamped his jaw shut, felt acid burn his insides as anger constricted his stomach.

"I don't need critical information. I'm out of the damn business."

"You might want this. Trust me."

"That'd be a first."

"I mean it."

Something in Roberts's tone caught Doyle's attention. He nodded at the couch.

"Sit down. I'll be back."

Doyle ground out his cigarette in a nearby ashtray and started up the stairs.

"Coffee smells great," Roberts called after him. "Okay if I grab some?"

"No."

Five minutes later Doyle returned to the first floor. He'd donned a pair of jeans, worn canvas sneakers and a Hawaiian print shirt. He left the tails pulled out from the waistband to hide the SIG-Sauer P-226 holstered in the waistband of his jeans, a round of 9 mm ammo chambered. Rounding the corner, he spotted Roberts staring at a painting, a cup of coffee clasped in his hands. Roberts toasted him with the mug, took a drink.

Doyle said, "Tell me what you want. I have a zero-tolerance policy for you."

"I see retirement hasn't mellowed you," Roberts said.

"And I see you're still full of crap. We both know I 'retired' so you bastards didn't make me station chief in Nigeria or something. If memory serves, you personally ordered my pension suspended. Something about incompetence, right?"

"Fortunately for you, the director thought otherwise."

"Yeah, fortunately. I'm living the life, as you can see."

Setting down his coffee, Roberts set himself into an armchair, crossed his legs, smiled at Doyle.

"That's because your wife is a successful real-estate agent. She had quite a year last year, by all accounts. Her best ever, actually."

Doyle placed his palm on his stomach as the burn intensified. Roberts was right; Nancy had unloaded a couple of homes for two senators, a retiring judge and a couple of lawyers. She'd earned—

Roberts finished the thought for Doyle. "She brought home—what?—a quarter of a million dollars last year. Bought herself a new car. A BMW, if memory serves."

Doyle felt his face flush hot with anger. "You prick. You'd better have a damn good reason for poking around in my private business."

"According to your tax records," Roberts said, "you have no personal business. You grossed ten thousand last year as a freelance writer, your old CIA cover. That's not even parking money in this town. Maybe the spy business doesn't look so bad now?"

"I'd rather starve than go back to what I was doing. You people bled me dry. And, when you were through, you tried to take away my shitty little pension. You couldn't even let me have that much."

"You were burned out. Ineffective. You should be grateful I didn't fire you before you could resign."

His fist clenched, Doyle crossed the room quickly, quietly. Halting within arm's reach of Roberts, Doyle stood at the side of the chair, positioning himself so the little bastard couldn't kick him. He knew Roberts viewed him as a dangerous man— and rightfully so—and he planned to press the advantage.

"The point," Doyle said. "Get to it. Now."

"Jon Stone has resurfaced."

Doyle kept his face impassive, but his neck and shoulders tensed at the mention of Stone.

"So tell him I said hi," Doyle said.

"There's more to it than that," Roberts said. "A lot more. This involves Thunder Hawk."

"Thunder Hawk is history. And good riddance to it."

"Hey, c'mon, Doyle. This is important. Lives are at stake here."

"Aren't they always? Look, I told you I'm out of the game. I don't care if he's selling the North Koreans the keys to the fucking White House. Not my problem."

"It is your problem, Doyle. It's everyone's problem."

Doyle opened his mouth to reply, but stopped himself. Something in Roberts's tone struck a chord within him, prompted a small chill to pass down his back. He backed into a chair, sat and stared the CIA man in the eye.

"What the hell do you mean?"

"James Lee is dead. Stone killed him."

Doyle felt his jaws clench. His first thought was of a drink, a nice cool beer, or maybe a bloody Mary. It was morning, after all. He visibly shook his head to clear away the thought. Forget it, he told himself. You fall off the wagon again, you can kiss everything goodbye. Nancy had assured him of that. She'd seen him through one relapse, had been a real trooper about it, too. But she'd made it crystal-clear that even if he thought he had another drunk in him, she was completely out of forgiveness. He sipped at his coffee to banish the cotton-mouth.

"What happened to Lee?" he asked Roberts. As the CIA man explained the assassination and Jennifer Kinsey's kidnapping, Doyle felt his stomach twist into knots.

"Kinsey was rescued last night. She told us about Stone's involvement. He tried to kill her, but a special ops team got there first, pulled her out."

"Stone?"

"Gone."

"Gone where?"

"It's classified. Whether I declassify it depends on you."

"Quit playing games. I'm in no mood."

Roberts leaned forward and addressed Doyle in a hushed tone. "I want to tell you. But we have something else we need to discuss first."

Here it comes, Doyle thought. "Shoot."

"I need you to come back in."

Doyle sat upright, as though jabbed with a needle. "I'm done. I told you that."

"I know what you told me. But just shut up and listen. We have reason to believe Stone is targeting other members of Thunder Hawk, too. Maybe picking them off one by one."

"And you base that on?"

"Sources."

Doyle's face reddened and he gestured toward the door. "Get out. Get the hell out now."

"I'm serious. I can't tell you where I heard any of this. At least not until you say you'll work with me."

"To hell with you."

"Doyle, you and I both know that if Stone comes after the old team, that will include you." Roberts nodded up toward the second floor where Doyle could hear Nancy blow-drying her hair as she prepared for work. "Both of you."

"No way. I can take care of myself."

"What about her? Can she take care of herself against Stone? That guy would kill her in a heartbeat, just for target practice. You want to leave her open to that?"

Doyle remained quiet for a moment. The son of a bitch knew his answer, probably knew it before he ever knocked on the door. Doyle exhaled loudly, let his shoulders sag under their newly acquired burden.

"What do you need me to do?"

THE GUY MADE Cameron Roberts's skin crawl. There was just no two ways about it. It wasn't his face. Hell, no. He looked normal enough. Middle-aged. Salt-and-pepper hair. Olive complexion. He looked normal enough. It was the man's voice, hollow, icy, and his presence, like a vessel of pure rage. Even as the man smiled at Roberts, a predator's eyes fixed on him.

Roberts didn't consider himself terribly intuitive, but the man seated across from him had a ghoul's soul.

And it fit. After all, the guy was dead. Just ask the Syrian government. Tariq Riyadh had committed suicide. Never mind that the two men were meeting in the office of an Islamic charity in Alexandria. Never mind that this ghost was grilling Roberts about the results of his appointment earlier this morning.

"He agreed, then?" Riyadh asked.

Roberts emptied the highball glass, let the contents burn its way down his throat. "Yes. He agreed."

"Excellent."

Yeah, flipping excellent, you nut job, Roberts thought. Avoiding Riyadh's gaze, he gave the man a halfhearted smile. Hauling himself to his feet, Roberts moved to the minibar across the room. Grabbing a bottle of bourbon by its neck, he upended it, filled the glass halfway. Replacing the bottle, he crossed the room, swigging the amber liquid as he moved. He swished it around his mouth, hoping to kill the bad taste that had settled there since he'd left Doyle's apartment.

"What's with the bar, anyway?" Roberts asked as he sank back into his seat. "I didn't think most Muslims drank, particularly during Ramadan."

Riyadh dismissed the question with a wave of his hand. "I try not to stand on ceremony," Riyadh said. "Except for a few trusted friends, I entertain my devout Muslim clients in another room. In here, I can drop the facade and do as I please." Riyadh paused, cleared his throat before continuing. "I presume you didn't come here to discuss my spiritual beliefs. You have the dossier?"

"Of course. I left it at the drop point as you instructed."

"Well done, my friend. You do good work."

His courage bolstered by alcohol, Roberts let his tone go nasty. "Spare me the compliments, Riyadh. Did you handle things as I asked? The transaction, I mean."

"You mean, the money transfer?"

"Of course."

Riyadh shook his head no. "I'm afraid there's been a change of plans."

"A what? What the hell are you talking about?"

"You and I both know how closely the CIA scrutinizes

every agent's finances. Even a small influx of money can—how do you Americans' say it?—raise a red flag, particularly when it's to an account in the Cayman Islands."

"An account that doesn't have my name anywhere on it," Roberts corrected. "Trust me, I know what I'm doing. It'd take the CIA years to find it. If they even decided to investigate me, which they won't. Why would they? My record's spotless."

Riyadh chuckled. "Oh, my friend, this is the CIA we're talking about. They investigate everyone, including their own people. Especially their own people. It's really only prudent that they do so."

A mixture of rage and fear roiled inside Roberts. He kept his face stoic, but let an edge creep into his voice.

"So how are you going to pay me?"

"We're not."

Roberts sprang up from his chair. "What? What the hell are you talking about? I put everything on the line here! I betrayed my country. My principles. And now you aren't going to pay me?"

Riyadh held up his hands in a placating gesture. "Please, please. Calm down."

"Go to hell!"

Riyadh leaned back in his chair. A smile ghosted his lips as he regarded Roberts. "Your fire impresses me. Stone said you had no backbone. Apparently, he sorely misjudged you."

"Stone's an idiot. And so are you if you think I'll let you get away with this."

"You hardly have any choice in the matter. Obviously you can't report my actions to anyone, lest you reveal your own crimes."

"You prick. I need that money. My son—"

"Is very ill. I know, I know. You've relayed this information to me before. I'm sure that's what you told yourself to justify sending another man to a certain death. You altruistically planned to save a young boy's life. How very noble."

"You—"

Before he could finish, nausea twisted at Roberts's stomach. He swallowed hard, trying to dispel the sensation, but found his insides continued to churn violently. A cold sweat formed on his forehead and his knees buckled, pulling him to the floor.

"What the hell did—" Roberts began.

"I do to you?" Riyadh said, his voice sounding far away. "Poison in the bourbon. I never liked you. And I only did business with you out of necessity—my necessity, of course. Plus, I just couldn't help myself. It seemed fitting for the CIA to betray itself as it betrayed me."

A buzzing filled Roberts ears and a black shroud settled over his vision. He started to say something but lost consciousness.

RIYADH WATCHED the CIA man's body convulse as, one by one, his critical systems shut down. As Roberts curled into a fetal ball, a line of spittle fell from his lips. With a final croak and a shudder, the man died.

The first of many to die, Riyadh told himself. Before all was said and done, he'd unleash a war, a clash of civilizations, a clash of continents. And he'd use the CIA—the very organization that had cheated him of wealth, of power, of family. To strike killing blows against the Middle East and Muslims everywhere. Enraged, the Middle East would retaliate with public condemnation of the United States and the CIA. Radical elements, perhaps even the governments themselves, would unleash a righteous retaliation that would cost American lives. And, this time, the U.S. would enjoy no moral high ground. How could it when it had unleashed hell on a culture, wittingly or unwittingly.

Riyadh clapped his hands together, smiled. Once he had expected to rule his homeland, to help rebuild it from the ruins created by Saddam Hussein. Now, too much time had passed and his home no longer was that. Military and social upheaval had turned the country upside down, changed it so that he no longer recognized it.

He no longer needed Iraq. He no longer thirsted for power; he craved revenge.

And he'd get just that.

CHAPTER NINE

Sevier Desert, Utah

It had to be him, Tom Roth thought. It just figured.

Crouched in the shadows of the concrete bunkhouse, Roth studied the dark figure in front of him, felt a pang of guilt for what he was about to do.

The man, an Uzi cradled in his arms, stood silhouetted against the full moon, blocking Roth's path to freedom. Like everyone else at the camp, the guy had sworn to kill anyone sneaking in or out after dark. That included police officers and federal agents acting without a warrant.

Unlike most of the other people, though, this soldier was just a kid, a misguided eighteen-year-old gullible enough to fall for the hateful rhetoric binding together the members of this group, Patriots of the New Dawn. Cody Peterson was a good kid from small-town Utah who'd gotten mixed up with the wrong people. Roth had talked to the kid a few times in the mess hall, on guard duty, that sort of thing. The kid spewed the same bullshit as the other forty-odd members of the group. But he did it with little conviction, sound-

ing more like tape recorder in playback mode than a true be-
liever.

Roth figured the kid just wanted to belong. The Patriots
had been more than happy to take him in, treat him like one
of their own. They'd done the same for Roth, a federal agent.
And now he was going to stick it right back up their asses,
show them the error of their ways.

But first he had to get out of the camp, and young Cody
stood in his way. And knowing what he knew, the horror
these people were about to unleash, Roth had no choice. He
had to leave this night, come hell or high water, and he'd kill
anyone, even a mixed-up kid, to get on the other side of the
gate.

A metallic clicking caused an icy sensation of fear to travel
down his spine. His breath hung in his throat as his mind raced
to identify the sound.

As the realization hit, a grim smile played on Roth's lips.
The kid was popping the magazine in and out of his weapon,
a nervous habit that had made him the target of blistering re-
bukes from the training officers and even from Mad Dog
himself. The leader's tirade had been the worst, leaving the
young man a quivering mass for a couple of hours.

Roth had wanted to intervene on the kid's behalf, but held
himself back. Getting in Mad Dog's face was something a cop
or a federal agent might do. But Roth's alias, Nick Anthony,
a dishonorably discharged soldier made homeless by a ram-
pant drug addiction, never would have stuck up for anyone,
especially a vulnerable kid like Peterson. So Roth, like the
others, had stood idly by while the kid got a tongue-lashing
from the crazy bastard running this little horror show.

Getting to his feet, Roth gripped the knife hard and started
for the young man. He had taken three steps when gravel
crunched underfoot, prompting the young man to turn toward

him. A moment of recognition flashed in his eyes and he started to smile. Then he saw the knife Roth held and panic seemed to overtake him. With unsure, jerky movements, he raised the Uzi and started to shout a warning.

Roth was on the kid in a second, his greater weight and strength knocking the young man to the ground. The young man brought his arm around, the Uzi held fast. Roth saw the muzzle tracking in on his head. He had no choice but to act. With a powerful thrust, he drove the blade into Peterson's throat, burying it up to the hilt.

Gurgling, Peterson dropped his weapon. His eyes widened and he pawed at his throat, trying to squelch the fire that suddenly seared through his windpipe. Nausea gripped Roth's gut as he watched the young man convulse for a few agonizing moments before surrendering his life.

Roth withdrew the blade, wiped it on Peterson's shirt and slipped it back into the scabbard on his belt. Tears stung the corners of his eyes as he studied his handiwork. Roth, a ten-year veteran of the ATF, had killed once before in the line of duty. But it was an older man, a gunrunner's personal bodyguard who'd decided he didn't want his boss to go to jail. The guy had been a stranger and the shooting happened at a distance. Even under those conditions, it had been a difficult, life-changing event. But the stakes had seemed high—his life or the other guy's. It had all seemed pretty cut and dried.

But compared to his current situation, saving his own life was unimportant. He knew something big was coming down, big enough to threaten the security of the United States. He didn't have many details. Just enough to paint a pretty grim picture. And he had to get the information out there or lots of lives would be lost.

Roth smiled grimly to himself. No pressure.

Hefting Peterson's Uzi, Roth made sure the weapon was

ready to go. Setting it aside, he stripped the young man of his radio, his ammo belt and the keys to the security team's Ford pickup. A chill shook Roth as the young sentry's open eyes stared into his own. Reciting a small prayer in his mind, Roth grabbed the kid's head and turned it away.

Pocketing the keys, Roth came to his feet. He didn't bother using the handheld radio to call for help. He knew it was programmed only for Patriot use. Instead, he needed to get to his Chevrolet Monte Carlo parked in nearby Milford. Inside the car, in a specially constructed compartment, he carried a secure phone, his identification and other tools of the trade. Once there, he could call for help, have the ATF shut down the entire camp within a matter of hours.

First he needed some wheels. Roth dragged Peterson's corpse to a large trash bin. Raising the lid, his heart skipped a beat as a rusted hinge creaked in protest. He held his breath for a minute, listened for any sounds that might indicate someone would come to investigate. Hearing none, he hefted the corpse and dumped it into the bin.

Sorry, Cody, Roth thought as he kept moving.

Whether from exertion, fear or both, Roth felt beads of sweat dappling his forehead, soaking his armpits. Gripping the Uzi, he started moving toward the motor pool, melting into shadows wherever possible.

How had he gotten himself into this? he wondered. Risk and high stakes always were givens in any undercover op. And infiltrating this particular militia with its anti-Semitic, antigovernment leanings hadn't sounded like a cakewalk. But it had seemed necessary. Word was that the group was working alongside a Los Angeles-based cell of Islamic extremists. The two sides traded weapons, intelligence and, sometimes, training.

Roth knew from the guys' tirades that Patriots' leader Mike

"Mad Dog" Pond hated Arabs, just as he hated all nonwhites. But he hated the Jews even worse, giving him common cause with the Arab terrorists. The worry had been that with Pond's military and intelligence ties, he might end up becoming a weapons conduit not only for extremists operating in the United States, but also for terrorists operating in the Middle East.

Roth's orders had been fairly explicit: nail down the contacts, gather evidence, but keep a low profile. Thus far, though, he'd yet to meet or even see any of Pond's Middle Eastern contacts. He apparently met them offsite, leaving at least once a week and usually not returning for at least a day.

Roth rounded the corner of the mess hall, halted in his tracks. Voices drifted out from the windows. Slipping up alongside the building, he strained to hear the conversation. From inside he heard a coffeepot gurgle and the steady thunk of a knife blade striking a cutting board. The rich smells of onions cooking, mixed with the aroma of brewing coffee, eliciting a grumble from his stomach as it reminded him that he hadn't eaten in nearly ten hours. Jesus, he thought, of all the times—

"Take this coffee to Peterson." Roth recognized the voice; it belonged to Frank Crawford, Pond's second in command. "Slow-witted bastard probably could use something to keep him awake."

"Kid's dumb as a post," said Marc Flynn, another member of the command staff. "Might be worth letting him drift off so we can report him to Mad Dog. I got a kick out of that last ass-chewing he got."

"Don't even go there," Crawford replied. "The mood Mad Dog's in, he's liable to kill the little bastard. And we need all the hands we can get with what's coming down during the next twenty-four hours."

"Going to be a damn bloodbath, ain't it?"

"It is."

"Serves the country right," Flynn said, "always sticking its nose where it don't belong."

A cold edge slipped into Crawford's voice. "Not the country, the government."

"Right, the government."

"We're doing this for the good of the country. Mad Dog said that himself. You remember that."

"I remember. I just said it wrong, is all."

"Well, say it right next time. Mad Dog hears you spouting that 'I hate the country' shit, he'll put one right between your eyes and laugh. We want to free the country."

"All right, all right. I get it." Flynn cleared his throat. "I don't much like the Arabs, either. I'd prefer to work with my own kind, if you know what I mean."

"Necessary evil. Besides, they've been awfully generous with us. You just remember that, too. Especially if you meet them. Now why don't you take Peterson some coffee."

"Right."

A tickle of fear passed through Roth's stomach. Coming up in a crouch, the Uzi held in front of him, he began to move back around the building. The door was on the side opposite him and he wanted to catch Flynn before the man discovered Peterson's absence and alerted the rest of the camp. Flattening against the wall, he listened as footsteps, presumably Flynn's, grew louder and a man's shadow loomed larger.

He struggled to keep his breath steady as the man neared. Sweat slicked his palm, forcing him to tighten his grip on the Uzi. Roth ticked off the options in his mind. The guy almost was on him, leaving no time to switch to the knife. The Uzi had no sound suppressor, making gunfire a last resort.

Flynn, a heavyset man who shaved his head bald, sounded

as if he was running a marathon as he walked in. Involuntarily, Roth's nostrils flared as he smelled the man, a mixture of hours-old beer and body odor. The guy's ample midsection had just poked past the corner when the radio on Roth's hip came to life.

"Peterson," Crawford's voice was sharp. "Peterson. This is command one. I'm sending you some juice to help get you through the shift. Do you copy?"

Crawford's voice rang loud and clear from Roth's stolen radio. He cursed as the sudden noise caused his quarry to stop short. Flynn dropped the coffee, the tin cup clanging to the ground, hot liquid splattering the earth and darkening the bone-dry dirt.

Damn, Roth thought.

He came around the corner, the Uzi tucked in at his side, and spotted Flynn filling his hand with a .357 Colt Python.

Unlike Peterson, Flynn was a combat veteran. Roth knew he had no time to take the man down quietly. He had to go for broke.

Centering the Uzi's muzzle on his opponent, Roth triggered the Israeli-made submachine gun. Orange flames blossomed from its barrel, flickering off the walls and splitting the darkness. The volley of slugs caught Flynn up close, tearing a tight pattern in his belly before hammering through his rib cage, shredding his vital organs and knocking him back several yards.

The gunfire still ringing in his ears, Roth vaulted over Flynn's corpse and headed for the fence. He felt himself struggling for breath, heard blood pounding in his ears. But his mind seemed somehow disconnected from the two kills. He had no time for remorse, only escape.

Sprinting along the concrete bunkhouse, he saw a shadow poke around a corner of the building and knew someone lay in wait for him. As he neared the building's end, Crawford reached around the corner and fired two shots at him. Roth, who'd switched the Uzi to semiautomatic mode, replied by firing three rounds of his own. The first two hit a concrete block and careened into the darkness. The third round tunneled into Crawford's eye. The impact knocked him out of sight.

His legs pumping, his lungs burning, Roth left the main compound behind and hurried for the motor pool. A chain-link security fence, topped with razor wire, surrounded the small group of trucks and cars. Roth knew he couldn't scale the fence, not without slicing himself to ribbons, anyway. But if he could shoot off the lock—

Before he finished the thought, he heard the growl of engines from behind. Staring over his shoulders, he spotted three sets of headlights, all growing larger as they neared him. He darted left, trying to avoid the headlights and to carve out a new path. The vehicles responded in kind, swerving, holding on to him as he ran, locked to him like a heat-seeking missile tracking an airplane.

Firing as he ran, he aimed just above the headlights of the vehicle closest to him. He hoped to drill a few rounds through the vehicle's windshield, hopefully killing the driver, or at least causing him to break off the chase.

Lead sparked against steel as the rounds glanced off the hood. Like a wounded animal, the vehicle's engine growled louder and sped up its pursuit. Turning ahead, Roth poured on the speed, even though he knew he had nowhere to run.

The white glare of headlights loomed larger as the vehicles gained on him. After three more steps, he felt something strike his hip, shatter his pelvic bone. The force shoved him several feet into the air, tossing him twenty yards before he struck the ground. The blunt force against his broken pelvis caused him to let out a shrill scream. A moment later the trucks circled him before coming to a rest. As the drivers braked, their wheels covered him in plumes of dirt and he had to shut his eyes to keep out the headlights' glare.

He heard one of the doors open. Dirt crunched under boot soles as someone came up next to him. A moment later blinding pain consumed him as someone drove a foot into his broken pelvis, eliciting a scream.

A silhouette stood over him. The man's form was backlit by the truck lights, making it impossible to see his face.

Roth recognized the guy in an instant.

"Nicky," Mike Pond said, referring to Roth's alias, "were you going somewhere, son? Where were you going? You know way too much to just go sneaking out in the middle of the night. C'mon and stay. We need to talk a little."

CHAPTER TEN

Ciudud del Este, Paraguay

Bolan squinted against the sunlight as he stepped from the Gulfstream C-21A jet onto the tarmac. Slipping a pair of aviator shades from his breast pocket, the Executioner donned them and scanned his surroundings for his contact.

A moment later Bolan spotted him, an Elvis-haired man with a long-sleeved Oxford-cloth shirt, drenched with sweat, hugging his paunchy middle. Bolan hefted his twin duffel bags, loaded with weapons and equipment, and started for the man. The guy, his own eyes obscured by sunglasses with oval-shaped lenses, rested against the roof of the Ford sedan, forearms folded over top of each other, keys clutched in his right hand.

As grim as hell, the guy scratched his mustache, staring at Bolan as the distance between them was closed.

"You Cooper?"

Bolan nodded. "Cal Rollins?"

"Maybe. Maybe I need to know you're okay."

Sighing, Bolan recited a coded message that was to verify his identity. Rollins replied with his own nonsensical phrase.

"Are we finished with the cloak-and-dagger routine?" Bolan asked.

Rollins frowned and pushed off the car. "Sure hot shot. You're too damn good to follow protocol, is that it?"

His muscles tensing for a fight, Bolan clenched his jaw, hesitating before replying. He shook his head. "Forget it. It's been a long flight. I just want to take care of business and get back on the road. It's been a long couple of days as it is."

"Whatever," Rollins said. He extended an arm, zapped the car with his keyless entry unit. The car chirped and the trunk sprang open.

"You can stow your gear back here," Rollins offered.

"I prefer to keep it close."

The CIA agent shook his head, closed the trunk with a slam. "Fine, put your bags in the back seat. Do what you want. I'm not here to be your skycap for God's sake."

Bolan slid his bags into the car and minutes later the two men were on the road. Lighting up a cigarette, Rollins hunched over the wheel as he drove, keeping his eyes locked on the road, only occasionally sneaking glances at small clusters of people walking the sidewalks or sitting at sidewalk cafés. Lifting two fingers from the steering wheel, the smoke pinched between them, he pointed at three men exiting a restaurant.

"See those three jerks?" he said. Without waiting for Bolan's reply, he continued. "Islamic extremists. They come down here all the time, buy weapons, meet with guys from similar groups. High-level people, every one of them. Know where the bodies are buried and all that."

"So?"

"So, these guys keep a low profile in the homeland. They're afraid an Israeli gunship might swoop down and stick a rocket up their collective asses. Probably right. Hell, given the chance, I'd fire the damn missile if I could."

"The point?"

"These assholes blow into town once or twice a month. They do their business, they buy bad stuff and use it to kill innocent people. Personally, I don't give two shits about their politics. I hate them for what they do. But I'm here to gather intelligence. So I gather intelligence and I tell Washington about their comings and goings. They file it away or use it for toilet paper or something, I don't know. Meanwhile, I watch creeps like that walk around, planning murder with complete impunity."

Bolan felt an angry heat rise from his neck, but he nodded, encouraging the guy to continue.

"You look like a guy who doesn't sit on his ass and watch people," Rollins stated. "You look like someone who's arrived loaded for bear. I'm not sure who you're gunning for in this town, but I assume whoever it is, is bad news."

"He is."

"Good," Rollins said, tapping his index finger against his forehead. "Then plant one right here—for me. Hell, take a couple more with you if you want, with my compliments. Then get the hell out of town."

BOLAN SAT ON A STOOL at the bar, a sweating mug of beer positioned in front of him. He watched as his target—a guy called McBain—threaded his way through bar patrons.

It had been about an hour since Rollins, the CIA man, had picked him up. Rollins had driven the Ford into an alley, then inside a garage. Within minutes the guy had lost the bushy black toupee, the mustache and fake paunch. He changed into jeans and a white T-shirt with a hole under the right breast, slipped a small silver stud earring into his left ear. As he had packed his former self inside a backpack, he'd shot Bolan a grin.

"Here's your second lesson," Rollins had said. "Things aren't always what they seem here. I'm just your ride and I did my job. If you get into trouble, don't call me. You're on your on."

Bolan had expected as much. "I'll try to manage."

The soldier turned away from McBain, watched the small bubbles ascend from the bottom of the mug and break the surface. The guy didn't look like much. He was bald and his fat body strained against the fabric of cutoff denims and a sky-blue T-shirt yellowed in places by sweat rings.

But, according to intelligence from Stony Man Farm, McBain was the man to know in Ciudad del Este. He put guns and rockets into the hands of users, hooked up hired guns with terrorists and criminals. He took undisciplined thugs, screened them and handed them over to Jon Stone for training. That made him Bolan's best resource for finding the rogue CIA agent. The soldier had considered using the front door, rousting Grant outright and striking a bargain with the guy—his life for a little information.

Bolan had decided on the stealthier approach. He wanted to take down Stone, sure. But he wanted more than a surgical strike. Stone had a school, a staff and students. If Jennifer Kinsey was to be believed, and Bolan had no reason to think otherwise, Stone had other highly trained CIA paramilitary operatives working for him, each willing to teach deadly skills to those who preyed on innocents. That meant dispatching Stone with a bullet wasn't enough. Bolan needed to apply some scorched-earth diplomacy to the man and what he'd built.

Bolan sipped his beer, felt the frothy mix burn a trail down his throat, cool his belly. The beer tasted good, but Bolan knew he'd take no more than a couple of sips and those for appearance sake. He needed to keep his faculties about him.

Setting the glass on the bar, he watched as McBain slapped a couple of guys on the back, then struggled up a flight of stairs and disappeared behind a door.

Since Stone had seen Bolan in Asia, the soldier had chosen to alter his appearance dramatically, dying his hair and eyebrows blond, using colored contact lenses to change his blue eyes to hazel, rounding out his cheeks with a pair of plastic implants and wearing lifts in his shoes so he towered over nearly everyone in the bar. He stared into his glass, watching his reflection undulate as the beer shook. The music, a mixture of techno pop and Arabic chanting, pulsed. Bolan caught snatches of conversation, a mix of English, Arabic and other languages. He strained his ears, listening for bits of gossip regarding McBain. Or himself, an obvious stranger, but heard nothing.

Bolan fixed his gaze on a mirror that ran the length of the bar. He kept his expression stony, disinterested, knowing that to do otherwise would mark him for what he really was—an enemy, an infiltrator—and probably antagonize the wrong people. He didn't need that sort of attention.

As he pretended to nurse his beer, Bolan felt a nagging intuition, a cold feeling in the pit of his stomach. He considered himself a soldier, not a detective, but he knew some pieces were missing.

Kinsey had been sure that Stone had instigated the attack on James Lee, possibly because of some bad blood between the men. Bolan found that scenario hard to swallow. For sure, Stone had connections, and a fair amount of cash. But from what Bolan had read in the intelligence files and had learned from Kinsey, Stone wasn't reckless. And shooting the former CIA director in cold blood was reckless. Stupid. If Stony Man Farm wasn't sitting on the information, Stone probably would find himself in the crosshairs of countless intelligence and law-enforcement agencies.

Had Stone considered his plan foolproof? Had he been blinded by overconfidence? It was possible, maybe even probable for a sociopath like him. But still, Bolan wondered whether that was the case. Stone had survived dozens of years in a very deadly game. So why take the risk? A point of pride? Revenge? Maybe, but Bolan doubted it.

Stone had to have some other motive, and likely it was money. If someone else were footing the bill, it might make more sense for Stone to stick his neck out. But who would pay Stone to assassinate a former CIA man? Unfortunately, probably a lot of people. Kurtzman was back in Virginia, along with the rest of the cyberteam, trying to pick up the money trail. Barb Price had promised to call Bolan with the information as soon as possible.

All Bolan did know was that he probably could scratch Tariq Riyadh off the list. Even if the guy still was alive, he probably wouldn't have the money necessary to pay Stone's price. So chances were slim and none that the guy was involved.

Bolan glanced at the mirror, caught a bit of motion as someone approached.

Right on time.

A hand, small and warm, touched his forearm. Turning his head, Bolan stared at the woman who'd been watching him ever since he'd entered the bar. She had brown skin and black hair that fell past her shoulders. Full red lips turned up into a smile as she looked at Bolan. Playing his part, Bolan let a corner of his mouth twitch up, as if it were all the smile he could muster, even for this exotic beauty.

"May I sit next to you?" she said. Wide eyes stared into Bolan's own. He didn't have to pretend to be intrigued. He also didn't have to pretend to be mistrustful.

"It's your ass," Bolan said. "Put it wherever you want."

He stared straight ahead.

She climbed onto the stool, not bothering to straighten her skirt as she sat. Crossing slender legs, she turned toward Bolan, leaning in close so her breath pushed hot into his ear. "My name's Elana."

"Good for you," Bolan replied.

The woman obviously was a pro and wasn't put off by Bolan's curt response. She set her hand on his thigh, sidled up as close as possible and continued speaking in his ear, ostensibly because of the background noise. Bolan's body reacted to her touch, and he felt light-headed. But he also knew what she was after, and it wasn't him or his money.

"You just in town?"

He nodded. "Just today. You the welcoming committee?"

Her smile widened, but still didn't reach her eyes. "If that's what you want."

"Maybe," Bolan said. "First I want to finish my brew."

STEPHEN ARCHER STOOD in a corner of the bar and watched Elana work her magic. The woman was a beauty, and apparently the newbie was playing right into her game. Good. As Stone's second in command, Archer made it his business to know who was moving into their territory. And considering the mayhem that had erupted in Asia, he was especially interested in any new arrivals.

He lifted his tumbler to his lips, drained the bourbon and water it contained, set the glass on a ledge that ran the length of the wall and signaled the waitress for another. Gnawing at the cold Cuban cigar, he watched the guy and memorized his features. He didn't match a description of the man who'd wreaked so much havoc in Afghanistan. But Archer knew that didn't mean anything. The guy was big, meaty in the shoulders, chest and arms. Tall and powerful-looking. Even some of the most hardened bar patrons, guys whose hands were drenched in blood, seemed to give this man a wide berth as he'd pushed through the crowd earlier and taken a seat at the bar.

Pulling a book of matches from his pants' pocket, Archer struck one and torched the end of his cigar. He stared through the silvery haze of smoke and watched Elana. The guy seemed disinterested at best. But if he had a pulse, Elana eventually would win him over. She could sweet talk him, get a little information, with a wink and a promise of more intimate time together. If not, Archer knew from personal experience that the woman could turn up the heat, get a man to admit to damn near anything she wanted.

A waitress brought Archer a drink. He took it, absently swirling the glass to melt the ice.

Archer's boss, Stone, was edgy and rightfully so. The covert operator in Afghanistan had blown open their operation, especially by rescuing the woman. She could identify Stone, thereby bringing attention to him and others around him. That made Stone a liability, which made him nervous. And since it always rolled downhill, Stone had ordered Archer to keep an eye out for anything suspicious. That included monitoring airfields and any other point of entry.

Then along comes this guy. A lot of people came in and out of the Tri-border region every day. But this particular man had come in on his own private jet. It was a military plane, but he was the sole passenger. That was enough to make anyone suspicious. Then a man—an American already marked as an intelligence agent—picks him up at the airport. Suddenly he becomes a whole hell of a lot more interesting than the steady stream of people coming in and out of this hellhole.

An anticipation of trouble caused Archer's stomach to

clench. Without thinking, he reached behind his back, fingertips grazing the butt of a Heckler & Koch VP-70 handgun through the fabric of his shirt. Satisfied, he sighed as he felt his stomach relax. Maybe the guy was something, maybe nothing. Regardless, Stone wanted some face time with him. And Archer intended to make sure his boss got exactly what he wanted. Chances were the guy was going to go out horizontal before all this was through. That suited Archer, too.

A hulking figure shoved its way through the crowd. Decked in a tank top and jeans with the legs cut off at the knees, the guy was corded with muscle. Red splotches from the heat colored his skin and sweat rolled from his forehead and shoulders. Plucking his sunglasses from his face, he gave Archer a look that somehow reminded him of a sphinx.

"This the guy, Archer?" Jack Reuben asked.

Archer shook his head yes. "Elana's been talking with him for about five minutes. I'm not sure whether he's said anything of value or not. We'll have to see."

"What if he doesn't tell the woman anything?"

"Fat chance."

"Just suppose."

"We wait until he leaves. Then we grab him, work him over. You bring the car battery and the cables?"

Reuben nodded. "Of course. What if he tells her something and it checks out? What then?"

"These are tough times, Jack," Archer said. "Tough for everyone. If the guy doesn't know anything. If he isn't anything, fine. He still goes down. No loose ends."

Reuben grinned. "I was hoping you'd say that."

"Glad you're so damn happy," Archer said. Reaching to his belt, he grabbed his mobile phone, flipped it open. "You got others out there?"

Reuben nodded. "Right. Three of us."

"Should be enough. I'll drop you a page when he leaves."

"SO YOU JUST CAME down here? No job, no anything?"

Pressing the mug to his mouth, Bolan tipped the glass, tightened his upper lip around its rim to staunch the flow of beer into his mouth. Slamming the mug on the bar, he licked his lips, wiped a bare forearm over his lips to dry them. He gave the woman a bored look.

"Yeah," he said. "No job. No nothing. Fascinating, ain't it?"

"You must have come here for some reason," she said. The woman's hand traveled a few more inches up Bolan's thigh, causing his throat to thicken and making it harder to feign disinterest.

"I've got my reasons. I just don't want to talk about them is all."

The woman smiled, then cocked her head to one side. "Okay," she said. "What do you want to talk about?"

"We could start with you telling me just how stupid you really think I am."

The corners of her lips turned down slightly, almost imperceptibly. Her hand slipped back toward Bolan's knee, her first nonorchestrated move yet.

"I'm not sure I know what you mean."

Bolan gave her a hard stare. "Look at you. You look at me. I just happen to walk into this bar. You—a beautiful woman— just happen to pick me out of a roomful of men to sidle up to. Then you start patting me down like I'm under arrest. And I'm supposed to believe it's because I'm so damn irresistible. Lady, please."

She withdrew her hand completely, placed it palm down on her chest. "You looked interesting. I just wanted to spend some time with you. That's all."

Bolan sneered at the woman. "I've got lots of faults. Stupidity ain't one of them."

Her cheeks flushed red and her eyes narrowed. "It's true," she said. "I just wanted some company."

"You a whore?"

"I don't have to take this," the woman said. Grabbing her small purse, she started to slide off the bar stool. Bolan's hand snaked out, came to rest firmly on her shoulder, stopping her dead in her tracks. Sinking back onto the stool, she set her purse into her lap, covered it with both hands.

"I asked a question," Bolan said. "You turning tricks?"

"No!"

"Which one of these jerks you working for?"

"I don't work for anyone."

Bolan gave her a nasty smile. "Yeah, and I'm here because it's the garden spot of the universe. How 'bout you quit lying to me?"

"Or what?"

Bolan let the smile widen. "Trust me, you'll know soon enough."

Inside Bolan's guts churned as he worked to intimidate the woman. He didn't like to lean on people who didn't pose a direct physical threat to himself or others. To do so, in his mind, made him as bad as the savages he hunted. He had his limits as to how far he'd take it and he hoped the woman wouldn't push him to that point.

The woman's eyes searched Bolan's own, apparently gauging his seriousness.

"Well, if you're going to do something to me," she said, "you'd better do it right now. If you try to drag me out of here, you'd never make it to the door."

"So you do have people in here."

She nodded.

"What's your gig? I walk out with you and your friends conk me in the head? Steal my wallet? Seems pretty small time to me, honey. Besides, if I had a fat wallet, I wouldn't be here looking for work, now would I?"

She said nothing.

Bolan took his hand off her. Swiveling back toward the bar, he stacked his forearms on top of each other, leaned forward, but kept looking at the woman.

"You go find your people," he said. "Tell them if they want to talk to me, to come here and do it. Tell them I'm thinking with my brain and I'm not falling for something this transparent. Or, hell, send them over and I'll tell them myself. I came here to speak to someone—one man—and every one else can kiss off."

"Which man?"

"Like I said, everyone else can kiss off."

A dark cloud passed across the woman's face. Her lips tightened into a small line, causing her chin to dimple. She started to turn away, paused and looked at Bolan, apparently waiting for his approval. He nodded and, seconds later, she was gone.

He watched as the woman stepped into the crowd. He tracked her movements by watching the crowd part, close back on itself. To Bolan's surprise, she didn't head toward McBain's office; instead she was moving toward a hard-looking guy leaning against a wall. Bolan ran through the photos supplied by the cyberteam back in Virginia. He recognized the man as Stephen Archer, a close associate of Jon Stone.

The woman began speaking with Archer, occasionally waving her arms and gesturing in Bolan's direction. Archer stole a furtive glance or two at Bolan but avoided making direct eye contact with him. During the conversation, McBain descended the steps, approached Archer and the woman.

Bolan watched as Archer dismissed the woman by jerking his thumb over his shoulder. She disappeared and the two men crossed the barroom, walking toward Bolan.

Grabbing a beer bottle by the neck, Bolan whirled on the bar stool as the men stepped up to him. He knew he could ram the tip of his steel-toed boot into McBain's groin before the man could walk another step. In a couple of movements, he could bust the beer bottle, carve a series of scarlet ribbons in Archer's face. Bolan had the Beretta 93-R snugged in the small of his back, under his gaudy print shirt. He also carried a hammerless .38-caliber revolver in an ankle holster. He left the handguns untouched. The soldier didn't want to incite a firefight in a crowded barroom, both because of the innocents peppering the crowd and because gunshots might provoke armed, drunken criminals to involve themselves, either for self-protection or just because they could.

And Bolan wasn't kidding himself. He knew he had no allies in this room. Despite his capabilities as a soldier, he also had his limits, knew and respected them. He had to shoot his mouth off just enough to pass as a hothead, but not enough to start a fight.

Archer positioned himself to Bolan's right. Hitching his thumbs into his belt loops, he skimmed cold eyes over the Executioner.

"Heard you want to speak to me."

"That what the lady told you?"

"Yeah."

"Then she lied. I didn't come to speak to you." Bolan nodded at McBain, who had crossed his arms over his chest, used his belly to support them. "He's the one I was looking for."

McBain snorted. "Me? Why me? Who the hell are you?"

"I came looking for work."

McBain tipped his head back, appraising Bolan with one eye. "Work? You a handyman or something?"

Bolan set the beer bottle on the bar, but kept his fingers loosely wrapped around the brown glass. "Of sorts. I do stuff for people that they don't want to do for themselves."

Archer plucked his cigar from his mouth and tossed it to the floor. "That doesn't narrow it down a hell of a lot, hotshot," he said. "Care to be more specific?"

Bolan shook his head no. "Not until I know who I'm talking to."

McBain gave Archer a nod. "He's with me. That's all you need to know. I can vouch for him."

Bolan paused for effect, then, as if the effort cost him, started to speak. "I do international military and security consulting. Up until recently I was in Africa. Then some things changed and I left."

Archer shot Bolan a suspicious look. "You on the run?"

The Executioner shrugged. "Not here I'm not. If you want my credentials, I'll get them for you. If you want to see my skills, I'll demonstrate them for you. If you want my damn life story, you're out of luck."

Muscles rippled under Archer's cheeks as his jaw clenched and unclenched. He gave Bolan a hard stare, which the warrior returned. Shoulder muscles bunched up under his shirt as he waited for Archer to respond, physically or verbally.

"You've got a mouth on you," Archer said.

"And a brain," Bolan said. "You want to treat me like some weekend warrior toadie, or something, then you can blow. You want to shut up and give me some work, then we'll talk."

McBain interjected, "There's plenty of people who do what I do. Why hunt me down specifically?"

"Hank Chesterfield sent me. He said you were the guy to

know in Paraguay, said you could hook me up with a merc school as a trainer or something."

At Bolan's request, the cyberteam had tracked down the names of mercenaries killed in Africa within the past week and cross-referenced them with McBain. Chesterfield, a former British SAS soldier turned mercenary, had fit the bill perfectly. According to intelligence reports, he had worked in Central and South America before moving to Africa, and recent phone records linked him to McBain. Bolan had studied the file on the flight over, learning as much as he could in as short a time as possible so that he could offer a credible story. If these guys probed too deep, Bolan knew he could derail their questions with an emotional outburst.

"Bullshit," McBain said. "Chesterfield's dead."

Bolan snorted and gave the guy a withering look. "Thanks for the news flash. I already know that. He died a week ago in Liberia. Guess a client decided to not pay him. He made an issue out of it and took one between the eyes. Rotten luck."

McBain scowled. "You seem broken up about it."

Bolan shrugged. "More work for me. It's not like he and I were tight or nothing. He and I were on a drinking binge in Monrovia, he dropped your name, told me to look you up sometime if I needed work. He always was a hell of a lot more helpful after a few drinks."

"Sounds like Chesterfield," McBain admitted.

"What kind of training you do?" Archer asked.

Bolan gave another shrug. "Small arms. Sniper work. Unarmed combat."

"Pretty good with the hands, huh?" Archer asked.

"I get by."

Archer sneered. "You don't look like much. And your story stinks. You come in here using a dead guy for a reference and we're supposed to believe that? Get the hell out of here. Or I'll throw you out."

Bolan got to his feet but let his arms hang loose at his sides, hands closed into fists. His breath came in smooth, easy pulls, even as adrenaline caused his heart to hammer faster inside his chest and his muscles to tingle with energy. He figured Archer was good, but Bolan knew he was better. He also knew that Archer was goading him, and he wasn't going to play that game.

Archer's voice had gained volume, prompting others around him to stop talking and look at the confrontation unfolding at the bar. Most watched for a few seconds, then returned to their drinks. Bolan guessed that fights were not uncommon in the bar, a favorite watering hole for all sorts of unsavory characters.

Bolan shifted his gaze from Archer to McBain and back again.

"I guess," the soldier said, "you better toss me. If you can."

Before Archer could make another move, Bolan heard the metal-on-metal of someone working a shotgun slide from behind him. A cold sensation washed over his insides and his breath caught in his throat. As good as he was, Bolan knew he'd never reach the holstered Beretta in time to free the weapon. He kept his hands at his sides, fists still clenched.

Bolan stole a glance over his right shoulder, saw the bartender cradling a shotgun and drawing down on him. Those who only moments ago had ignored the fight, now watched with keen interest.

Bolan's adversaries broke into wide grins.

"First rule down here," Archer said, "we don't fight fair. Now get the hell out of here before you get your backside blistered by 4-aught buckshot."

"Fair enough," Bolan said. "You can pay for my beer then."

Never raising his hands but giving Archer and McBain a wide berth, he started for the door. As he crossed the barroom, he caught sight of the woman who only moments before had come on to him. He flashed her a grin and she flashed him the finger.

Stepping out of the darkened bar, Bolan shut the door behind him and leaned his weight against it in case anyone tried to follow him out. He squinted against the afternoon sun, feeling practically naked as his eyes refused to open as they adjusted to the onslaught of light.

A tense moment later he cracked open an eye. As he did, he heard a rush of breath and caught a glint of sunlight on metal as a knife blade carved out a deadly arc for his head.

CHAPTER ELEVEN

Stepping onto the sidewalk, Chris Doyle closed the cab door behind him. He watched as the driver—a stout man wearing a ball cap bearing the Chicago Bulls basketball team's logo—rounded the rear of the old Chevy, jabbing a key into the lock and disappearing behind the trunk lid. A moment later the man, his cheeks reddened with effort, moved the bags to the sidewalk and set them down.

Doyle reached into the pocket of his summer-weight suit and began fishing for money.

The driver smiled at him. "You pack very heavy."

Doyle returned the smile. "I've got heavy work to do here."

"Of course you do. You look very important."

Doyle handed him enough to cover the fare and the tip. "Looks can be deceiving, friend."

The man took the wad of cash, then looked at it and back at Doyle. "You're very generous. How long will you be in town. Do you need to hire a driver?"

Doyle shook his head. "I'm just here long enough to stop in on someone," he said. "Then I have some business in Bogotá to which I must attend."

"When do you leave? I will be here to ferry you to the airport."

"Friday," Doyle said, lying. "I leave Friday."

The man clapped his hands together. "Friday it is. I will be here for check-out time."

Doyle felt a pang of guilt. He'd tipped the guy well and chances were the driver just wanted to pocket a few more bucks from a good customer. But there also was a chance the guy was pumping Doyle for information. He hadn't been out of the field so long that he'd forgotten a basic piece of trad-ecraft—misdirection. Give five different people five different answers and you leave a twisted, confusing trail that ulti-mately leads nowhere.

"Thanks for the ride," Doyle said.

Stepping between his satchels, he grabbed each by its han-dle and brought himself erect. Immediately sweat began to roll down his temples. Spotting a luggage cart, he set the bags on it, rebuffed offers of assistance from a bellman and pushed his luggage into the hotel lobby. Minutes later he'd checked in under the name of Sean Gillis.

Pushing the cart through the lobby, he threaded between other hotel residents and employees, smiling and nodding to several of them. Doyle knew he had to walk a fine line. He wanted to be a benign presence, friendly and forgettable, like a ghost that spent eternity sleeping in the attic rather than dragging chains across the floor.

Reaching the elevators, he pulled back on the cart to curb its momentum, jabbed the up button and waited.

To his left stood the bar. Even without looking directly at the dark grotto, he knew it was there. His nostrils flared at the smell of the stale beer and the clinking glasses sounded like angelic chimes to him. His tongue seemed to swell, stick to the roof of his mouth. And a voice told him that a beer—just one—might ease the discomfort. After all, it was a hell of a trip….

He shook his head. As he did, the elevator doors parted, allowing him inside. He felt like a guy being plucked from a forest fire, saved by a last-chance grab at the bottom rung of a dangling rope ladder.

But the flames sure as hell were still licking at his feet.

He'd finally shut himself inside his room. One after the other, he lifted the bags and set them on his bed. Inserting a small key into the first bag's key hole, he twisted the key a quarter turn to the left, then two more quarter turns to the right, left the key in the hole as he looped the end of each index finger around the latches and popped them open simultaneously. His right eye screwed shut, his left open just a slit, he lifted the suitcase lid.

Nothing.

Only after he performed the same ritual on the second bag did his breathing return to normal. The Agency had rigged both bags to deliver focused but deadly charges—complete with small bits of razor wire—if they weren't opened correctly. Doyle had been briefed on the locking mechanisms back in Virginia but had received the bags during a hand-off outside the local airport. At least his superiors knew better than to stuff a passenger jet with explosives-laden suitcases, he thought sourly.

Reaching into the suitcase to his right, Doyle extracted a .40-caliber Glock sheathed in a nylon shoulder rig. Wriggling out of his jacket, he unwound the straps and slipped on the holster. A pair of extra clips rode on the rig's opposite side. He took a couple of practice draws, familiarizing himself with the gun's weight, the ease with which it slid loose from the holster. Satisfied, he holstered the weapon and secured it with the Velcro-tipped strap. He strapped a Beretta .380 to his ankle as a backup piece.

Rummaging through the same suitcase, he found the other tools he'd requested: a stiletto wrapped in a wrist sheath, an Uzi and an Ingram machine pistol. Strapping the stiletto around his forearm, he felt nausea and dizziness begin to overtake him. Pushing back one of the suitcases, he sat on the bed, wrapped his arms around his middle and rode out the upset stomach.

He'd sworn he wouldn't do this. He'd vowed years ago to walk away. No more killing, no more globetrotting. Nothing. For him, it all seemed to go hand in hand. He'd spent three months in a hot jungle training guerrilla fighters. He drank. He'd watched an Islamic terrorist spin back as a bullet drilled through the confluence of the guy's nose and his forehead, and Doyle drank.

And drank. And drank.

Doyle had been left with no choice but to leave the CIA. He'd realized long ago that he couldn't stay and stay sober. And civilian life hadn't been a picnic, either. Sometimes when he slept, he saw their faces, eyes bulging, skin turning a sickening shade of pale as their life fluids drained from them. Yeah, in his dreams it always featured an all-star cast, he thought sourly. The Saudi stockbroker making trades for al Qaeda, the Colombian rebel who'd kidnapped and ultimately killed a U.S. diplomat's wife and baby, that poor Iraqi kid sent by Doyle and Stone to die on a suicide mission.

Doyle had the touch of death, but he no longer wanted it. He no longer wanted to take people's lives. He'd stopped believing in fighting the good fight long ago. And he knew he'd be a liar if he said he was here fighting for ideology.

He was here for Nancy. Period. Though he initially figured that his former boss had been full of crap, Doyle had run some traps with his old contacts within the Agency and nailed down at least bits and pieces of it, enough to confirm the theory that Stone was gunning for old members of Thunder Hawk.

Doyle had wasted all of about thirty seconds trying to figure out the *why* behind Stone's crusade before scuttling the effort. Stone was an animal; a psychopath; a mindless killing machine who probably had snapped under the weight of his own bloodlust. So Doyle was here to put the poor bastard out of everyone's misery.

Truth be told, though, Doyle knew he had purely selfish reasons. If he were alone, he'd probably kick back in Virginia and wait for Stone to hunt him down. If he were alone, it wouldn't much matter if Stone hunted him down, perhaps even killed him. If Doyle were alone, he knew he could take life, or leave it.

But he wasn't alone; he had Nancy and he couldn't risk Stone coming for her. Faced with that reality, he'd had to shove his morals aside and take Stone out. Kill or be killed. It was that simple. Making sure he kept things at that level would make this whole nightmare pass much more quickly.

He hoped.

Rising from the bed, Doyle moved to the cramped washroom. Standing at the sink, he ran cold water into it. He formed a cup with his hands, filled them with water and splashed it over his face, cooling it. Sometimes he just spent too damn much time thinking, he told himself. Drying his hands and extinguishing the bathroom light, he walked back into the main quarters, grabbed his jacket and slipped it over his slight frame.

A cold feeling had settled into his gut and his scowl and the lines on his forehead deepened. Given his choice of targets, Stone ranked at the bottom of the list. Not that he felt any lingering loyalty or friendship for the man. Just the opposite; he hated the son of a bitch. But Stone was dangerous. While Doyle had spent the last few years in rehab and piecing together some semblance of a normal life, Stone had been

pulling illegal ops and training people to kill. If he was to succeed, Doyle knew a fair fight was out of the question. He'd
already accepted that fact, as he'd accepted that he'd freshen
the bloodstains on his hands, add new nightmares to the endless images already haunting him.

So quit whining. It's time to play hunt the psycho. Shut up
and do it.

Stepping into the hall, closing the door behind him, Doyle
scanned the hallway, but saw nothing unusual. He spotted a
maid's cart positioned next to an open door. A woman
hummed from inside. A tray of dishes set next to another door,
awaiting pickup. Elevators stood at the end of the hall, a
muted ringing audible as they stopped on other floors.

Since he'd used the elevator before, chances were any tail
might expect him to use the same mode of transportation. Instead he pulled open the heavy steel door leading into the
stairwell and began hoofing it. This was a smart precaution,
if he wasn't being monitored on security cameras or by multiple tails. If he even rated a single tail. He was considerably
less conspicuous than a team of Marines, which probably
would have been the better solution to the Stone problem. But
with Jennifer Kinsey's rescue, chances were Stone was expecting some kind of reprisal. If the guy had more brains than
testosterone, he probably wouldn't have even returned to
Paraguay.

Doyle hoped Stone hadn't gotten more sensible in his old
age.

He passed through the stairwell and the lobby without incident. Slipping on a pair of sunglasses, he exited the hotel
and began walking the streets, following a predetermined
route. He felt the familiar flutter of excitement pass through
his belly and for a moment the adrenaline rush carried him
away. There had been something about living on the edge, he

decided as he pushed through a crush of pedestrians. Something pleasant, if not fleeting. Doyle wasn't one to take particular pleasure in life. But the closer he'd come to death, the more alive he'd felt.

But it came with a price, he reminded himself. Most of the time he could rationalize the bloodshed. Most of his targets had had it coming. But his battle hardly had been a clean one, and occasionally civilians had gotten caught in the cross fire. A little boy in Somalia. A schoolteacher in Afghanistan. A pair of servants working for a Saudi financier. All dead, by his hand. Accidentally, of course. But that did little to lessen the guilt that gnawed at his insides like a rat chewing the plastic sheath from a live wire.

Those deaths had driven Doyle into retirement and the confines of the bottle, turned him against his country, his values, and caused him to question his own humanity.

So this time he had a chance to do it right. Take out a single threat, go home in one piece and forget about the spy game once and for all.

At least he hoped so.

But he also knew it'd get dirty in the process.

Case in point.

He stood outside the import-export house and stared through the rectangular pane-glass window. Persian rugs rolled tight lined the window and a series of custom-made lamps hung from the ceiling, each pulsing with light. Hamid Gul, the store's proprietor, obviously was doing well for himself, Doyle thought. Not surprising, since he had the rugs stuffed with processed heroin before importing them from Afghanistan.

Thumbing open the strap holding his pistol in place, Doyle pushed open the door and stepped inside the building. The stench of musty fabric and incense assailed his nostrils as he entered. Doyle swept his gaze over the store, but saw no customers. He locked the door behind him and pulled the SIG-Sauer.

Stepping between racks loaded with rolled carpets, Doyle ducked, moved toward the back of the store. From behind a curtained door situated behind the counter, he heard the murmur of voices. A male voice was gaining in volume.

"I know nothing of this Jon Stone," Gul said. "Why do you threaten me? I just sell rugs. I don't want any trouble. Please leave my store and we forget all this."

The short hairs along Doyle's neck stood as he listened to the exchange. Even if the words hadn't been a direct tip-off, the tautness of Gul's voice telegraphed that his visitor likely had a weapon of some sort. Doyle tightened his grip on the SIG-Sauer and thumbed off the safety.

Another voice sounded from the back of the store—a decidedly feminine voice.

"You're full of shit, Gul," she said. "And I'm out of patience. So you'd better start talking before I spray brains over this room."

A grin tugged at the corner of Doyle's lips. Well, I'll be hanged, he thought. It's her.

BEFORE HE COULD IDENTIFY the object slicing out a collision course for his head, Bolan folded at the knees, let the arm pass harmlessly over his head. As his eyesight returned, he saw a pair of tree-trunk legs in front of him. Drops of perspiration landed on him as his assailant grunted, struck at empty air. Even as Bolan's mind identified the weapon as a dual-edged knife, his right arm rocketed forward and he buried his fist into the man's groin.

Looking up, Bolan saw the guy's cheeks redden and his eyes bulge. The man doubled over. As he did, Bolan already was shooting up to his full height. The Executioner reached out, grabbed the man's ears and jerked the man's head down hard. Bolan simultaneously brought up his knee and buried it into the man's face, splintering the cartilage forming the man's nose.

Giving the guy a hard shove, Bolan already was on the move, seeking his next attacker. From his peripheral vision the warrior saw something coming at him. Taking a step back, Bolan rested most of his weight on his rear foot. Despite the Executioner's speed, his attacker still landed a glancing blow off his chin, whipping his head right and knocking him off balance.

The big American staggered back. The coppery taste of blood filled his mouth and he spit it out without thinking.

Apparently sensing an opening, Bolan's assailant cocked his arm back, prepared to fire another punch. The arm flew forward. Bolan caught his balance and knocked the arm aside. The guy followed up with a left jab. Twisting at the waist, Bolan dodged the blow. Planting his right foot between the man's legs, he fired elbow into the man's throat. Hard bone connected with soft flesh, sending the guy back gagging. Bolan was ready to finish the guy off when more motion to the left caught the Executioner's attention.

Even as Bolan whirled to meet his latest attacker, his fingers scrambled for the Beretta. A slender guy with a crew cut and goatee was moving toward the fighters. The warrior noted that the guy's own hand was obscured behind his back as he looked for something.

The Beretta came free and Bolan jabbed the muzzle into the guy's face.

"Don't," the warrior cautioned.

The guy didn't. Instead he raised his hands. Bolan's combat senses begged for his attention; he felt a presence closing in from behind. As the Executioner stepped off the bull's-eye, the man in front of him dived away and scrambled for his gun. Bolan whirled, gun hand already extended, and caught another man closing in, a shotgun held fast against his shoulder.

Bolan triggered the Beretta and a triburst of 9 mm Parabellum slugs drilled into the man's skull. In a final death spasm, the man's finger tightened on the shotgun. The weapon belched smoke and flame as it discharged skyward. Even as the wild shot continued to reverberate, Bolan heard screams as onlookers suddenly began to panic.

Muttering a curse, the soldier turned back toward his previous attacker. Red-faced and sweating, the guy stood at a forty-five-degree angle from Bolan, a mini-Uzi trained on him. Archer stood several feet away from Bolan, far enough away to have the drop on Bolan's back. He was pointing a H&K VP-70.

Two more men, each brandishing an M-4 rifle, aimed their weapons at Bolan from a second-story window.

Archer grinned at the soldier. "Care to step inside?"

Bolan ran the numbers. He could take out Mr. Goatee, definitely. Then he had to readjust his aim, draw down on a guy that already had him dead to rights and trigger the Beretta before his opponent—a CIA-trained killer—could fire his own.

Yeah, right.

Bolan knew he was good, better than most. As a soldier, he knew better than to expect a sure thing. But only a moron would expect him to pull off that kind of shooting and walk away unscathed. And even if he could, Bolan knew at least one of the second-story assassins would core a round through his head before he could defend himself.

At the same time, the sirens sounded closer with each passing second.

No, he didn't want to step inside.

He tossed his weapon in the dirt.

"You win, Archer," Bolan said, starting for the bar.

CHAPTER TWELVE

Stony Man Farm, Virginia

Barb Price watched as Aaron Kurtzman's fingers glided over the keyboard. Occasionally he emitted a small sound or swore under his breath, but otherwise he remained silent as he went about his task. Briefly, Price saw the FBI logo flash on the screen before Kurtzman chased it away with a few more deft keystrokes.

Flashing through more screens, he let out a low whistle. "Shit," he said.

Price set her hand on his shoulder, squeezing the muscle lightly to remind Kurtzman that he wasn't alone in the room.

"Come on, Aaron," she said. "Enough muttering. What the hell's going on?"

Kurtzman snapped his head toward Price. He shot her an embarrassed grin.

"Sorry, Barb," he said. "Got a little absorbed in things."

"Tell me about it."

Kurtzman turned back to the computer, leaned his bulky torso into his wheelchair's backrest. With his right index finger, he indicated a spot on the screen.

"Whenever a federal agent or U.S. police officer gets killed, we get a notice from the Justice Department," Kurtzman said. "It's a courtesy thing that Hal set up."

"Right," Price said. "I scan through it at the end of the workday. So what's got you so enthralled, Aaron?"

"This," Kurtzman replied, tapping his finger against his monitor. "Seems a federal agent named Tom Roth turned up dead several hours ago. In the Utah desert, no less."

Price felt a chill race down her spine. "Dead from what?"

"Gunshot wound to the base of the skull. Close range. Other details are sketchy. These files don't indicate the nature of his mission. Or even if he was on one, for that matter. Akira's following up on that."

Price turned toward Akira Tokaido, another member of the Farm's cyberteam. The young man stared into his monitor, bobbing his head in time with music blasting through his earphones. Tokaido had pulled his earphones off his head and looped them around his neck. Despite the distance separating them, Price could hear the wailing of an overdriven electric guitar as clearly as if she wore the headphones herself.

"Got anything for us, Akira?" Price asked.

"Still pretty sketchy," he said. "From what I've pieced together, Roth was operating deep undercover. He had penetrated this militia group—Patriots of the New Dawn. Until the last twenty-four hours, he'd been filing regular reports with his bosses. Then he missed his check-in call. His handlers were concerned, but before they could do anything, a couple of hikers found Roth's body."

The churn in Price's gut worsened. "What about the Patriots' compound?"

Tokaido shrugged. "It's a ghost town, nothing but tire tracks and empty buildings. Nobody's quite sure where these folks went, obviously."

"What do we know about these people?" Price asked.

"They're as hateful as hell. They hate the government, hate blacks, hate Jews. I doubt if I'd rate an invite to their annual dinner, either," said Tokaido, who was of Japanese descent.

Kurtzman's voice sounded from behind Price, prompting her to turn back toward him. "This is interesting," he said.

"What?"

Kurtzman punched a few buttons on his keyboard. A moment later a hard-looking man, unshaven, with a bottomless stare, appeared on the screen.

Kurtzman poked the image with his index finger. "This guy's the brains behind the Patriots. His name's Mike Pond. But everyone calls him, Mad Dog."

"Original," Price muttered.

"Aren't they always? Seems Mad Dog's new to the militia business, but not new to armed conflict."

"Former military, I assume."

"Give the lady one of Hal's half-chewed cigars," Kurtzman quipped. "Former Air Force Special Forces. He usually handled intelligence work during insertions. Guy speaks four languages and has dual degrees from Oxford in history and physics. His IQ is off the charts."

"You'd never know it to look at him," Price said.

"According to these records," Kurtzman continued, "the guy's built like a beanpole, but he's an expert in small arms and unarmed combat. He's also a little on the crazy side."

Price's brow furrowed, but she didn't turn away from Pond's image. "Crazy?"

Kurtzman scrolled through a file, reading, absorbing and reciting it in a matter of seconds. "Unstable. Guy slapped a female officer when she criticized his haircut. He enjoyed it so much, he hit her two more times."

"A real man's man."

Kurtzman shrugged. "The guy's a loon. The Air Force did the right thing. They canned him. So he did what any other red-blooded American with lots of combat experience would do."

"Oh, no."

"Right. He joined the CIA."

"Let me guess. During James Lee's tenure, correct?"

"Right again."

"It could be a coincidence," Price offered. She knew her words rang hollow even as she uttered them.

"It's a nice thought, anyway," Kurtzman replied.

Price continued to stare at Pond's image, even as she weighed what she knew. So far, she had one dead CIA director, killed by a former subordinate, and now a second operating a militia that possibly had just killed a federal agent.

"When did Pond leave the CIA?"

"December, 2000."

"Why?"

Kurtzman shook his head. "Can't tell, Barb. Other than what I've shared, this guy pretty much is a closed book."

"Akira, chart the distance between the Patriots' stronghold and Hal's offsite."

"Already did. Fifty miles as the crow flies."

The computer genius turned toward Price. "You thinking we should drop Hal a line?"

She nodded in agreement. "The chances of anyone actually getting close to the facility, let alone doing any harm, are slim and none. But Hal would want to know anyway."

Ciudad Del Este, Paraguay

THE JEEP CHEROKEE shuddered as it rolled over a pothole, causing Bolan to grind his teeth. He sat at the rear of the SUV, next to Archer, who had the snout of Bolan's Beretta 93-R centered on his chest. Handcuffs held Bolan's hands behind his back, the steel rings digging into flesh.

"I'll say this for you, Cooper—you got good taste in hardware. I may keep this as a memento."

Bolan stared out his window and let out an irritated sigh. "Stick the thing in your ass for all I care."

Bolan felt the anger radiating from the other man as he absorbed his prisoner's reply. Ultimately the soldier had elected to surrender back at the bar. Besides being outgunned, instinct told him that an encounter with the local police probably would work against him. When Archer had dismissed the investigating officers by handing them money, Bolan knew his instincts had been right.

Now he was starting to have second thoughts. But he banished them almost as quickly as they came. He needed to keep his mind on the task at hand. Besides, he'd prepared for this contingency.

Without looking at Archer, Bolan asked, "Where are we going?"

"You wanted to meet my boss, you're going to meet my boss."

"Aren't I the lucky one?" Bolan turned away from the window and stared straight ahead. His torso bobbing back and forth, his stomach lurching, as the Jeep rolled over more rough terrain. A heartbeat later, Bolan caught something flying at his head. Even as Archer's knuckles brushed against his chin, the soldier rolled with the blow, letting Archer believe he'd hit Bolan fully.

He whipped his head around, pinned Archer under his gaze. "What the hell'd you do that for?"

"Just warming you up, Cooper. When Stone gets hold of you, you'll get the beating of a lifetime. Unless he decides to just put one between your eyes."

DOYLE ROUNDED a cluster of Persian rugs, his weapon extended. He sighted down the barrel of his handgun, ready to pull the trigger at the slightest provocation. Still, he couldn't help but grin as he saw the woman standing in front of him.

Jennifer Kinsey. Just as he thought.

Pointing the pistol skyward, he cleared his throat. Kinsey and Gul simultaneously whirled toward him. Kinsey centered the barrel of her handgun on his chest. Recognition flickered in her eyes for a moment before her gaze again grew cold. Damn, the woman was a pro. She wasn't going to acknowledge that she knew him in front of an asset.

"Drop the gun," she said.

"What's in it for me?"

"Your life."

"Not much of a prize, most days," Doyle said.

"Drop it."

Doyle bent, set the pistol gently on the floor. He kicked it just far enough away that he could recover it by diving for it.

Kinsey stared at Doyle another moment. As she did, Gul stepped toward her. Doyle started to react, muscles tensing, lips parting to shout a warning. Spotting his change of expression, Kinsey's hand slipped under her light jacket and reappeared with a pistol. She jabbed the gun in his face. He stopped cold and raised his hands higher.

"Nice moves, Gul," Doyle said.

"Shut up," the man replied. "Just shut up."

Kinsey looked back at Doyle. "You two know each other?"

"Sure," he said, grinning. "I know all the lowlifes in town. Can I put my hands down?"

Kinsey stared at him for a moment, then nodded. She turned to the other man. "Keep your hands up."

Gul complied but shot Doyle a look. "What do you want with me, you crazy bastard? I told you to stay away."

Doyle shrugged. "I couldn't understand you through all those broken teeth. My mistake."

An image of Gul's face, bloodied and bruised, flickered across Doyle's mind. He quickly dismissed it, but the memory caused his gut to twist so hard that he felt as though he might break in two. The old thirst slipped in again. Seeing Kinsey—Jennifer—after all these years didn't help matters, either.

Neither did knowing what he'd have to do before all this was over.

Kinsey spoke, pulling him from his thoughts. "You two met before?"

Doyle nodded. "Hamid was selling pirated athletic shoes and jeans, then funneling the money back to Palestinian terrorists. I encouraged him to stop, told him we'd have a more forceful discussion if it continued."

"You beat me!"

"Did you stop?"

"Yes."

"Don't argue with results," Doyle said, forcing a grin.

"They said you'd retired."

"I did.

Kinsey poked the barrel of her pistol between Gul's eyes. "I don't have time for you two to reminisce. And I don't plan on splitting a knuckle on your ugly face. I came to ask questions and I want some answers."

Gul stiffened. "I'll tell you nothing."

Doyle watched as Kinsey's eyes narrowed and instantly knew her prisoner had said the wrong thing.

"You talk," she said, "or I'll perforate your spine with a 9 mm slug." She turned toward Doyle. "And you, get the hell out of here." She motioned for the door with a nod. "I don't know who you are and I don't care. I have personal business to discuss with this guy and I don't need gawkers."

"Fair enough," Doyle said. He stepped toward his gun, but stopped when Kinsey drew down on him again.

"Leave it," she said.

"As you wish, my queen."

Kinsey scowled. Doyle turned on his heel and walked out the door.

Lighting a cigarette, he walked through an alley and to the rear of the store, saw that it had no back door. He returned to the mouth of the alley and stood flush with the building, waiting for Kinsey to step outside. By the time he lighted a second smoke, she walked outside and started toward him. Sunlight glinted from the mirrored lenses of her sunglasses.

Doyle stepped into her path and she halted inches from him.

"You probably thought I'd sneak out, didn't you?" she asked.

Doyle shrugged. "Don't break your arm patting yourself on the back. There's only one door. I checked."

Kinsey gave Doyle her best smile. Reaching up, she nabbed the cigarette from between his mouth, stuck it into her own and let her eyes linger on his. "Good to see you, Doyle. I thought you quit the trade. I heard you lost it or something. That true?"

"I quit. I had to come back. It's complicated."

Kinsey pursed her lips, exhaled a column of smoke. She cocked her head to one side, smiled. "You miss me?"

"Cut the crap, Jen. You're better than this. You want to play that game, do it with someone else. We aren't going there again, period."

Her eyes narrowed. "So you're not happy to see me?"

"I didn't say that. All I'm saying is the Thunder Hawk days are over. So quit acting like they're not. I didn't travel halfway around the world to rekindle things with you. And I'm not picking up my career where I left off, either. I'm here for a reason."

She crossed her arms over her chest, but her gaze didn't waver. "And that reason is?"

"Same as you."

"Which is?"

"Jon Stone."

Doyle saw something flicker in her eyes at the mention of the name. Anger? Fear? Damned if he knew—or cared for that matter. She stared at her feet as she spoke. "You heard about James?"

Sunlight burned the back of Doyle's neck. And the longer he stood in the open, the more antsy he became. He was on Stone's territory now and he knew death could lay in wait for him anywhere. "That's why I'm here," Doyle said. "Couple of suits from Langley told me about his murder, said a witness put Stone at the scene. The working theory is that Stone is gunning for members of the old team."

"And you buy that theory?"

Doyle shrugged. "Doesn't really matter what I buy, does it?"

"Why would he just start a rampage against us?"

"Because he's a psycho? Hell, Jennifer, I don't know."

Kinsey shook her head. "It doesn't add up," she said. "Stone's crazy, but he isn't a moron. I'm not sure he'd draw the U.S. government's wrath just for the sake of doing it. He's got a pretty good thing going down here to just screw it up like that."

Reluctantly, Doyle nodded in agreement. "So if not for revenge, then why?"

"Why does Stone do anything?"

"Money."

"Right."

Turning away, Doyle began to walk down the street. Kinsey fell into lockstep next to him.

With an open hand, Doyle wiped the sweat from his neck, stared at his glistening palm for a moment before drying it on his suit jacket. "Gul tell you anything?"

"Yes."

"And that would be?"

"Later," Kinsey said. "First, tell me why you're here."

"Because Stone—"

"Cut the bullshit, Chris. You'd just as soon crack open a beer and wait for Stone to come to Virginia. You quit and swore never to return."

Doyle pushed his sunglasses back up on the bridge of his nose. "Couldn't stand it anymore, Jen. It all started to feel like climbing a ten-thousand-foot sand dune. I'd take a step forward, kill a terrorist or an arms dealer, and two more people would step in and replace him. Or I'd find out that the people I was hunting were doing business with someone else in the Company."

Kinsey nodded.

Doyle continued. "After a while, it all seemed like a farce. I believed in Thunder Hawk's role as a counterterror unit, felt we were fighting the good fight. But when the bad guys kept multiplying and Lee abdicated all responsibility, I decided I'd had enough."

"You were disillusioned."

Doyle grinned. "Idealists get disillusioned. I just wanted a vacation."

"You didn't answer my question."

"What?"

"Why are you back? I know you hate Stone, but, come on. You said it yourself—you gave up the fight. Why step back into the breech?"

"I've got my reasons."

"Nancy?"

"How did you know my wife's name?"

"You and I used to sleep together. I make it my business to keep up on these things."

For a moment, Doyle felt violated. Then, in spite of himself, he grinned. Welcome back to the wonderful world of espionage, he thought.

THE SHOVE SENT Bolan hurtling forward. His knees struck the earth and a moment later pain lanced through the joints. With his hands still tied behind his back, Bolan was unable to stop himself as his body pitched forward. From behind him, he heard Archer snicker.

Muscles coiling, the soldier strained against his bonds, used his left leg to roll himself on his back. He glared at Archer, who seemed genuinely pleased with himself.

"Nice moves, Coop," Archer said.

"Take off the cuffs and I'll show you some real moves," Bolan replied.

"Enough time for that later," Archer said. He gestured toward Bolan and two men moved to the Executioner. Each grabbed an arm and hauled the soldier to his feet. "First," Archer said, "I want you to meet someone."

One of the men shoved Bolan forward and he continued up the steps. Sweat trailed down his forearms, burning flesh worn raw by the handcuffs. He'd lost his aviator shades during the battle in the city and he squinted against the sun's onslaught as he approached what he guessed was Stone's house.

The home had been built on a hill on the outskirts of Ciudad del Este. Surrounded by acres of verdant jungle, it was accessible only by a gravel road. The group already had passed through a reinforced steel gate to access the grounds. A concrete wall surrounded much of the property.

Bolan heard the pop of automatic weapons from somewhere behind the property. Elsewhere, he heard a man shouting orders in Pashto, a native language of Afghanistan, and heard the steady pounding of multiple footsteps.

"Yeah," Archer continued, "Stone wants to meet the man that killed one of his mercs. Donaldson was the guy whose head you ventilated. He was one of Stone's better men. Lots of money invested in training that guy."

"A lot of money wasted, you mean," Bolan said. "If that's the best you people have to offer, maybe I ought to look for work elsewhere."

Archer shook his head. "You just don't get it, cowboy, do you? I ain't bringing you here for a job interview. Stone wants to find out more about you, then he'll likely kill you."

"Yeah, you mentioned that before," Bolan said. "I'm not dead yet. And truth be told, if I was you I'd worry more about someone else." Still flanked by two hardmen, Bolan reached the front door and stopped. Another man stepped up to the door, passed a security card through the reader and waited for the bolts to slide back.

"And who should I be worrying about?" Archer asked.

Bolan gave him a pointed look. "I'd worry about the guy who sent Donaldson out to get killed."

Minutes later Bolan found himself in a massive room. Mounted heads from lions, rhinoceroses and bears hung from the wall. Hunting rifles mounted on plaques were positioned on the walls, too. As he scanned the weapons, Bolan's mind immediately began to name them and to recall ammo specs, muzzle velocities and effective distances even as he surveyed his surroundings, searching for potential points of cover. The mounted weapons, he knew, would do him little good, unless he wanted to bludgeon someone. Chances were, they weren't loaded. He did, however, spy an M-14 with an attached bayonet and tucked away the knowledge.

He heard the click of heels on ceramic tile and turned. Elana, the woman from the bar, entered the room. Raking back some of her hair with her fingertips, she tucked it behind an ear and smiled at Bolan.

"You should have talked to me," she said. "It would have made things much easier."

"I didn't get the idea that talking was your strength," Bolan replied. The woman glared at him, started to say something but stopped as heavier footfalls announced another arrival.

A hulking form stepped from the shadows, slowly coming into view. Bolan knew from the files supplied by Stony Man Farm that Stone was a big man, but he hadn't realized how much so until the guy came within a few yards of him. The man stood a couple inches taller than Bolan. The fabric of his T-shirt strained against massive pectorals and thick shoulders. Bolan saw a pair of auto-loading pistols hanging from the guy's belt, in cross-draw fashion. Though they were indoors, mirrored sunglasses obscured the guy's eyes.

Without looking at Elana, he jerked a thumb over his shoulder. "Get your tail out of here," he growled.

Elana did as she was told.

Boots thudding against the floor, Stone walked to within a foot of Bolan and studied him like a sculptor studying a statue. The scents of cheap cologne and sweat assailed Bolan's nostrils as the guy gave him a once-over.

His arm firing out like a piston, Stone struck Bolan in the chest with an open palm and sent him reeling backward. The soldier stumbled a couple of paces before he could stop himself.

Stone turned to look at Archer. "This is what you got so damned excited about? This is the guy who killed Donaldson and beat up my people? What are you, Archer, an old woman? He's not so tough."

Archer's face remained inscrutable as he returned his boss's stare.

"The guy's something," Archer said.

"Bullshit."

"It's true. He moves like a damn machine. You ought to see him in action."

Stone looked at Bolan a second, then back at Archer. "He tougher than you? Is that what you're saying? I got the wrong guy in charge here?"

Bolan saw Archer tense, his eyes narrow just a little. "I'm not saying that," Archer said.

"Then what are you saying?"

"The guy's good. That's all I'm saying."

Stone turned back to Bolan. Crossing the room in a couple of long strides, he put himself in the soldier's face. "That true? You some kind of badass or something?"

"You tell me," Bolan said. "You're the one keeping me in handcuffs. You must be afraid of something."

Harsh laughter exploded from Stone's mouth. He wheeled, walked a couple of paces away before spinning back toward Bolan.

"You got a hell of an attitude there," Stone said. "Who sent you? The Company? Washington wanting to keep an eye on Jonny, see what he's up to these days?"

"Go ask Washington," Bolan replied. "I came here looking for work. Nothing more, nothing less."

Like a dog responding to a whistle, Stone cocked his head

to one side. The mercenary screwed one eye shut, regarded Bolan with the other. "And you knew to come looking for me," Stone said. "What a coincidence."

Bolan shook his head. "I don't know you from Adam. I came here looking for McBain, because an old friend suggested it. Far as I'm concerned, you're just another steroid stallion with a crew cut. If I wanted to work with someone who's all mouth and no ass, I'd go do security for a Colombian drug cartel or something."

"You got any other skills? Besides talking trash, I mean?"

"I got skills, same as your other guys. Only difference is I'm better than your guys."

"That so?"

Bolan flashed a wicked grin. ""Go dig up Donaldson and ask him."

"Hell, I'll do you one better," Stone said. "I'll let you show me."

With a nod, Stone dispatched one of his men to release Bolan. The guy removed the handcuffs, then backed up several steps. Bringing his hands in front of him, Bolan took turns rubbing his wrists even as he swept his gaze over the men surrounding him. Six guys, each a trained warrior, each armed, ringed him.

Bolan let his arms hang loose at his sides. He softened his gaze, noticing everything but fixating on nothing. Even as his heart pounded in his chest, he slowed his breath, taking it in even, deliberate pulls. The way he saw it, he'd have enough time to get one guy, maybe put him down with a knife-hand strike to the throat before the others gathered on him. Or shot him. Sweat rolled down the warrior's neck, traced the length of his spine as he waited for Stone's next move.

"See, here's the deal," Stone said. "I had some bad luck recently in Afghanistan. Real bad luck that cost me some good men, put me in a bad way with a client."

"Business sucks," Bolan said.

Stone snorted out a small laugh. "Problem is, I never saw the bastard who did all the damage. Not face-to-face, anyway. So he could be anyone, anywhere. Then you come dancing in here, wanting to work with me, and I'm supposed to welcome you with open arms? Forget it."

Stone's hand dipped into his holster. In a blur of motion he fisted a Smith & Wesson Combat Magnum, aimed it at Bolan's head, thumbed back the pistol's hammer. A cold sensation passed through Bolan's stomach, but he kept his face impassive.

"And I'm looking at you, and I'm seeing that you've got red cheeks," he said. "Red like you got a bad case of windburn. Maybe like you were crawling around in some snow-covered pass in the mountains of Afghanistan."

"Bullshit," Bolan replied. "I haven't been to Afghanistan in years."

"Maybe, maybe not. But I don't intend to take the chance. So here's what I'm going to do—"

"So you really believe that the CIA can't track down Stone without your help?" Jennifer Kinsey asked.

Doyle shrugged and pondered the question. In the meantime, he piloted Kinsey's extended-cab pickup through the streets of Ciudad del Este. Kinsey had returned his Glock, and Doyle had stopped by the hotel to gather up the rest of his gear.

"I hadn't thought of it," he said.

"Bullshit. You think of everything, you damn cynic."

Keeping his eye fixed on the road, Doyle sighed and shook his head slowly. "Okay, I wondered about that. Does the Agency have dozens of agents capable of doing this job as well or better than me? Hell, yes, they do. But I know Stone as well or better than most of the other agents. And who's to say someone else isn't working the case, too."

"Another agency?"

Doyle shrugged again. "Maybe. Probably. I mean, Lee's assassination was big news, and it sets a bad precedent if the perpetrators get away with it. So, yeah, there's probably a lot of people looking into it."

"Which brings me back to my original question."

Doyle felt his face flush hot with anger. "What the hell's your point? That the CIA is using me? I've realized from the get-go that that's a possibility. Hell, I'd almost guarantee they are. So what's my other option? If he came after my wife, and I didn't act, what does that say about me? This may be a game to you, but to me it's damn serious."

Kinsey's face reddened. "It's serious to me, too, dammit. I was there when they killed Jim, remember? And I almost lost my own life in the process. Don't forget that."

Scowling, Doyle nodded. "Understood."

"I just want to make sure you know the score, that's all," she said. "If we're going to work together, I want to keep things honest between us."

"That's a first," Doyle said.

"Shut up, Doyle."

They traveled the next twenty minutes in silence. Finally, Doyle turned to Kinsey and watched as she studied a map. With the crumpled document fanned open on her lap, she traced her fingernail over about three inches of paper, peered through the windshield before turning to Doyle.

"Pull over here," she said, pointing at the roadside.

Doyle cut the wheel right and took the truck off the road. Slipping the transmission into park, he turned to Kinsey.

"How close?" he asked.

She pointed northeast, into a line of trees bordering the opposite side of the road. "About a mile that way," she said. "If Gul was telling the truth."

"Good luck," Doyle said. "That guy never tells the truth."

"Well, if he betrayed us, I already repaid him in advance."

Doyle didn't bother asking her to elaborate; in his gut, he already knew what she meant.

"I guess we hoof it from here," Doyle said.

Disembarking from the truck, Doyle reached into the rear, removed his gear bag and slung it over his shoulder. Kinsey, her own weapons bag hanging from her shoulder, met him on the other side of the vehicle. Doyle watched as she aimed a small key fob at the pickup. An instant later the truck's headlights flashed and the vehicle emitted a small chirp.

Reaching into her pants' pocket, Kinsey withdrew a matching fob and handed it to Doyle, who took it. He gave her a questioning look.

"In case we get separated," she said. "You need this to unlock the truck. If the truck doesn't get the signal, it'll blow up, even if you have the right key."

Doyle nodded and pocketed the device. The pair crossed the road and slipped in among the trees. Setting his bag on the trunk of a fallen tree, Doyle opened it and withdrew a pair of camouflage coveralls. Slipping out of his street clothes, he rolled them up, then stepped into the coveralls. He turned and found Kinsey, stripped down to her underwear, donning a similar outfit. His gaze lingered as she wriggled into the coveralls, the movements causing supple calf, thigh and back muscles to play under ivory skin.

She turned and caught his stare. Blood colored his cheeks, caused them to burn hot. "Sorry," he muttered. She came to her full height, zipped up her uniform and turned to face him. Her smile was surprisingly gentle.

"We don't want to go there, do we?" she asked.

"No. Definitely not."

"Not that it wasn't fun. We had some good times, right?"

"Sure," he said, nodding. "Some very good times."

"But we're all done with that."

"Right." Damn, where was she going with this? Crouching next to his duffel bag, Doyle grabbed the Uzi. As he stood, he slammed home a magazine, charged the weapon and strapped it over his shoulder. He'd grab the Barrett a .50-caliber sniper rifle, locked and loaded it in a moment.

She took another step closer. Doyle felt a warm sensation blossom in his stomach before spreading to his crotch.

"And you have no feelings for me?" she asked.

Doyle stepped away from her. Was she trying to seduce him? Maybe so, maybe no. But he knew better than to play. In this business, an impromptu dalliance could lead to a knife in the back, figuratively and literally, either from your lover or someone else while you're distracted. Forget all the spy movies where the guy gets laid at every turn. In the real world, at least in espionage, sex and emotions were weapons, just like guns and knives.

Besides, he reminded himself. Time had passed and he was a different man. A married man.

"Why do you ask?" he said, his voice not betraying his inner struggle.

Her look hardened. "Because I want to know where your head's at."

"More of your full-disclosure crap?"

She licked her lips, kept her eyes locked on his. "Sort of. I'm not trying to rekindle anything here. But you need to know the score. If something happens to me and you have a chance to escape, you take it. We aren't the Navy SEALs. We do leave our fallen behind, if necessary. In fact, I'd prefer you put a bullet in me, just to make sure I'm dead."

Doyle shook his head. "You know I can't do that."

"Trust me," she said. "Stone held me captive for several hours. I can say with authority that I would rather die than live as his prisoner. I took a hell of a beating and he threatened to do a hell of a lot more to me. Sick things. And I believe he would, given enough time."

She paused. She blinked hard as if to banish the memories and her lips tightened into a thin, bloodless line. She gave her head a quick shake, fixed her gaze back on Doyle.

Before he uttered a word, a series of gunshots reached his ears, sudden, violent, ripping apart the silence. Tearing his attention from Kinsey, he tracked the echoes of the initial blasts, tried to pin their origination point. In an instant realization swept over him. He felt the small hairs on his arms and neck rise.

Stone's house, and it sounded as though someone was already serving up big helpings of hell there.

CHAPTER THIRTEEN

Grimaldi heard his opponent before he saw him. The hard guy protecting the perimeter stood less than six feet tall and was whipcord-thin. The guy held a Colt Commando by its pistol grip, canting it at a forty-five-degree angle as he trudged through the jungle, silent other than the occasional snapping of a plant stalk or twig. In surroundings as full of life as these, though, the noise didn't sound any more out of place than the trill of exotic birds.

Ever since their arrival in Paraguay, the pilot had trailed Bolan at a distance, planting tracers on Archer's vehicles while Bolan worked the barroom in hopes of gathering some useful intel. Grimaldi also had made a couple other modifications that he hoped to put into play—after he determined Bolan's status.

Grimaldi raised his Beretta 92, outfitted with its custom sound suppressor, and drew down on the guard. As his finger tightened on the trigger, the man's walkie-talkie crackled. The ace pilot froze, straining to hear the radio traffic.

Dipping his head to one side, the guy reached up, keyed his shoulder microphone.

"Go ahead," the guard said.

"We've got a visitor on the grounds. Break."

"Acknowledge. Go ahead."

"Not sure if he's traveling alone. Switching to two-minute radio checks. Also, expect Protocol Orange."

"You're clear."

Grimaldi checked his wrist chronometer, pegged the time of the last check-in. As he did, the guy switched his rifle to a two-handed grip and started forward. Sighting down the Beretta's barrel, Grimaldi squeezed the trigger. The weapon sighed, spit a 9 mm round that punched into the back of the man's skull. The guard pitched forward, hit the ground in a boneless heap. Grimaldi rose to his feet but stayed low. A moment later the pilot knelt next to the corpse, stripped it of radio gear. He added the gear to his own equipment.

With fast, precise movements, Grimaldi dragged the corpse from the trail, hid it behind the trunk of a fallen tree.

Holstering his Beretta, the Stony Man pilot fisted an Ingram submachine gun. Decked out in camou fatigues, his face stripped green and brown with recently applied combat cosmetics, Grimaldi tried to keep his movements as silent as possible. A second Ingram SMG hung from a strap, bouncing against his hip with every footfall. A second Beretta rode in his shoulder holster.

In his backpack, he carried a pair of holstered Israeli-made Desert Eagle handguns that he planned to pass to Bolan as soon as he found the guy.

Looking at his chronometer, Grimaldi saw that a minute had passed since the guard's last check-in. The way he figured it, if these guys were on high alert, a failure to reach someone probably would set off the alarm bells sooner than Grimaldi wanted. Stepping off the trail, he moved out of plain sight and headed toward Stone's house.

His eyes and weapon moving as a single unit, he swept the area ahead of him, but he saw no threats. Despite his load of weapons and equipment, Grimaldi moved fast, covering ground with long, reaching steps. His shirt, soaked with sweat, matted against his body, particularly under the Kevlar vest that sheathed his torso. The damp air was like a tangible presence that surrounded him, stifled his breathing even as his hyperalert body clamored for more oxygen.

A sound to his left caused him to freeze. Bringing around the Ingram, he scanned his surroundings, even as he used his free hand to turn down the volume on his walkie-talkie. Other radios crackled and his murmured. He saw a pair of shapes moving through the foliage and closing in on his position. His grip tightened on his weapon as he waited for a chance to identify his targets.

"I'm not a damn babysitter," one of the men said, his voice just above a whisper.

"Shh, we're not supposed to talk."

"To hell with it and to hell with their protocols."

A tinny voice erupted from their radios. "Kane's still not responding."

Kane? Was that the guy I just killed? Grimaldi wondered. He looked down at the radio, saw a name—Myers—etched into its metal skin.

The guy who had been griping activated his shoulder microphone, spoke. "Clear. What about Anderson?"

"Negative."

"You want us to head out to their zone?"

"Negative. Keep the circle tight. Find Kane. I'm going to raise Myers. His GPS indicates he's sitting when he should be moving."

"Probably taking a leak."

"Whatever. Myers? You out there?"

Grimaldi froze. He'd just lost thirty seconds he'd been banking on. Judging by the radio traffic, someone else was also taking Stone's people out of commission. But who? Grimaldi saw the two men approach and knew he had no time to waste solving puzzles; he need to get to his friend ASAP, give the guy some backup.

That meant going for broke.

The men stepped into view, walking several yards apart. Each swept his muzzle over his surroundings. As far as Grimaldi could tell, neither had spotted him. Good. He'd take every second he could get.

The pilot raised his weapon, locked on the man coming in from his right flank. He triggered the sound-suppressed Mac-10. The weapon spit a sustained burst of .45-caliber slugs. The rounds caught the advancing gunner in the right hip and Grimaldi raked the weapon upward, stitching the man's torso to the left shoulder. The man jerked wildly under the on-slaught, and finally, mercifully, folded on himself as the leaden storm came to a halt.

Turning at the waist, Grimaldi stared through a haze of gun smoke, caught his other adversary darting right. As the guy moved, muzzle-flashes erupted from the barrel of his M-16. A swarm of 5.56 mm slugs sizzled overhead, forcing Grimaldi to hurl himself forward, even as he prodded his own weapon to life.

The Ingram's short burst flew wild, cleaving the air just to the guard's left. Judging by his controlled reaction, the guy was fire-tested. Even as he crouched and moved, he read-justed his aim, trying to get Grimaldi dead to rights. Another burst chewed into the dirt just ahead of the Stony Man pilot, whipping up small brown geysers of earth, thrusting dirt into Grimaldi's unprotected eyes.

Grimaldi fired the Ingram and this time trapped the guy in

a withering hail of gunfire that tore through flesh and bone, stained the ground crimson. Even as the man fell, his hand still twitching in his death throes, Grimaldi scanned his surroundings for his next opponent.

Nothing.

Yet.

Using an earpiece from his own radio, Grimaldi fitted it into his pirated radio. He turned up the volume, continued toward Stone's compound.

"Gunfire in the southern quadrant. Two hundred yards from the main compound."

A series of voices acknowledged the traffic.

"We have three men missing," the dispatcher continued. "Jakes. Torez. Didn't log a response from you. Status report."

Grimaldi muttered a curse. Probably his dead guys. Now the others knew where to start hunting. Instead of proceeding forward, he walked to his right, covering what he guessed was the length of a football field. After that, he again changed directions and headed back toward the house.

"Jakes. Torez. You copy?"

After a brief silence, the dispatcher said, "Protocol Red in place."

Protocol Red? What the hell did that mean?

A scant moment later the pilot got his answer. A humming sounded in the distance and he froze. It gained in volume, quickly changing to an insistent buzzing before intensifying into a mechanized thunder he knew all too well.

Motorcycles—coming right for him.

"SOUNDS LIKE a bad deal to me," Bolan said.

Stone shrugged. "Only deal you're going to get. Either you tell me the truth or I spray your brains all over this room. It's your call."

"Killing me won't change my story," Bolan said.

Stone smiled. "Hell, I don't need to change your story. I already got the whole thing, every last detail, from an old buddy."

Bolan's blood went cold. Old buddy? Had they captured Grimaldi? Instinct told him that, even if they had, Grimaldi would die before selling out Bolan. No question. That only left one guy.

Without breaking Bolan's gaze, Stone extended his arm in the direction of one of his men, made a beckoning motion with his first two fingers. The guy disappeared from a room for a minute, then returned with another man, a prisoner, and Bolan immediately felt his stomach lurch. Crimson stained most of the man's T-shirt. Blood trailed from dozens of cuts and abrasions on the man's head and neck. Both eyes had swollen shut, the flesh surrounding them damaged from repeated blows. The scent of singed flesh from where the man had been tortured, probably with a blow torch, filled the room. Bolan wanted to look away, but knew he couldn't.

It was Rollins, the CIA guy.

Stone's man dumped Rollins on the floor. The CIA agent whimpered, curled into a ball. Bolan figured the guy's body and mind were so overloaded with pain, weakened by blood loss, burns and blows, that he was incoherent, probably— hopefully—slipping into the merciful confines of shock.

Rage coursed through the warrior's body.

Stone walked up to the CIA agent, kicked him hard in the kidneys. Rollins gasped automatically, writhed.

"He says he knows you."

Bolan remained silent, kept his face impassive. Nausea pushed at the back of his throat even as a tingle of fear raced down his spine.

Stone continued. "He says you came here to kill me."

Stone paused. "Got nothing to say, huh? No sweat. See, here's the deal. This guy's with the CIA. I used to be with the CIA, so I know better than to trust him. Maybe he was lying, telling us what we wanted to know, just to save his miserable skin. What do you think, Arch?"

Archer shrugged. "Makes sense to me."

Stone returned his attention to Bolan. "From what our boy Rollins says, you're a federal agent, but not CIA." Stone tapped the Detonics's muzzle against his temple. "I racked my brains, trying to think of who might want to kill me. You know what I realized? That it just doesn't matter."

Stone pointed the pistol at Rollins. Bolan's muscles bunched as he prepared to make a last-ditch attempt to save Rollins. The warrior didn't kill innocents, and he wouldn't stand by and helplessly let someone else do the same.

Before he could act, the pistol cracked once and a .45 slug slammed into Rollins's battered skull, killing him instantly.

Stone aimed the still-smoking weapon at Bolan. "It just doesn't matter."

The walkie-talkie clipped to Stone's belt began to beep. Cursing, Stone grabbed the device, freed it from his belt, lifted it to his lips. He kept the pistol trained on Bolan's chest.

"Go ahead," Stone said.

As Stone listened, Bolan saw his enemy's face redden with each passing moment. "Well, keep looking for them," Stone said, finally. "If they're slacking off, put a bullet in their head. Quit bugging me with the little crap."

His lips formed a grim line as he listened a few more beats. "We knew our visitor was dirty. We saw someone else leave the plane, but he disappeared before you morons could tail him. So maybe he's here. Deal with it."

Stone swore again and returned the walkie-talkie to his belt. As he did, the sharp crackle of autofire sounded in the distance.

One at a time, he pointed the gun at three of his men. "You, you, you. Get out there. We'll deal with this." Nodding, the men began to move, passing in front of Bolan as they went. Keeping his hands raised, Bolan stepped back, as though giving them room to pass. His moves brought him several inches closer to one guard, but put more combat stretch between him and two of Stone's shooters. All the men were focused on Stone as the man continued giving direction.

Whirling, Bolan caught the guard closest to him, drove an elbow smash into the guy's face. The shooter let out a pained grunt and took a step back. Even as he did Bolan, fisted the guy's shirt, dragged him close and drove a knife-hand strike into the guy's midsection, driving it upward into his diaphragm. The guy's eyes bulged. Using his free hand, Bolan grabbed the man's shirt and heaved him behind a nearby couch.

Stone's men responded immediately. Bullets scorched the air around Bolan as he took a step forward, threw himself on top of the injured guard. The guy struck out at Bolan weakly, but the soldier batted the blow aside. Slipping the struggling man's mini-Uzi from a shoulder rig, Bolan hit the guy in the temple with the weapon, putting him out of commission.

Even as Bolan rolled off the downed guard, lead stingers ripped through the couch, tearing fabric and splintering the wood frame inside. Bolan came up in a crouch. To his right stood two gunners, each tracking in on him with their assault rifles. The men, clustered together, a deadly mistake in a live fire situation. Bolan stoked the Uzi to life, raked its deadly fire over the gunners. The 9 mm missiles sliced through air, stopping only after they tore through flesh and blood, toppling both of Bolan's opponents.

Before either corpse hit the floor, Bolan darted right, the Uzi popping as it uttered sharp, short bursts of fiery death.

Bullets sizzled the air just inches from Bolan's face, a grim reminder that he faced overwhelming odds. The warrior spun, surveyed the room. Stone had disappeared. Archer was firing in Bolan's direction, trying to use the Beretta to kill him. Two other gunners stood at opposite points of the room, trying to catch their former prisoner in a cross fire. Bolan guessed the sixth man, as well as Archer, had bolted with Stone.

A 20-round magazine jutted from the pistol grip of Bolan's Uzi. He guessed he'd already exhausted more than half of that. Stealing more from the dead men was out. By the time the warrior reached the bodies and liberated more ammo, he'd end up dead, body rent by relentless automatic fire.

A good soldier knew when to retreat. Now was that time.

Whirling, Bolan raked the Uzi in a long arc. As the weapon belched fire and spit brass casings, he headed for the stairs. As the soldier took the first step, the Uzi cycled dry and he tossed it. Bullets nipped at Bolan's heels, splintering wood paneling as he sprinted up the steps.

Just before he reached the top, Bolan's combat instincts kicked in and he came to a dead halt. Bullets cut through the air in front of him. Finally, someone had gotten the bright idea to shoot ahead of him rather than behind him. Wood chips and plaster dust rained on the warrior as autofire shredded his surroundings. He waited out the onslaught, pulling himself into a ball to present a smaller target. Fire consumed his flesh and breath exploded from his lungs as a slug grazed him, opening a gash in his back. Bolan grunted, but kept his jaw clamped shut to stifle a cry of pain.

The blistering weapons fire stopped for a moment and Bolan guessed his attacker's gun had run empty.

"There, he's there," someone shouted.

Getting to his feet, Bolan scrambled up the remaining steps as more gunfire began peppering the area around him.

To his right another set of three steps led onto the upper floor. As Bolan started up, a bulky figure stepped into view.

Lunging forward, Bolan struck the man in the midsection, knocking him back like a linebacker striking a tackle dummy. Bolan came down on top of the guy, drove his fist into the man's face, once, twice. His adversary brought his arm, tipped by a boxy silver shape, around toward Bolan. The Executioner thrust out his own arm, steely fingers tightening on the man's wrist. With his other hand, Bolan gripped the man's hair, yanked his head up, smacked it against the floor. With a groan, the guard's eyes rolled into the back of his head as he fell unconscious.

Bolan rapidly snatched the man's pistol—a stainless-steel Kimber .38 auto-loading pistol—from still fingers. The Executioner took the man's gun belt, looped it around his own waist and holstered the .38. Bolan next took the guy's main weapon, a Colt Commando, and web gear carrying four 30-round magazines for the Colt and a pair of flash-bang grenades.

A creak of wood caught Bolan's attention. He turned, spotted a shadow growing larger on a wall as someone crept up the stairs. Holding the Colt at hip level, he centered the muzzle on the opening that led from the stairs into the entryway where he stood. His ears still rang from the earlier onslaught of gunfire and his back stung like hell. That he was walking was enough proof for him that the bullet had sliced open skin, but missed anything vital. He'd lost some blood, but not enough to weaken him—yet.

A figure flashed into view, face partially obscured by the wall, arm extended, pointing a revolver in Bolan's direction. The Colt came alive in Bolan's hands. Dragging the chugging weapon vertically, the warrior caught the hardman in his exposed arm and face. As the guy screamed, he dropped his weapon, disappearing from view.

The repetitive thud of running footfalls echoed behind Bolan, snagging his attention and prompting him to whirl. A door opened behind him and a pair of hardmen tumbled through it, assault rifles grinding out short bursts of fire.

Dropping into a crouch, Bolan fired the Colt. Jagged yellow flames leaped from the weapon's ten-inch muzzle as the Executioner laid down a sustained burst that sent both men lunging for cover. One of the gunners shoved a nearby table onto its side, used its top for cover. The second shooter sprinted from behind a red-leather chair, darting for the more stable shielding provided by a heavy wooden cabinet. Bolan twisted at the waist, laid down a barrage of fire that caught the man in midstride, causing him to jerk about as bullets riddled his body.

Crouching, Bolan crossed the floor in quick strides, the Colt churning out more 5.56 mm tumblers as the warrior pinned the second shooter in his hiding place. While Bolan focused on this attacker, two more men rounded the stairwell and rushed into the room, shooting.

Bolan yanked loose one of the flash-bang grenades, activated it and tossed it toward the new arrivals. Then he covered his ears. One of the men started to shout a warning, but it melted into a stifled yelp as the bomb detonated, filling the room with a supernova of white light and a thunderous report.

Slamming a fresh clip into the Colt, Bolan proceeded toward the shooter behind the overturned table. Smoke from gunfire and the stun grenade hung heavily in the air, obscuring his vision. A heartbeat later the shooter rose from behind his cover, assault rifle extended in a one-handed grip, eyes narrowing in on his attacker. Already prepared, Bolan responded an instant sooner than the other man. A volley of hot lead erupted from the Colt, opening a half dozen crimson holes on the man's torso.

The warrior spun toward the incapacitated gunners and saw that one of the men had raised himself into a sitting position. Even as Bolan caught the gunner, the man triggered his AK-74 and tried to eliminate his adversary through some spray-and-pray shooting. Hurling himself behind a chair, Bolan waited out the withering salvo of gunfire.

Glimpsing the man's outstretched legs, Bolan raised his weapon and fired a burst. The rounds found their target and geysers of blood sprang from the man's shredded limbs. He jerked in place, his screams creating a sickening harmony with the gunfire.

The warrior surged toward the remaining gunner. The guy apparently had recovered enough from the flash-bang grenade to react, bringing a big-bore revolver to bear on Bolan. The soldier stepped out of the line of fire, simultaneously triggering the assault rifle. Bullets tore into the other man's chest. A shocked look ghosted the man's features for an instant before life drained from him.

A car engine turning over, followed by the screech of rubber against pavement, drew Bolan to a nearby window. He saw a red Corvette shoot around the circular driveway that led away from the rear of the home. Was it Stone? There was no way for Bolan to know for sure at that distance.

Moments later he was heading back down the stairs, reloading his weapon on the run, hoping that perhaps he could hotwire a second car and give chase.

Rushing through a set of double doors, Bolan found himself on a large concrete deck built around an Olympic-size pool. He raced along the pool, heading for a staircase that led to the next level.

The scuffling of feet to his left drew Bolan's attention. He caught sight of Archer closing in on him. Before Bolan could act, the guy collided with him, wrapping his arms around the

Executioner's midsection and throwing him off balance. The impact caused him to drop his submachine gun.

A heartbeat later Bolan felt warm water close around him. Archer's weight and force drove both men into the pool. Bolan caught a fleeting breath before he submerged, feeling Archer's hands close around his throat, the balls of his of thumbs pressing in on his windpipe.

Archer's face, twisted with rage, registered with Bolan. Black spots quickly began to interrupt his vision as oxygen-starved lungs burned through what remained of his air.

CHAPTER FOURTEEN

Grimaldi slammed a fresh clip into the Ingram and gritted his teeth as the whine of motorcycle engines grew louder.

Wheels slashed a path through the undergrowth, like a lumbering predator closing in on prey. Grimaldi's mouth went dry and his grip on the Ingram hardened. Doubtless, the rattle of gunfire had drawn this new pursuit in motion.

The ace pilot's gaze darted left, then right, as he weighed his best method of escape. If it was one or two gunners, he could stand his ground, take them out. If it was more, he'd require a miracle. A grim smile ghosted his lips and he patted a small electronic device in his pockets. What he had there wasn't a miracle, but it would suffice under the circumstances. If he could get to the right spot.

The first cycle crested the horizon, angling in on Grimaldi from the right. Hunched over the handlebars, the driver navigated the big machine, while a second guy swept his submachine gun over the area, looking to acquire a target. Sunlight poking through the canopy of leaves overhead glinted off the chrome headlight fixture. Reflexively, Grimaldi blinked, the motion almost causing him to miss the ruby dot of a laser sight that had settled on his upper bicep.

Thrusting himself sideways, Grimaldi cut loose with a punishing burst from the Ingram. The rounds flew wide, nicking leaves and tree bark, but missing his target. Even as the ace pilot smacked against the ground, he adjusted his aim and fired again. The impact of his slim frame striking the ground knocked off his aim by a couple of inches. But, though the bullets missed their intended targets, the burst did throw off the gunner's aim for a precious second.

The big cycle rammed down an incline before climbing another small hill. Gunning the engine, the driver rode the cycle up the hill, took the vehicle airborne. Dirt fell from the tires, raining onto the ground as the vehicle passed over Grimaldi's position.

As the vehicle passed overhead, the Stony Man pilot fired the Ingram, raking it over the motorcycle and its passengers. Bullets pounded into the big machine's power plant, chewed through the diver's legs and the rear gunner's stomach.

The flesh of his thighs savaged by the storm of lead, the driver screamed and let go of the handlebars, grabbing for his legs as though flame engulfed them.

Letting the spent SMG fall loose on its strap, Grimaldi drew the Beretta 92, swung the weapon into target acquisition. The cycle crashed to the ground, the impact kicking up a spray of dirt and knocking loose the rear gunner's corpse. The driver struggled for a moment, simultaneously grabbing for his side arm and trying to free himself from the wreckage. Even as a black .357 Colt Python came in to view, its barrel tracking in on Grimaldi, the ace pilot triggered the Beretta twice. The cyclist caught both rounds in the forehead, the 9 mm hollowpoint rounds ripping away the back of the man's skull.

Taking up the Ingram, Grimaldi recharged the weapon and holstered the Beretta. He scoured his surroundings for the next threat and didn't have to wait long for it. A pair of motorcycles, each bearing two hardmen, materialized from opposite sides, each chewing out a deadly path toward the Stony Man warrior. Grimaldi dipped his empty hand into his nylon satchel, fished out an M-68 frag grenade. Using his teeth to pull the pin, he tossed the bomb toward the biker approaching from his right while assaulting the other cyclist with a sustained burst from the Ingram.

Apparently spotting Grimaldi's arm motion, the biker to his right gunned the cycle's engine, causing it to hurtle toward the pilot like a missile. The grenade hit hard ground behind the cyclist, causing the impact detonator to ignite the object, peppering the blast radius with shrapnel. The cyclist's companion uttered an anguished cry as he bore the brunt of the shrapnel. The driver seemed unfazed as stray bits of razor wire sliced through the leather of his jacket and chaps but apparently missed skin.

At the same time the burst from Grimaldi's Ingram drove the second cyclist off course as the man swerved to miss the volley of slugs. The man expertly laid down his cycle, the movement saving him and his companion from a volley of bullets. Even as Grimaldi readjusted his aim, the motorcycle's passenger popped up from behind the downed vehicle. In a heartbeat, an Uzi came into view, registering with Grimaldi, spurring survival instincts into overdrive.

The hardman moved fast, trying to lock the Uzi on Grimaldi while the pilot brought his own weapon to bear on his adversary.

Grimaldi's fast reflexes bought him a microsecond's advantage. He took it, dropping the guy with a short burst to the face. Without losing a beat, he raked the Ingram over the driver, who was struggling to free an auto-loading pistol from a hip holster. Flame leaped from the Ingram's barrel as it unleashed its fury on the cyclist. The bullets ripped into the man's chest, stitching from the man's lower ribs to his opposite shoulder.

As the din of gunfire subsided, the distant rumble of more vehicles approaching reached Grimaldi's ears. Reloading on the run, he moved into a thicket, melting into the verdant background as best he could. This time the engine noises seemed to originate from the same direction as the main home and barracks building. With stealth and silence, Grimaldi moved through the foliage, staying parallel with a dirt road worn into the ground through frequent travel. About thirty yards in the distance, he saw Stone's roof and knew he was getting close to Bolan.

A pair of Hummers rolled down the trail toward him, kicking up clouds of dust, their growling engines growing louder with each passing moment.

A pair of motorcycles, each carrying a driver and a gunner, flanked the big vehicles. A line of hard-looking men, armed with AK-47s and decked out in olive-drab fatigues, had fanned out behind the vehicles. Grimaldi pegged those men as Stone's students, judging by their no-frills attire, their matching weapons and a lack of other equipment.

A pair of scouts, each wearing fatigues patterned with jungle camouflage, Colt Commando rifles sweeping over the dense greenery, walked point. Both men wore radio systems similar to those of the other jungle fighters already encountered by Grimaldi.

The pilot guessed he had almost two dozen men, each packing enough firepower to ventilate the pilot, bearing down on him. Twenty-four to one. Though a veteran of countless combat missions, both in the ground and on the air, Grimaldi wondered if he was good enough to single-handedly take out that many fighters.

Hardly.

Fisting a pair of field glasses and raising them to his eyes, he scanned the first Hummer's interior, then the second. He saw no sign of Bolan in either vehicle.

That, Grimaldi decided, was a good thing. In the distance he heard the chatter of gunfire emanating from the house. The grin widened almost imperceptibly. That had to be Bolan. At least, he hoped so.

Give them hell over there, Sarge, Grimaldi thought. I'll do the same over here.

Reaching into his pocket, Grimaldi pulled out the small detonator he'd been carrying and rested his thumb on the toggle switch. While Bolan had been scanning the scene inside the bar, Grimaldi had planted C-4 plastic explosive charges on the undercarriage of each vehicle, molding chunks of it around the big combat vehicles' gas tanks.

The plan had been simple. If Bolan got into trouble, he'd signal Grimaldi, who'd blow up the vehicles to create a diversion. Judging from the gunfire, Bolan was alive and kicking. Maybe caught in a gunfight. But Grimaldi knew no one was better at emerging from such scrapes unharmed.

Besides, a little diversion still might help both their causes.

Grimaldi waited until the small knot of men and vehicles rolled within several yards of him before detonating the explosives. The C-4 blew immediately, setting off twin peals of thunder, as roiling, black-tinged columns of fire erupted underneath each vehicle. The initial explosions tore through the gasoline tanks, igniting the stored fuel, creating a secondary blast that thrust the Hummers' flaming skeletons into the air for an instant before gravity dragged them back to earth. Cries of pain filled the air and Grimaldi saw more than one man, his body engulfed in flames, bolting into the nearby forest.

The shock waves accompanying the blasts punched through the line of mercenaries, staggering men, causing several of them to drop their weapons as they cupped their hands over their ears, protecting them from the concussive blasts. Grimaldi emerged from his cover, firing a line of bullets that punched through a pair of the burning men, hopefully ending their suffering prematurely. Swinging the Ingram, he caught two more men, blood streaming from their ravaged eardrums, fleeing. The Ingram churned through several more rounds. The bullets cleaved into the men, caused them to jerk under their hellish volley for a brief moment before they folded in on themselves in lifeless heaps.

The remaining cyclist gunned his engine, the vehicle slicing its way toward Grimaldi. Whirling toward the deadly combination of man and machine, Grimaldi triggered his weapon, swept it in a wide arc. Bullets collided with flesh, the hot lead ripping into the man's throat and chest. Pulling both hands from the handlebar grips as though scalded, his hands went to his wounds as the driverless cycle rolled over a large stone, sending the vehicle hurling off in a new direction. The Ingram spit out another short burst that killed the rear gunner even as the man tried to simultaneously hit Grimaldi with a hail of autofire from his Colt Commando and grab for the handlebars of the careening motorcycle.

The bike struck a tree and erupted into flame. A man— whether driver or passenger was unclear—stumbled from the wreckage, his body sheathed in fire. The Ingram's muzzle tracked in on the man, barked out a short volley of slugs that caught the man midstride, tunneled through his flaming torso, quickly ending his suffering.

The burning vehicles pumped black smoke into the air,

fouling it with the nauseating stench of burning fuel and tire rubber. Mercenaries lay prone on the ground, their weapons spitting fire and lead. Others sprinted away, distancing themselves from the chaos.

Bullets blistering the air around him, Grimaldi raked the Ingram in long sweeps at the line of prone gunners. His initial burst fell short, chewing up the ground a few yards ahead of the mercenaries. A second sweep caught one of the gunners in the face and shoulders, his body shaking as bullets pierced it. Simultaneously, Grimaldi reached into his satchel, fisted a fragmentation grenade, aimed it and lobbed the bomb at the remaining gunners. It erupted with a peal of thunder and hurled shrapnel into the air, leaving behind two more dead men. Another man rounded the flaming hulk of one of the damaged Hummers, his arm raised as he prepared to hurl something at Grimaldi. The Stony Man pilot snap-aimed the Ingram, unloaded the weapon in the man's direction, cutting him down with a punishing onslaught.

Ejecting the spent clip, Grimaldi snatched another, started to feed it into the Ingram. A one-two punch from an unseen source hammered into his ribs, staggering him. White-hot lancelets of pain radiated through his midsection. His mind blanked for a moment as his body sought the refuge of shock. As he stumbled backward, then fell to the ground, he was vaguely aware of another round burning just inches from his face as he dropped into a heap.

With one Ingram empty, the pilot desperately scrambled to grab the second SMG, still secured around his neck by a strap. Even as his fingers encircled the weapon's handle, Grimaldi heard more shots, flinched. Autofire raked the air above him, lashing out at an unseen target before quieting. A loud thump, like a body colliding with the ground, reached Grimaldi's ears.

As his fingers gripped the Ingram, he heard the crunch of footsteps behind him. He rolled onto his stomach, bringing the machine pistol to bear on the person. Before he could acquire a target, though, a booted foot lashed out, knocked the Ingram from his grip. Moving with the speed of a striking cobra, Grimaldi fisted his Beretta, raised it as his eyes rested on his opponent. He caught a slight whispering sound, then felt a sting in his neck. The shadow disappeared again. A moment later, Grimaldi felt his vision blur, his mind begin to slow. He tightened the grip on his pistol as though it might steel his grip on consciousness. Dart. A damn dart. In his neck. Like a zoo animal. Nice job, Jack.

His assailant knelt beside him. Grimaldi felt his eyes slam shut. He tried to will his arms to move, found them heavy, unresponsive. A voice, distinctly feminine, sounded in his ear.

"Sorry, flyboy. Appreciate your help. But you've outlived your usefulness." Before Grimaldi could react, his blurred vision went black.

BOLAN'S EVERY CELL cried out for oxygen as he grappled with his assailant. Steely fingers, unyielding in their grip, seemed to flatten his windpipe. The weight of Archer's stout frame, Bolan's own weapons and equipment, dragged him under, held him down for what seemed like forever.

The icy-eyed warrior didn't thrash wildly, knowing it would deplete his remaining oxygen, drive him more quickly into panic, unconsciousness and, ultimately, death.

Instead he made a grab for the .38 Kimber, began pulling it from his holster. Seeing the movement, Archer released his grip on Bolan's throat, grabbed the warrior's wrist to keep him from freeing the pistol. The soldier brought up his foot and planted it in his adversary's chest. Coiling steely muscles, he shot his leg out hard, the force thrusting Archer away.

The Executioner planted his feet on the pool's concrete floor, used them to hurtle himself toward the surface. Light shimmered above him as he shot upward through the water. As his head broke the surface, he opened his mouth, pulled greedily at the air. Just a couple of feet away, Archer's head popped up from the water as the guy recharged his lungs.

Around the pool stood three hardguys, the cold muzzles of their AK-47s focused on Bolan, ready to take him out in a heartbeat. The Kimber had slipped from Bolan's grip as he'd worked toward the water's surface.

Grabbing a second breath before the added weight of weapons dragged him back under, Bolan grabbed at Archer's belt, dragged the guy down with him. The way he saw it, Bolan knew that the closer he got to Archer, the less attractive a target he posed for the men gathered around the pool.

So Bolan's chances of survival dropped to less than zero once he went back up for air.

Archer's right hand moved quick. Sunlight reflecting off silver registered with Bolan, kicking his combat-hardened reflexes into overdrive, moving him into action. The warrior whipped his torso aside, letting a blade slip a hairbreadth from his flesh, the resistance from the water providing Bolan the critical edge he needed for survival.

Bolan's own hand fired out, fingers extended in a knife-hand strike. The fingertips just missed Archer's windpipe as the guy jerked his head back to avoid the hit. In a rush of bubbles, Archer brought down his knife, the blade carving out a downward arc as it plunged toward Bolan's throat.

Thrusting his hand out sideways, the Executioner caught the guy's wrist, stopping it cold. A stream of bubbles rolled from the corner of his mouth as it quirked up in what almost seemed to be a lopsided grin. Bolan saw the guy's shoulder jerk, caught the upward momentum of a second knife thrusting up from down low, blade cocked horizontally to fit between his ribs. Grabbing Archer's other hand, stopping the knife thrust, Bolan drove his foot into the man's gut a second time, watched as his air escaped from his mouth in a roar of bubbles.

As Archer's mind dealt with the change in circumstances, Bolan shifted his weight and pushed the guy under him. The man was robbed of air, and his arms jerked wildly as he tried to break free of Bolan's grip. The warrior's temples throbbed from lack of air. The muscles of his cheeks burned as he kept his mouth clamped shut, despite his body's cries to open it, gasp for air even though he knew there was none.

Bolan's weight dragged both men to the pool's bottom. Pushing hard, Bolan held one of Archer's arms at bay while hammering the other against concrete. Archer released his grip, letting the knife fall from his fingers. It collided with a muted clank against the pool. At the same time, Archer's other hand fought harder, trying to stab downward as he held it fast. Letting his adversary's empty hand go free, Bolan's hand jabbed out, fingers weaving into the man's hair, tightening. With a violent yank, he brought Archer's head forward, thrust it back, cracking bone against concrete. Panic registered for a moment in Archer's eyes. Striking the man's head against concrete twice more, Bolan saw the sheer terror drain away, followed by any other signs of life. Bolan's vision began to cloud and his lungs ached for oxygen.

With a series of powerful kicks, Bolan distanced himself from the body, hand outstretched for an object dropped earlier by Archer during their struggle.

The Beretta 93-R. His Beretta.

Bolan snagged the handgun in his grip, kicked toward the surface, lungs on the edge of bursting. Muffled cracks sounded from above. Bullets lanced through the water, slicing paths around Bolan as he neared surface. The warrior's vision blackened as his head and gun hand broke through the water.

Even as he swung the pistol, acquired a target, he heard gunfire erupt all around him, saw death reach out, ready to claim its next prize.

DOYLE RAN through the jungle, gasping for air, cursing his two-pack-a-day cigarette habit. His leg muscles, toned from hours of walking, handled the exercise with relative ease. His lungs, though, burned as he gulped at the humid air.

As he closed in on Stone's house, Doyle heard the gunfire intensify. An icy wedge of fear buried itself in his gut. Blood roared in his ears and he knew the sensation was less about exertion than it was fear.

As he rushed headlong into a hellground, doubt gnawed at him. He hadn't seen live fire in years. He'd kept up his martial-arts training, occasionally spent an afternoon at the range. But he was out of practice, no doubt about it.

What the hell had he been thinking, trading in his cushy existence for this fool's errand? What if he died here, in the middle of nowhere, with Nancy believing he was on a business trip, never knowing what happened to him? He imagined the pain he'd cause her, the unanswered questions his disappearance would cause.

But maybe it was for the best. With him in Paraguay, face-to-face with Stone, he could end the cycle early. If he died, so be it. Stone likely wouldn't give his wife a second thought. If he could kill Stone, so much the better.

Setting his jaw, he drove himself forward. Kinsey, obsessive about weight and fitness, had outpaced him easily, disappearing into the tangle of limbs and brush that lay ahead. A fleeting image of her as she'd changed clothes flitted through his mind, but he banished it immediately. The job, he told himself. Focus on the job. That woman, your past in general, is a train of thought you don't want to board. Focus on your surroundings, act like a damn professional. Your life depends on it. More important, Nancy's life depends on it.

The access road led to a clearing. Plumes of roiling smoke, black, heavy, rolled past and distant gunshots continued to fill the air. Slowly he stepped into the open area and spied Kinsey ten yards distant, hunched over a man lying on his back. With a flick of her arm, she tossed something into a nearby tangle of trees, grass and weeds.

Apparently sensing Doyle's approach, she whirled, leveling her Glock at him. Holding up his hands in mock surrender, he flashed her a grin. She relaxed visibly, lowered the weapon.

When he came to her side, she whispered, "You shouldn't sneak up on me like that."

"Sorry. Next time, I'll let you shoot me."

"Jerk."

Doyle stared down at the slender man, saw his chest rising and falling. "He's still breathing."

"You're brilliant."

"I'm serious. Since when do you take prisoners? This guy could come to, get frisky and take us out from behind."

She shook her head. "He won't."

"How do you know?"

"I just do. Trust me."

"You know him?"

Crimson swept through her cheeks and she gave him a hard look. "Damn it, Chris."

Shaking his head, he put some edge into his voice. "Forget it. I don't like your behavior. And until I start liking it again, we don't take another damn step. You either have my back or you don't. I can either trust you or I can't."

"Well, which is it?"

"You tell me."

"I know him, okay."

"He on our side?"

She shrugged. "I'm not sure. But he wouldn't hurt us."

"So why knock him out?"

"He's probably on our side, but that doesn't mean he won't get in our way. I assume he and his partner are here for Stone, but I can't guarantee they wouldn't interfere with us."

"Partner? He has a partner? Lady, you've been holding on me. It's time to start talking."

Briefly she explained about her rescue in Afghanistan, about the last-minute intervention by federal agent Matt Cooper.

"This guy was with him?"

"Right."

"So we may have a Justice Department agent running loose around here? In addition to Stone, his mercenaries and his students."

"Right."

He sighed. "It was never dull with you, Jen. Looks like some things never change. Better give me a physical description in case I run across this guy."

She did and he memorized it. "But trust me," she said, "you don't just run across this guy. You collide with him, like you collide with a freight train."

"Bad?"

"Yes, definitely."

Getting to his feet, Doyle looped his arms underneath the unconscious man's midsection, hefted the guy until he was on his legs and his feet touched the ground. He dragged him into the undergrowth, laid him out prone, where he could sleep off the drug without catching anyone's attention. Slipping a canteen from his belt, Doyle laid it on the guy's stomach, in case he woke up thirsty or, worse, dehydrated from the heat.

But Doyle also realized that if the guy really was a spook, he probably would rather die of thirst than risk a drink from a foreign canteen. But it made Doyle feel better not to leave the guy in a lurch.

More shots sounded from the house. Moving as one, Doyle and Kinsey melted into the jungle and beat a path toward Stone's villa. It took another four minutes to reach it. They stopped at a line of trees bordering the open spaces around the house. Kneeling, Doyle appraised the opposition. Three nervous-looking gunners stood outside the house, each scanning his surroundings for intruders. Using a series of hand signals, Doyle indicated that he'd take the two men closest two him. She flashed him the okay sign and headed off to take out the other man.

Moving to his right, the Uzi in his grip, Doyle remained under cover until he no longer was in the guards' line of sight. Stepping into the open, he sprinted across pavement, trying hard to keep his footfalls soft as he closed in on the house. From behind the villa, he heard more gunshots, then the sound of something solid—and heavy—striking against the water.

He felt a sick twist in his gut as realization dawned on him. He planned to gun down both men in cold blood, shoot them in the back like a cowardly train robber from the Old West. Raising the Uzi, he triggered the weapon, unleashing a sustained burst. Bullets cleaved through the air, pounded into the men. The dying hardmen shivered under the onslaught, staggered as though jerked around by invisible strings. When Doyle eased off the trigger, the men collapsed to the ground.

Clenching his jaw, he turned away, started for the front door. As he did, Boyle heard the rattle of more gunfire just ahead. Flattening against a wall, he watched for Kinsey, felt his breath stop as he waited. A moment later he caught a slender shadow's approach, then saw Kinsey step into view. She flashed him the okay signal, which he returned.

With Doyle taking the lead, they slipped into the house. The Uzi held firm against his side, Doyle stepped through the entryway and into the main room. The sight of bullet-pocked walls, some smeared with bright red swaths of blood, greeted him. Overturned furniture. Dead men, bodies ravaged by gunfire, lay around.

Voices drifting through an open window caught Doyle's attention. Crossing the room, he stepped to the window, stared down at the Olympic-size pool surrounded by a concrete deck and potted trees and plants. A male, his face frozen in a shocked death mask, bobbed on the surface. Doyle zeroed in on the corpse, recognized it as Archer, his old teammate. Two men, automatic weapons in hand, stood poolside, each drawing down on a lone figure. A third stood on the opposite side of the pool, gun poised to fire.

"That's him," Kinsey said in a harsh whisper. "The guy from Afghanistan."

"Which one?"

"The guy in the pool. He looks different, but I think it's him."

Doyle started to question her but stopped himself. If she was right, a possible ally was about to take a bullet.

Raising the Uzi to shoulder level, Doyle squeezed the trigger. The first burst fell just short of the target but distracted the man, buying the guy in the pool a moment. Adjusting his aim, Doyle fired again, drilled a short burst through his target's stomach.

At his side, Kinsey's own weapon barked and one of the gunners fell. Even as the third man watched his comrades fall, he darted left, his AK-47 spitting flame and hot lead. The man in the pool raised his handgun, fired it. Flame spit from the muzzle and a line of three red dots sprouted in rapid succession on the runner's back. The force of the bullets shoved the man forward, causing him to fall face forward. The Kalashnikov slipped from dead fingers, skittered a few feet away from the corpse.

The rustle of fabric sounded behind Doyle, catching his attention, causing him to wheel toward it. He turned, saw Stone approaching, handgun Detonics .45 leveled in front of him, muzzle locked on Doyle's forehead.

"Hi, Doyle," Stone said. He thrust himself to the side, felt a searing pain split open his skull. An instant later he heard the crack of a pistol, sounding impossibly far away. It was the last thing he heard before a yawning abyss of darkness swallowed him up.

BROGNOLA STIFLED a yawn as he combed through a stack of intelligence reports handed to him by Barbara Price shortly before he'd left Stony Man Farm the previous day. Despite the Virginia facility's state-of-the-art computer systems and its crack cyberteam, Brognola preferred paper—paper reports, paper folders, paper messages. Kurtzman, Tokaido, Delahunt and Whethers ribbed him mercilessly about this, he recalled with a grin. Let them. He was an old warhorse, set in his ways, and he had no intention of changing.

Shifting in his chair, he set the papers on a nearby seat, stretched his arms and sighed. It'd been twenty-four hours since he last slept and the endless cups of coffee had ceased to perk him up, but instead were leaving him drained and tired. He chewed his unlit cigar, leaving the end a ragged mess.

Leaning back, he balled his hands into fists and pressed

them against his eyes, setting off an explosion of tiny yellow sparks. His chest caved as he let out a deep sigh. They'd flown into Utah the previous night, but Brognola had elected to stay off the Citadel grounds until the last possible instant. He hated meetings, hated sitting, hated talking about problems rather than solving them. He hated pressing the flesh and playing politics. Like others at Stony Man Farm, he preferred action to talk. He set his hands in his lap, reopened his eyes.

Orders were orders, he told himself. Be a good soldier and shut up.

He'd stayed in a hotel the previous night and kept in contact with Stony Man's duty officer. Knowing Striker was in the field, putting it on the line for his country, made it hard for Brognola to sleep. He liked to lead by example. And sawing logs while his people dodged bullets in developing countries set a pretty damn bad example.

Besides, there was that damn phone call to think about.

Brognola heard boot heels slamming against the floor. Turning his head, he cast a glance behind him and saw a man dressed head-to-toe in black, a pistol holstered at his side, approaching. The handgun was a 10 mm Delta pistol. Brognola knew this because he'd signed the damn requisition order himself, under the guise of ordering them for Justice Department agents that openly existed on the payroll. The blacksuit was a team leader named Chet Collins. A former member of New York City's emergency response team, Collins stood bolt upright, stared at a point over Brognola's shoulder whenever he addressed the big Fed.

"We arrive in ten minutes, sir," he said.

Brognola nodded. "And quit calling me 'sir,' for God's sake. I keep thinking you're talking to my father. Call me Hal."

A relieved smile spread over the guy's features. "I can do

that, Hal." He spun on a heel and rejoined his team. Like most of the blacksuits, Collins would take a bullet for Brognola or any of the other farm operatives, to protect the operation itself. Brognola couldn't, in good conscience, treat them like cattle.

Pulling the cigar from his mouth, he held it a few inches from his face, rolled it between his fingers and studied it. Before trying to turn in for the night, he'd spoken with his wife, Helen, said good-night to her over the phone, as he had so many times before. She'd tolerated a lot during his career, the long hours, middle-of-the-night phone calls ripping them from sleep and the danger to them and their family. But a brush with the killers he hunted on a daily basis had only steeled her resolve that he should continue his work, continue hunting the killers, terrorists and criminals that had preyed on innocents such as her and their children. She never pressured him to retire or to take an easier, less demanding job. Or, at the very least, to ask for an extra week of vacation. She had his back and he loved her for it.

But last night she'd uncharacteristically expressed worry over this trip, even hinted that he might want to bow out.

"I can't put my finger on it, Hal," Helen had said. "I just have a bad feeling about it."

"Woman's intuition?" he'd asked. He kept his tone light, trying to allay her concerns.

"Maybe," she had said, her voice taut. "Do you really have to go?"

"I do. The Man put in the request himself. He's kind of hard to say no to."

"I understand."

"No, you don't."

He'd heard the smile in her voice. "You're right. I don't. But I also don't want to be a controlling shrew, trying to decide your every move for you. I don't want to be that person."

"Couldn't be one if you tried."

"I'll work on it."

It had been his turn to smile. "You get too rough and I may have to spend more time at the office."

"Impossible. A week's only got seven days." She'd paused for a moment. When she spoke again, she'd sounded serious. "Hal?"

"Yeah?"

"I love you."

"Hey, you, too. Listen, it'll all be fine, Helen. I promise. In a couple of days, I'll be back at the house, leaving coffee cup rings on every flat surface I can find."

Letting his fists fall into his lap, he stared at the ceiling, hoping he could make good on his pledge to Helen.

Unconsciously he wrapped his fingers around the revolver holstered on his right hip, adjusted it. When he'd grabbed the.44-caliber Charter Arms pistol from his desk drawer, he'd told himself that he did so out of habit. Where he was going, the most likely threat was a lethal case of boredom.

At least, he hoped so.

Eight minutes later Brognola began to collect his papers, stuffing them into his briefcase. He grabbed his jacket and slipped it on. As he waited to arrive, he studied the cramped, rectangular surroundings he and the team of blacksuits rode in. The space resembled a typical office, with fat couches and armchairs, tables and lamps, even a dorm fridge. However, all the furniture was bolted to the floor and once Brognola settled in, he'd had to strap a seat belt over his lap.

From the inside, the space screamed Corporate America. Dark wood paneling covered the walls and red leather chairs and couches, each soft as a pillow mattress, were positioned around the room. Aside from the insistent hum of big diesel engines, the occasional sense of accelerating and halting, the

oddity of seeing all furnishings bolted into place, it'd be easy
to believe you were sitting in a luxury office inside a sky-
scraper in some tony part of Manhattan.

Brognola, of course, knew better. The office had been built
inside a semi-trailer, part of a fleet of similarly built convey-
ances used to transport high-ranking government officials to
and from Brognola's destination. The Citadel. The exterior
carried the logo of a waste-removal company created more
than two decades ago by the Justice Department for use in
sting operations. More recently it had been conscripted for
the second, but equally important, duty.

The facility sat on a parcel of land composed of sweeping
canyons, winding rivers, expansive deserts and lengthy buttes.
In the 1940s, the federal government had seized the property.
Within weeks it had been separated from the world with miles
of electric fence and restricted air space. If Brognola remembered his cloak-and-dagger lore correctly, the military had
planned to use it as a top-secret testing site for cutting-edge
jet fighters, but later had scrapped the plan.

During the past several decades, the government had
needed to drive away the curious and concocted a lie to do
so. It listed the land as a dirty site, one contaminated by
countless nuclear weapons tests and fields of buried radioactive waste. For nearly six decades, the government had pro-
tected the property, but left it unused.

That was before September 11, 2001.

After the murderous terrorist attack, shaken government
officials had sought a way to insure continued leadership
should another attack succeed in wiping out the executive or
legislative branches.

The Citadel and the sites that followed were outfitted as
proxy command centers for government and military operations. They also were used to host high-risk meetings, partic-

ularly those presenting a tempting target to terrorists. Federal officials used the trucks to move people in and out without raising suspicions. After all, what was more natural than cleanup crews at a waste site?

Through the trailer's reinforced skin, Brognola heard the brakes hiss as the truck stopped. Faint voices reached his ears as the engines continued to thrum, powering the climate-control system.

Releasing his seat belt, he stood, stretched his legs. As the circulation returned to his lower extremities, a small groan escaped his lips. He was getting too damn old for this, he told himself. Maybe he should retire, open a bait shop or something.

Like hell. Like his old friend, Mack Bolan, and the other men and women of Stony Man Farm, he had too damn many battles left to fight.

And, God willing, win.

He heard the whine of power tools as crews worked to remove the reinforced steel panel that covered the trailer's rear. The designers had placed hidden escape hatches throughout the trailer, along with dozens of gun ports and an elaborate camera system that allowed security guards to view the exterior, but they sealed up the most obvious entrance in case someone tried to hijack the vehicle.

The crews opened the rear door and Brognola felt a rush of heated air flood inside. Peering into the huge truck bay, he saw several plainclothes agents—probably Secret Service—and several members of the facility's elite guard team.

The Man stepped up to the truck and shot Brognola a grin. "Enjoying the ride, Hal?" he asked.

"I'm starting to feel like a box of canned goods back here," Brognola said, returning the smile.

Stepping from the truck, he shook hands with the President before doing likewise with the top brass for the State Department, the National Security Council and the CIA. Unlike previous CIA leaders, the current director, apparently less concerned with territory disputes and more concerned with national security, treated Brognola with a measure of respect, which Brognola returned, albeit grudgingly so.

Moving at a brisk pace, the President led Brognola and the other government officials through the bay. After hurried walk to an elevator and a quick ascent to another floor, he ushered them into a conference room. Upon entering, Brognola saw several men seated around a conference table. He knew from his previous discussions with the President that the men represented the governments of Egypt, Jordan, Morocco, Saudi Arabia and Kuwait, all U.S. allies in the Middle East.

After greeting three members of Saudi Arabia's royal family, he clasped hands with a small, bookish-looking man with a broad smile. When he spoke, his English was impeccable.

"Khalid Haddad," the man said. "It's a pleasure to meet you."

"Likewise," Brognola said. "You're an assistant minister for Saudi intelligence, right?"

"Yes, yes," Haddad said, nodding vigorously. "Your department's reports have been invaluable in helping us prevent two separate al Qaeda strikes within our country, just within the past six months. We've kept it quiet, of course."

"I'm glad we could be of service."

"I attended university in your country many years ago. I love it here. It's like a second home to me."

"We're glad you're here," Brognola said. "We consider our partnership with the Saudis invaluable to our own security. It's a symbiotic relationship."

His diplomatic skills tapped, Brognola clapped the man's upper arm, gave him a smile and continued on. After a few more introductions he hurried to the buffet table where he poured himself a cup of coffee, black, from a silver pot. Sipping it, he stared over the rim at the assembled group. Having this much power in a single room made him edgy, even in a high-security facility such as this. He'd offered the President extra protection from Able Team and Phoenix Force, but the Man had declined, asserting the warriors might be better employed somewhere else.

Shrugging, Brognola acknowledged the wisdom of that. The guys were more than glorified bodyguards.

But...

Ah, forget it, he told himself. He was just letting Helen's fear cloud his judgment. He was probably still edgy from sleep deprivation and caffeine.

CHAPTER FIFTEEN

Fatigue burned at Bolan's muscles as he climbed the stairs. He'd continued to lose blood from the wound in his back and that, combined with the various other beatings he'd suffered, had left him feeling light-headed and exhausted.

Both Kinsey and the other guy had turned away too suddenly. As he took two more steps in a single stride, the soldier heard the unmistakable report of a handgun. Reaching the top of the steps, Bolan rounded a corner, saw Stone positioned twenty feet from Kinsey, his Detonics aimed at her head.

Bolan started to raise the Beretta. A mirror positioned behind Kinsey betrayed Bolan's movements. Even as he drew down on Stone, the big psychopath whirled toward him and triggered the handgun. Bullets lanced through the air around the soldier, chewing into walls and woodwork, forcing him to flatten against the floor. He squeezed the Beretta's trigger, unleashing a pair of 3-round bursts in Stone's direction. He heard the larger man grunt, and Bolan started for his feet. A glance showed that Stone had drawn his second pistol, trained it on Kinsey. The weapon cracked three times, drilling through her shoulders before tearing out the other sides. An almost-inhuman scream escaped the woman's lips as she sank to her knees, her face immediately ashen, frozen in shock. Stone fired again, this time, hitting her in the head. The bullet's force punched into her, thrust her onto her back.

Stone emptied one of the .45-caliber pistols at the Executioner. As grim as hell, Bolan came up in a crouch, ready to deal death on the murderous maniac. Flipping the fire selector to single-shot mode to conserve ammo, the soldier snap-aimed the Beretta and fired. Propelled by a 120-grain cartridge, the subsonic Parabellum round burned just past Stone's ear. The pair of Detonics wielded by Stone chugged in unison, the onslaught of bullets driving Bolan back to the ground. He rolled from his position just as a hail of .45 rounds pounded into it. A sudden silence fell over the room, followed by the clank of ejected magazines hitting the floor. Using an armchair for cover, Bolan came up looking for Stone, but saw that the man had disappeared from view while reloading his weapons.

Bolan guessed he had three rounds left in the Beretta. He'd lost the spare clips when Archer had taken him prisoner. He had plenty of ammunition for the Kimber, but no weapon. Great.

Staring down the Beretta's barrel, Bolan searched for Stone. The man came out from behind an overturned couch, riddling Bolan's position with a storm of hellfire. The soldier dived right, emptying the Beretta in Stone's direction.

The warrior heard a door slam. Ears straining for any sign of Stone, Bolan heard nothing other than the groan of Kinsey's partner.

Bolan immediately went into triage mode. He first knelt next to Kinsey, checked her pulse and found none, as expected. He studied her slack, waxen features for a moment. His gut brimmed over with rage as he looked at her. Not only had Stone killed her, he'd done so slowly and methodically. Leaving her helpless so she could do nothing but wait for the end. The man was an animal, pure and simple. And Bolan needed to take him out.

He moved to the unconscious man and knelt next to him. As best as Bolan could tell, a bullet had grazed the man's temple, knocking him unconscious. Blood saturated his hair, matting it against his skull. But at least this one was still alive, Bolan thought. Snatching a knife from the man's equipment belt, Bolan cut two lengths of fabric from a nearby chair. Folding the first into a makeshift compress, he applied it to the wound, secured it with the second strip of cloth.

As he rose, a dark cloud passed over Bolan's features as he realized Grimaldi was nowhere in sight. Bolan had heard his friend activate the explosive charges in the Hummers. And Bolan guessed the gunplay he'd heard earlier had resulted, at least in part, from Grimaldi stirring up trouble. Still, he wanted to find the guy.

Stripping away the useless gear he carried, Bolan turned to Kinsey and unhooked her gun belt. Gently sliding his fingers under the small of her back, he lifted her, causing her lower back to arch slightly as he pulled the belt to him. A pang of guilt registered with the warrior as he handled her, taking her weapons. Slipping the Beretta into the waistband of his blue jeans, at the small of his back, the warrior picked up both her Glock and her Uzi, checked their loads and started to come to his feet.

The growl of motorcycles called Bolan to the window. He saw Stone, flanked by two thugs, navigating a Harley-Davidson down a winding length of asphalt that led into the forest and out of sight. Raising the weapon, Bolan locked the muzzle on Stone's back, trying for the biggest target possible from this distance.

Bolan snapped off three shots, all intended for Stone. However, at the same split second, one of Stone's thugs swerved into the line of fire and caught the bullets, the .40-caliber slugs perforating his spine. The driverless cycle plowed into a tree, mangling the steel and chrome beast, tangling the corpse in its twisted remains.

Stone was gone, the whine of the cycle's engine fading into the distance.

Bolan figured he could scare up another vehicle. He could give chase to Stone, hunt the man down and end all this. Or he could find Grimaldi, make sure his comrade was okay.

"He's outside."

The words surprised Bolan, caused him to spin toward the source. He saw the injured man had awoken. He stared at Kinsey, screwed his eyes shut as if to banish the image. He opened them again, stared at the dead woman, the corners of his mouth twitching with grief.

"Jennifer. Jesus—"

"Who's outside?" Bolan asked.

The man just continued to look at Kinsey.

"I said—"

"I heard what you said, dammit. Your buddy's outside. We hid him in some brush. He was fine. Jesus, my head hurts."

Bolan grabbed the guy by the arm and hauled him to his feet.

"Hey, what the hell?" the guy started to protest.

"We need to find him."

"What about her?"

"She's dead."

The guy's face reddened. "No kidding. I mean, what about the guy who did this? It was Stone, right?"

Bolan nodded. " It was him, but he's gone."

The guy yanked his arm hard, trying to free it from Bolan's hold. The Executioner released his grip on the man's arm, but continued to fix a hard stare on the guy.

"I'm going after Stone," the man said.

"No," Bolan replied, "you're not. You want your pound of flesh? Fine. But you track it down later. Right now, you're going to show me where my friend is. After that, I ask the questions and you answer them."

The guy gave Bolan a hard look. The warrior sensed the man's body tensing, preparing to lash out.

"Don't make this any harder on yourself," Bolan said.

The man looked at Kinsey, let his gaze linger a moment before turning back to Bolan.

"I don't think this could get any harder. Are you the guy from Afghanistan?"

Bolan nodded.

"Then let's go find your friend."

Salt Lake City, Utah

MACK BOLAN WHEELED the black rental onto the ramp leading into the underground parking garage. Driving one-handed, he fished in the breast pocket of his denim shirt and brought out a security card, the kind with a magnetic strip on the back. Braking at the card reader, he jammed in the card, waited for the arm to raise, allowing him access to the garage.

Navigating the car to a predetermined spot, Bolan slipped in between two other vehicles, killed the engine and the lights before exiting.

Obscured by aviator shades, Bolan's ice-blue gaze roved over his surroundings. Tactically, he hated parking garages. Too many nooks and crannies to hide an adversary. Too many innocents milling in and out, should the place erupt from a cold, concrete bunker into an all-out firestorm.

But he also figured the garage offered the optimal insertion point for the job at hand. Stone probably would have people working the lobby, guys who'd not hesitate to take out a few bystanders in their quest to save Stone's worthless hide.

No way.

Crossing the garage in long steps, Bolan reached a bank of elevators, swiped his card again to gain entry. Stepping inside the elevator, he punched the appropriate button and stepped back from the control panel. Staring at his shoes, he dipped a hand inside the black, calf-length leather coat, pretending to reach for something in his inside pocket when, in fact, he was keeping his hands within reach of the Beretta, which rode snug in a leather shoulder rig. A micro-Uzi rode counterpoint in the double shoulder rig while Bolan carried the .44 Desert Eagle on his hip.

Working around the clock, Kurtzman and the rest of the cyberteam had dug up this small lead on Stone. He occasionally used the alias James Crockett. A Crockett with the same fake social security number had an apartment registered in this building, a thirty-story high-rise apartment in Salt Lake City. According to the computerized tracking system employed by building security, Crockett had used his card to enter the building within the past twenty-four hours. If the computers were to be believed—and Bolan had little choice but to do so—Crockett hadn't left the building since.

Bolan checked his chronometer and saw that he had two minutes.

He'd known from the start that a man like Stone would post guards throughout the building. And it was a sure bet that the paranoid bastard also had tapped into the security camera feeds so he could monitor whatever activity within the building he wished. So the Stony Man team had crafted a simple but, Bolan hoped, effective plan. Kurtzman had hacked into security's computers, giving him the ability to disable the system remotely from Virginia with a few keystrokes. The connection was passive until Bolan inserted his forged security card, alerting the Stony Man team that he'd made it inside. Once Stony Man received the signal, it overrode the security cameras, causing them to play the last sixty seconds recorded in an endless loop, until Kurtzman instructed the computers otherwise.

They'd agreed to hobble the system for four minutes and no more. From all indications, the security team was legit and the residents counted on them for protection. Bolan knew he couldn't in good conscience leave the residents unprotected any longer than necessary.

The elevator car came to a halt. The doors slid aside, allowing Bolan to proceed into the hallway. Moving along the corridor, he stepped into a nearby stairwell, ascended the remaining three stories to the twenty-ninth floor. Checking his chronometer as he moved, he saw that he had another ninety seconds before the cameras came back to life.

Exiting the stairwell, Bolan drew the Beretta, held it flat against his thigh as he drifted toward his meet with Stone. The corridor led to a dead end, breaking off in either direction like a T. The soldier stopped at the edge of the hall, stood flush with the corner. He listened for a moment, heard a cough, the scratch of a lighter wheel rolling, the click of the torch's stainless-steel cover closing.

A moment later the scent of cheap cologne and stale cigar smoke reached Bolan. He risked a look around the corner, saw a lone gunner puffing on a thin cigar. With one hand jammed into his pocket, the hardman held the cigar about a foot away from his face and studied it. A quick check of his chronometer told Bolan he had thirty seconds before the cameras again went live.

Bolan needed to move.

Rounding the corner, he glided along the wall, the plush

carpet conspiring with his thin-soled athletic shoes to muffle his approach. As Bolan's shadow overtook the guy, the guard spun, his hand scrambling inside his jacket for a weapon. Grabbing the guy's shoulder, Bolan wheeled the guard toward him, using the man's momentum against him.

Get control of the gun! The words resounded in Bolan's head as he grabbed the wrist of the guy's gun hand, applied enough pressure to hold it in place. The guard opened his mouth, possibly to scream. His face froze in horror as the Beretta's muzzle came to rest on the tip of his nose. The guy stiffened and his eyes widened with fear.

"Drop it," Bolan said, "or I drop you."

The handgun fell to the floor with a dull thud.

"Go," Bolan said, giving the guy a hard shove. The man raised his hands, started backpedaling. Scooping up the guard's pistol from the floor, Bolan walked in lockstep with the guy, escorting him down the corridor toward a nearby stairwell. The Executioner ground the Beretta's muzzle against the guy's ribs, but otherwise kept the weapon out of view.

Bolan could only hope that Stone or one of his men wasn't watching the security monitors, wondering why the guard suddenly had abandoned his post.

Once they reached the stairwell, Bolan opened it and shoved the man inside. At that moment the guy decided to play it tough. Wheeling toward Bolan, he produced a six-inch knife from under his coat, jabbed the blade in Bolan's direction.

The warrior stepped back, let the knife slice through the space formerly occupied by him. At the same time, the warrior pushed into the guy's space, smashing his nose with a back fist. The man's head snapped back, exposing his neck, and he groaned. Controlling his force, Bolan drove an elbow into the man's throat, sending him reeling back, gagging. Sinking to his knees, the guard grabbed at his throat, gagged. In the meantime, Bolan scanned the area for security cameras, but saw none.

Aiming the Beretta dead center on the crown of the guy's head, Bolan spoke, his voice as icy as arctic winds.

"Get up."

Casting Bolan a weary glance, the guard came to his feet but continued massaging his throat with his fingertips.

Bolan nodded in the direction of the apartment. "Crockett in there? In the apartment?"

The guy remained silent.

"Pick your allies wisely. That blood spot that was your nose makes a sweet target."

The guy tried to sneer, but moving his shattered face thus caused him to wince.

"You shoot that gun in here, everyone will hear it," the guard said. "They'll be on you like flies on—"

Bolan shrugged. "Subsonic ammo. Suppressor. Your friends won't hear a thing. You've got one card left. Now I suggest you get smart real quick and play the damn thing. Otherwise, I'll ventilate your head and go about my merry way."

"He's inside."

"How many others?"

"Five."

"Guards?"

"Right."

"No one else?"

"Nah, man. Nada."

Holding the man's gaze, Bolan considered his words. After years of conducting field interrogations, Bolan had developed a sixth sense about when someone was lying to him. His gut said this guy was telling the truth. Faced with a certain death, the man apparently saw no benefit in lying.

"Face the wall," Bolan said, underscoring the command with a gesture from the Beretta. "Lace your hands behind your head."

"Man, I'm bleeding here. How about a little consideration?"

"How about I give you a third nostril?"

The man shut up and did as he was told. Within seconds Bolan had secured his hands with a pair of plastic handcuffs. He hit the guy once in the head. The man sagged, unconscious.

Patting down the man, Bolan found a security card, but no other keys. He dragged the man's inert form into a corner. Although leaving a man unconscious and beaten in the open was a risk, Bolan had no other option. He needed to move and to move quickly. He didn't want to lose Stone again.

The man had a lot to answer for.

Back at Stone's door, Bolan inserted the card in the reader, then waited. When the door unlocked, he popped it open and surged inside. The entry led him into the living room, which Bolan found populated by a pair of gunners, one seated on the couch reading a magazine, the second fixing himself a drink at the bar. Both men carried handguns in shoulder holsters.

A sawed-off, double-barreled shotgun sat on the cushion next the thug seated on the couch.

The guy made a play for the 12-gauge room sweeper, but stopped short as a trio of Parabellum rounds tunneled through his forehead and crashed through the back of his skull in a spray of blood and brain matter.

The second man dived behind the bar, left the contents of his overturned drink to wash over the bar's surface, drip onto the floor. Bolan shut the door behind him, listened for the thud of the automatic dead bolt slamming home. The last thing he needed was someone—friend or foe—coming through the door as bullets were exchanged.

Bolan glanced left at a line of floor-to-ceiling windows that opened into Salt Lake City's skyline. He saw the reflection of the man huddled behind the bar, gun in hand, waiting for a chance to shoot. Raising the Beretta, Bolan ripped off four more 3-round bursts. The bullets drilled through the bar, tunneled into the hidden gunner, the force knocking the man back against the wall in a dead heap.

Scanning the room for other adversaries, Bolan ejected the Beretta's clip, fed the pistol a new one. Extending the weapon in a two-handed grip, the warrior exited the living room, headed into a hallway. A man armed with a silenced MP-5 submachine gun wrapped himself around a corner, drew down on Bolan. The Beretta sighed again and three bullets slammed into the man's face, showering the wall behind him with crimson.

The Executioner saw a closed door at the end of the hall. As he approached, he heard a loud thump, followed by a shower of glass shards falling to the floor, cracking into even smaller pieces. What the hell? Cautiously stepping forward, Bolan closed in on the door, fired into the lock and let the door swing free. He stepped inside just in time to find all hell breaking loose.

THE WIND WHIPPED through Doyle's clothes and pinched the flesh of his cheeks as he stood on the roof of the thirty-story tower. He gave the nylon rope one last tug to check its stability. Satisfied, he clipped the rope to the harness wrapped around his midsection and backed toward the edge of the roof. Seating himself on the parapet, he turned, dangled his legs over the edge and began to slide his rear end off the ledge. As he hung in space, he twisted himself and began to climb down the side of the building. Almost immediately, the muscles of his arms, chest and shoulders began to burn and he wondered again whether he should've let Cooper do this.

Wind occasionally grabbed him, swinging him around and causing his stomach to lurch. Each time he considered giving up, he recalled Jennifer's corpse, skin waxen, body torn by bullet holes. He cared for the woman and felt as though a hole had opened up underneath his heart and swallowed it up. Still, as tragic as it was, she'd known the score before she'd ever set out looking for Stone. She'd had an even chance against the guy, but lost. But if Stone hadn't been looking to kill Doyle before, he would be going forward. And if the crazy SOB went after Nancy—

Climb, you crazy bastard.

Using the rope and pulley system moored to the roof, Doyle continued to lower himself hand over hand until he reached the ledge that ran above Stone's apartment window. Unlimbering the MP-9 submachine gun, he gripped it with one hand while holding the rope with the other.

He had about three seconds to make it work. He uttered a short prayer and started to lower himself.

Suspended from the rope, he took a second to look through the window. Despite the cold, the skies were clear blue, the sun a brilliant yellow. Doyle knew he cast a shadow. He figured that, at any moment, Stone would turn to see who was outside his window. Setting his feet to the glass, Doyle bent his knees and kicked off the surface. As he did, he unloaded the MP-9 into the window, shattering it and causing shards to fall both into the apartment and down to the street.

As the window disintegrated before him, Doyle went through the open space and into the apartment. Landing on his feet, he swept the SMG's muzzle over the room. Stone was up and out of his chair in a heartbeat. He hefted the chair over his head and, like an enraged gorilla, flung it at Doyle.

Doyle sidestepped the chair, but had blown his easiest shot at Stone. A pair of gunners also swung into action, each scrambling for hardware and running for cover.

Stone was fastest on the draw, though. The big man raised a Detonics .45 and squeezed off three shots at Doyle.

Doyle dived out of the gunfire's path. As he lay on the floor, bullets streaking overhead, he unhooked the rope from his harness and cast it off. Stone shot two more rounds at him while backing toward the door. The hastily placed rounds flew wide of Doyle and tunneled into a couch.

Before he could counter, more shots thundered at him from the right, forcing him to ignore Stone. A man stood in front of the shattered window, his pistol blazing. Doyle crawled several feet to his right, drew down on the man and cut loose with a burst from the MP-9. The bullets struck the man in the chest. The force caused him to backpedal several steps until he reached the shattered window. He teetered for a moment before tipping backward and plummeting through the opening.

As the gunfire intensified, the door snapped open and Cooper lunged through it. Another of Stone's men unloaded his weapon at the federal agent. The rounds chewed through drywall and wood, raising clouds of white dust. Cooper, the Beretta in his grip, sent the man to hell with a well-placed burst from his weapon.

Trying to make a break for the door, Stone ran across Doyle's line of sight. Doyle locked the muzzle on Stone's legs. The weapon stuttered out a line of lead that chewed into his adversary's calves and knees, stopping his advance. He shook like a man wrapped in high-tension wires and then sank to his knees and rolled onto his back. He'd dropped the pistol, but his fingertips skittered madly over the floor as he tried to recover it.

Doyle got to his feet. A red haze had blinded him and he wanted nothing more than to kill the man.

Slowly.

Not now.

Soon enough.

Cooper needed him alive as much as Stone needed him dead. Doyle knew he could wait two minutes. Jennifer would want him to.

Blood matted the fabric of Stone's tattered pants and pooled on the floor around him. He sucked wind as though he'd just run a marathon, and rivulets of sweat rolled down his face, which was fast going from ruddy to pale.

Cooper stepped up to the man and stared down at him. Doyle anticipated the kill and could hear a rush of blood in his ears, the sensation of sweat collecting between his shoulder blades before trickling down his spine.

"Who's footing your bill?" Bolan asked.

"Go screw yourself," Stone rasped. "Get me a doctor and we'll talk."

The big man shook his head. "Not part of the plan, Stone. You talk first, and then we'll see what we can do for you."

"I get a doctor first or I don't talk."

A shudder passed through Stone, who'd propped himself up on his elbows to stare at the men. He laid down and breathed harder. Blood spurted from one wound more heavily than the others, and Doyle realized he'd hit an artery. The guy would be dead in minutes.

Bolan shook his head. "No deals. Now, who's paying the bills? Who hired you to kill James Lee?"

Stone started to hyperventilate as his body fought for oxygen. He shuddered again and went silent as he slipped into shock. Doyle stripped off his coat and draped it over the man, to help keep him warm. He knew he was too late, but had to try anyway. Within moments, Stone lost consciousness and a death rattle escaped his lungs shortly thereafter.

CHAPTER SIXTEEN

With Doyle just a step behind, Bolan pushed aside a pair of glass doors and made his way into the Salt Lake City office of Helpers Alliance International. His eyes hidden behind aviator shades, he swept his gaze over the room, looking for hostiles, but found none. He approached a desk occupied by a pretty brunette. Tethered to her phone by a headset cord, she was typing something into a laptop. The nameplate on her desk read Stacy Nelson.

She turned, gave Bolan an appraising look and flashed a smile. "May I help you?"

"Mohammed Nasrallah," Bolan said.

"Is he expecting you?"

"No."

"I'm sorry," she said, her lips curving into a slight frown, her voice lowering into a hushed, conciliatory tone. "He's extremely busy and he only sees people by appointment. Would you like to schedule one? For next week, perhaps?"

"No."

The woman stiffened a bit but kept her smile. "Excuse me?"

"I said no. I'm with the Justice Department," Bolan said. "I want Nasrallah. Now."

"But, sir—"

"Lady, are you interfering with official business?" Doyle interjected. "'Cause if you are…"

Doyle let the sentence trail off, leaving her to fill in the potential consequences. Apparently she imagined something dire. Turning, she jabbed a red-lacquered nail into a button on her phone, waited for a reply. As she did, she tapped her pencil eraser against the desktop, tugged at a loose strand of hair with the other hand.

Bolan smiled inwardly. As a rule, he preferred to do his fieldwork alone. He relied on Stony Man Farm for research and intel. Occasionally, if he found himself outgunned, or two hotspots erupting simultaneously, he conscripted the warriors of Able Team and Phoenix Force. But he preferred to travel light and fast. Still, Doyle seemed a decent guy, skilled and able to think on his feet.

"Hi, Janice, this is Stacy. I have two men here to see Mr. Nasrallah." She paused, chewed on her lower lip as she listened. "Yes. I understand that he's busy. These men are from the Justice Department." Another pause. "Yes, the Justice Department. No, I didn't catch their names."

She looked expectantly at Doyle and Bolan.

"Cooper," Bolan said.

"Rossington," Doyle added.

She turned back toward her phone and Bolan found himself admiring her profile. "Agents Cooper and Rossington. No, I don't know what they want here." Another few heartbeats of silence hung in the air, before the receptionist spoke again. "Right. I'll send them back."

Pulling the headset from her hair, she raised her slender form from behind the desk. With a sweep of her hand, she indicated an oak door. "This way, please."

A minute later Bolan found himself and Doyle in a large

office lined with bookshelves. A massive desk stood in a corner, a mural-size map of the world decorating the wall behind it.

"Mr. Nasrallah will be right with you. Please have a seat."

"Thanks," Bolan said. "I prefer to stand. Our business here is short."

She offered the men drinks, which they declined. She turned and left, probably grateful to distance herself from the situation.

A door sounded behind them. Bolan and Doyle turned in unison. The man looked first at Bolan, gave him a brief nod. He turned to Doyle and Bolan noticed his gaze lingered a moment on Doyle's face. He then turned, as though suddenly bathed in blinding rays of light, looked again at Bolan and held out a hand.

The soldier took it, noticing the skin felt cold, moist against his. The man obviously was nervous. He didn't bother to offer a handshake to Doyle. Bolan's gut told him something was going on, though he was unsure what.

The man broke the silence.

"I'm Mohammed Nasrallah," he said. He waved his hand at a group of armchairs situated around a coffee table. "Please sit."

"As we told the young lady," Bolan said, "we won't be here long. We just have a few questions to ask."

A cloud of anger passed over the man's features, but he kept his tone even. "Certainly."

"You know James Crockett?" Bolan asked.

Nasrallah nodded. "Of course. He does security consulting for us."

"Security consulting?"

"Yes. We send aid workers all over the world. Unfortunately, because of the nature of our work, we have to send them to some of the world's worst places. Mr. Crockett would research such places, advise our people on the dangers, train them in basic self-defense, that sort of thing."

"Is that all he did for you?"

Nasrallah's brow furrowed. When he spoke, he forced the words through clenched teeth. "What do you mean? What else would a security consultant do?"

Doyle broke in. "I think what Agent Cooper is asking, and delicately so, is did Crockett train mercenaries for you?"

"Certainly not!"

"No need to get uptight," Doyle said, softening his voice. "We're just trying to get some information, that's all."

"You insult me. You insult my organization with such questions."

"Sorry," Doyle said, shrugging. "Do you know a Jon Stone?"

Nasrallah shook his head. "Should I?"

"Maybe."

"Why?"

"How did you meet Crockett?" Doyle asked.

"Before I answer more questions, I should call a lawyer."

Doyle kept his tone soothing. "Why do that? We aren't here to charge you with anything. We just want to talk. Why waste the money?"

A smirk spread across Nasrallah's features. "Am I now to believe you're trying to help me?"

"We're just looking for information, sir. That's all."

"What did Mr. Crockett do?"

"He was training mercenaries," Doyle said. "He also murdered a federal agent."

"Training mercenaries? That's impossible."

"Do you know a Jon Stone?"

Nasrallah scowled. "You already asked me that once. I know no such man. You don't believe me?

"That's Crockett's real name," Doyle said. "But, of course, you already knew that."

"I knew no such thing. Anyway, what are you talking about? Crockett wasn't using an alias."

"How do you know?"

"We kept records for him, for payroll purposes, of course. Social security numbers, driver's license. The standard things one collects for employment."

"Those things can be forged."

"Yes, yes. I know that."

"But you didn't know Crockett was an alias?"

"I just answered that."

"Of course you did."

As Nasrallah spoke, Bolan noticed that the man never once looked at Doyle, even though the former CIA agent asked most of the questions. Bolan also saw that, although the man had salt-and-pepper hair, and wrinkled skin on his hands, he had no crow's feet around his eyes.

"Can we see the records for Mr. Stone?" Doyle asked. "I mean, Mr. Crockett."

Nasrallah shook his head. "I told you, I don't know a Jon Stone. You can contact my lawyer if you want any of our papers. We're nonprofit, but we do have some rights."

"No one's denying that," Doyle said. "Perhaps you'd like to call your lawyer."

Nasrallah nodded. "Yes, as a matter of fact, I would."

Doyle shrugged again, gave him a benign smile. "Knock yourself out."

Spinning on a heel, Nasrallah walked to his desk. Grabbing the phone receiver from its cradle, he punched in a number, waited.

"Charles? Mohammed. I have a situation."

As Bolan and Doyle listened, the man explained the bare essentials regarding his visitors and their questions.

"A private line. Of course I have one. Wait a minute."

Putting his lawyer on hold, Nasrallah turned to Bolan and Doyle. A smile that didn't reach his eyes was plastered across his face. "Excuse me. I need to go somewhere else and speak."

"Whatever," Bolan said.

After Nasrallah left the office, Doyle walked to the coffee table. With a handkerchief, he grabbed a spoon that rested on a saucer, wrapped it in the cloth and stuck it in a pocket. Nasrallah entered the room just as Doyle straightened.

"My lawyer says to tell you nothing. If you have further questions, you can call him."

Bolan felt his muscles tense as the man gave him a smug smile. His expression grim, the soldier nodded. If he wanted, he knew he could press the issue, count on Brognola and the Justice Department to bail him out. Until he had a compelling reason to do so, though, he decided against.

He still found the Arab's behavior curious. After his initial introduction to Doyle, the man had elected to focus his attention on Doyle during the entire conversation. Curious behavior, but it wasn't criminal by any stretch. Besides, the way Bolan figured it, he had more to gain by leaving the guy alone.

So, yeah, he'd keep his cool. But he'd also drop a bomb on Nasrallah, so the man lost his.

He looked at Doyle and cocked his head toward the door. Doyle headed for it, with Bolan following behind. As the Executioner reached the door, he turned to Nasrallah and locked eyes with the man.

"A little friendly advice?" Bolan asked.

Nasrallah scowled, but nodded his ascent.

"Start looking for a new security consultant," Bolan said.

Nasrallah's brow furrowed. "Why? What happened to Mr. Crockett?"

"He's dead."

"What?"

"Dead. In his apartment. How do you think we got your name? We found your business card in his place."

Stepping through the door, Bolan slammed it behind him and went to catch up with Doyle.

TEN MINUTES LATER, Bolan and Doyle had returned to the parked rental car.

Reaching under the seat, Bolan extracted a nylon briefcase, unzipped it and folded over the flap, revealing a laptop. Raising the lid, he booted up the machine. Seconds later he began punching buttons, opening various program windows and punching in a series of codes.

"What, are you checking e-mail or something?"

Bolan shook his head. "Now that we've lit a fire under Nasrallah, I expect him to react. Usually that means a phone call. My people can trace all calls coming in or out of the building, patch me into the calls he makes. Before we ever walked into the building, they'd already tracked down his cell phone, office and home numbers. If he uses any of these, we can intercept the satellite transmissions and listen in."

Bolan pressed a few more keys on the laptop, waited.

"Sharp," Doyle replied. "Nice job shaking him up in there. You're about as subtle as a hydrogen bomb, Cooper, you know that?"

Bolan shrugged. "My methods are effective, at least as effective as stealing a man's silverware."

Doyle grinned. "Pretty sharp, huh? I figure maybe your people can lift some fingerprints off here and see what's shaking with this guy."

Bolan nodded. He knew they could drop it off at the FBI field office later and, using Brognola's contacts, process any prints found on the utensil.

The laptop emitted a pinging sound. Bolan looked at it, saw that it was alerting him to an intercepted phone call. A moment later voices sounded over the speakers.

"—you mean, Stone is dead?"

"The agents said he was dead. He died this morning."

"Died, or killed. There's a difference."

"Of course, there is. Do you think I don't understand that?"

"How did they connect you and Stone?"

"The agent said they found my business card in Stone's apartment."

"That's sloppy. I expected better."

"Stone sometimes acted in such a manner. He could be a loose cannon."

"I was talking about you."

"Oh."

"This upsets me greatly. Did you give them any information? Anything that might hamper our cause?"

"Nothing of substance," Nasrallah said. "I told them that Stone, or his alter ego, anyway, worked for us as a security consultant. I swore I knew nothing about him. They seemed to accept that."

"For the moment."

"For the moment," Nasrallah agreed. "In another twenty-four hours, it won't matter. They'll have much more important things to worry about. By then, I'll be gone and no one will ever connect you to any of this."

A cold edge crept into the other man's voice. "So you say."

"It's more than words, my friend. I swear this to you. You have done so much for me, for our cause. On my family's honor, I would die before I'd betray you."

"Oh, man, here comes breakfast," Doyle said. Bolan gestured for him to keep quiet.

"I will hold you to that." Nasrallah terminated his phone connection.

Bolan considered the implications of what he'd just heard. Obviously, Nasrallah knew more than he'd let on during their face-to-face. The soldier had suspected as much and wasn't surprised to have his belief confirmed. He also wasn't surprised to learn that the man was no good, or that he had someone backing him in his covert play.

The computer pinged once more, bringing Bolan from his thoughts. Nasrallah once again began to speak.

"We must accelerate things."

"By how much?" another man asked.

"We need to move tonight."

"You're kidding. Why the hell would we want to do that?" Bolan noticed Doyle's brow crease as he listened to the exchange. He made a mental note to ask him about that.

"We've gained attention from the authorities."

"Authorities? You mean, like cops, federal agents, what?"

"The latter."

"Damn Feds. They're like a bunch of leeches. It's getting so a decent person can't do a damn thing in this country without getting an eyeball from those bastards."

"You can do this, right? You can move up the timetable, I mean."

"Look, Nas, we've got problems of our own here."

"Problems?" Nasrallah replied. "What sort of problems?"

"We've been infiltrated. Lord, man, didn't Stone tell you this? What's that asshole doing?"

A rumble escaped from Nasrallah's throat as he cleared it. "Stone's dead."

The other man paused, exhaled deeply.

"Dead? Great. When the hell were you going to tell me this?"

"Soon," Nasrallah said. "And what do you mean 'infiltrated'?"

"Just like it sounds. An unfriendly has been bunking with us for months. I suspected it for a while, but couldn't nail it down." He chuckled. "Last night, I nailed it down, but good, eliminated the problem forever. You ought to thank me. I had a heart-to-heart with the dumb SOB, found out he knew enough to derail the whole operation. Then I removed him from the equation."

"Was that wise?"

"Oh, what, so now you're an expert in tradecraft? Look, I was doing this shit while you still were meandering around the damn desert with your nose up your psycho boss's rear. You just prance around in your Italian suits, begging for money and leave the real work to me. Trust me. I did some checking. No one knows we deactivated the guy."

"Fine," Nasrallah said, sounding unconvinced. "Did you get the package?"

"Yeah. It's pretty sweet stuff, probably the best I ever handled. And, just as soon as you and I end our little telethon here, I'll go get bundle number two. Just say the word and we'll deploy."

"I'm giving the word."

"So it's in play?"

"Yes."

"Good. Hey, look, don't sweat it. My people do good work, even without Stone. You'll get everything you wanted and more out of this little psycho wet dream of yours. Believe it."

"This is a mission of honor."

"That's what they all say. I don't care about your motives. Just make sure you pay me."

"You know I will. You just complete your mission."

"Always," the man said before terminating the call.

The computer indicated to Bolan that Nasrallah's phone once again had gone inactive. The soldier turned to Doyle. "Sounds pretty damn cryptic."

"It's worse than that," Doyle said. "I recognize that other guy's voice. It belongs to Mike Pond. He was another member of our team, the one Jennifer told you about. We called him Mad Dog. He made Stone look like sanity's poster child."

"Wonderful. Tell me what you can about him."

"Ostensibly, he's a militia leader."

Bolan cocked an eyebrow. "Ostensibly?"

"Mad Dog is a narcissistic bastard. He doesn't care about anything or anyone other than himself. I seriously doubt he gets worked up over injustices—real or perceived—by the government. He probably just gets off on being the boss of something. It's probably a kick for him to take a bunch of guys and mold them into his own warped image."

"And get paid for it."

"Exactly."

Yanking the handle, Bolan opened the car door, stepped one foot on the curb. "Looks like this gives us enough to grab Nasrallah," Bolan said. "Let's go."

SEATED IN THE SECURITY ROOM, Donald Blair watched as the two Justice Department agents exited Nasrallah's office. Two other hard-eyed men stood by. Blair's small eyes betrayed nothing as strategically placed cameras allowed him to watch the visitors as they proceeded through corridors, boarded an elevator and headed for the ground floor.

Blair watched the men exit the elevator and move through the lobby, approaching the glass doors leading to the streets.

The big guy looked dangerous. The smaller man looked like a whole lot of nothing.

The phone next to him rang. "That's them," Nasrallah said. "The big man is the one I hired you for. His name's Cooper. But I want you to take out the other man, too. Rossington I think he said—"

"I don't need names. And a second kill will cost extra."

"Dammit, there's no time for this. Move!"

Blair rolled his eyes and shook his head. "I'll get you the little guy, but it's for the same terms as Cooper."

"Fine, just move!" the other man said, his voice sounding like a hiss. Nasrallah slammed down the phone, causing Blair to hold it a few inches from his ear. He stared at it for a moment, chuckling. Killing the phone's power, he pocketed it.

Rising from the chair, Blair hooked two fingers under the collar of his suit coat, yanked it from the seat back it was draped over. He slid on the jacket, letting it cover the twin Berettas he carried in a custom-made dual shoulder holster. He slid into a black overcoat.

Snatching up a folded copy of a newspaper, he exited the room. His associates fell in behind him, walked in lockstep with one another. Blair covered the corridor in quick, reaching strides, his mind already shifting to the kill. Even if Nasrallah hadn't regaled him with all the bullshit campfire stories about the guy, Blair would know with one look that his opponent wouldn't be an easy hit. Cooper oozed confidence, moved with a tiger's grace, despite his bulky frame. The guy was like a physical manifestation of the Grim Reaper.

Rossington looked nondescript, perhaps even a little goofy, the kind of man you'd jostle on a bus and not apologize to. But, as the cliché went, appearances could be deceiving. If he was keeping company with Blair's first target, then he had to have some sharp edges of his own.

To hell with it, Blair decided. He could dull anyone's edge. He stepped onto the elevator, punched the lobby button, waited breathlessly for it to reach the ground floor. It was just the three of them in the elevator, and Blair had deactivated the security camera that monitored the interior. Sliding a hand under his multiple layers, he fisted a Beretta. Opening the newspaper into a single fold, as though he'd bought it at a newspaper box, he laid the Beretta inside it, folded the paper over the weapon and slid it under his arm. Just another executive planning to hide in his office, sipping coffee and scanning the sports pages, avoiding real work as long as he could.

The terse conversation with Nasrallah moments earlier already had slipped his mind. Blair considered this, the hunt, the most important thing. He loved the adrenaline rush, the accelerated heartbeat and the heightened senses that marked the chase. Sure, the kill was fine, sometimes even pleasurable. But it was tracking him, seeing the fear in his eyes just before the kill, that kept Blair coming back to work every day.

A fast walk across the lobby brought him to the revolving doors. He pushed through them, all but ignoring his two associates. He didn't need to. Angelo and Tommy were sharp, dependable, ruthless. Sometimes, he thought, they even earned their keep. He had more men waiting outside, ready to ring the targets in so Blair could deliver the killing blow.

Shooting through the revolving doors, he ran his gaze over the street, seeking his targets. Simultaneously his ears sorted through the urban orchestra resounding around him—the hum of car engines, the honk of horns, the occasional hiss of a bus's brakes and the pleasant odor of diesel fumes.

Turning left, he started down the street. As he did, he caught a glimpse of his target's towering form looming over passersby. The guy was climbing into a car. Using hand signals, Blair sent Tommy across the street, while he and Angelo continued down the other side.

Less than a minute later he was within thirty yards of the target's car. Cooper sat in the driver's seat and stared down at something. Rossington sipped coffee and stared out the passenger-side window. Blair ducked into a doorway situated just across the street from the black sedan. In the meantime, Angelo continued along the sidewalk. Blair knew the other man would head several yards past the car before doubling back to approach it from the rear. Tommy would hit it head-on.

Both men appeared to be staring at something. After a few minutes they conversed a bit before Cooper popped open his door and stepped from the car. When Rossington joined him on the sidewalk, the two men started back toward Nasrallah's building. Blair grinned. He knew Nasrallah would be long gone before these men reached him. He hadn't worked with Nasrallah long, but he considered himself a good judge of character. He'd judged the Arab and found him to be a coward.

Blair let the newspaper fall to the ground. A gust of wind grabbed it and dragged it away, scattering the individual sheets. Stuffing the pistol into his pocket, he crossed the street at a jog, threading his way through lines of cars halted for a traffic light.

Falling in behind Cooper and Rossington, he gripped the Beretta. Hooking his index finger around the front of the trigger guard, he edged along the line of storefronts, keeping the men in sight. Whenever he got too close, he dropped back, allowing them room to move. Like a fisherman feeding out line to a potential catch, he wanted the men to believe they were calling their own shots, controlling their own destinies.

Nothing could be further from the truth.

The cold pinched the skin of his cheeks and caused the interior of his nostrils to swell. Regardless, he felt invigorated as he brushed his way through pedestrians, closed in on the two men. A bicycle cop passed and Blair nodded at him, giving him a crooked smile.

The cop nodded dutifully back before pedaling away.

The targets stopped for a moment, stared into a shop window, exchanged a few words.

CHAPTER SEVENTEEN

As he and Doyle hurried back to Nasrallah's office, Bolan replayed the telephone conversations between the Arab, Pond and the other man over and over in his head. Something was coming fast and furious, an unexpected twist in what had first seemed to be a simple payback strike against James Lee. Bolan gave Doyle a hard stare and said out loud something that had been bothering him ever since their meet with Nasrallah.

"Nasrallah recognized you. Why?"

It was Doyle's turn to scowl. "What the hell are you talking about?"

"Come on. I let you do most of the talking so I could check out the office, but he barely looked at you."

Doyle shrugged. "What do you want? Maybe he likes taller men."

"Not funny."

Doyle jammed his hands into his pockets and looked at the ground as he walked. "Okay, I noticed it. The truth? There was something familiar about him, too. Damned if I can put a finger on where or when, but I know I've met him before. It wasn't the face. Maybe it was the eyes or something."

"The face wasn't his. He had no crow's feet and no wrinkles. But his hands had small wrinkles and a few liver spots. I'd bet he's had plastic surgery of some sort. So if you met him before, he likely doesn't look the same."

Doyle nodded, but said nothing.

A gust of icy wind blasted down the street. Bolan gritted his teeth, flinched as it stabbed into him. His combat senses told him to halt and he did. Stopping in midstride, he cast a sideways glance into a music store's front window, feigned interest and approached the store. Ignoring the propped-up guitars and squat black amplifiers, he checked the street scene reflected back at him from the window for threats, but saw nothing.

Still, his combat senses were telling him to watch his back.

He knew what to trust. Not his eyes and ears. Though both were highly attuned, perhaps more so than those of others, Bolan considered them tools, much like the weapons he carried. His gut had never led him astray, but instead had helped him weather countless battles. He knew better than to ignore his intuition.

And right now it told him he was in someone's crosshairs, figuratively if not literally. It made sense. He'd just rousted a man with deadly ties and stayed where the man could find him.

"What's the problem?" Doyle asked.

"Someone's coming for us."

"Big surprise, especially with the bomb you dropped on Nasrallah before we left. You made anyone yet?"

"Negative. I'm going by intuition."

Doyle nodded, apparently satisfied with the explanation. Bolan continued to run his gaze over his surroundings, using window reflections to monitor his rear flank. The Executioner undid the first few snaps on his coat, allowing him better access to his weapons.

A heartbeat later his mobile phone trilled in his pocket. Reaching his hand inside, he withdrew the phone, flipped it open.

"Go."

"Striker," Barbara Price said, "we've got something."

"Nasrallah?"

"Right. The Bear's been tracing the numbers. I guess Mr. Nasrallah's been showering Stone with cash for the last two years."

"Stands to reason," Bolan said. "He told us Stone—or his alias, anyway—has been working with them as a security consultant for some time now. He said it's just business, all aboveboard."

"You belicvc that?"

"No."

"You shouldn't. Last year, Helpers Alliance International stuck more than one million dollars into a series of Cayman Island accounts owned by Mr. Stone under his Crockett alias. They did likewise for a man by the name of Mike Pond. Only in Pond's case, the amount climbed to about five million."

"Pond's former CIA."

"Your tag-along told you that?"

"Affirmative."

"Let me guess, they used to work together."

"Right."

"I can see why the government broke them up. It's like Psychos Inc., or something. Anyway, we found something else interesting about Mr. Pond. Seems the Feds were investigating his militia group, Patriots of the New Dawn. Their undercover guy turned up dead last night. Not coincidentally, I'm sure, the group pulled up stakes and left. The FBI's hostage rescue tcam stormed the grounds earlier this morning."

"Find anything?"

"Nothing but empty concrete buildings, dirty dishes and a few pamphlets."

A chill raced down Bolan's spine, caused him to stiffen. Stopping dead in his tracks, the Executioner turned in time to see a hard-looking guy shoving his way through the crowd and moving in Bolan's direction. The soldier made eye contact with the guy and he froze in his tracks.

A scream sounded behind the Executioner. Stabbing his hand into his jacket, he whirled toward the sound.

CHAPTER EIGHTEEN

As he turned Bolan saw a man walking toward him, arm extended, pistol clenched in his fist. In one fluid motion, the Executioner drew the Beretta and fired. The weapon coughed out a round of subsonic ammunition and opened his opponent's forehead; he crumpled into a boneless heap.

Even as the man collapsed, more screams erupted from behind. Bolan turned toward the noise and spotted two more men pushing through the crowd, their weapons visible.

The warrior glanced at Doyle, saw he'd drawn his Glock. The former CIA agent fanned the weapon over the crowd, the first joint of his index finger looped around the front of the weapon's trigger guard. Catching sight of the handgun, pedestrians froze before either ducking or turning and running, several of them screaming as they got out of the way.

Bolan grabbed a fistful of Doyle's coat and tugged on it. The former CIA agent turned and Bolan motioned toward a nearby alley with his head. Both men circled around a panel truck parked in between the buildings and started down the alley. Bolan surged ahead, covering the distance in smooth strides, while Doyle fell a few paces behind. Both men crunched discarded newspapers and aluminum cans under-foot as they covered the distance.

Bolan spied a wino, a gray-bearded man dressed in a tat-tered high school varsity jacket, a bleach-spotted sweatshirt and torn jeans. The man lay to Bolan's left, on a bed of trash bags. Almost immediately the alarm bells sounded in his head.

A new belt. Scuffed, dirty tennis shoes with new soles.

Hand inside the brown paper bag, rather than around it.

"Doyle, watch—"

In a flurry of motion, the wino came up from a lying posi-tion and swung the paper-bag-covered hand in Bolan's direction. Without losing stride, he locked the Beretta's muzzle on the man, double tapped the trigger. Instantly a red hole opened in the bridge of the man's nose, while a second devastated his forehead.

"Nice moves," Doyle said.

The men sped to the other end of the alley, but found it blocked by a parked semi-truck. Realizing he'd been led into this situation, Bolan bit off a curse and turned toward the sound of footsteps slapping against pavement.

A jagged line of gunners spread across the alley, weapons raised and tracking in on Bolan and Doyle.

From his peripheral vision, Bolan saw Doyle drop into a crouch, dart right and take up refuge behind a garbage Dumpster. He reached around the refuse container, Glock in hand, and fired off three rounds. In the meantime Bolan sprinted to a recessed doorway to gain better cover. He switched the Beretta to 3-shot mode. Peering around the wall with one eye and holding the Beretta at arm's length, he fired. The Beretta spit out a triple load of death that hammered one man in the chest, the rounds leaving three vertical holes as the Beretta's muzzle climbed. Even as the guy fell to the ground, Bolan was swinging the pistol in search of a new target. A thug armed with a machine pistol crouched next to a stack of cardboard boxes. He snapped off a line of bullets that hammered into the bricks just a few inches from Bolan's face. The near miss briefly drove the soldier under cover. Going down on one knee, Bolan wrapped himself around the doorway and caught the shooter in his sights. The Beretta sighed and dispatched another trio of deadly messengers that ripped into the man's throat. He dropped his weapon and started to grab for the wounds. Death overtook him before his curled fingers could reach his shredded throat.

The warrior drew himself into the doorway and changed the Beretta's magazine. Switching it to his left hand, he fisted the Desert Eagle with his right and cocked back the hammer. Submachine gun fire pounded relentlessly against Bolan's position, chewing apart brick and filling the air with grit.

The warrior came back around the doorjamb and pinned the shooter in his gunsights as the man tried to reload. The Desert Eagle thundered twice, hurling forth a pair of .44 Magnum hollowpoint rounds that caught the shooter in the head and reduced it to a red mist.

Doyle's own weapon continued to bark and, from what Bolan could tell, he'd downed two other attackers.

The sudden rattle of Bolan's combat sense prompted him to turn his eyes upward, to the roof of the building next to him. Above stood a man, body wrapped in a long coat, a Beretta clutched in each hand. He triggered the weapons in unison. Bolan thrust himself forward, tucked and rolled, as bullets pounded his former position. He heard Doyle swear and an instant later he sprinted into view. Doyle turned in midstride and squeezed off a shot just as a bullet caught him in the thigh. He stumbled backward, fell onto his rear even as the Glock barked twice more.

Bolan was on his feet and heading toward his partner. The shooter spun toward him and drew down on the Executioner, the Berettas spitting bullets. The hot lead sizzled just past Bolan's ears and under his arms, piercing his coat. He brought up the Desert Eagle, caught the shooter in his sights and fired.

The hollowpoint round punched through the right lens of the man's sunglasses and into his eye. The man's body went limp as the bullet tunneled through his head, the raw force knocking him off the parapet. He took a loose-limbed dive from the roof and landed in a pile of bagged garbage.

Doyle limped up next to Bolan. He stared at the corpse for a moment, looked at Bolan and whistled.

"Looks like the rats'll eat good tonight," he said.

"Come on," Bolan replied. "We need to see a man about a spoon."

Stony Man Farm, Virginia

DRESSED IN JEANS, worn leather sneakers and a flowered shirt, Carl Lyons strode into the War Room, placed a foam cup of coffee onto the circular table, fell heavily into his chair and sighed. When Hermann "Gadgets" Schwarz and Rosario "Politician" Blancanales, his comrades from Able Team, and Barbara Price, ignored his arrival, he sighed again, taking the volume up a notch.

The others exchanged glances. Price who was sitting next to Lyons, was using her laptop, a projector and a screen, to provide the others with mission notes. She turned, gave Lyons a withering look.

"You're late," she said.

Lyons's face reddened, making his blond hair seem more pronounced. "Hey, you ought to just be glad I made it here at all."

Blancanales and Schwarz shifted around their chairs. This time, Price didn't bother to turn around. "Pray tell, why is that?"

For an instant the strain in her voice registered with Lyons. To hell with it, he decided. She was always uptight. "Hey, I got a life. I had to cancel a date. You know, I need to work off a little steam sometimes."

Blancanales snickered. "A date? Make sure her pimp gives you a refund."

Schwarz chimed in. "And get one for that shirt, too."

Both men laughed out loud and Lyons felt his ears begin to burn. He slammed an open palm on the table, creating a sound that cut through the room like a gunshot. "Hey," he said, "I'm serious."

The men of Able Team ignored the outburst. Price stiffened. "Carl," she said, "I'm about to work off a little steam of my own. And guess who's going to get it?"

"Shit," Lyons said.

Keeping her back to him, Price punched a key on her laptop. An image of an unshaven man with what Lyons liked to call "Psycho Eyes," popped onto the screen.

"Who's the hairball?" he asked.

"Mike Pond," Price replied. "People call him Mad Dog."

"And we care about him why?" Lyons asked.

Price explained about the slain federal agent, Pond's militia and his CIA connections.

Lyons shifted a little in his chair. "Sorry to hear about the guy getting capped. And Lord knows I like nothing better than tangling with cop killers. But can't the Feds handle that? I mean, it sounds like a no-brainer. Guy's undercover, he gets killed, lean on the people he was investigating."

"It's more complex than that," Price said.

Lyons rolled his eyes. "Isn't it always?"

Price turned to face the three men. "The group has its headquarters within a reasonable distance of the Citadel, a high-security meeting facility in the Utah desert."

Blancanales spoke. "The one they built after September 11?"

"The very same. The Feds built it in a remote corner of Dixie National Forest in southwest Utah. It's supposed to provide the President with a safe alternative to meeting at Camp David. They can fly him out west, then shoot him to the facility via Marine One, minus the company of the White House press corps."

Lyons spoke up. "So if Pond and his people are so dangerous, why didn't the U.S. government evict them from their property? Declare eminent domain or something and seize the land? Hell, that nut job ought not be anywhere near the Citadel."

Price shook her head no. "The powers that be considered it, but deemed it a bad move. They couldn't make a case for seizing the property, because it really has no value for public projects such as highways. And, since they had no firm evidence of the militia members breaking any laws, they knew any other efforts to shut them down would get mired in court challenges. Besides, no one's even supposed to know the Citadel exists. Send in the lawyers or the black helicopters and every conspiracy theorist in the country will start scouring the area."

"So they figured it best to keep their heads down," Lyons said.

"Precisely.

Schwarz leaned forward and rested his elbows on the table. "Why the undercover op, then?"

"Like I said, they had no solid evidence. But Pond's CIA connections made everyone uneasy. The guy knew how to do an arms trade and he didn't care who got the weapons. Mix his connections, his training, with his hatred for the U.S. government and you've got a recipe for disaster."

"So did our dead guy find anything?" Schwarz asked.

"From what the field agent—Tom Roth—learned, they were buying some small arms from Mexico—AK-47s and

Ak-74s, handguns, possibly even a couple of pounds of C-4 plastic explosives. They brought it through the same underground tunnels used by a lot of drug dealers."

"And that wasn't enough to bust them?"

"Roth never saw the illegal arms or saw them smuggled into the camp. He only heard about them. Pond was smart. He knew that no matter how quiet, how covert, a militia is, it always runs the risk of being penetrated by undercover operatives. So he saved the real training for a select cadre of warriors. Everyone else got some bullshit weekend warrior boot camp. Until Mad Dog signed off on them personally, most trained with single-shot Uzi carbines and 9 mm Berettas. No one saw automatic weapons or anything else that might raise an eyebrow, until he agreed to it."

"And Roth hadn't earned that level of trust," Blancanales stated.

"Apparently not. He'd only been in there a few months. Pond wasn't the type to fast-track anyone."

"Imagine," Blancanales said, grinning, "a homicidal maniac with trust issues. No offense, Carl."

"According to a hostage Striker rescued in Afghanistan, she, Pond and some other men involved in this once worked for the CIA. They were part of an elite team called Thunder Hawk."

"Thunder Hawk? Nice name," Lyons groused. "If you're a damn comic-book character."

Price's lips tightened as she apparently fought back a smile. "They did lots of wet work, primarily overseas. Kind of like a poor man's Stony Man Farm, actually. Unfortunately these folks didn't have quite the same compunctions against taking innocent lives as we did, so the CIA disbanded them."

"Good riddance," Lyons said. "So is their nasty nature what's got your and Hal's shorts in a bunch?"

"Not exactly. Remember James Lee?"

"Former CIA director," Schwarz offered.

"He was murdered in Pakistan," Price said.

"Right, the papers, television and radio said it was the work of Islamic extremists," Schwarz said.

"They were wrong—at least partially so," Price stated. "The same woman who told us about Thunder Hawk identified another former team member at the murder scene, a man named Jon Stone."

Schwarz smoothed his mustache with his thumb and fingertips. Thought lines on his forehead deepened. "Not a coincidence," he said. "Can't be."

Price nodded in agreement. "Were pretty sure of that, too. Striker is in Salt Lake City right now with another agent. They killed Stone, but a search of his apartment turned up a card belonging to a Mohammed Nasrallah."

"And he's who?" Blancanales asked.

"I'm getting to that," Price said. "He's a high-level executive with Helpers Alliance International, an aid organization."

"Stone doesn't sound like the charitable type."

"He's not. But apparently the organization is charitable to him. Once we had the name, it was easy work for Aaron to background the organization, profile its executives and track its financial comings and goings."

"Let me guess—Stone was feeding at the trough," the Latino said.

"Right. And, not coincidentally, we believe, the same organization was dumping money into Mad Dog's coffers. Last week alone, it wired $5 million through various shell entities into a front business that Mad Dog uses to launder money for his militia work. And those were just the ones Aaron could decipher. There could be more."

Lyons snickered. "Get out, a militia with a front business."

"A bank, no less."

Lyons knew the surprise registered on his face. "Wow. So why do it? Give them money, I mean?"

"We're not sure," Price replied. "The militia group espouses lots of anti-Semitic claptrap. And the Alliance gets its share of anonymous donations from the Middle East and some Arab-Americans, all with clean records, but radical anti-Israel views. Treasury's been watching the Alliance, the charitable group, for years, but it has managed to stay within the bounds of legal behavior. So that's all Treasury can do—watch."

Lyons flashed a humorless smile. "I assume we're not being sent in to watch these guys."

"You three will concentrate on the militia, not the charity. Aaron did some first-rate hacking and got us some leads. I guess Pond sometimes uses calling cards to pay for his long-distance calls. Couple of months back, he got sloppy and used a credit card issued to one of his old aliases from some convenience store somewhere. It was a common name, Smith or something, so he probably figured he was safe. But the Company got wind of it and logged the calling-card numbers."

Lyons yawned. "Fascinating. And the point is?"

Price's expression hardened for a minute. She turned, opened her mouth to reply, but Blancanales cut her off. "Please, Barb, you're straining Carl's gnat-size attention span. Smaller words might help, too."

A grin twitched at the corners of her mouth. "He used one of those cards today. From a hotel in Enoch, Utah."

"Which, if I remember my geography, is near the Dixie Forest," Schwarz said.

"Exactly."

"I take it we're heading to Enoch, then," Lyons said.

"Next flight out," Price stated.

"Which is when?"

"Immediately."

Enoch, Utah

SEVERAL HOURS LATER Carl Lyons scowled as he watched the one-story motel from across the street. Judging by the single car, a rusted Chevrolet Impala, parked outside the motel, there were plenty of empty rooms, which meant the militia members had already hit the highway. He shoved a fast-food biscuit stuffed with cheese, eggs and sausage into his mouth, chewed, swallowed hard, and tore off another piece with his teeth.

"Ironman, my friend, you are one unhappy-looking guy."

Lyons cast his gaze in Blancanales's direction. The Latino was grinning, enjoying his partner's short fuse, as usual. Lyons tried to show his displeasure by scowling, but his full mouth made it difficult. He grunted instead.

"That's the understatement of the damn century," he said. "I feel like we're pissing into a gale-force wind here, sitting on our duffs, gawking at this damn fleabag. We ought to be kicking down doors for pity's sake."

Blancanales looked over his shoulder at Schwarz, who also was smiling. Lyons steeled himself for the next salvo of sarcasm about to erupt in his direction.

"Someone's getting cranky," Blancanales said to Schwarz.

"Hey, give the guy some credit," the electronics genius replied. "It's been a whole hour. I expected him to crack fifty-five minutes ago."

Lyons wadded up the fast-food wrapper, threw it in to Blancanales's face. Throwing his hands up to shield himself, Blancanales laughed, which frosted Lyons even more. Wiping the biscuit grease on a napkin, Lyons turned his attention back to the motel.

"We've waited long enough. That's all I'm saying. I think the only people left here are a couple of hookers sitting in the coffee shop."

"You see hookers?"

Lyons rolled his eyes. "I was a cop, remember?'

With a deep, audible exhale, he popped open the door, stepped onto the asphalt and unbuttoned his sheepskin coat, making sure his weaponry remained in reach. His favorite .357 Magnum Colt Python rode on his right hip in fast-draw leather. He also carried twin 9 mm SIG-Sauer P-226 pistols in a double shoulder rig. The weight in his front pockets—a collection of speed loaders and spare magazines—caused the sheepskin to pull tight as it fell below his hips.

"Hey," Schwarz called, "where the hell are you going?"

"I'm doing a little recon work."

Blancanales climbed out of the car. "I'll go, too. You behave better with a babysitter."

Rounding the car, Blancanales gave Lyons a pat on the back. For all their ribbing, the men were good friends, comrades who'd fought side by side and spilled blood for the same causes. Each man respected the other and, if necessary, would die for them.

Lyons hoped today wasn't that day.

Walking along the length of the motel, Lyons peered into the windows. In almost all of them, he found the curtains drawn back, exposing empty rooms with beds unmade and white towels piled on the carpet. He saw no maid cart anywhere, which didn't surprise him at all.

"Empty," he said.

"Every last one," Blancanales agreed.

"Talk to the manager?"

"Sounds like a plan."

Approaching the main office, Blancanales pushed open the glass door, ushered Lyons inside with a sweep of his arm. The big ex-cop moved inside. As he did, he noticed that Blancanales was sweeping his gaze over the parking lot, watching their backs. Before he stepped inside, the Latino touched the brim of his baseball cap, a signal to Schwarz that all was okay.

The room stank of cooking grease, cigarette smoke and too sweet perfume. A young woman, pretty, wearing low-rider jeans and a too small T-shirt, smiled at the men as they entered. Lyons indulged in an appreciative look before reminding himself she was half his age.

"Can I help you?" she asked.

Lyons pulled a fake Justice Department ID from his wallet, flashed it quickly at the young woman before jamming it back into his pocket. Blancanales did likewise. The young woman's eyes widened.

"We're federal agents, ma'am," Lyons said. "We need to ask some questions."

"Am I in trouble?" the young woman asked, a slight tremor in her voice.

Blancanales grinned disarmingly at her. Lyons knew the handsome Latino was more skilled at putting people at ease, particularly women. The guy exuded charm and charisma that eluded Lyons.

"Should you be in trouble?" Blancanales asked, his tone light.

"No, of course not," she said. Her shoulders relaxed visibly and her smile returned, lips parting slightly, Lyons noticed. "Though I'm not adverse to trouble, the good kind, I mean."

Jesus! Lyons thought. His stomach roiled and his impatience rose up from within like a Cobra coiling to strike. He cleared his throat, turned to Blancanales.

"Questions," he said.

Blancanales gave him a sour look, but nodded. He returned his attention to the young woman, who seemed unfazed by Lyons's behavior.

"What's your name, ma'am?" Blancanales asked.

"Amanda. Amanda Cornett."

"Amanda, we're looking for someone," Blancanales said. "Several someones, in fact." He paused until the girl prompted him with a nod. "You had a group of men stay here last night."

"Yes?"

"Are any of them still here?"

She shook her head. "We're completely empty. They checked out this morning, every last one of them."

"All at the same time?"

She nodded. "Yeah. They left about 5:00 a.m., one right after the other, just like a convoy or something."

"Did you see them leave?"

"Yeah, I was here. I work the night shift. I usually get off about 7:00 a.m., but I'm picking up extra shifts right now. I've got a baby to support. The father—he's not my husband—is a jerk. He took off, left me with the baby. He told me he loved me, you know, and then—"

"So you're working a double shift? You must be exhausted."

Her eyes brightened a bit. "I am. These double shifts are a killer, you know. Sometimes I'll lock up the office, sneak off to one of the rooms and take a nap." She gave Blancanales a conspiratorial wink. "That's our little secret, right? I don't want that in any of your reports, okay?"

Cornett laughed and Blancanales fell right in with her. Lyons clamped his jaws together so hard, he thought the bones might crack.

"I understand you get tired," Blancanales said. "Hey, you're a working girl. I'd be flat on my ass if I had your schedule. You weren't taking a nap when they left, were you? I mean, you did see them leave, right?"

Nodding vigorously, she said, "Oh, of course I did. I was

in here, working. Otherwise I couldn't have checked them out of their rooms. Besides, you know, when you have a six-month-old, you learn to watch things very closely. Even when you're asleep."

More laughter sounded. Lyons's hands balled into fists. Pulling in his lips, he trapped them between his teeth, putting his acid tongue on ice. Blancanales's methods weren't his, but they worked. Experience told him so. He needed to stay patient, he really did.

But ten seconds later, when she started to ask Blancanales whether he had children and where he lived, Lyons thought he might have a stroke.

"Ma'am," Lyons said, "how did they pay for their rooms? Credit card? Cash? Debit card?"

"Credit card," Cornett replied, her smile dimming. Her look hardened and her forehead creased slightly. "Just what did you say these guys did, anyway?"

Lyons hesitated for a moment as he tried to conjure up a plausible lie. Blancanales beat him to it.

"Drugs," Blancanales said. "Major, major drug dealers."

"Drugs? You're kidding," she said, shuddering. "If I'd known that, I would have contacted the police."

"Of course you would have," Blancanales said soothingly.

Weary of all the daytime talk-show coddling, Lyons pressed his line of questioning. "About the credit cards, do you have paper copies, or do you run it through an electronic reader?"

"Electronic reader."

"I want the merchant's receipts for anyone signing for those rooms. And I want them now."

"I don't know," she said, the corners of her mouth turning back into a frown. "Don't you need a search warrant or something for that?"

"I don't need a search warrant for anything," Lyons said, his face flushing red. "So get off your—"

Blancanales interrupted. "Agent Irons wants to assure you that a search warrant isn't needed in this instance. You could just show us the information. Of course, if it makes you feel better, we could get the proper paperwork. But only if it makes you feel better. My advice? Why hassle yourself? I mean, as it stands, you show us the receipts, we look at them, and we're gone. If we request a search warrant, we have to go see a judge, swear out affidavits, bring in attorneys, the whole nine yards. Who knows? The judge might even want to see you."

The woman gave Blancanales a sympathetic look. "Gosh, that's a big headache just to look at a few pieces of paper. I'd hate to put you through all that. Besides, if a judge wanted to talk to me, well, I just can't afford to miss work."

"You've got bills to pay," he said.

She beamed. "You really understand my situation, don't you?"

"Absolutely."

Turning back to the computer, the woman hummed while punching a few computer keys. "Just a second." She disappeared into a back room. A moment later Lyons heard the slap of plastic on plastic, followed by a mechanical thrumming. The woman returned, arms crossed over her chest, a pile of papers held tightly to her, like a schoolgirl carrying her books.

She handed them to Blancanales, who took them without looking at them. He tucked the documents under his arm.

"Thanks very much," he said. "By the way, what kinds of guests were they?"

"Male."

"No, I mean were they quiet, rowdy, mean, nice—what?"

"Oh, they were quiet," she said. "Bobby—he owns the

place, you know—he doesn't let people pull crap. Not like a lot of places do, anyway. If people get rowdy, we're supposed to call the police. Or we call Bobby. He's a big guy, mean as hell if you cross him. He runs a tight ship. If he had his way, he wouldn't even let guests bring in alcohol."

"Lots of scruples for a guy who rents rooms by the hour," Lyons muttered.

"He's nicer than you," she shot back.

"Big accomplishment," Lyons said, shrugging.

Blancanales interrupted. "Was there anything else that you recall? Anything that struck you as odd?"

She screwed up her face as she considered the question. "They had a lot of luggage. I mean, lots. But they didn't have suitcases. They carried everything in duffel bags, like my brother does when he comes home on leave. He's in the Army. Were you ever in the Army? You look like you might have been."

"A while back," Blancanales said, urging her on with a gentle nod. "What else do you remember?"

"They had these long, rectangular boxes."

"Any writing on the boxes? Logos?"

"No. It just had black bars where words might have been, like maybe they were covering up the lettering. And they acted strange about it. I mean, really strange."

"How so?"

"They carried them all into their rooms, whereas most people would have left them in the car. And they were really sneaky about it, too. While they were unloading them, one of the guys came in and talked to me. Kept asking me questions about my baby and stuff." She jerked a thumb over her shoulder, directing them to an unframed picture propped against a coffee cup. A baby dressed in pink pajamas, her head topped with honey-blond hair smiled up from the picture.

"After a while," she continued, "I got the feeling he wasn't really interested in what I was saying. It was more like he was pretending to be interested. You know what I mean?"

"I sure as hell do!" Lyons said.

"Anyway," she said, "as soon as they hauled everything in, the guy disappeared. Come to think of it, he said something about knowing Bobby, like maybe that was supposed to intimidate me."

"Did it?"

She shrugged. "A little. Like I said, he has a mean temper."

"What's Bobby's last name?" Blancanales asked. "Just for my records, of course."

"Bobby Shepherd. He lives in town. He's got a nice wife and he works hard. This is just a sideline business for him, you know."

"Really?"

"Sure. He works for Paladin Corp., it's that defense company. They make all kinds of secret stuff that no one talks about. They have a shipping center and a bunch of offices on the outskirts of town. I asked Bobby once what they make. He said he could tell me, but he'd have to kill me."

"He was kidding, then."

"Yes," she replied, her voice unsure. "You're sure he's not in trouble?"

"Of course."

That seemed to relieve her a bit. Lyons's anger churned around in his stomach. The longer they talked about Bobby Shepherd, the more afraid she seemed to become. Sure, she was a royal pain in the ass. But no one should have to put up with that kind of crap, especially when they had a kid to feed.

A lull in the conversation had settled. Blancanales broke it by clapping his hands together once. He extended one to the young woman, gave her a warm smile. She shook hands with both men, but let her gaze linger on Blancanales.

A few moments later the men were back outside, each scanning the area for possible enemies, as much out of habit as necessity. Lyons couldn't get that damn baby's face off his mind.

"Maybe we ought to go see Bobby Shepherd," Blancanales said. "The girl said he might know the guests."

"This time," Lyons replied, "I do the damn talking. No more of this coddling crap."

"Hey, cut me a break. She's a sweet kid."

"Silence is golden," Lyons said. "She ought to learn that."

"Carl, you are one crabby dude. You know that, amigo?"

"Yeah. I'm an ass, but I kind of like it that way."

"Such self-awareness. It's an inspiration to us all."

"YEAH?"

"Bobby? This is Amanda. Amanda Cornett at the motel."

"What?"

"I need to tell you something. A couple of federal agents stopped by here this morning. They asked me some questions about those guys who stayed here this week."

Cornett held the phone receiver a few inches from her ear, chewed on her lower lip as she waited for his reply. His voice, a cold, heartless rasp, made her feel queasy. She knew the imminent torrent of verbal abuse would leave her feeling even worse.

She knew it was coming. It always did. Here she was, the mother of his child, not one he claimed, but his child, nonetheless, and all she got was abuse. Abuse and a shitty job that barely paid minimum wage. She hadn't wanted to call, but she'd been unable to stop herself. She knew he'd find out; he always did. Whether it was flirting with a man or spending money, he knew about it.

"What'd you tell them?"

"Nothing. Not a blessed thing."

"Did you mention my name?"

"No. Never."

"You better not be lying to me. You remember what happened the last time you lied?"

"Yes, I remember." She shuddered as a phantom ache radiated from her ribs, her stomach, her throat, all the places he'd hit, kicked or squeezed.

"If I find out different," he said. "We're going to have a talk. You and me. Understand?

"What did they look like?"

She told him. He slammed the phone in her ear and she winced. Her lips quivering, she put her head in her hands and began crying uncontrollably. She hoped that someday the bastard would get his, particularly before she got hers.

BOBBY SHEPHERD'S FACE glowed red as he stared at the phone. Stupid bitch! Her and her damn mouth. She was going to bring the whole thing crashing down around them. And then everyone would look at him, blame him for the failure. Not with the people he'd fallen in with. It was a group of killers, every last damn one of them, and he had no desire to end up in a desert somewhere, dead, all just because that little whore couldn't keep her mouth shut.

He made another quick call and ended it within thirty seconds. Opening his desk drawer, he reached inside and pulled out a pearl-handled Smith & Wesson .38-caliber revolver. The nickel-plated beauty was wrapped in a leather snap-draw holster, scratched and scarred from years of use, first by his father, then by him.

Pond and the others laughed at the weapon. They called it a lady's gun. But it had been a gift from Shepherd's daddy, God rest his soul, and Shepherd was proud of it.

Drawing the gun, he stared at it. He broke open the cylinder and emptied the shells into his hand, jammed them in his pocket. He reached into the lap drawer of his desk and extracted a box of hollowpoint shells. Setting the box and palming six rounds, he loaded them into the weapon and closed it with a flick of the wrist.

The way he saw it, the girl probably was telling the truth. He figured she was too damn stupid and scared to lie about something so serious. But he also knew he couldn't just ignore her, hope she kept her damn mouth shut. Once things went down, every alphabet-soup federal agency with investigative powers would be hunting for answers. And, if the feds sensed she knew even a little bit, they'd be back pumping her for information. One slip of the tongue and he'd find himself up to his neck in trouble.

Hell, he already could be in trouble.

All because he couldn't keep it in his pants.

With a grunt, he came to his feet, threw back his shoulders and strode to the coatrack. To hell with it, he decided. He wasn't going to burn for treason just because that little whore couldn't keep her damn mouth shut. Daddy always told him that a man had to protect his family, no matter what. As far as Shepherd was concerned, that included waxing a mouthy little slut who didn't know when to shut her mouth.

So he had his why and the how was even easier. When he'd first knocked her up, the girl had got all teary-eyed and begged him to marry her. He'd held off as long as he could to keep the sex coming, but when she'd finally demanded an answer, he'd told her no. To mollify her, he gave her a job at the motel and slid her a couple hundred bucks under the table every month, besides, all without his wife's knowledge, of course.

He hadn't paid a lot of attention to her likes and dislikes. However, he had realized one thing about her: she was a hopeless romantic, blinded by some fantasy that someone might love and take care of her.

That had rendered her an easy target the first time. It'd be just as easy today. He shook his head dismissively and marveled at his luck.

Her weakness would get him exactly what he wanted. He'd take her somewhere isolated under the pretext of talking things through. When they were alone, he'd put one through her head, dump her in a ravine and get on with life. Maybe he'd even take one last turn with her first, before he waxed her. Hell, he'd do it afterward for that matter, just for a little change of pace.

He grinned at the thought. You are one sick bastard, Shepherd, he told himself as his posture straightened a little.

And to hell with the baby. She was an accident, a bastard child and a drain on his hard-earned money. He'd made plenty of it, running Paladin's warehouse, especially when he fudged the inventory and made covert weapons sales to psychos like Pond and Stone and that damn Arab they'd been palling around with.

Clutching the lapels in his big hands, he tugged hard to bring the collar from his beefy neck. He made a show of rolling his head, like a boxer warming up for a prize match. Reaching for the knob, he cut his grasp short when it turned on its own. Jamming his hand inside his jacket, he gripped the revolver but didn't draw it. If this was the boys from the Justice Department, and they wanted to play rough, he'd show them just how lethal he could be.

CHAPTER NINETEEN

Lyons, Blancanales and Schwarz walked through the pair of glass doors to Paladin's offices and hurried to the guard station in the main lobby.

Blancanales was the first to reach the desk, a tall semicircle, its interior stuffed with phones, monitor screens. A pair of walkie-talkies jutted from a battery charger, emitting occasional radio traffic. Blancanales slammed his fake Justice Department ID on the desktop, let the guy bend to study it. Lyons and Schwarz also held their IDs out for scrutiny as they scanned the area.

During the ride over Blancanales had contacted Aaron Kurtzman and gotten the basics on Bobby Shepherd. A former college football player, the guy had a master's in business administration and a high-level security clearance. News of the latter had been a mixed bag for Able Team. It had allowed them access to Shepherd's file, which included vital statistics and a recent photo, all downloaded by the Farm into Schwarz's laptop. At the same time, it also meant that the guy had access to any weapons that came through the local Paladin warehouse before they were distributed to American,

Mexican, Canadian and European military bases. If he really was associated with Pond and the others, such access was a nightmare waiting to happen.

A fleeting glance at his comrades told Blancanales that they shared his apprehension. Though they hadn't completed the puzzle, their findings, along with those of Striker and Stony Man Farm, painted a damn bleak picture. From the motel clerk's description of the militia's so-called luggage, it sounded as if the militiamen were carrying crated weapons, big ones, too. If they were and Shepherd was in tight with them, and handing out weapons, it was a safe bet that the bad guys were capable of unleashing hell.

Blancanales had a sixth sense when it came to dealing with people. Almost inexplicably, he knew how to approach damn near every person before they uttered a word or acted in a telling way. The former Black Beret also was a master negotiator and diplomat, hence the nickname Politician.

With the motel clerk, he sensed a vulnerability best exploited with gentleness. His gut told him the guard was a bulldog and in need of a slap on the nose.

"Justice Department, in case you can't read," Blancanales said. "We're looking for Bobby Shepherd."

"Do you have an appointment?"

Blancanales nodded toward his ID. "I just gave you my appointment. Now tell me where I can find him."

The guard reached for the phone. "I'll call him."

Blancanales's hand darted out, fingers encircling the guard's wrist before the man could grasp the telephone receiver.

"If I wanted you to call him, I would have asked. Now we can do this one of two ways. You either direct us to Mr. Shepherd, or you harass us and force my hand. If you do the latter, I guaran-damn-tee you won't like the results. By lunch I'll have this place crawling with people like me. We'll be seizing records. Interrogating everyone from the president down to the janitor. Holding press conferences. And it'll all be on you."

Scowling, the guy pondered Blancanales's words. Picking up his ID, he studied it for a few seconds, even matching the picture with the face of the man in front of him. Lyons and Schwarz tossed their IDs and waited while he repeated the process.

"Office 313," the guard said. "Elevators are down the hall and to the right."

Collecting their IDs, the Able Team warriors caught the elevator and rode it up one flight. Stopping on the second floor, Blancanales stayed in the car while Lyons and Schwarz exited and hurried for the stairs. Blancanales wasn't sure whether the guard would call Shepherd's office to warn him of their impending arrival, if for no other reason than to exert some power and control over the situation. But, if they faced an ambush, he didn't want Able Team clustered together, ready to be picked off with the single sweep of a submachine gun. They'd hit the guy from several points.

Blancanales carried a pair of Beretta 93-Rs in a double shoulder rig underneath a jacket custom tailored to hide such a setup. As the elevator slid into place, he unbuttoned his trench coat and his suit jacket. Drawing one of the Berettas, he slipped it into his coat pocket and kept it in his grip. If necessary, he'd shoot through the trenchcoat, but he didn't want to create a panic by waving a gun around.

As he stepped from the elevator, a well-coiffed young man who apparently bathed in designer cologne, and a pretty brunette in a red business suit brushed past him. As the elevator doors closed behind him, he looked left, then right, but saw no one else in the corridor. A brass plaque on the wall indicated that rooms 312 through 330 were to his right. Moving quickly down the hall, he came to room 313, where he heard a man's voice, muffled by the door. The voice was loud and agitated, but, despite the volume, Blancanales could only discern a few words, Amanda's name among them.

Shoe leather squeaked from behind and he whirled toward the noise. He caught Lyons and Schwarz proceeding down the hallway toward him. Like him, both men had their weapons in reach, but kept out of sight.

Blancanales heard a phone receiver slam into its cradle. Footfalls thudded against the floor, growing louder with each passing instant. Grabbing the door lever, he pressed it down, even as he shoved his body weight against the door. Lyons and Gadgets were at his back as he went in.

According to records supplied by Kurtzman, Shepherd had been a hell of an athlete in his youth. In an instant Blancanales was able to size the guy up. He still had the thick neck, the meaty shoulders, arms and legs of a college athlete. But he had gone soft around the middle, looking as though someone had inserted a sack of beach balls where his stomach should be.

Regardless, the guy was big and angry.

And he was bringing a silver revolver into play.

Blancanales was on him in a second. He grabbed the man's wrist, pinned it to his chest with a steely grip, stopping the weapon from joining the fray. He hated getting so close, especially considering the size advantage the other man enjoyed. He had little choice. He needed to keep the gun out of the equation, at least until he could bring his own to bear, show his opponent who was in charge. They needed some answers, which meant they needed to bring this guy down but keep him alive. And, perhaps more important, they didn't want the risk or exposure that a shootout might bring.

Sensing a shift in the big man's weight, Blancanales swiveled his hip, used it to stop the knee driving toward his groin. His leg fell numb, but he continued to press his attack. He heard the door slam from behind. Drawing the Beretta, he shoved it upward until the barrel pressed into the soft flesh of the man's neck. In the same instant Lyons's Colt Python and Schwarz's Desert Eagle came into view. The guy's body went slack and he let Lyons wrest the pistol from his grip. Lyons handed the weapon to Schwarz, who studied it for a moment before slipping it into his coat.

"Seems like you ought to wear a dress, if you're going to carry something like this," he said.

Scarlet splotches spread over the man's cheeks, betraying his rage, but he said nothing.

Lyons reached around, grabbed Shepherd by the collar and shoved him into a nearby couch. The big man collided with the furniture, knocking it back against the wall and causing a pair of framed college degrees to shake. With surprising speed, the guy hit the couch, rolled and sprang up, a big fist cocked back and ready to strike. Lyons met the attack with a side snap-kick that stopped the guy in midlunge, sent him sprawling back on the couch. This time, the man remained still, except for his chest, which expanded and contracted like an accordion as rage and exertion cut his breath short.

The feeling had returned to Blancanales's hip. He perched himself on a corner of Shepherd's desk, crossed his arms over his chest and pinned the guy under his gaze.

"We're with the Justice Department, Mr. Shepherd," he said. "We need to ask you about your guests at the hotel and the crates they were carrying."

"Go to hell," Shepherd replied. "I've got rights. I want my goddamn lawyer. And I want him now! Until then, I don't have to say shit."

"You make a good argument. But it's flawed."

Shepherd cast Blancanales a wary look. "What are you talking about?"

"See, a lot of federal agents get hung up on procedural stuff like Miranda rights and that crap. We don't. It slows us down too much. We need to move fast, for reasons I think you already understand."

Lyons pulled a switchblade from his pocket and clicked it open. "What he's trying to say is, we don't give two shits about the Fourth Amendment, the Bill of Rights or any of that other stuff. Now, either you cough up some information or the next thing you'll be hearing is your last rights."

The big man studied Lyons's face for several tense moments, obviously trying to gauge his sincerity. Apparently somewhere in Lyons's hard stare, he got his answer. Staring down at his lap, he muttered, "Okay, tell me what you jerks want to know."

LATER, BLANCANALES and Schwarz, each gripping their prisoner by the arm, led Shepherd from his office to the lobby, while Lyons walked point. All three men wore grim expressions as they individually mulled the information they'd just heard. Shepherd had verbally drawn for them a blueprint for hell, a series of events slated to happen that even in the best-case scenario could leave hundreds dead and destroy America's credibility on the world stage.

Not a squeamish man, Lyons nonetheless found himself suppressing a shudder as he considered the worst-case scenario: a world divided with thousands, perhaps tens of thousands, dead, and a yawning gap opened between America and the Middle East.

As they moved through the lobby, the same baby-pink guard stepped into their path, told them they needed to fill out the appropriate paperwork before they exited the grounds. His patience worn thin, Blancanales opened his mouth, ready to unload on the guy.

He shouldn't have bothered. Lyons handled it for him.

"Look, we've got a national security situation on our hands. A very dangerous one, and one that could have been prevented if you'd been doing your damn job," said the former cop. As he spoke, he jabbed a finger into the man's chest every few words for emphasis. "Either get the hell out of my way or I'll personally bust you as an accomplice. I'll have the judge set the bail so damn high that Ross Perot couldn't pay it. Then you'll get to spend the next twenty years to life in a max-security pen, bent like a divining rod over an aquifer. Do I make myself clear?"

"Crystal," the guard said.

The men stepped into the late-morning sun and hurried to the parking lot. Stuffing Shepherd into the back seat, Schwarz climbed in beside him and shut the door. Lyons slid into the driver's seat while Blancanales rode shotgun.

As they drove, Blancanales called ahead to the local police department, and, using their Justice Department authority, got permission to incarcerate Shepherd until the FBI or Marshal's service could come pick him up. Knowing what they did, the three comrades had agreed to lose Shepherd as quickly as possible so they could move into action.

Blancanales glanced at Lyons, saw concern etched on his features, knuckles white as he held the steering wheel in a death grip. A green traffic light beckoned them into the intersection and Lyons guided the vehicle through.

A silver flash winked in Blancanales's peripheral vision. Turning, he first saw a chrome bumper, followed quickly by the outline of a white pickup as it lurched into the intersection, carving out a path toward the car. Before Blancanales could shout a warning, the truck slammed into their rental's passenger's side rear panel. The force thrust the car, tires screeching against asphalt, into a 180-degree. Before Lyons could regain control of the vehicle, a second truck rocketed from the opposite direction, landing another strike on the car's back end that sent it spinning across the intersection. Steel ground against steel as the rental slammed into a parked car, pinning Shepherd's door shut. Lyons mashed the accelerator to the floor but found the car unresponsive.

"Shit!" he said through clenched teeth. "Out! Go!"

Even as Able Team responded to the sudden onslaught, a hit squad of six men disgorged from the twin trucks. The gunners, all armed, went for broke, unloading automatic weapons and big-bore pistols into the vehicle. Relentless salvos of lead pierced the windshield, eroding the safety glass like loose dirt struck by a fire hose. More rounds flattened the tires, drilled through the grille. The engine block bore the brunt of the attack, stopping rounds before they could penetrate the car's interior.

Blancanales grasped the door handle, yanked up on it and threw himself against the car door. As his weight carried him through the door, he reflexively thrust his hands out to break his fall. He felt stones and broken glass shred the flesh of his palms as he slid to a stop, the crown of his head coming to within an inch of smacking into a car bumper.

A heartbeat later, the Stony Man warrior got up onto one knee, the twin Berettas clutched in his hands as he acquired a target. He caught a pair of gunners crossing the road in long strides. One man cut loose with an Uzi. The weapon spit a relentless stream of 9 mm Parabellum rounds that scorched the air around Blancanales before slamming into concrete sidewalks and steel lampposts.

Raising the Beretta in his right hand, he squeezed off a single shot, drilling a round into the man's forehead. The bullet exploded from the rear of the man's skull, leaving a soft-ball-size exit wound in its wake. The force caused the man to pitch backward.

Prodded by instinct, Blancanales wheeled his upper torso to the two-o'clock position. He spotted the second gunner threading between abandoned cars, apparently trying to strike the Latino's rear flank. Raising the Beretta, he caught a view of the man's midsection through car windows. Locking the Beretta's muzzle on the running man, Blancanales squeezed off two more shots. The bullets pounded through the windows before drilling into the thug's midsection, the force spinning him and knocking his bloodied torso against an automobile.

Blancanales heard a pistol's sharp report to his left. Turning, he saw Lyons a dozen or so yards away, crouched behind the nose of an abandoned black Cadillac. Like Blancanales, the blond warrior was selecting his shots carefully. The Python spit flame and smoke as Lyons capped off a second round. The bullet cored through a shotgun-wielding thug who'd broken cover so he could close the distance between himself and Lyons. The bullet punched into the man's nose, snapped his head back and knocked him backward.

A third figure sprinted from a recessed doorway. Sweeping his Uzi in a wide arc, the guy laid down a barrage of fire that drove Blancanales and Lyons to ground. Blancanales muttered a curse as the shooter drained an entire clip of ammunition, unleashing an unforgiving salvo that shattered storefront windows and careened off brick.

As quickly as it began, the Uzi's lethal onslaught ended. Blancanales knew that the Israeli-made SMG firing wide open burned through a clip in about three seconds. He guessed that the gunner had done just that and was reloading, preparing to hammer them with renewed fury.

Footfalls struck the concrete, warning Blancanales of an attack. He started to pop up from behind the car so he could grab a quick look. A hard rain of lead drove him back under cover.

Before he could counterattack, the Latino heard twin thunderclaps explode from across the street, followed by the dull thudding of bodies hitting the pavement. Within an instant, the gunfire hammering his position had stopped.

Blancanales chanced a look around the car's front bumper, saw Schwarz across the street, Desert Eagle extended in both hands, smoke rolling from the barrel. Blancanales flashed him a thumbs-up before the men turned their attention back to the battle at hand. Schwarz apparently had run down the street, crossed it and caught the gunners from behind by sneaking through an alley or a business.

In the distance, Blancanales heard the wail of sirens, and cursed. The law's impending arrival created more distraction and complication for the trio of warriors as they finished their work. Though he didn't doubt the approaching officers' skills, he didn't want the local police on the firing line any more than he did other noncombatants. They also didn't have time to be detained by the police and, if taken into custody, would have to rely on Washington to bail them out.

If what Shepherd said was true, they had much bigger worries than a few low-level gunners stupid enough to risk an attack in the open.

Despite the cold, he felt heat building up under his coat as his body reacted to the stress of combat. To gain flexibility, he slipped off his trench coat and suit jacket. Both had been stripped of any identifying markers, including brand tags.

The gunfire lessened and Blancanales chanced a look around the car's front end. He saw one man closing in on him while another laid down cover fire. Snap-aiming the Beretta, he fired two shots, cored both through the man's side. The one-two punch of hollowpoint and hardball ammunition pummeled the man's rib cage and brought him to a violent halt as the life drained from his face. He folded to the ground, a bloodied heap.

A thug came up from behind a Honda, a big-bore revolver clasped in both hands, arms resting on the car's hood for support. Blancanales heard the roar of Lyons's Colt Python and saw the enemy gunner go down as the Magnum slug tunneled through the man's head, taking part of the skull with it. A flash of red prompted Blancanales to turn. He caught another thug, his body wrapped in a crimson ski jacket, closing in, trying to acquire a target with his auto-loading pistol.

The man fired on the run, the impact of his footsteps throwing off his aim. The bullet sizzled just past Blancanales's ear even as he squeezed off two rounds with the Beretta. The bullets slammed into the man's rib cage, killing him instantly.

The men of Able Team scoured the area for more threats, but found none. Rubber screeched against asphalt as police cars swept into the area from different directions. Even as the officers closed in, guns drawn, Blancanales, Schwarz and Lyons holstered their weapons and raised their hands into the air.

CHAPTER TWENTY

After his morning break, Brognola ducked into his room. Just moments before the meeting adjourned, he'd received a page from Barbara Price, and he wanted to return it immediately. Upon entering the small room, he loosened his necktie and checked out his surroundings. The place definitely had a postapocalyptic coldness about it. He found nothing but a bed, a dresser, a desk, a couple of chairs and small tables. A secure phone, a blotter and a lamp topped the desk. Not even a damn coffeepot, he thought mournfully.

Dropping into the chair, he picked up the phone receiver and dialed a number. The call passed through a series of cutouts before Stony Man's mission controller answered on the other end. The pair exchanged greetings and got down to business.

"Striker called from the field," Price said. "He nailed James Lee's killer and it wasn't al-Shoud, at least not directly. It was an American and Striker chased the guy from Pakistan to Paraguay all the way back to the States. Salt Lake City, in fact."

The guy was in Utah? The uneasy feeling returned. Brognola didn't believe in coincidences.

"Tell me what you know," the big Fed stated.

"The dead guy is former CIA."

"Okay," he said, grinding his teeth.

"It gets worse."

"Doesn't it always? Lay it on me."

She told Brognola about the slain federal agent, the Islamic charity funneling money to Stone and Pond, the two cryptic phone calls by Nasrallah and the attempt to assassinate Bolan and Doyle.

"Did Striker nab Nasrallah?"

"Negative," she replied. "He was too busy dodging bullets to snag the guy."

"Nasrallah's gone?"

"Right. A commercial helicopter picked him up from the rooftop, flew him to parts unknown. By the time the police caught up with the craft, Nasrallah was gone. Pilot probably took it down in a parking lot or field somewhere, dumped Nasrallah and flew to the nearest airport."

"You guys working the pilot?"

"Striker is."

Brognola allowed himself a grim smile. "That poor bastard's toast. He'll probably cop to being Jack the Ripper by the time Striker finishes with him."

"Most likely," Price replied. "Hal, with all this stuff going down, do you think it's wise for the summit to continue? You've got a lot of players concentrated in a small spot. Maybe it'd be best to shut things down, just in case."

"Point noted," Brognola said. "I'll raise it up the flagpole and see if the Man salutes. But I'm not sure he will. So far, all we have is circumstantial evidence and no direct links to this summit. He may be reluctant to push the panic button."

"Are you sure that's wise?"

"No," Brognola said honestly.

Price was hardly passive, but she chose her battles carefully. That she had reservations about his approach gave him pause. And he couldn't blame her; he also had a bad feeling he couldn't shake. But feelings weren't facts, particularly in politics, and the President would want some hard evidence before shutting down such critical talks.

Brognola sensed her apprehension. "I'll make a hard case for closing things down. In the meantime, why don't you put a team of blacksuits on alert? I'll ask the Secret Service guys to send some folks out here, too. We'll lock this place down tight."

"Sounds like a good decision."

"Keep me posted on what Striker learns from the pilot."

"Understood."

"Brognola out." The big Fed set the receiver back on the phone on the desk and rose from his chair. He was already practicing his pitch for the President, knowing it'd be a tough sale. The Man didn't like to show signs of weakness, didn't like to blink against threats. Brognola respected him for it.

But it sure as hell made his job that much harder.

A knock sounded at the door; he crossed the room and opened the door. Khalid Haddad stood outside, the same appeasing smile fixed to his face.

"Mr. Brognola? May I come inside, please?"

"Don't mean to be rude, but I'm a little busy," Brognola said. "I, uh, have some news from the home office that I need to communicate up the chain of command."

A look of concern washed over Haddad's features. His eyes narrowed slightly. His reaction didn't surprise Brognola. After all, the guy was responsible for the prince's security.

"It's nothing serious, I hope."

Brognola shook his head and donned a halfhearted grin. "No. In fact, it's probably nothing at all. Just the usual government hooey. I'm sure you understand."

Haddad nodded. "Of course. We have similar challenges

in the kingdom. If I may press, I do need to speak with you. It involves critical intelligence I just received from home regarding a potential terrorist incident, one that possibly could occur on American soil. It's time-sensitive information."

Brognola ground his teeth and tried to still his impatience. He needed to speak to the President immediately. But the note of urgency in Haddad's voice was unmistakable. The big Fed couldn't turn the guy away without arousing suspicion, which was out of the question. Until they knew more, Brognola didn't want to create a panic.

Besides, the guy's news obviously was important, too. Brognola could spare a couple of minutes, particularly if it meant saving lives.

He nodded toward the room. "Come in," he said.

Haddad entered and Brognola shut the door behind him. The Saudi official ran his eyes over Brognola's room and winked. "I see you have the same lavish accommodations as me," he said.

"You had some information?"

"Of course, please sit down."

"I'll stand."

"Our intelligence services have intercepted cellular phone calls from a known terrorist within our country. He was telling a comrade of a series of synagogue bombings planned for New York. I have sketchy details, but my people can get you more information. They have names of the New York operatives, addresses, everything you could wish."

"Who do we call?"

Haddad gave Brognola a contact. He memorized the name, reached into his jacket and withdrew the mobile phone. He planned to call Price. He'd pass the information to her so she could coordinate an intervention. That'd still give him time to huddle with the President and to discuss security measures for the summit.

He jabbed two numbers. Before he hit a third, a sharp pain exploded at the back of his head. The phone dropped onto the desk as he stumbled forward, reaching out for something to hold on to. As his fingertips grazed the edge of his desk, a second blow came, stronger than the first and Brognola pitched forward, unconscious.

HADDAD TRIED TO REACH OUT and grab the big American before he fell face-first into the floor, but missed. He stared down at the man who lay in a crumpled heap, blood already seeping from broken skin and matting hair against his skull. Haddad glanced at Brognola's desk and saw the phone, revolver and other items that lay there. He pocketed them and returned his attention to the American.

He'd stopped by the room, expecting to ask Brognola to eat lunch with him so they could discuss the United States and, more specifically, Haddad's time there. The fawning gesture was part of a wider effort to deflect suspicion away from him until things began to happen. However, he could tell from the American's demeanor that the man knew something. Maybe he didn't know everything. But he knew enough to pose a potential threat to the plan's laid down by Tariq Riyadh and Jamal Aziz.

If Haddad was right, he'd just preserved what was a very important plan. If not, well, in an hour it wouldn't matter because everyone on the grounds would be dead.

As expected, the steel truncheon had knocked Brognola unconscious. The easy rise and fall of his chest told Haddad he remained alive. He planned to change that, too. One more blow to the head would kill the American and eliminate him as a threat.

With a foot, he shoved Brognola into a space next to the queen-size bed, putting him out of direct line of the doorway.

He stepped toward the body and started to raise the truncheon. The door latch clicked and Haddad's blood froze. He tossed the truncheon onto Brognola's body and turned to the door. A trim young man, black hair plastered in place by styling gel, poked his head in. He gave Haddad a surprised look and ran a cursory glance over the room.

Haddad recognized the young man as a presidential aide named Welch. "Where's Mr. Brognola?" he asked.

"We were talking and he said he had to leave," Haddad stated. "You just missed him."

The aide let out a low whistle. "Our next meeting starts in five minutes. If he isn't there, it's going to be his rump. The President is not going to like this one bit."

Haddad gave the young man a consoling smile. "I'm sure you'll find him."

He'd put a tone of finality into his words and had expected the aide to leave. Instead the younger man stood in the doorway, looking expectantly at Haddad and making him feel self-conscious.

"Yes?" Haddad asked.

"Let's go."

"What?"

"The meeting. C'mon, let's go."

Haddad smiled. "I can find my own way, I assure you."

The young aide shook his head. "Forget it. With all due respect, the President told me to round up any stragglers and get them in there. I'm afraid that includes you."

Haddad started to protest, but stopped himself. The longer the young man lingered, the greater the odds that he'd see Brognola. And, if the young man returned to the meeting and mentioned that he'd seen Haddad alone in Brognola's room, it surely would raise questions. No, it was better that he accompanied the young man now.

He took one last look at Brognola, who lay facedown in a pool of blood. Don't worry, he told himself. By the time this oaf wakes up it will be too late. Far too late.

Salt Lake City, Utah

MOHAMMED NASRALLAH'S pilot sat at the interrogation room table, scratched at its painted surface with a thumbnail. His hands were cuffed in front of him and the chain dragged the tabletop, rattling as the man chipped away at the paint.

Powerful arms crossed over his chest, Bolan stood over the man and stared at him. Doyle was positioned in another corner, puffing on a cigarette and watching the guy who'd been placed in FBI custody.

"Where's Nasrallah?" Bolan asked.

"Gone."

"Gone where?"

"Screw yourself," the man said. "I want a lawyer."

Bolan felt the doomsday numbers falling to zero and he needed to get some information. He stepped to the table, grabbed a file folder from its top and hurled it at the guy. The file fanned open and papers spilled from it, covering the table and falling onto the floor.

"Says in there your name is Wazir Ginzarli, a former Iraqi military pilot. According to the file, you're wanted in Europe for smuggling guns and drugs."

"That's not my name. My name is—"

"Already heard that line of bullshit," Bolan said.

"I want my lawyer."

"You mentioned that," Bolan said. Resting his palms on the table, he leaned in closer to Ginzarli. "Unfortunately for you, I'm happy to violate your civil rights. That includes freedom and a right to life."

The man stared into Bolan's icy gaze and seemed to get it immediately.

"Nasrallah?" Bolan asked.

The man shook his head. "I don't know. A car was waiting for him when I touched down. He's probably long gone by now."

"And where were you supposed to go after you dropped him off?"

The man stared at the table. "Nowhere. I was supposed to return the helicopter to the airport and go home."

Bolan knew in an instant the guy was lying.

"Wazir," he said, "you're pissing me off. I'm a bastard when I get pissed off."

The man's lips tightened into a bloodless line. "Some plot of government land," he said finally. "They store radioactive materials there. I was supposed to drop in, pick someone up and get out." He gave Bolan the coordinates, which he immediately recognized as those belonging to the Citadel.

"Who were you picking up?" Bolan asked.

"Mike Pond."

"Anyone else?"

He shook his head. "There wasn't supposed to be anyone else. I was supposed to take Pond to Mexico and disappear myself. Nasrallah gave me a nice severance check. He told me to leave America today and never come back. He didn't say why."

BOLAN AND DOYLE stepped from the interrogation room. Bolan pulled his mobile phone from his jacket pocket, activated it and called Stony Man Farm. Price answered on the first ring.

"Find anything, Striker?" Price asked.

"Your gut feeling was right. We've got something going on at the Citadel," Bolan replied.

"Any idea what?"

"Not one hundred percent. But mix that with the fact that Stone and Pond have been storing up weapons and you get a dark picture."

"We found one other wrinkle," Price said.

"Go."

"The Feds checked the fingerprints on Nasrallah's spoon. They aren't his."

Bolan frowned. "Then whose are they?"

"Tariq Riyadh, former member of the Iraqi Parliament. The same guy who allegedly shot himself in Syria."

"Which explains why he knew Doyle."

"Right. From what we've been able to glean from intelligence files and newspaper reports, Nasrallah's home was destroyed by fire about a month after Riyadh killed himself. The cover story was that he'd survived but had been burned badly enough to require major reconstructive surgery to his face."

"So he didn't look like Riyadh or Nasrallah."

"Precisely."

"Get hold of Able Team," Bolan said. "Get them to the Citadel. And I need a chopper here, too. Fast."

"Right, Striker. One's already on its way. We lost contact with Hal a little while ago. He shut off his priority phone and has been incommunicado."

"Hal never shuts off his priority phone," Bolan said.

"Exactly. That's why we scrambled a chopper. We figured you'd want to check on him. We're also contacting the Citadel's security."

They ended the conversation. Bolan turned to Doyle.

"Looks like you did know Nasrallah, as Tariq Riyadh," Bolan said.

"Why the hell not?" Doyle said. "It's been like old home

week around here as it is. Might as well add him to the list. It was the spoon, wasn't it?"

Bolan nodded.

Doyle grinned. "See, and you scoffed. You could learn a thing or two from me."

Bolan returned the grin. "I have no doubt."

"So what's next for us?"

Bolan shook his head. "Forget it. You came out for Stone. You got him. Now go home to your wife. Have a nice life and all that."

"I want to see this through."

The Executioner shook his head again. "From what you've told me, you've got a good thing going in real life. You left the cloak-and-dagger stuff for a reason. So don't forget that reason. Besides, what's the use in going off to slay a dragon for your princess, if you end up coming back in a body bag? And there's that graze to your thigh."

Doyle crossed his arms over his chest, stared at the floor and scowled. Finally he shook his head slowly. "You're right. I'm done."

The two men exchanged goodbyes and Doyle left. Bolan, in the meantime, heard the thrumming of a chopper as it descended upon the roof. Without hesitation, he moved to the stairs and, running, ascended them two at a time. Another battlefield lay in front of him.

SERGEANT FREDERICK Montgomery wheeled the white Jeep Cherokee along the thin strip of asphalt running parallel to the Citadel's security fence. The radio offered an occasional burst of chatter and the heater's low hum intermingled with the rumble of the Jeep's power plant. Unlike the other guys, Montgomery enjoyed patrolling the perimeter and having the chance to stare over the wide expanse of Utah desert with its

sparse greenery and open skies. Montgomery was an intro-
vert, a guy who liked to be alone, particularly alone with nature or his guns or his books.

Like all other military personnel on the base, he wore a security guard uniform and his only visible weapons were a
Beretta 92 holstered on his belt, a collapsible nightstick and
a canister of pepper spray. Underneath the coat, he carried a
micro-Uzi and spare clips for the weapon in a leather rig. His
Jeep bore the Carville Industries logo as did the patches on
his uniform. The vehicle, like the uniforms, was nondescript,
except for the thin bar of yellow lights bolted to the cab.
When it came to the public and the Citadel, it was all about
misdirection.

The way he saw it, he had it knocked with this latest assignment. Not that he'd ever tell that to his colonel. Hell, no.
Bastard had an aversion to pleasure, particularly other people's pleasure. He treated Montgomery and the other security team members—all highly decorated, highly trained
combat veterans—like a bunch of raw recruits. He tried to
break their spirit, mold their minds. Every day was the first
day of boot camp for that guy.

Montgomery didn't consider himself particularly mallea-
ble and, at thirty, he was too damn old, too damn jaded, really, to blindly pledge allegiance to anyone.

The old man had been wound tighter than usual this week.
Not surprising, with the President and a bunch of heavy hitters from the Middle East on post. Even if the summit was
top secret, it still made a tempting target for every whacko
trying to make a point with a truck bomb or a sniper rifle.
That, combined with the Secret Service, the Justice Department and the CIA breathing down your neck, offering to help,
was enough to make anyone crazy.

Screw him. That's why the colonel got the big bucks,

Montgomery thought as he spied something in the distance. His brow furrowed slightly and he braked the vehicle. As he reached for a pair of binoculars resting on the passenger's seat, he scrunched up his eyes and tried to get a clearer image. Bringing the binoculars to his eyes, he adjusted them until his view of the distant object clarified.

It was an SUV. The hood was raised and white smoke billowed from the engine compartment. Montgomery also saw two men. One stood next to the vehicle's left headlight, peering into the engine compartment and waving his baseball cap over the engine in a futile attempt to dissipate the smoke. The second man stood with his back to the vehicle, fists cocked on his hips as he stared into the fenced compound, apparently expecting help to magically appear out of nowhere.

Plucking the microphone from the dash radio, Montgomery held it to his lips, pressed the call button and identified himself.

The dispatcher, a husky-voiced woman, said, "Unit 81, go ahead."

"Got a stranded civilian at Gate 13. Appears to be two male occupants."

"Anything suspicious?"

"Negative. They just look ticked off. They're probably as anxious to leave as we are to see them go."

"You're clear. Please advise—do you need backup?"

Montgomery lowered the microphone and pressed it, speaker down, into the folds of his black leather jacket and weighed the question. Given his druthers, he'd rather handle it alone, but he knew better than to do so. The colonel would have his ass for lunch if he engaged strangers without backup, particularly with all the heavy hitters on the ground.

Returning the microphone to his lips, he said, "Right, backup and also a courtesy cab so we can chase them away before they ask questions." He eased off the brake, letting the Jeep creep toward the stranded motorists.

"Unit 93 is in the area," the dispatcher replied. "I'll assign—"

Another woman's voice broke in. "Unit 93 clear on last traffic. Mark me en route. I have an ETA of two minutes."

The dispatcher acknowledged the traffic, announced the time and the radio went silent. As he approached the men and their car, he identified the make, a GMC. He also got a better look at the men. The one scrutinizing the engine was short with wide shoulders and a thick neck. The other man was average height and rangy, with big fists and feet. Both wore jeans, red-laced hiking boots and waist-length winter coats, one red, one blue.

In the distance Montgomery saw Corporal Toni Edwards closing in from the opposite direction. He parked the Jeep, opened the door and set one foot on the ground as he waited for her arrival. In the meantime, he called in the Oldsmobile's license plate number to dispatch. As Edwards's vehicle drew in closer, he stepped from his vehicle, rested his right hand on the butt of the Beretta and strode to the gate, donning his sunglasses as he did. The guy with the concrete-block fists smiled and waved at him, like a castaway hailing a passing freighter.

"Man, am I glad to see you," he said. "We've been out here for about fifteen minutes, just hoping someone would come along."

Montgomery kept his expression stony and the fence between them.

"ID."

The guy stuck a plastic card through a space in the gate. Montgomery took it and nodded at the other man. "Him, too."

"C'mon, Josh. The guy wants to see your driver's license."

The guy, who until now had been staring mournfully at his crippled engine, turned to the other men. Walking stiffly to the fence, he handed Montgomery his ID, wheeled back around and returned to the SUV.

The guy with the big hands jerked a thumb over his shoulder. He said, "Don't mind Josh. He's all pissed off. That hunk of junk is his baby."

Montgomery nodded. Before he could reply, though, he heard the crunch of boot soles to his left, heralding Edwards's arrival. Except for her seemingly ever present campaign hat, she wore the same uniform as him. She positioned herself several feet away from Montgomery, so they wouldn't present too easy a target, should things go bad.

Splitting his attention between the strangers and the IDs, he thumbed the talk button of his shoulder microphone. When a dispatcher responded, he recited the names and social security numbers on the cards.

"Sir, you realize this is a restricted facility, don't you? We could arrest you for trespassing."

The guy's smile faded some. He combed his fingers through the thick mop of black hair topping his head, left the hand in place as he gave Montgomery a worried look.

"Hey, guy," he said, "we're not looking for trouble. We just took a couple of wrong turns, is all. If it were up to me, I'd be ten miles away, in a diner somewhere sipping coffee, smoking a cigarette, you know what I mean?"

"Sir, you do realize this area is dangerous?" she said.

The guy shrugged. "No. I mean, I know it now. I didn't when we got lost."

"We post signs, sir," Edwards continued. "Did you see them? We do so for your protection."

The guy offered what Montgomery guessed was supposed

to be a disarming grin. "What, are you folks storing dead aliens here, or something? Is this like Area 51?"

"We store radioactive waste here," Montgomery said, nodding toward a sign posted on the fence. "It says so right there. You did read the sign, didn't you?"

Chastened, the guy stared at the ground. "Yeah, I read it. Look, we screwed up, okay? We're stuck in the middle of nowhere, with a dead car and no phone. Give us a hand and we'll be out of your hair in no time, guaranteed."

"We're going to have to search the vehicle."

The man raised his head, a surprised expression on his face. "Search the car? What for? You think we came out here to steal something? Like steal some toxic waste or something? Good Lord!"

Montgomery kept his voice even. "We're going to search the car. We're also going to search the two of you."

Shoulders sagging in defeat, the guy made a sweeping gesture with his hands. "Shit, you want to search us? Fine. But when you're done, do me a favor, huh? Get me a ride the hell out of here. I don't want to be here any more than you want me here, okay? I don't need radiation screwing up my chromosomes or any of that crap."

Montgomery ignored the man and, after swiping his security card and undergoing a retinal scan, he opened the gate. He knew Edwards would watch his back for him as he went through the protocols necessary to deactivate the alarms and the electric charge buzzing through the fence.

He looked at Josh, the man next to the SUV, and started to open his mouth. He wanted the guy to turn around and step away from the vehicle while they searched it. As he started to speak, the man turned toward him, a black object held in both hands. Everything slowed for a moment as Montgomery grabbed for his Beretta, darted right and started to shout a warning.

He cleared his holstered arm, raising the weapon in a tight arc, just as he'd done so many times in training. He didn't think about it; he just did it. In an instant he saw orange-yellow flame blossom from the black object and an instant later he saw no more.

MIKE POND FISTED the 9 mm Ruger, aimed it at the female guard and fired two shots dead center into her chest.

The woman, saved by her Kevlar vest, fell to the ground, but was grabbing for her side arm. Pond pushed his way through the gate and was on her in seconds. Pinning her shooting arm under her knee, he drove a fist into her face, knocking her head back against the ground. His lips curled into a snarl and he hit her once more, this time just because he could.

The woman bucked underneath him, trying to throw him off. He knew what he was about to do was risky. Every guard here was drilled in the martial arts and, quite possibly, his equal in a fight. Even as he thought this, he felt the woman's weight shift. Her ankles wrapped around his face and she began pulling him back, hard enough that it felt as though his spine might snap.

He pointed the gun in the approximate direction of her head, which only made her pull harder. If necessary, he'd shoot her right here, right now. But he hoped it didn't come to that. As her ankles dug into his windpipe and small white lights began to swim in his eyes, he caught a brief impression of a shape hurrying in from behind. A moment later he heard a scuffling noise and then a short cry of pain. Her ankles loosed. Reaching up, he forced them apart and freed his neck.

Grabbing a small throwing knife from his belt, he jabbed the blade into the woman's hip before she could try a similar hold on him. He looked down at her face, red, sweaty, and saw a large gash had been opened on her temple.

He glanced over at the other man, who clutched an Ingram in his hands.

"I kicked her in the head," the guy explained.

"Subtle," Pond replied. He turned back to the soldier and pinned the Ruger's muzzle against her forehead. Fear flickered in her gaze for a moment as she glanced up at the weapon, but was replaced by a steely toughness when she looked back at him.

A voice sounded over her walkie-talkie. "Units 81, 93— check." Pond saw a glimmer of hope in the woman's eyes as she heard the call.

Pond shook his head. "Forget it," he said. "You're going to call in and say everything's okay. I know you Corporal. Edwards. I know all about you. Where you live, where your family lives, every last detail. You're tough and I see you're not afraid of me. Hell, you're probably not afraid to die, at least no more than any other sane person. But can you say the same for your family? You'd make the ultimate sacrifice for your country. But what about them? You think they want to die in their sleep? Killed by me or my guys?"

He held her gaze as the words sank in. He was lying, but she didn't need to know that. Her mouth tightened into a hard line and he detected a hint of skepticism.

The dispatcher spoke again, this time her voice more urgent. "Units 81, 93—check."

"It's your call, Corporal."

Switching his gun to his free hand, he gripped the shoulder mike, edged it closer to her lips, and thumbed the talk button.

"Units 81, 93—check."

"We're okay," Edwards said.

Releasing the button, Pond kept the pistol trained on her as he hauled himself to his feet. He could tell the gears were clicking in her head, and he guessed she was weighing her options for escape. He admired her fire, but he knew she was trouble. Sure, she was cooperative now, but only by necessity. She wasn't cowed and, given a chance, he knew she'd try to upset his plans.

If he let her, which, obviously, he wouldn't.

The Ruger barked once in his hand. The Parabellum round drilled dead center into the soldier's face, tearing away the back of her head and staining the ground with a supernova of red.

Pond stared at the corpse and laughed. "Who's your daddy, bitch?" he yelled. He looked at the other man, grinned. "I do good work, don't I?"

The blood had drained from the guy's face, leaving him pale, as he stared at the corpse. "You the man, Mad Dog," the guy said, his voice taut with fear.

"Bet your sweet tail, I am," Pond said, laughing.

He unclipped his mobile phone from his belt, dialed in a number and waited two rings for an answer.

"Yeah?"

"Go," Pond said. "Pass it on."

Terminating the call, he closed the phone and slipped it inside his coat. He looked over at the other man—some candy-ass named Campbell—and snapped his fingers. The guy turned to him, swallowed hard, but kept his mouth shut.

"You wanted war, didn't you?" Pond said. "Well, welcome to war." He jerked his thumb over his shoulder. "Now unload the trucks. We've got just a little while before it breaks out all over."

CHAPTER TWENTY-ONE

"You're sure of this?" the Saudi prince asked.

"Yes," Haddad said, nodding. "Our intelligence officers tell me there will be a coordinated attack on several members of the royal family within days."

At Haddad's request, the two men had moved into a private conference room to discuss an urgent security matter. The prince, seated at the head of the table, considered Haddad's news. Haddad kept his expression stony as the prince chewed absently at his lower lip, causing his chin to dimple.

"I suggest you return home to lead the investigation," Haddad said. "But it is, of course, your call as to how we should proceed."

"You're my most trusted aide. And I believe you are correct in your suggestion. I must return home immediately, if for no other reason than to comfort the others with my presence. The royal family must be together at such a critical time. But the summit—"

"I can handle the summit," Haddad said.

"You are a good friend," the prince said. "I'm sure you'd rather be home with your family at such a critical time."

"One must make sacrifices to serve the kingdom,"

"Of course."

The two men stood and embraced. A lesser man might feel guilty for deceiving an old ally, a man who gave his trust so easily, Haddad thought. That's what separated Haddad from the weaklings populating the Saudi government. He'd long ago cast aside such useless emotions as guilt or loyalty. It galled him to no end to grovel before the royal family like some trained animal. After all, the only thing separating them was an accident of birth. He had come from an upper-middle-class background while they'd been born into royalty. Haddad knew he'd worked hard for everything he possessed while those he served enjoyed wealth and power through a simple fluke of nature.

Of course, some might view such thinking as envy, but Haddad knew better. He was a man of intelligence, dignity and grace. He simply wanted to claim what was his, no more, no less.

"I have a helicopter waiting for you," Haddad said. "We must take the elevator to the helipad."

"Of course."

The bodyguard exited the room, followed by the prince and Haddad. The aide herded them into the elevator and they rode in silence as the car climbed to the roof.

Stepping from the elevator, they passed through a security center, where more than a dozen soldiers in camouflage fatigues, faces awash in the bluish of glow of computer monitors, scanned their equipment for threats to the facility. Situated next to the security room, partitioned off by a glass wall, was the air-traffic-control center. Haddad watched as another dozen or so soldiers wearing headsets went about their tasks, seemingly with a mechanical precision, almost an air of boredom.

He knew the boredom would be short-lived. Soon enough the sky would catch fire and the Citadel would do likewise in short order.

After they made it through the various security procedures, the three men were allowed onto the roof, which doubled as a helipad. He saw the chopper, its rotors already whirling, as the pilot waited for his passengers.

The prince turned to Haddad. "I already gave my regrets to the President. You will, of course, repeat them. And extend to him an invitation to visit the kingdom sooner rather than later."

Haddad assured the other man of this and walked him to the helicopter. The bodyguard, a well-muscled Arab dressed in a black business suit and aviator shades, kept a hand inside his jacket as he walked in lockstep with the prince. Two more bodyguards already standing on the roof also fell in with the prince as he hurried to the aircraft.

Haddad stopped several yards short of the chopper as the prince boarded it. With the leader safely inside, the pilot powered the engine, causing it to gain volume until Haddad needed to cover his ears with his palms. The rotor wash intensified, whipping his coattails around his waist and kicking up dust. He squinted against the dirt particles pelting his eyes, but remained on the roof until the chopper gained some altitude, turned and headed northeast from the Citadel's main compound.

To do otherwise would be unseemly, disrespectful. He needed to play the role of loyal aide to the last. If that meant enduring a few moments of minor discomfort to deflect suspicion, he'd do it.

He kept his gaze fixed on the chopper for a few moments more as it gained distance and altitude, growing smaller with each passing second. Slipping a hand into his coat pocket, he pressed a preset number, knowing it would send a page to Pond and the others, alerting them to the prince's pending arrival.

He hurried back through the security center, down the elevator and to his room. As he entered, he swept a scornful eye over the sparse furnishings and felt another wave of anger swell in his gut. He knew for a fact that the prince didn't suffer such a perpetual state of lack. No, he, like others in his family, lived with only the best, while Haddad and others like him suffered in silence and obscurity.

Hefting his suitcase from the floor, he laid it flat across the bed and opened it. He pulled a penknife from his pocket, opened the blade and jabbed it into the seam joining the liner to the suitcase's hard shell. He traced the blade along the contoured edge and folded down the lining, revealing a secret compartment built into a false bottom in the case. He inserted two fingers and a thumb into the space. Extracting a small box-shaped item, he set it next to him on the bed and checked his watch.

Four minutes.

The countdown to hell finally had begun.

BROGNOLA WOKE UP in a world of pain. He tentatively cracked an eye as consciousness returned. A deep groan escaped his lips. The back of his skull pounded. His nose, which he apparently had used to break his fall after blacking out, throbbed worse than his head. His lips felt warm and slimy. Almost unconsciously, his tongue darted out and he tasted blood. Rolling onto his back, the big Fed willed himself to rise into a sitting position, trying to reconstruct the minutes before he blacked out.

Correction: not blacked out, knocked out.

Realization dawned on him. Haddad! The bastard had

knocked him unconscious. Why Brognola still was alive was a mystery. By all rights, he knew he should be dead. Haddad should have killed him as he lay on the floor, helpless.

Brognola touched his fingers to the back of his head, jerked them away almost the same instant. Even the slight pressure sent searing jolts of pain from the point of impact.

Price's warning returned to him, causing him to forget his injured head and broken nose. He came stiffly to his full height and set a palm on his desk to steady himself. He glanced at the desktop, hoping to find his revolver sitting where he'd left it. Seeing the weapon gone, he bit off a curse. A glance at his laptop told the big Fed that Haddad also had destroyed the computer. Brognola's mobile phone also was missing.

Stumbling to the door, he pulled down on the latch and drove his shoulder into the door to open it. Spotting a pair of female guards, he called out to them as he moved into the hallway. They turned in unison, surprise registering on their faces as they saw him. Brognola imagined he looked shocking as hell. Blood covered his face, neck and shirt. Crossing the corridor, one of the women moved next to him. Grabbing his wrist, she lifted his arm and tried to drape it over he shoulder.

He shrugged her off.

"Forget about me," he said. "We need this place locked down, pronto."

BROGNOLA KNEW he was living dangerously, but he also knew he didn't care. He stuck his face, bloodied and battered, to within an inch of the colonel's and spit out a question.

"He's where?"

The colonel didn't bat an eye. "Gone," the guy said. "He left a few minutes ago on a helicopter. This isn't a damn prison. If someone wants to go, they go."

"Did they say where they were going?"

"If I was a betting man, I'd say Saudi Arabia."

"You need to put this damn place on lockdown," Brognola said. "ASAP."

The colonel crossed his arms over his chest. "By who's authority?"

A third voice rang out. "Mine."

Both Brognola and the colonel stiffened. Looking over the soldier's shoulder, Brognola saw the President, grim-faced and ringed by Secret Service agents, approaching. At the rear of the crowd, Brognola spotted Schwarz in full combat gear.

Soldiers straightened and threw the Man crisp salutes as he passed. The colonel turned on a heel and did likewise.

"At ease," the President said. "We have a situation here. Until I say otherwise, we are in a lockdown situation." He pointed a finger at Brognola. "And this man's in charge."

The colonel turned back toward Brognola, nodded. Though the big Fed detected anger in the guy's stare, he didn't take it personally. He'd feel the same if someone tried to usurp command of Stony Man Farm.

"Let us know what you need," the soldier said. "We'll crawl through hell to protect this man and the others."

"I don't doubt it. First thing is send your people through every nook and cranny of this place. Khalid Haddad, the prince's aide, was the one who clocked me. If he's still here, then that dumb bastard has to be up to something bad."

The colonel nodded again. "We're on it."

"And the President's right—put this place on lockdown. No one comes in or out unless I okay it."

"Understood."

The colonel waded into his people and began shouting orders. Schwarz walked up to Brognola and gave him a tight smile.

"You all right?"

"Yeah. I wasn't a pretty boy before all this started. Helen might like the change. How did you get in?"

"When we lost contact with you, Barb said to hell with protocol and contacted the Man directly. His people vouched for me when I arrived."

Brognola cocked an eyebrow. "Do they have your real name?"

"Hell, no. They think I'm part of the FBI's Hostage Rescue Team or something."

Brognola nodded. "You have an extra gun I can borrow?"

"Always." Reaching behind his back, Schwarz brought around a SIG-Sauer P-229, chambered for .357 cartridges. He slapped it onto Brognola's palm and, a moment later, supplied him with three 12-round clips.

Schwarz cocked his head toward the bustle of activity as soldiers and civilian workers busied themselves with the lockdown.

"You stuck here?"

"Negative. They've got this in hand. I need to see someone about a broken nose."

"Paybacks are hell, aren't they?"

"Damn straight."

A KNOCK AT THE DOOR caught Haddad's attention. He fisted the American's revolver and held it close to his thigh as he approached the door. With his free hand, he slipped the detonator into his pocket.

Fear overtook him, seizing his breath and causing his mind to race. Had the American awakened already? He cursed himself. He should have returned to the man's room and killed him while he'd had the chance. It was the only sensible thing to do. Instead he'd become overconfident, believing that the blow would leave the man down for hours.

A second knock, this one more urgent, sounded. Unconsciously he clicked back the pistol's hammer, but continued to hold it out of sight.

"Coming, coming," he said. "Who is it?"

"Us."

Opening the door slowly, Haddad peered around it and saw three men standing in the corridor, looking expectantly at him. All three were members of the security team and were armed.

"All's ready?" Haddad asked.

One of the men nodded. "Yes. We must go."

Haddad released the hammer on the revolver and pocketed the handgun. He followed the other men to an elevator. Stepping inside, the four men rode it to the bottom level and exited, stepping into a large corridor of seemingly endless white walls and glaring fluorescent lights. Haddad noticed the cameras poised overhead and tugged one of the men on the sleeve. When the man looked at him, he nodded toward the camera.

"Won't they see us?"

The man shook his head. "We overrode the camera. Everyone's too busy to notice."

Haddad was unconvinced but continued on, anyway. At this point he had little choice. Coming to a door, one of the men swiped a security card through a reader. The bolt slipped back, sounding like a gunshot in the otherwise quiet corridor. The man opened the door and they slipped into the room, Haddad bringing up the rear. He ran the ball of his thumb over the detonator's smooth plastic surface as he shut the door behind him.

CHAPTER TWENTY-TWO

Pond and his group of killers scattered over the butte, taking up positions as they waited for the chopper's approach. Kneeling, Pond lifted one of the SAM missiles onto his shoulder and waited for the critical moment. Another man, similarly armed, settled in next him, ready to unleash a second missile should Pond's shot miss.

Fat chance, he thought as his index finger caressed the weapon's trigger fondly. He'd spent hours training with the damn thing back at Langley and could hit a mosquito at two hundred yards. Plus, Riyadh had provided the right motivation for him—$2 million in cash—to blow the Saudi prince from the sky. As anticipation fluttered in his gut, he had to laugh at his good fortune. He'd have done it for half the price.

He had just received Haddad's page, letting him know the prince had taken off from the ground. Now he needed word from his spotters, informing him that the craft was within the SAM's three-mile range.

A voice boomed into his earpiece. "Sir, we've got a problem."

Taking a hand from the launcher, Pond keyed the headset. "Problem? What kind?"

"We've got choppers swooping into the area. From what we can tell, they're landing, then popping back into the air to run patrols."

"So what? They do air patrols over here all the time. What's the problem?"

"Patrol choppers usually have the refuse company's logos plastered all over them and they keep the weaponry damn near invisible. These babies are Black Hawks, armed to the teeth and not afraid to show it."

"You got an ID on them?"

"Negative, sir. No logos or other telltale markings. They're federal, of course, but there's no way to discern which agency they belong to."

"Okay," he said. "Keep your damn head on. What about the target? Is it still in the air?"

"Affirmative. It circled the main compound a couple of times, but it's now en route. It should be in range within sixty seconds or so."

"Clear," Pond said. "Tell me when it is."

"Understood."

Pond felt his heartbeat begin to accelerate as he considered the news. The Feds took great pains to make the place so bland as to be almost invisible. That usually included keeping combat choppers, Air Force One and Marine One out of the Citadel's air space, no matter what. Considering the group assembled here, and the world situation being what it was, a change in policy wasn't out of the question. But it damn sure made him nervous.

"Thirty seconds, sir," the spotter said.

"Clear."

Pond tightened his grip on the launcher and waited. Keep your eye on the prize, he told himself. In a few seconds he'd shoot the Saudi prince from the sky and collect millions for it. Then they'd move into phase two of Riyadh's twisted little plan and unleash a sweet little bit of carnage that wouldn't soon be forgotten.

"Fifteen seconds."

The tickle of anticipation became almost unbearable and Pond swallowed hard as he ticked off the seconds in his head. He slowed his breathing, shrugged just slightly to put the launcher in a better position for accurate fire.

He counted down eight more seconds, tightened his trigger finger, but almost imperceptibly so. Suddenly he heard a grunt and a hot, sticky substance splattered over him, covering portions of his hands, face and coat. In the next breath he heard metal clatter against earth and felt deadweight fall against him. Reflexively he removed a hand from the launcher, jabbed out an elbow to knock away the sudden burden leaning against him. He looked down and felt his breath catch. Blood clung to his skin and clothing. The guy charged with watching his back laid next to him, a ragged hole visible in place of the soldier's ear. In the same instant, he lowered the SAM, unlimbered the Uzi hanging around his neck and lunged sideways. A salvo of bullets ripped through the air, missing his head by inches.

Looking up, Pond saw a vision from hell approaching from the north. A big guy clad head-to-toe in black surged forward.

The man's handgun spit a pencil-thin line of flame as its handler peppered the air just above Pond with another punishing salvo of slugs. Pond snap-aimed the Uzi and let it rip at full-auto. The weapon churned out loads of hot brass and flame as Pond dragged it in an arc. The other man dived out of Pond's line of fire and disappeared from view for a moment.

An instant later the bastard was back in view, this time

clutching a small assault rifle at hip level. The short barrel already was tracking in on Pond, about ready to deal death upon him, when he got a break. Autofire carved out a path toward the soldier, forcing him to break off his attack. Pond watched as the guy lowered into a crouch and quickly downed two gunners with a couple of well-placed blasts.

Feelings of relief clashed with rage as Pond realized how close he'd come to getting killed. Judging by the guy's size, the ease with which he'd approached and his skill with a gun, Pond guessed this was the Justice Department bastard Stone and Riyadh had been wetting their pants over. Pond snorted. Didn't look like much of anything to him.

The thrum of chopper blades sounded closer and Pond cursed. He wanted to take the soldier down, sure. But even more, he wanted to finish the mission. Otherwise, he walked with empty pockets.

Even with his three kills, the guy still was outnumbered six to one. Besides, you could wax men like that anytime. How often did you get to kill royalty and make millions to boot? Not often enough, he decided. He let the Uzi fall loose on its strap as he moved to the discarded launcher. The insistent crackle of gunfire told Pond that the Justice guy already had all the trouble he could handle.

THE ONSLAUGHT of bullets forced Bolan to make a hard choice. He had wanted to kill Pond—whom he recognized from photos supplied by the Bear—but the gun-wielding thugs descending on the Executioner had made themselves a priority.

Muzzle-flashes winked at Bolan as the shooters unloaded their weapons at him. The bullets stabbed into the ground at his feet and kicked up geysers of dirt. The warrior triggered the Colt Commando and swept the short-barreled assault rifle in a figure eight. The hail of 5.56 mm rounds drilled the men, jerking them around as if they'd had contact with live power lines as scarlet dots appeared on their chests.

Sensing motion to his right, Bolan turned and spotted a hardman positioned on a pile of rocks. The Executioner was already moving as the man's Uzi came to life, rattling out a line of bullets that pierced the spot occupied by Bolan only a heartbeat ago. Experience told the warrior that he could trade shots with this guy all day and never score a hit because of the rocks. He also knew instinctively that the numbers were counting down toward zero fast, and he had no time for prolonged gun battles.

Crouching behind a rock, he pulled a 40 mm high-explosive round from his satchel and thumbed it into the M-203's breech. Snapping the launcher shut, he fired the grenade at the shooter. The blast hit quick and hard, showering the area with bits of dust and rock. Peering from behind his cover, he saw the blast had flung his enemy's body into the open, leaving his clothes and flesh afire, his head twisted at an unnatural angle.

Bolan turned away from the grisly sight and snapped a fresh magazine into his assault rifle. The beating of rotor blades reached his ears and prompted him to move. He guessed that was the Saudi chopper, hopefully with the Black Hawk helicopters escorting it up and away from danger. But, as it was, the Executioner's kill zone stood right in the chopper's planned flight path. And in the heat of battle, he'd lost track of Pond and had to assume the guy still had a missile launcher. Bolan knew from previous intel that at least a couple of other militiamen also carried similar weapons.

So the Saudi's chopper needed a little ground support, at least until it got downrange.

Getting to his feet, Bolan broke away from cover and

began his desperate hunt for Pond. A few long strides into his advance and the warrior heard a sound that chilled him.

An engine's growl.

Not a helicopter engine, but that of an automobile, the rasp of tires kicking up dirt from the rear wheels.

Bolan spun toward the sound. He caught sight of an SUV, militiaman at the wheel, carving out a deadly path toward Bolan.

Shouldering the Colt Commando, Bolan laid down a sustained burst at the approaching vehicle. With precision borne of experience and skill, Bolan kept his weapon trained on the driver as the vehicle bore down on him. The volley of slugs hammered through the safety glass, creating a half dozen or so spiderwebs before several rounds punched into the driver. His lifeless body slumped over the wheel, knocking the car into a skidding turn that slammed it into a pile of boulders. It exploded a moment later, pumping roiling columns of flame and oily smoke into the sky. Undulating waves of heat rose from the burning vehicle, causing the air above it to shimmer.

The chopper, audible for at least the last forty-five seconds, came into view and passed overhead. Two Black Hawk helicopters glided over the battle zone just on the craft's tail. Bolan figured that Pond had missed his initial shot and decided to nail the craft once it gained an appropriate distance. The doomsday numbers were about to tumble to zero, unless Bolan made another kill.

CHAPTER TWENTY-THREE

The Black Hawk helicopter touched down on the butte, scattering plumes of dirt as it settled onto a tabletop-like surface.

Lyons headed for the door, taking a mental inventory of his weapons as he did. His Colt Python hung from one fast-draw leather holster and a Browning Hi-Power rode counterpoint on his left hip. His M-16/M-203 combo hung from a strap on his neck. He clasped an Ithaca 37 shotgun, a stakeout model with a 4-round tubular magazine and pistol grip.

For quiet work, a Hell's Belle Bowie knife hung heavily from Lyons's belt. The quintessential packhorse, Lyons also bristled with flash-stun and fragmentation grenades and plenty of extra ammunition. The weight of the equipment rode easily on his six-foot, two-inch frame.

Blancanales shot up from his seat in tandem with Lyons. Like his teammate, he carried an M-16/M-203 combo. Twin Berettas were holstered on his hips. An Applegate-Fairbairn commando dagger hung point-up on the warrior's web gear, which was strapped over a Kevlar vest. Both men wore black Nomex suits.

Lyons and Blancanales jumped from the chopper, came

down crouching and fanning the muzzles of their weapons over the terrain. They saw nothing. The pair distanced themselves from the chopper and Lyons signaled for it to take off.

Whether these nut jobs would succeed in a mass assassination was debatable. But Lyons knew it really didn't matter. It only took killing a few of the right people—Arab leaders— and Riyadh won the game. Like his fellow Stony Man warriors, Lyons knew he couldn't stomach that.

The chopper had deposited the battle team about a half mile from their targets. A satellite scan had located a cluster of heat signatures on a ridge that overlooked the Citadel. Because several guards were missing and possibly held hostage, Lyons had pressed for them to delay an air strike on the assembled warriors. The way Lyons saw it, a precision strike was the best way to go. Blancanales, Schwarz and Striker all had agreed. Anyone else with an opinion was cordially invited to go to hell.

Lyons and Blancanales broke into a run and minutes later came to rest about two hundred yards from the Patriots' last recorded position. Dropping behind a stand of fallen rocks, the Stony Man warriors scoured the area with hawklike intensity. Lyons spotted two sentries. One stood about twenty yards away, panning the horizon with a pair of binoculars. The second was fifty yards distant, but stared almost directly at Lyons. Fortunately the man was too absorbed in his cigarette to notice the intruders.

A pair of the Citadel's security officers lay on their stomachs, hands bound behind their backs, at the smoking man's feet. Their waxen faces stared at Lyons, slack jaws hanging open as though they continued even in death to cry out. An image of their last moments, bound and staring into their killer's face just before they took a bullet flashed in Lyons mind, filling him with rage and disgust.

Lyons glanced at Blancanales. The grim set of his old friend's jaw, the hatred burning in his eyes, betrayed the hatred in his heart for these callous killers.

The Able Team leader unleathered the Browning and threaded a custom sound-suppressor into its barrel. They needed intel on troop strength assigned to this particular area. However, the distance between them and their targets made a quiet takedown with prisoners impossible. It was all or nothing, and Lyons could live with that.

He cast a glance at Blancanales who had fisted a Beretta. Lyons knew the weapon was loaded with subsonic ammo, making it capable of silent death. They were ready to take the war to the killers.

Lyons, his shooting arm extended at the shoulder, uncoiled from behind his cover and drew a bead on Mr. Cigarette. The guy's eyes widened like saucers. With fast, practiced movements, he raised his weapon and lunged to one side, trying to make himself a more difficult target. In the same instant, his mouth opened, presumably so he could shout a warning to his buddy.

He was fast, sure. But against Lyons he might as well have worn cinder-block shoes.

The Browning coughed three times in rapid succession. Two rounds punched into the man's nose, hurling his head back like a haymaker to the jaw. The third bullet pierced the man's throat. The man retreated a couple of steps on wobbly legs. Limp fingers released the machine pistol, the cigarette long gone, as he dropped onto his rear and tipped to one side.

From the corner of his eyes, Lyons saw Blancanales's weapon flash as it spit a pair of 9 mm rounds at the second target. The rounds pounded into the man's forehead and exploded out the back in a shower of blood and brain matter that covered the wall of sandstone at his back.

Moving with urgent strides, the Able Team warriors stepped from the line of rocks, grabbed their kills and dragged them into hiding. Within seconds they were continuing their march toward their adversaries. Lyons had switched back to his shotgun, while Blancanales had traded his Beretta for the M-16. Edging along a wall of smooth, orange-brown rock, they covered half a football field's distance before the sound of voices caused them to stop. Lyons tried to discern the words, but the rush of high-altitude winds made such a task impossible.

Ahead lay a slim passage between two boulders. The shotgun held in front of him, Lyons moved into the space, his senses alert to any possible danger. The smell of wintergreen chewing tobacco and aftershave reached his nostrils. The slap of footsteps, the jangle of metal gear caused him to tense.

"Jimmy, get your ass over there. We got about five minutes until we smoke them bastards out of their bunker. Then it's time for a little target practice."

Lyons saw a man's shadow split off from the one cast by the rocks. "Shit, I just get a chance to relax and now I gotta move again."

The first man's voice took on an edge. "Quit your damn whining. We don't get a second chance on this. If Mad Dog heard you, he'd put a damn bullet through your head. Hell, I've got half a mind to do it myself."

"All right," Jimmy said. "Don't get your shorts in a bunch. I'll go. Just let me take a damn leak."

Prying himself away from the rocks, the man started toward Lyons's position. Flattening himself against the wall, Lyons waited for the man to round the corner. His hand stabbing out, Lyons grabbed a fistful of the guy's shirt and yanked him out of sight. He slammed the bastard hard against the rocks, causing his breath to explode from his lungs, then jammed the shotgun barrel up under the man's chin. As silent as a whisper, Blancanales was next to him.

Lyons eyes bore into the other man's. "You're dead," he growled. "A fucking ghost."

The guy opened his mouth, whether to speak or to scream was unclear. Regardless, Lyons rewarded his prisoner's initiative with a knee to the groin. Breath exploded from the man's lungs and his eyes bugged out of his head. His lips moved, but only a croaking noise came out.

Lyons gave the man a second to regain his voice, then asked, "How many?"

The guy hesitated. Lyons pressed the shotgun muzzle into the soft flesh underneath the man's chin and used the weapon to tip the guy's head back at an uncomfortable angle.

"How many? Or do we make it minus one?"

"Twenty."

"Turn around," Lyons said.

"Why?"

"Because otherwise I'll use the contents of your head for wall decor. Got it?"

The thug searched Lyons's eyes for a moment, apparently gauging his resolve to kill, and apparently saw it went off the charts. Lyons noted the change and backed up a step from the prisoner. Leaving his hands in the air, the guy turned to face the rock wall. Lyons raised the shotgun, holding it like a baseball bat, barrel pointing behind him. He brought the weapon down hard against the man's skull. Upon impact, the man groaned and sank to his knees, unconscious. He pitched forward and slammed his face into rock. It took Lyons only a few seconds to bind the man's hands with plastic handcuffs and gag him with duct tape.

They moved forward again, ready to hit the next battleground. "Unless I miss my math, twenty against two is pretty bad odds, amigo," he said.

"You scared?" Lyons asked.

"Shit," Blancanales said, grinning.

Lyons couldn't help but return a muted smile of his own. He knew that what both men lacked in numbers they made up for in sheer audacity. Maybe they'd fall in this fight, maybe not. Regardless, they'd heap a merciless beating upon their opponents, like a hurricane tearing through a village of grass huts.

Stepping between snarls of sagebrush and stands of long grass, they reached a line of Douglas fir trees and melted into the cover they provided. Lyons veered left, while Blancanales headed right, disappearing from view within seconds. It never ceased to amaze Lyons how Blancanales, a man who'd grown up on the mean streets of East L.A., negotiated jungles and forests as easily as he did alleys, drug houses and posh office spaces. Like a chameleon, the man fit in everywhere, making him one of the most versatile warriors Lyons ever had encountered.

Lyons felt moisture and heat collecting underneath his Kevlar vest as he wound his way through the trees. About ten yards distant, he spotted the white chassis of two pickups, their hue a stark contrast to the earthy oranges, greens and browns that surrounded him.

He also heard the noises of animals—human animals.

"We've lost contact with three units," a voice said. "Permission to send out a search team."

"Negative," another voice said. "We don't have the horses to spare. We've got two minutes before ignition. Once that happens, I need anyone who can carry a gun ready to rock and roll on those bastards down there."

"Permission to speak freely," the first voice said.

"Denied."

The guy pressed the issue, anyway. "Look, Pond's team's taking fire, too. We've got enemies working the area, and they're more capable than this first line security. We could have people crawling up our tailpipes even as we speak."

The second speaker's voice took on an edge. "De-fucking-nied. Can I make it clearer?"

A pause. "You're the boss."

"Damn straight. Now get me status reports on the snipers along the ridge."

"Understood."

Moving in a crouch, Lyons crept forward a few more steps, bringing him within a few feet of the clearing. Peering out, he saw six more dead guards piled up like deadwood, clothes bloodied from bullet wounds in their foreheads or the backs of their necks. From what Lyons could tell, there were no hostages to save. Just corpses.

Lyons knew he could do nothing to help the unfortunates who'd fallen, but he sure as hell could get them a measure of justice.

Surging forward, he broke from the line of trees. One of the militiamen whirled toward Lyons, raising a Galil assault rifle as he moved. Lyons swung the shotgun in target-acquisition mode, squeezed off a shot that tore into the man's head, causing it to disappear in a spray of blood and gore. As Lyons pumped a fresh round into the Ithaca's chamber, he sensed motion to his right and dropped to one knee. The movement saved his life. Bullets blistered the air just inches above his head. Lyons snapped off another round from the riot gun, the blast taking a shooter off at the kneecaps. The shotgun roared twice more and blasts shredded the midsections of two more gunners.

A volley of bullets sliced in from the right, passing inches from Lyons's head. He let go of the shotgun and dived forward, fisting the Browning in his right hand as he landed flat on the butte's rocky surface. He fired three shots, nailing one of his attackers in the face. The other two men cut loose with bursts from their machine pistols, forcing Lyons to change tactics. Grabbing a fragmentation grenade from his combat webbing, he yanked the pin with his teeth and heaved the grenade at the shooters. The explosive overshot Lyons's targets by several yards, but the blast wrought its damage anyway as bits of razor wire tore through his opponents, shredding skin and clothing, and dropping them to the ground.

Lyons heard gunshots sound in the distance and guessed that Blancanales was waging his own war. In quick succession, he reached under the dashboard of each truck and ripped out handfuls of wires, disabling both vehicles. Slamming the second truck's door behind him, he was on the run again. He heard the staccato report of his teammate's assault rifle and a tight smile played on his lips. He'd only taken down seven fighters. That left Blancanales with thirteen heavily armed gunners to handle all by his lonesome.

BODY FLATTENED against a rock, muscles tensed like those of a mountain lion ready to strike, Blancanales stared down at the army of murderers ready to ply their trade.

The militiamen had formed a ragged lined along a ridge overlooking the Citadel, separating themselves into pairs. Four of the men lay prone, each holding an M-24 sniper rifle propped up on a bipod, while four others acted as spotters. Two men held SAM launchers, and the remaining soldiers stood like bookends at either end of the serpentine line of gunners, MP-5 submachine guns held at the ready as they monitored the team's exposed flanks.

"What the hell was all that gunfire?" one of the snipers asked.

His spotter, a barrel-chested man with his face covered in camouflage paint, smacked him lightly on the helmet. "Focus. Our rear flank's covered. You just watch the targets. We have two minutes until ignition."

Noting that he had a clear field of fire, Blancanales triggered his grenade launcher. The weapon hurled a 40 mm round that landed next to the sniper team. Immediately roiling clouds of smoke rose up from the ground and the men began to fire wildly and scatter. Blancanales thumbed a high-explosive round into the launcher, fired again, planting a grenade into a knot of four men. An orange fireball tinged with black smoke erupted, the force of the blast tearing through the men, ripping away limbs and silencing a sickening outburst of death cries. The blast's force snagged one man, lifting him off his feet and hurling his battered body over the ridge and into a two-hundred-foot freefall.

Blancanales switched the M-16 to full-auto, slid from his perch and hit the ground running. The assault rifle's muzzle flashed orange as it ground through the contents of its 30-round magazine. Bullets from the M-16 careened off rocks and the din of autofire, both from Blancanales and his opponents, seemed to swallow every other sound.

The Stony Man warrior swept his assault rifle in a figure eight, peppering a trio of shooters. The tumblers stabbed into flesh and caused the men to jerk crazily until he eased off the trigger, ending the punishing salvo.

He spied two more men, the nervous sniper and his brusque spotter, on their feet and splitting apart. Each man was trying to plant Blancanales in their gunsights as they ran. The M-16 flared to life once more, and he buried a swarm of 5.56 mm tumblers into the sniper's head. The man wilted under the hail of gunfire, his body collapsing backward until only a leg jutting from behind a tangle of sagebrush was visible.

Blancanales whirled toward the second attacker, but the sudden movement combined with the burden of his equipment caused him to stumble forward. He threw a hand out to break his fall and bolts of pain knifed up and down his hand and arm as he struck the rock. Blancanales clamped his jaw and ignored the pain. Bullets hammered into the ground around him, splintering rock and pinning Blancanales down.

Manipulating the M-16 with one hand, he aimed the assault rifle at his opponent and opened fire. The man tried to readjust his own aim and take out Blancanales, but he moved a fraction of a second too slow. The hellfire unleashed by the Able Team commando's weapon burned into the man's legs, tearing apart flesh and sinew. The man's screams filled the air as he suffered under the searing volley of bullets. He fell to the ground, writhing. Switching the assault rifle to single shot, Blancanales fired a single round into the man's head, ending his suffering for good.

Blancanales ejected the assault rifle's spent clip and scrambled for a new one. Instinct told him to look up and, when he did, he spotted an MP-5's blunt, black barrel tracking in on him.

A cold sensation washed over him as he realized he could never reload and fire in time. In a stretched moment, his mind sized up the situation.

No time to reload.

No time to move.

He was dead. He'd failed.

A burst of autofire rang out to Blancanales's left. He flinched for a moment until he realized the shots weren't intended for him.

He watched as someone peppered the shooter with a hail of scorching lead, burning the guy down a heartbeat before he could shoot Blancanales. The man's head disappeared in a crimson burst as the fusillade of bullets found its mark. Even as the corpse folded in on itself, more bursts from the unidentified shooter hammered into a knot of gunners, raising the body count by three.

Lyons strode onto the killing ground, white smoke still rolling from the barrel of his M-16. He studied the tangled pile of dead fighters for a moment before turning to Blancanales and grinning.

"I'm incredible," he said. "Just admit it."

Blancanales shook his head. Experience told him that only one thing was worse than dying: being saved by Carl Lyons and having to listen to him gloat.

HAL BROGNOLA MOVED DOWN the sterile corridor in the Citadel's lowest level, traveling just a step behind Gadgets Schwarz. He gripped the SIG-Sauer with both hands. Sweat slicked his palms and he felt traces of moisture collect between his skin and the SIG's textured grip. His heart hammered in his chest as they closed in on their target. The big Fed's mind wandered to the ramifications of a possible failure. He shook the thoughts away.

The stakes were too big to consider such an outcome.

Brognola watched his comrade move down the hall first. The big Fed hated letting one of his people walk point for him, and had argued vehemently against it. But Schwarz's practicality ultimately had won out. He had a tactical vest; Brognola didn't. There'd been no time for them to track one down big enough to fit over his stocky torso, not with what was about to go down.

Schwarz stopped, turned to Brognola. "How much farther?" he whispered.

Brognola took a moment to study the corridor. "End of the hallway, second door on the right."

Schwarz nodded. After having his gun and mobile phone stolen, Brognola finally had caught a damn break.

A tracer embedded in Brognola's mobile phone allowed the cyberteam to track his movements in the field. The tracer had been intended as a security tool, but Brognola hoped it might yield another benefit. According to Kurtzman, the phone had been moving and, at last check, was in the Citadel's bottom level. Most likely, that meant Haddad was down here somewhere.

Both men had donned headsets and hooked into the Farm's War Room before pursuing the man.

Kurtzman's voice came on the line. "Anything?"

"Shh!"

"Sorry."

Brognola and Schwarz arrived at the door. The Able Team commando took one look at the elaborate series of locks, card readers and retinal scanners, and shook his head. He gave Brognola an expectant look, prompting the man from Justice to back up a few paces. "Get the control center here to override the lock," he demanded.

"Clear," Kurtzman said.

A series of lights began blinking on the locking mechanism and the bolts slammed back with a thud. Schwarz didn't wait for Brognola's order before throwing open the door and moving inside.

"Freeze. Federal agents," Schwarz yelled.

Almost as soon as he had uttered the warning, the Able Team warrior's Desert Eagle thunder four times.

Brognola already was in motion. The SIG-Sauer extended, he filled the doorway and caught a third man, dressed in a Citadel security uniform.

Friend or foe? Brognola barely hesitated. The guy was about to plug a federal agent, and a close comrade. As far as Brognola was concerned, that bought him a one-way ticket to the graveyard. The SIG-Sauer bucked twice in his hands and the .357 Magnum slugs pounded into the man's center mass and shoved him back several feet. The guy, who apparently wore Kevlar plating under his leather bomber jacket, swiveled toward Brognola. The SIG-Sauer cracked once more, gouging a hole in the man's throat.

Brognola heard the slap of footsteps against the floor. Spinning toward the noise, he spotted Khalid Haddad making a run for the door. As he closed in on the big Fed, Haddad brought up his hand, which was filled with the Justice man's revolver.

Brognola's and Schwarz's guns sounded as one. Bullets punched into the guy's legs and hips, causing him to drop the gun and knocking him off course. But he remained alive for questioning.

Schwarz was already across the room and kicking the pistol farther from Haddad's reach.

Brognola straddled the guy, who lay on the floor, writhing in pain. Dropping onto him, his weight agitating Haddad's injuries, Brognola searched through his jacket and found the detonator, which he passed over to Schwarz.

"We want to know where you folks hid the charges. You're going to tell us. Understand?"

"Yes," Haddad managed to reply, forcing the words through clenched teeth.

BOLAN RAN FOR THE ROCK FORMATION where he'd last seen Pond, trading the MP-5 for the Colt as he covered the ground in long, easy strides. The towering rock stood twenty yards ahead and jutted into the sky at least a few dozen feet. Mea-

suring half as thick as it was tall, the formation provided perfect cover for Pond. Just beyond lay a sheer two-hundred-foot
drop. The cliff overlooked the main road leading to the
Citadel.

Reaching the massive stone, Bolan edged along its perimeter, using the MP-5's barrel to run point for him. Rounding
the rock, he spied Pond crouched on one knee and drawing a
bead on the fleeing Saudi helicopter. Just as the Executioner
squeezed the MP-5's trigger, Bolan felt something strike his
kidneys with the force of a runaway truck. Staggering forward, he dropped to his knees and fought the urge to vomit.
His vision blurred, his nerves alive with pain, he did the only
thing he could.

He fought on.

Snap-aiming the MP-5, he fired the weapon with one hand
as he threw himself into a sideways roll.

Raking the weapon back and forth horizontally, Bolan riddled Pond with 9 mm slugs. The miniature missiles drilled
through flesh, causing the man to jerk crazily as bullets whipsawed his body.

Knowing another shot to the back was imminent, Bolan
continued to roll. As he did, his fingers scrambled for a throwing knife. He unsheathed the weapon and rolled onto his
back, catching sight of the shooter and heaving the knife.
Rolling end over end, the blade crossed the gap between
Bolan and his enemy and bit deep into the man's throat.

Dragging himself into a sitting position, the warrior stared
at the carnage around him. The downed Black Hawk chopper was visible in the distance, pumping plumes of smoke into
the air as fire ravaged the craft and the remains of its crew.
An image of Jennifer Kinsey, the woman Bolan had been sent
to save, dead at the hands of Stone, flashed through his mind.
And he pondered the danger that Riyadh and Aziz's plan had

posed to his old friends Hal Brognola and Able Team, the President and a host of foreign leaders who'd entrusted the United States with their security.

As Bolan got to his feet and reloaded the MP-5, he heard Lyons's steely voice sound in his earpiece.

"All clear, Striker," Lyons said. "We've shut these bastards down good. And everyone's present and accounted for. It's time to go home."

"Later," Bolan said. "This isn't over for me."

CHAPTER TWENTY-FOUR

The black BMW bearing Tariq Riyadh drove onto the isolated runway, slid into place next to a large jetliner and came to a stop. Seated in the back, Riyadh produced a white silk handkerchief from his jacket's breast pocket and wiped it over his forehead, which was beaded with perspiration. It had been a week since the debacle in the United States and, after barely escaping, he'd taken up refuge in Africa. He'd hoped within days to change his appearance with more cosmetic surgery and then disappear again. Perhaps he could once again seek refuge in Syria. Or maybe he could travel to Libya, Somalia or one of the half dozen or so other countries that would welcome him.

Those had been his plans. A last-minute phone call had changed everything, including his status as a free man.

Three Africans rode with him in the BMW, two in front and one in back. The man seated next to Riyadh was a middle-aged Somalian, known to him only as Abdul. Abdul stood nearly seven feet tall, was thin as a dagger's edge and equally deadly. It had been his reputation for unfeeling brutality and ferocity that had prompted Riyadh to hire him. Riyadh considered Abdul's reputation to be quite impressive in the part of the continent that got most of its notice for dismemberments, rapes, murders and other atrocities.

It was precisely these qualities that had prompted Riyadh to hire the man and his associates as security guards. The need for protection had been obvious. He feared Justice Department Agent Matt Cooper, if indeed that was his real name. Riyadh also feared Jamal Aziz's wrath.

He'd decided it best to hire a security team to watch his back as he regrouped. Abdul and his associates had come highly recommended by an old associate, a man Riyadh had trusted. Unfortunately, Riyadh realized too late that his trust had been misplaced.

"Don't be so nervous, my friend," the African said. "Mr. Aziz very much wants to see you. That's why he went to the trouble of finding you."

"Shut up, you bastard!" Riyadh said. "I hired you to protect me. Instead you betrayed me. You're a dishonorable man."

Even as he spoke, Riyadh heard the brittleness of his voice and felt ashamed. Abdul gave him a vacant stare before breaking into another smile. It seemed to Riyadh that the other man found his sense of betrayal, his fear, to be interesting, but alien. Certainly not something the man would dwell upon.

The driver stepped from the car, hurried to Riyadh's door and opened it. Immediately, Riyadh felt a slap of hot air against his skin. The whine of the plane engines stabbed into his ears and drowned out all other noise. Reaching down, the driver gripped Riyadh's bicep and dragged him roughly from the rear of the car. His captors had elected to not bind his hands, something that only further injured Riyadh's pride. Did they consider him so weak, so compliant, that he'd simply walk to his death without putting up a fight?

They should have known better, Riyadh thought. He was, of course, a diplomat first. He'd tried talking the men into letting him go, promising them money, weapons, drugs, all considered universal currency. They had spurned every offer. Riyadh had figured as much; it's hard to outbid a billionaire, after all.

But he wasn't afraid to fight, either. He'd rather resist here on the airfield, die on this isolated strip of pavement in the middle of an African desert, than stand in front of Aziz and give the man the pleasure of ordering his death, witnessing it.

No way.

Riyadh drove an elbow into the man nearest him. The strike hit the man's stomach, caused the guard to grunt. But he held his ground, grabbed Riyadh by the jacket and shoved him face-first into the BMW. Riyadh struggled against the strong hands holding him down, but to no avail. The man held him in place like an anchor.

From the corner of his eye, Riyadh saw Abdul round the rear of the car. Something big and blunt pounded into Riyadh's kidney. Nausea immediately overtook him. The man struck the same spot once more and Riyadh inhaled sharply, ground his teeth to stifle a yell. The men pulled his arms behind him, cuffed his wrists and began walking him to the airplane.

He climbed the stairwell leading up to the plane, stepped inside the cabin and felt a sudden rush of cool air envelop him. A moment later he was in the first-class cabin with Aziz. He saw a different man than the one he'd seen a week ago. Dark circles outlined Aziz's eyes and a trace of fear blemished the Egyptian's hard stare.

Abdul shoved Riyadh into the room and led him to within a few feet of Aziz. A sharp kick to the rear of his knees caused

Riyadh to fall to the floor. A hand grasped the back of his collar and lifted him, like a mother dog hoisting a puppy by the
scruff of its neck. Riyadh found himself on his knees, eyes
locked with the Egyptian's. A guard grabbed Riyadh's arms
roughly and a moment later his handcuffs had been removed.

"So good to see you," Aziz said.

"Go to hell!"

"I've lost a great deal, my friend," Aziz said. "The authorities have snatched up ninety percent of my money, as well
as stocks, cars, houses and businesses. I find myself on the
run, like a common criminal. This disappoints me greatly."

"You knew there were risks."

"At the same time, the word's out on what we tried to do.
Middle Eastern intelligence services have been telling anyone who will listen about my involvement in this. I'm fast losing my standing among my own people. Not only am I poor,
but I'm an outcast."

"It wasn't my fault. The American—"

Aziz shook his head, disgusted. "Blame. Isn't that always
the last refuge of the weak, the incompetent?"

"You failed, too," Riyadh countered. "Your assassin had
the chance to kill the agent. He didn't."

"And he paid for it with his life. But I had no hand in seeing him die, so it's of little comfort knowing that he did. You,
on the other hand—"

The door slammed shut behind Riyadh, sharp, loud, like
a gunshot. He stiffened, as though tensing his muscles would
stop sure death.

Aziz laughed. "You know what's coming, don't you? You
realize that if I have nothing else, I'll at least know the man
who brought me to ruin died as I looked on."

The engines had continued to grow louder as the plane prepared for takeoff. A dull tone sounded from somewhere in the

cabin, indicating that the craft was about to begin taxiing down the runway.

Aziz nodded at the Africans. "Please, gentlemen, take a seat. There's no rush in dealing with Mr. Riyadh. I'd much rather kill him on the ground than soil the airplane's carpet."

"Where are you taking me?"

Aziz smiled, lifted a plastic bottle of spring water to his lips. Riyadh watched the little man's Adam's apple dance up and down as he took a long pull from the bottle. Setting it back into a nearby cup rest, he dabbed at the corners of his mouth with a cloth napkin. Folding the napkin, he flattened it with his palm and returned his attention to Riyadh.

"Libya," he said finally. "I may not have much money, but I have more than enough to buy asylum, particularly from a country at odds with the United States."

When he spoke, Riyadh's throat ached, his tongue felt swollen. Tremors began passing through his knees. "And what about when we get there? You'll kill me then?"

Aziz shrugged. "Eventually. First, of course, I want you to spend some time in one of their prisons. They have a man there, he's very good at inflicting pain. From what I understand, after a week or so, you'll be begging to die."

Alternating currents of fear and rage shot through Riyadh's body. "I did as you said. You cannot punish me for that."

Aziz shrugged and downed more of his water. Riyadh wasn't sure what enraged him more: his own helplessness or the Egyptian's indifference. Both stoked within him a homicidal rage that he could barely hold in check.

Two guards helped Riyadh to his feet. They crowded him, shoved him across the cabin to a seat well away from Aziz. A punch to the head, so fast he didn't see it, caused him to sway and reach out for support. He found nothing and started to sink to his knees. However a pair of big hands fisted the fabric of his jacket and held him aloft before pushing him into the chair with a hard shove.

As he landed in his seat, he cupped his hand over his aching jaw, trying to quell the fiery pain engulfing it. The coppery taste of blood registered with his tongue, and he swallowed hard.

Had he been a religious man, he might have praised Allah for his luck. His captors had searched him well. They'd taken his SIG-Sauer P-229 he'd taken to carrying ever since he'd arrived in Africa. They also had found the SIG-Sauer P-239 he'd carried around his ankle and a dagger strapped to his other ankle.

But they'd left him with one weapon. He'd sewn a razor blade into the lining of his suit jacket. It wasn't much, practically nothing, in fact. But, if after the plane landed, he could grab Aziz and threaten to drag the blade over the parchment-like skin of the bastard's neck, perhaps the men would let him go. After all, if Aziz died, they got no money, thereby making the very man bent on killing him Aziz's best insurance policy.

As the plane continued to gain altitude, Riyadh laid his forearm over his lap and let his hand dip inside the jacket. Running his thumb over the coat's silky lining, he felt something rigid resist his thumb's pressure. Pinching the blade between his thumb and his index finger, he sliced the edge against the fabric. Moments later, a pointed end of the razor blade broke through the cloth. He sawed the blade against the fibers for a few seconds more, creating a large enough slit to pass the blade through.

He heard the click of a seat belt clasp and froze. A moment later Abdul stared down upon him from behind the seat.

"What are you doing?" he demanded. As he leaned over Riyadh, he stabbed out a hand and made a play for the Iraqi's wrist.

Abdul stopped in midlunge and Riyadh suddenly found himself drenched in blood. The big man folded at the waist and his torso draped partially over the seat back, apparently caught on one of the headrests. Riyadh saw the small red hole in the man's throat, his features frozen in surprise. The pop of a handgun hit Riyadh's ears even as he stared at the corpse.

Shock overtook Riyadh. Shifting his gaze to the front of the cabin, he saw a vision of hell.

It was the American, dressed head-to-toe in black, a pistol clutched in each hand. Riyadh clutched the razor blade, but held his position, waiting for the man to step in closer.

PISTOLS EXTENDED, Bolan stepped into the room, knowing he had to make quick, precise kills. He carried a pair of .38 revolvers, each loaded with minimum-charge cartridges and bullets designed to shatter against the cabin walls of the airplanes.

He saw the second and third guards clawing for hardware. The .38s barked in unison. A man to Bolan's right began to draw a weapon, even as he shot up from his seat. Before he freed the weapon, he caught a .38-caliber slug in the eyeball. Bolan followed up with another shot to the throat that put the man out of commission permanently.

Simultaneously the warrior's second pistol discharged a pair of bullets. One plowed into the empty seat beside the shooter, while the second lanced into the man's mouth and buried itself into his spine.

The warrior caught a flicker of motion behind the curtains separating Aziz's personal section of the plane from the rear quarters. Just as a man pushed his way through the curtains, an Uzi in his grip, Bolan dived to the ground. The .38s popped again and a pair of rounds punched into the man's groin. Dropping his weapon, he folded in on himself and lay on the ground, writhing in pain. Bolan walked to the man, kicked his weapon out of reach. As he did, he saw a shape brush past him. Bringing up the pistol, the soldier held his fire. The runner had already made it through the curtained entrance and into the back section of the plane.

Bolan approached the well-dressed Arab and drew down on him.

"Mr. Aziz."

"You've come to arrest me?"

"Not even close."

Aziz clawed his jacket pocket, hoping to free a pistol, but the .38 cracked once and the bullet crashed into Aziz's nose, opening a geyser of blood as the force shoved his skull against the headrest. Wheeling around, the Executioner sought Riyadh but saw the man had fled.

Bolan holstered one revolver, but held the second just above waist level, his forearm pressed in against his abdomen. He walked sideways, edging along the rows of seats until he reached the exit. He fisted his Colt Combat knife with his left hand, ready for close-quarters combat.

He waited a moment for takers, but found none. No big surprise there. Few sane people would walk through a narrow door into a room where others obviously were armed and willing to shoot. But Bolan knew there were two more guards on board. He'd counted them before he and Grimaldi had secured the original crew and taken over the plane.

Gripping a flash-bang grenade from his gear, the warrior covered his ears and activated the bomb, rolling it under the curtain and into the plane's rear section. The weapon popped once and Bolan knew the effects in such close quarters would be devastating. Standing flush with the edge of the door, he reached up and ripped down the curtain. A pair of wild shots sizzled through the entrance, causing Bolan to grind his teeth. The bullets smacked harmlessly into the backs of seats.

Moving in a crouch, Bolan cornered the door frame. He spotted one man, obviously disoriented, arm extended, pistol held at shoulder-level, preparing to fire it. Bolan fired the .38 and cored a round into the man's armpit, causing him to drop his weapon and protectively pull his arms in on himself. Bolan fired the pistol's final cartridge, cored a round through the man's throat and dropped him. A second man came around a seat back, the muzzle of his pistol tracking in on Bolan's middle as he tested himself against the Executioner's reflexes. He needn't have bothered. The soldier's weapon cracked once more and the man lay stuck between the seats, a crumpled heap.

Bolan continued his march through the airplane, icy blue eyes seeking more adversaries. Riyadh was in here, maybe armed, maybe not. Either way, Bolan had come here to send the guy to hell.

The big soldier heard labored breathing two rows ahead. He leveled the pistol in that direction.

"Come out, Riyadh," the Executioner said, his voice icy. "It's over."

Bolan lifted his foot to step forward. As he did, the plane shuddered and began pitching side-to-side as it flew into a patch of turbulence. The craft's sudden heaving threw Bolan off balance. He stumbled left and the force thrust him into one of the seats. The instant his knees touched the seat, he pushed himself back to his feet.

He sensed the approach before he saw it. Something bit deep into the muscles and sinews of his forearm, causing him to drop the pistol. Whirling, he saw Riyadh's eyes, clouded by rage, staring into his own. Bolan whipped around at the waist. He brought the knife around in an arc and buried the blade into Riyadh's throat, waiting for the man's body to go limp.

A moment later the man fell to the floor in a boneless heap.

Pulling a field dressing from a pocket in his blacksuit, Bolan began to bandage his injured forearm. He stared at the man who'd nearly brought two cultures to the precipice of war and wondered how many more men like Riyadh existed, men ready to murder, rape and pillage so they could advance their own cause, be it greed or revenge.

How many existed?

Bolan already knew the answer.

Too damn many. That's why he'd keep fighting his War Everlasting.

PROMISE TO DEFEND

The elite counter-terrorist group known as Stony Man has one mandate: to protect good from evil; to separate those willing to live in peace from those who kill in order to fulfill their own agenda. When all hell breaks loose, the warriors of Stony Man enter the conflict knowing each battle could be their last, but the war against freedom's oppressors will continue....

STONY MAN®

*Available
October 2005
at your favorite retailer.*

SKYFIRE

Wind of a grim conspiracy comes to light, and the levels of treachery go deep into America's secret corridors of power. When the Cadre Project was created decades ago, it served to protect the U.S. government during the Cold War. Now it's a twisted, despotic vision commandeered by a man whose hunger for power is limitless, whose plan to manufacture terror and lay a false trail of blame across the globe may find America heading into all-out world war against the old superpowers.